PROMISE NOT TO TELL

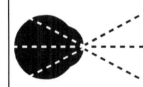

This Large Print Book carries the
Seal of Approval of N.A.V.H.

PROMISE NOT TO TELL

JAYNE ANN KRENTZ

LARGE PRINT PRESS
A part of Gale, a Cengage Company

GALE
A Cengage Company

Farmington Hills, Mich • San Francisco • New York • Waterville, Maine
Meriden, Conn • Mason, Ohio • Chicago

GALE
A Cengage Company

Copyright © 2018 by Jayne Ann Krentz.
Large Print Press, a part of Gale, a Cengage Company.

LIBRARY OF CONGRESS CIP DATA ON FILE.
CATALOGUING IN PUBLICATION FOR THIS BOOK
IS AVAILABLE FROM THE LIBRARY OF CONGRESS.

ISBN-13: 978-1-4328-4688-6 (hardcover)

ISBN 13: 978-1-4328-4689-3 (pbk.)

Published in 2018 by arrangement with The Berkley Publishing Group, an imprint of Penguin Publishing Group, a division of Penguin Random House LLC

Printed in the United States of America
3 4 5 6 7 8 23 22 21 20 19

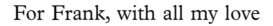
For Frank, with all my love

ACKNOWLEDGMENTS

I am very grateful to Donald Castle for the consulting advice he provided for the tech-related scenes in this story. Any and all mistakes are strictly my own. Thanks, Don! You're the best nephew in the world!

CHAPTER 1

Hannah Brewster splashed the accelerant around the inside of the small cabin, working feverishly because time was running out. She was certain now that the demon would come for her that night. He had been stalking her for weeks.

She had spent many agonizing hours trying to decide what to do. In the end she had finally understood that she had no alternative but to destroy her creation. It was her only hope of keeping the promise she had made all those years ago.

She set the empty container down on the floor next to the door and picked up the box of matches. She was surprised to see that her hands were once again steady, just as if she held a brush and stood in front of an untouched canvas. Tonight she would paint a picture with fire.

Afterward they would say she was crazy, that she had finally gone over the precarious edge that separated sanity and madness. But the truth was that her mind had not been this clear in a very long time. She knew exactly what she had to do.

A few weeks ago, when the monster had come to the island the first time, she had tried to convince herself that she was hallucinating. Again. These days the past came and went in visions that were so real she often got confused. It had been twenty-two years, after all, and everyone claimed that Quinton Zane was dead.

But two weeks ago she had spotted him again. She had tried to convince herself that she could not trust her eyes. But that night she had sensed that she was being watched. She had known then that she could no longer deceive herself into thinking that she was hallucinating. The truth was always shatteringly clear at night.

At midnight she had picked up a brush, her hand firm and steady, and begun to paint her final picture. She had continued painting every night until her creation was finished.

And then she had waited for the demon to return.

For the past several days she had made the long walk into the small village every afternoon to watch the ferry dock. She stationed herself inside the shop that sold herbal teas and studied the handful of visitors who arrived. It was February and still quite chilly in the Pacific Northwest. At this time of year there was never more than a handful of tourists.

She had spotted the demon immediately, even though he had tried to disguise himself with dark glasses, a stocking cap and a black parka. He could not fool her. She might be plagued with visions, but even her hallucinations were clear and detailed. She was an artist, after all.

Quinton Zane was after the secret she had kept for so long. He was relentless. Now that he had found her, he would not stop until he forced her to give up the truth. After he had gotten what he wanted from her, he would kill her. She wasn't afraid of dying. She had, in fact, been contemplating the prospect of making the final transition ever since Abigail had died. That had been just before Christmas. But she had made a promise twenty-two years ago and she had done her best to keep the vow.

The real problem was that she feared she was not strong enough to resist Quinton Zane. The bastard could make you believe anything he wanted you to believe. She had fallen under his spell once and paid a ter-

11

rible price. She could not risk getting sucked back into his web. She had a duty to protect the children. She was the only one left who could warn them.

The odor of the accelerant fumes was almost overpowering. It was time.

She struck one of the matches. When the flame was steady she stepped outside and tossed the match through the doorway of the cabin.

For a few seconds nothing happened. Unnerved at the thought of failure, she plunged her fingers into the box for a second match. At that instant the fire exploded, roaring to life. The wild flames illuminated the interior of the cabin and her final painting in a hellish light.

She watched the inferno through the doorway, studying the image with a critical eye. She had been forced to paint the picture on the wall because she had not had a large enough canvas.

The fire devoured the cabin and the painting. The heat was intense. Instinctively she moved back several more steps, welcoming the chill of the night air off the cold waters of Puget Sound.

She stood, transfixed by her act of destruction. Scenes from the past and the present fused in her mind. She thought she heard children screaming but she was certain that was a memory, not her present reality. There were no children nearby. She had chosen the cabin because of its remote location. She had been aware that her nighttime habits would disturb neighbors, even here on the island, where eccentricities were not only tolerated but also expected. Abigail had been the only one who understood and accepted her weird ways.

So, no, there were no children screaming. But her heart was pounding and her breath was tight in her chest, just as it had been that dreadful night all those years ago.

She watched the fire and waited. She was certain that he would soon appear.

Quinton Zane emerged from the dense shadows of the thick woods that surrounded the cabin. It was as if he had walked straight out of one of her paintings, straight out of the past, straight out of her nightmares.

She could not let him touch her. He was too strong, too powerful. If he got his hands on her, he would force the truth from her. She might be crazy, like everyone said, but she knew how to keep a secret.

"Stay away from me," she warned. She was amazed at the calm fortitude in her voice. "Don't touch me."

But Zane broke into a run, moving toward

her. His tall figure and broad shoulders were silhouetted against the storm of flames just as they had been that long-ago night when she had watched him stride through the burning compound.

He was strong. He could easily outrun her. She would not stand a chance.

He was calling to her now, telling her to come to him, promising safety, security and an end to the visions, just as he had promised all those years ago. But she knew he lied.

She made her decision.

"You were a fool to come back," she shouted. "The key belongs to the children. Did you really think that they would forget what you did to their families? You're a dead man. You just don't know it yet."

She turned and fled into the night. Footsteps pounded behind her.

The edge of the cliffs was lit with moonlight and fire. She had walked to that edge many, many times in the years she had been living on the island. So many nights she had stopped there, looked down at the dark, deep water far below and thought about how easy it would be to take one more step.

In the past she had always turned back. But not tonight. A sense of deep certainty came over her.

She realized somewhat vaguely that she was still holding the box of matches. She would not need them anymore. She tossed them aside and kept going until there was nothing but air beneath her feet, until she was flying away from the demon.

The last thing she heard was Quinton Zane's scream of frustrated rage. She knew then that she had defeated him, at least for the moment. It was up to others to stop him. She had kept her promise and she had sent the warning. She could do no more.

She knew a split second of peace.

The dark sea took her.

CHAPTER 2

"You saved my life, Mr. Salinas," Virginia Troy said. "I'm embarrassed to admit that it took me this long to track you down so that I could thank you. Embarrassed to tell you that I came looking for you now only because I need your help."

"No need to apologize," Anson said. "I was just doing my job that night. You were a little kid caught up in the craziness. There was no reason you should have come looking for me as an adult."

The last time he had seen Virginia Troy she was a child of nine, one of the eight children trapped in the blazing barn. He'd used his vehicle to crash through the locked doors, tossed all eight kids into the SUV and reversed out of the inferno, a hound out of hell. Shortly after he had gotten them all to safety, the barn had collapsed in on itself.

He'd saved the kids but he and the local

firefighters had not been able to save all of the adults. Virginia Troy's mother had perished, along with several other people.

Quinton Zane had kept the women away from their children at night. They had been locked in separate quarters. Zane had torched the entire compound before he vanished. It was a miracle and a tribute to the first responders that several of the cult members had made it out alive. The following morning, when they had surveyed the ruins, it was clear that Zane had not intended for any of his followers to survive. Each one was, after all, a potential witness.

"I have never forgotten what you did that night," Virginia said. "Afterward my grandparents tried very hard to erase that part of my past. The stress of losing my mother and finding themselves stuck with the task of raising me eventually broke up their marriage. My grandmother still won't talk about it. But for the rest of my life I will remember that you saved all of us who were locked up in that barn."

"Can't blame your grandparents," Anson said. He was aware of a great heaviness settling on him. "There was a lot of pain going around. You lost your mother that night. They lost a daughter."

"Yes."

Something about the bleak tone of Virginia's voice told him that she wasn't only mourning the loss of her mother all those years ago. He had a feeling that she carried another kind of burden as well. He recognized survivor's guilt when he saw it because it was close kin to the kind of guilt he felt when he looked back on that night. He had not been able to save everyone in Quinton Zane's compound.

For a while he and Virginia sat quietly, facing each other across the desk. He did not try to restart the conversation. Once upon a time he had been a cop. He understood the value of silence.

A mid-February rain beat steadily, lightly, against the windows. He had lived in Seattle for several months now, but this was his first full winter in the city. He was starting to think of it as the Season of the Deep Gray. The skies were overcast most of the time, and when the sun did make short, fitful appearances, it was low on the horizon. The weak, slanting light was often blocked by the gleaming new office towers. The boom in high-rise construction in recent years had created dark canyons in much of downtown.

It should have been depressing, he reflected. Instead, there was a sense of energy about the city. He had been surprised to discover that something in him responded to the vibe. He wasn't the only one. The region was home to innumerable start-ups. The new gig economy was going full blast. Businesses of all kinds were enthusiastic about setting up shop in the city. New restaurants and coffeehouses opened every week.

Seattle was infused with a frontier spirit. That was as true now as it had been in the gold rush and big timber eras. But these days there was a hell of a lot more money around. That, he told himself, ought to be good for the investigation business — the business in which he and two of his foster sons, Cabot and Max, were engaged.

His job was to ensure that Cutler, Sutter & Salinas prospered. When the door had opened a short time ago, he'd hoped that the representative of a corporation or maybe a lawyer needing discreet services for a wealthy client would walk into the office.

Instead, Virginia Troy had entered the small reception lobby, bringing with her the long shadows of the past.

He hadn't recognized her, of course. She had been one of the youngest kids he brought out of the burning barn all those years ago — a wide-eyed little girl so trau-matized by the events that she had not even

19

been able to tell him her name for several hours. Cabot, who had been orphaned that night, had supplied him with Virginia's name.

Virginia was thirty-one now. No wedding ring, Anson noted. That did not surprise him. There was a cool reserve about her. She wasn't exactly a loner, he concluded, rather someone who was accustomed to being alone. He knew the difference.

She was the kind of woman who caught a man's eye, but not because she was a stunner. Attractive, yes, but not in a standard-issue way. She wasn't one of those too-beautiful-to-be-real women like you saw on TV. Instead there was something compelling about her, an edge that was hard to define. Probably had something to do with the bold, black-framed glasses and the high-heeled boots, he decided.

Most men wouldn't know how to handle a woman like Virginia Troy. Sure, some would be damned interested at first, maybe even see her as a challenge. But he figured that, in the end, the average guy would run for the hills.

A short time ago, when she had walked into the room, she had taken a moment to size up everything in sight, including him. He had been relieved when he and the expensive new furniture appeared to have passed inspection.

Although his name was on the door, technically speaking he was the office manager, receptionist, researcher and general gofer. Max and Cabot were the licensed investigators in the firm. Both had complained mightily about the stiff rent on the newly leased office space, as well as the money spent on furnishing the place, but Anson had refused to lower his newfound standards of interior design.

Before embarking on his career in office management, he had never paid any attention to the art of interior design. But after hiring a decorator and immersing himself in the finer points of the field, he had become convinced that the premises of the firm had to send the right message to potential clients. That meant leasing space in an upscale building and investing in quality furniture.

The result, however, was that Cutler, Sutter & Salinas now had to start making some serious money.

Virginia crossed her legs and gripped the arms of the chair. Anson knew that she was ready to tell him why she had come looking for him.

"I own a gallery in Pioneer Square," she

said. "One of the artists who occasionally exhibits her work with me died a few days ago. The authorities have ruled the death a suicide."

"But you don't believe it," Anson said.

"I'm not sure what to believe. That's why I'd like to hire you to investigate the circumstances."

The door opened before Anson could ask any more questions. Cabot walked into the room carrying two cups of coffee — one balanced on top of the other — and a small paper sack emblazoned with the logo of a nearby bakery. He was slightly turned away from the desk because he was using the toe of his low boot to close the door. He did not immediately notice Virginia.

"The Coffee Goddess said to tell you she's got a new tattoo that she might be willing to show you if you'll let her surprise you with one of her own custom lattes," he said. "Evidently she's tired of you ordering regular coffee instead of one of her specialties. Says you need to be more adventurous."

Anson felt himself flushing. He cleared his throat, but before he could warn Cabot that there was a client in the room, the client spoke.

"Some things are best appreciated in their

purest, most essential forms," Virginia said.

Cabot turned very quickly to confront her. Anson stifled a sigh. *Confront* was the operative word when it came to Cabot. Not that he was *confrontational* in the sense that he was always looking for a fight. If anything, he usually came across as unnaturally aloof and unemotional. It took a lot to make him lose his temper, and on the rare occasions when that happened, you didn't want to be standing in his vicinity.

The issue was that he regarded anything or anyone new, unknown or outside his normal routine, as a potential problem at best and, at worst, a threat until proven otherwise. The result was that he *confronted* situations and people until he could decide what to do about them.

He also had a bad habit of being attracted to women who thought they needed a man to rescue them. Unfortunately, that type of woman was attracted to him — but never for long. Anson had observed that needy women were happy enough to use Cabot for as long as he was useful, but sooner or later they found themselves dealing with the whole man, not just the rescuer part. And Cabot was nothing if not complicated. His relationships, such as they were, usually ended badly.

The swift, sure way he moved to deal with Virginia said a lot about the man, Anson thought. Most people would have lost the top cup of coffee with such a sudden turn, but Cabot had excellent reflexes and an innate sense of balance. He'd had those talents from childhood and had honed them over the years. Some men ran or lifted weights to stay in shape. Cabot had a black belt in an obscure form of martial arts.

He contemplated Virginia now with a cool, calculating gaze. People often got nervous when Cabot fixed his attention on them. It was the primary reason why Anson or Max usually took on the task of dealing with new clients. Those seeking the services of an investigation agency were already uneasy when they came through the door. There was a general consensus that Cabot might scare off new business.

Virginia seemed unaffected by the infamous Cabot Stare. If anything, she appeared amused.

"Sorry," Cabot said. "Didn't know we had a visitor." He held out one of the paper cups. "Want Anson's coffee? It's straight. No sugar, no mocha, no foamy milk, no chocolate sprinkles, no caramel."

Anson winced. Some people might have assumed that Cabot was trying to make a small joke. They would have been wrong. Cabot was inclined to take things literally. He often spoke the same way. He possessed a sense of humor but you had to know him really well before you could tell when he was joking and when he wasn't.

Virginia glanced at the cup Cabot was offering and then looked at the other cup.

"Out of curiosity, what are my options?" she said.

Cabot's brows rose. "Options?"

"You've got two cups of coffee," Virginia said with an air of grave patience. "You just told me that one is straight. I am inquiring about the status of the second cup."

"That would be mine," Cabot said. "It's straight, too. Anson's the one who taught me how to drink coffee."

"I see," Virginia said. "Thank you, but I'll pass."

Cabot nodded once, as if she had just confirmed some conclusion that he had made. He placed one of the cups down on the desk in front of Anson. Every move was fluid and precise. There was no wasted motion.

"You're the fully-loaded-latte type," he said.

"Actually, no," Virginia said smoothly, "I'm not."

She did not elaborate.

Cabot's eyes tightened a little at the corners. He did not take his attention off Virginia. Anson recognized the expression and suppressed a small groan. Cabot's curiosity had been aroused. It was a fine trait in an investigator but it could also cause problems.

Cabot was not the subtle type. What you saw was pretty much what you got. That was, of course, why he had trouble when it came to his relationships with women. They were inclined to believe they could smooth out the rough edges and still keep the tough, strong core. Big mistake. And then, inevitably, they concluded they no longer wanted to deal with the inflexibility that was a part of that core.

"This is Virginia Troy," Anson said before the situation could deteriorate further. "One of the kids in the barn."

He did not need to say anything more.

Cabot went very still.

"Virginia," he said. He spoke very softly. "I remember you. Little kid. Dark hair. Big eyes. You had a book that night. You wouldn't leave it behind."

On the surface his tone was devoid of all inflection. Anson wondered if Virginia heard the echoes of the nightmares that moved in

26

the depths.

"And I remember you," Virginia said. Her voice was equally neutral. "You were the one who told the rest of us to go low to avoid the smoke."

Oh, yeah, Anson thought. She had sensed the bad stuff, all right. He could hear the same grim echoes in her words.

"I assume you're here because of what happened that night," Cabot said.

That was Cabot for you, Anson thought. He had the gift — or the curse, depending on your point of view — of being able to put a couple of stray facts together and add them up in a hurry.

"How did you know?" Virginia asked. Curious, but not surprised.

"No other reason you would show up now, after all this time," Cabot said.

"No, I suppose not," Virginia agreed. "I was just telling Mr. Salinas —"

"Anson," Anson said.

She dipped her head slightly in acknowledgment of the invitation to use his first name.

"I was just telling Anson that my grandparents encouraged me to put the past behind me," she said. "I have tried to do that."

"Didn't work, though, did it?" Cabot said.

Some people would have been offended by the observation. Virginia gave Cabot a wry smile.

"No," she said. "Did it work for you?"

"No," Cabot said. "Gave up trying a long time ago. Makes more sense to acknowledge the power at the core and channel it."

Virginia studied him intently for a moment and then she nodded. "I see."

"Don't mind him," Anson said. "He says things like that from time to time. It's martial arts crap — I mean, philosophy."

"Sort of like saying that 'some things are best appreciated in their purest, most essential forms,' " Cabot said, deadpan.

Anson groaned. But Virginia did not miss a beat. To his amazement, a smile came and went in her cool green-and-gold eyes.

"I see that martial artists and art gallery owners have a few things in common," she said. "We both get to say pretentious stuff that sounds way more insightful than it actually is."

Cabot looked intrigued by the concept that they might have something in common. "Do you say pretentious stuff a lot?"

"Mostly just when I'm trying to sell some art. You?"

"Mostly just when I'm trying to sound like I'm a hotshot private investigator."

Time to move on, Anson decided. He sat forward and clasped his hands on his desk. "Virginia owns an art gallery here in Seattle. She wants us to investigate the death of one of her artists who was living on an island in the San Juans. Says the local authorities are calling it suicide. She has her doubts."

"What does this have to do with the past?" Cabot asked.

"If I'm right," Virginia said, "if Hannah Brewster was murdered, then I think we have to consider the possibility that Quinton Zane is still alive."

CHAPTER 3

She had their full attention now.

Virginia watched the expressions on the men's faces with a sense of relief. She had hoped that they would at least listen to her wild theory, but Anson Salinas and Cabot Sutter were doing a whole lot more than just hearing her out. They were one hundred percent focused, a couple of natural-born hunters who had just sensed prey. She reminded herself that they were both ex-cops.

"Correct me if I'm wrong," she said, "but I have the impression that you're not altogether surprised to hear me say that Zane might still be alive."

"Anson and my brothers and I have never found hard proof that he's dead," Cabot said. "Until we get solid evidence, we're working on the theory that he's alive."

"I don't remember you having brothers at Zane's compound," she said.

This time Anson responded. "Max Cutler and Jack Lancaster. After the fire they didn't have much in the way of family. They came to live with me. I did the foster parent thing."

Paternal pride was infused in Anson's voice.

"So I've got brothers," Cabot said. "And a dad."

"I understand," Virginia said. "All of you have questioned Zane's death?"

"Over the years we've chased down every rumor — every hint — that he might still be out there somewhere," Cabot said, "but if he is, we're almost certain he's operating outside the country these days."

"A few years ago there was a pyramid scheme in New York that looked like it had his fingerprints all over it," Anson said. "But by the time it came to our attention, whoever was running the scam had vanished."

"Generally speaking, we keep our little conspiracy theory a family secret," Cabot added. "We've learned the hard way that it gives other people a bad impression. They tend to regard our interest in Quinton Zane as an unhealthy obsession."

"Anything connected to Quinton Zane is, by definition, unhealthy," Virginia said. "But just so you know, I share your obsession."

"We're listening," Cabot said.

He angled himself onto the corner of Anson's desk, one foot braced on the floor, and peeled the plastic lid off his coffee. His movements were deceptively relaxed. He had no doubt been born with that fluid co-ordination, Virginia thought. But his actions were infused with an aura of control and power that told her he had worked to hone his natural talent.

Mentally she did the math and concluded that Cabot was in his early thirties, two or three years older than she was. The tall, lanky boy with the very serious eyes had matured into the kind of man who probably wasn't the life of the party. He would, however, be the kind of man you'd want at your back in a bar fight.

His dark hair was cut ruthlessly short and his lean profile had hardened into pure granite. His eyes were a feral shade of amber brown and still unnaturally intense. Hannah Brewster would have said that Cabot had the eyes of an old soul. But that wouldn't have been entirely accurate. He had the eyes of a man who took the world very seriously.

There was no ring on his hand. That surprised her because everything about him intrigued her. Surely she wasn't the first woman to find him interesting. On the other hand, Cabot Sutter would definitely not be the easiest person on the planet to live with. There was a gritty, uncompromising vibe about him that, sooner or later, would probably convince a lot of women that he was more trouble than he was worth.

She understood the reaction. She was a little screwed up herself, with a history of failed relationships testifying to the fact that a number of men had decided that she was more trouble than she was worth.

"As I told Anson, Hannah Brewster was an artist," Virginia said. "She was also quite eccentric. Some would say unhinged. I occasionally exhibited some of her work in my gallery."

"Was she any good?" Cabot asked.

"Hannah was quite good but her work is . . . disturbing. It's too raw and too dark and too personal for most people. Hannah painted to exorcise the demons of her past — our past. She was there, you see."

"She was a member of Zane's operation?" Cabot asked.

"Yes. She was my mother's closest friend in the cult. I'm sure you remember her. She did much of the cooking and cleaning."

Cabot glanced at Anson. "See if Brewster's name is on our list."

Anson was already at work on his computer.

Virginia watched him. "You've got a list of the cult members?"

"It's not a complete list," Cabot said. "Nobody used last names, remember? And Zane confiscated everyone's ID. Most of the documentation that he collected disappeared with him that night."

"I interviewed the survivors after the fire," Anson said, "but they were all traumatized. Some refused to identify themselves. Others were afraid. Most just took off and disappeared. I had no legal grounds to hold them. We've done our best to compile a list of cult members but, as Cabot said, we don't think that it's complete, not by a long shot."

A page came up on the screen. Cabot uncoiled and rounded the desk so that he could read over Anson's shoulder.

"There's no Hannah Brewster," he said. "There is a Hannah Parker, though. She just disappeared after the fire. No family ever came forward to ask about her."

"That's her," Virginia said quickly. "She changed her name. She was always terrified that Zane might come looking for her. That's why she lived off the grid on Lost Island. No phone. No computers. No credit cards. No bank account. To my knowledge, the only piece of tech that she possessed was a digital camera that I gave her about a year ago."

Anson whistled softly. "All because she was afraid Zane might find her?"

"Yes," Virginia said.

"Sounds like Hannah Parker Brewster would have fit right in with our little crowd of conspiracy theorists," Anson said.

Virginia nodded grimly. "Definitely."

Cabot fixed her with his intent gaze. "If she didn't trust technology, why did she accept the camera?"

"She didn't consider it a risky device. It was just a camera, after all. She used it to take photos of island scenes. She painted the scenes on notecards that were then sold to tourists at one of the island gift shops. That was how she survived, you see — selling boxes of notecards to visitors. She never signed those pictures, and the people who operate the gift shop kept her secret."

Cabot got a thoughtful look. "If Brewster went to ground on that island, how did you find her?"

"I didn't," Virginia admitted. "It never even occurred to me to look for her. When I was growing up, my grandmother made sure that I had no connection with anyone who had been associated with Zane's operation. Not that anyone ever came around asking about me, as far as I know. But about a year and a half ago Hannah showed up at my gallery."

Anson peered at her over the rims of his glasses. "Why?"

"She wanted to give me some of her serious paintings — not the notecard scenes. I knew her pictures would be tough to sell — they are quite large, for one thing. But when she told me who she was, and after I saw the paintings, I couldn't turn her away. I assumed she needed money, so I took the pictures and gave her an advance. She accepted the payment but she insisted on cash. I don't think she really cared much about the money, though. She just needed to get rid of her pictures."

Anson's bushy brows formed a solid line above his forceful nose. "Why would she do that if it wasn't for the money?"

"Her paintings were scenes from her worst nightmare," Virginia said.

Understanding heated Cabot's eyes. "Scenes from her time in the cult."

It wasn't a question.

"Specifically scenes from the night Zane torched the compound," she said.

Cabot's jaw tightened. "I see."

36

"Before she died she gave me a total of ten pictures of that night," Virginia continued. "Each one is a little different, each is from a slightly different perspective. But if you saw them, you would recognize the setting immediately. She called the series *Visions.*"

"Did you ever sell any of her pictures?" Anson asked.

"No. After the first couple of pictures were delivered, Hannah decided that she didn't want them sold to what she called 'outsiders.' She insisted they were only for those who understood their true meaning."

"Survivors of the cult," Cabot said.

"Exactly," Virginia said. "In the end, I just collected them one by one. I keep them in a storage locker in my shop."

"You don't hang any of them in your own home?" Anson asked.

"No," Virginia said.

"Of course not," Cabot said. "They're your nightmares, too. Who wants a nightmare hanging on the living room wall?"

Virginia gave him a long, level look. "You are very perceptive, Mr. Sutter."

The corner of his mouth may or may not have twitched a little. "What can I say? You caught me on a good day."

"I assume you only bill for services rendered on your good days," she said politely. "I wouldn't want to pay for time spent working on your off days."

"I'll keep that in mind," Cabot said. "And the name is Cabot."

Anson cleared his throat and looked at Virginia.

"Did Hannah Brewster always deliver the paintings to you personally or did she ship them to you?" he asked.

"She brought the first couple to me but I realized she truly hated having to leave the island," Virginia said. "The outside world terrified her, so I offered to make the trip to Lost Island to pick up the pictures whenever they were ready. She was very relieved."

Cabot raised his brows at that. "If Brewster didn't use a phone or a computer, how did she let you know when a painting was ready for you?"

"Hannah had a very close friend on the island, Abigail Watkins, who ran the Lost Island B and B. Abigail did have a phone — a landline. She needed it for business purposes. She called me to let me know whenever Hannah had finished a painting. But aside from that landline, Abigail didn't use any tech, either."

"You say this Abigail Watkins was a good friend of Brewster's?" Cabot asked.

"Yes. But I should mention that Watkins wasn't Abigail's real last name. She changed it years ago."

"Why?" Cabot asked.

"Because she was connected to Zane's cult, too, right from the start when he set up his first compound at the old house outside of Wallerton. Maybe you remember her as well. She was a little wisp of a woman who worked in the kitchen most of the time. Very delicate. Very lovely. Almost ethereal. She and Hannah were responsible for the cooking and housekeeping."

Cabot's eyes went cold. "Zane ran his cult like the business it was — a classic pyramid scheme. And, like any smart CEO, he only wanted people who could help him grow his empire. Everyone he lured into the cult had a purpose. Some of his followers handed over their life savings to provide him with capital. Others had business or technology expertise. And then there were the bastards who served as his enforcers."

"Yes." Virginia shuddered at the memory. She and the other kids had been terrified of the thugs Zane used to patrol the compound grounds. "Abigail was one of Zane's earliest followers — maybe the very first."

Cabot glanced at Anson. "We should add Abigail Watkins's name to our list."

"Right," Anson said. He swiveled around in his chair to face his computer.

"You can mark Abigail Watkins as deceased," Virginia said.

Anson and Cabot shot her sharp, questioning looks.

She shook her head. "No conspiracy theory involved. Abigail died of cancer in early December. It was very sad. Hannah nursed her to the end. They were quite close."

Anson nodded once and then went to work entering Abigail Watkins's name to the list.

Cabot turned back to Virginia. "What makes you think that Hannah Brewster's death wasn't suicide?"

"It's her last painting that worries me," Virginia said. "I need to show it to you."

Cabot glanced at her large black leather tote. "Did you bring it with you?"

"I have a picture of it. I never got the original. Hannah painted it on the wall of her cabin. It was destroyed when the cabin burned to the ground."

Cabot watched her intently. "How did you get a picture of the painting?"

"Hannah used the digital camera I gave her to take a photograph of it. Then she mailed the camera to me. According to the time-and-date stamp, she took the photo at three o'clock in the morning of the same day that the cabin was later destroyed — the day she died."

Anson frowned. "Any other photos on the camera?"

"No, just the one. At first glance it looks very much like the others in the *Visions* series. But there are some significant differences. As I told you, the paintings are all scenes from the night of the fire at the California compound. They all show a demonic figure striding through an inferno. In most of the pictures it's easy to identify the figure as Zane — at least it's easy for those of us who remember him. Hannah usually depicted him with shoulder-length black hair swept straight back from a sharp widow's peak, and he's always dressed in black from head to toe. Always wearing a steel key ring."

"That sounds like Zane, all right," Anson said. "He used to come into town occasionally to pick up packages or get gas for that big black SUV he drove. I remember those fancy black leather boots he wore. The bastard had a real flair for the dramatic."

Cabot's eyes narrowed faintly. "I remember that damned key ring. He kept the keys to every building in the compound on it.

41

You could hear those keys clashing whenever he got close. That's how you knew when he was nearby."

"I remember that sound, too," Virginia said. "At night, after he locked us into that horrible barn, I could hear the keys as he walked away."

She saw no point in mentioning that she still heard the clash and clatter of keys in her nightmares. She could tell from the way Cabot's hand tightened around his coffee cup that he, too, heard the terrible music in his dreams.

"Go on," Anson prodded gently.

Virginia willed herself to stay focused. She had to convince Anson and Cabot that there was enough evidence of murder to make them take the case. She could not afford to have them conclude that she was as unhinged as poor Hannah. The suggestion that she suffered from a form of PTSD had been made by more than one person in her past, including a couple of therapists and some ex-lovers. She had to tread carefully.

She reached into her tote, took out her tablet computer and opened the image of Hannah's last painting. She put the device on the desk so that Cabot and Anson could see the screen.

"There's a frantic kind of energy about

this final painting that makes me think she did this in a great hurry," Virginia said. "As you can see, she used one entire wall of her cabin as a canvas. It was as if she was trying to create a life-sized version of what she saw in her mind."

Cabot and Anson studied the photo for a long time. She could tell by their grim expressions that they saw what she saw — a disturbing vision of the past fused with the present.

The scene showed a large, dark, demonic figure striding through a storm of flames. There were eight smaller figures clustered on one side of the painting, reminiscent of a Greek chorus. Virginia knew they were intended to represent the children, including herself and Cabot, who had been trapped in the barn. They stared at Quinton Zane, silent witnesses to the horror he had unleashed upon them.

After a time Anson looked up. His eyes were bleak. "Was there an investigation into Brewster's death?"

"It was minimal at best," Virginia said. "They believe she jumped off a cliff near her cabin. Her body washed ashore the following day. The island is very small. Only a couple hundred people live on it, so there is no local police presence. The authorities were called in from one of the larger islands. They determined that there was no indication that Hannah had been attacked. She hadn't been shot or stabbed. There were no signs of a struggle."

"Not a lot of high-end forensics available out there on those small islands in the San Juans," Anson observed. "And water washes away a lot of evidence."

"Believe me, I understand why the authorities went with the verdict of suicide," Virginia said. "Everyone who knew Hannah was aware that she had some serious mental health issues. In addition, she was grieving the loss of Abigail, her only real friend. I might have bought the official conclusion myself, if she hadn't sent me this last picture."

Cabot examined the image again. There was a heightened intensity about him now that stirred the hair on the back of Virginia's neck. It was not unlike the highly charged vibe she occasionally experienced around some of the artists she represented. The aura of fierce concentration that shivered in the atmosphere told her that Cabot was doing his own kind of art.

"I'll be damned," he said at last. "She really nailed the bastard, didn't she?"

"I can see why it would be hard to sell

pictures like this one," Anson said.

Cabot glanced up briefly, his eyes tight at the corners. "You said this one was different from the others that Brewster painted?"

"I took a picture of the previous painting, the one I got a few months ago," Virginia said. "You can compare the two and see for yourself."

She opened the other picture on the screen so that Anson and Cabot could view both side by side.

"In theme and design it's clear that the final work was intended to fit into the *Visions* series," she said. "However, some of the details are different. Take a close look at the figure."

She waited to see if they understood the significance of what they were viewing. In the hellish scene, a man dressed in black strode through a storm of flames, a devil walking through his empire.

"It's not like looking at a police sketch," Anson said. "There's no real detail in the face. Hard to be sure of the age. But if you know something about the situation and the man, you can sure as hell tell it's Zane. Amazing."

"Hannah was a skilled artist," Virginia said. "She could do traditional portraits. She did two of her friend, Abigail, for example. I have both of them. But when it came to the *Visions* series, she took a more abstract approach — probably because she was working from memories and dreams. She didn't have any photos of Zane or his followers."

"No one does," Cabot said grimly. "At least, none that we've been able to discover. How did you end up with the portraits of Abigail Watkins?"

"Abigail left them to Hannah, but Hannah couldn't bear to look at them after Abigail died. She insisted that I keep them. She said maybe someday someone would remember Abigail and come looking for the pictures. I doubt that will ever happen, but I promised Hannah I'd look after them. I store them in the same locker where I keep the *Visions* series."

Cabot's gaze sharpened. "Tell us about this picture of Zane."

Virginia took a deep breath. This was it, she realized. She had to convince them that she was not the victim of an overactive imagination.

"Hannah used certain elements and details to identify her subjects. It was a form of iconography. The keys dangling from the steel chain on Zane's belt are a typical example."

Cabot studied the image. "They tell you the figure is Zane."

"Without a doubt," Virginia said.

Anson pointed to the cluster of eight small figures in the background.

"The kids in the barn," he said. "You and Cabot and Jack and Max and the others."

"Yes," Virginia said. "We are almost always depicted in the same pose and in the same positions in the paintings."

Cabot looked up. "Almost always?"

"This final picture is a little different. One of the girls is holding a book. You'll notice that she is standing at the front of the group. That figure is me and that placement is new. In previous pictures I'm shown in a less prominent position on the canvas."

"You're holding that book," Cabot said. "The one you carried out of the barn that night."

"My mother gave it to me the morning of the day she died. It was an illustrated book filled with basic math lessons. She made it herself. Hannah illustrated it."

Anson's jaw tightened. "Those eight little figures represent the innocent victims."

Cabot contemplated the cluster of children for a moment and then shook his head. "I think they somehow serve as a sort of judge and jury in the paintings. The kids

47

are condemning Zane for his crimes."

"I agree," Virginia said. "Aside from Zane, there are no other grown-ups in the pictures. Just the kids. I'm very familiar with Hannah's work. When it comes to her art, I'm the expert. She knew that. I'm sure she expected me to get the message that she was sending in this picture."

"You said that in the other paintings the figure intended to represent Zane had dark hair down to his shoulders," Cabot said. "This shows him with short hair."

"Yes," Virginia said. "The short hair cut in a very modern style was the first thing that jumped out at me."

Anson rubbed his jaw. "No boots. Looks like he's wearing running shoes. And a black parka. The hood is pulled up over his face."

"There's a small portion of a car in the background," Cabot said. "Looks like a late model. Silver or gray. Definitely not Zane's black SUV."

"There are no cars in the earlier pictures," Virginia said.

Cabot took one last look at the photos and then he fixed Virginia with his intent gaze. "You think she actually saw him before she died, don't you?"

His tone was exquisitely neutral, but that very quality told her just how much control he was exerting over his own reaction to the painting.

"Yes," Virginia said. "Here's the thing about Hannah Brewster. She had trouble dealing with reality, but that was why she painted. She said it was the only way she could get at the truth."

CHAPTER 4

Anson contemplated the image again. "There's no indication of the age of the figure in this sketch. Zane was in his mid-twenties when he fired up his cult. He'd be in his forties now."

"He did such a good job of deleting his own past that we've never even been able to pin down his age," Cabot said. "Are you sure Hannah Brewster never left the island after she delivered those first two paintings to you?"

"I can't be absolutely certain but I seriously doubt it," Virginia said. "Hannah wanted to stay hidden. Why do you ask?"

Cabot pointed at the vehicle in the background of the painting. "If you're right — if Brewster did see Quinton Zane — then he must have taken a ferry to the island. Those communities in the San Juans are small. There's a possibility that someone else noticed him, too."

Relief crashed through Virginia.

"Does this mean you'll take my case?" she asked.

"Oh, yeah," Cabot said. "We will definitely take the case."

The icy certainty in the softly spoken words sent a flash of unease through Virginia. There was a fine line between keeping an open mind and full-on obsession, she thought. She ought to know. She had been walking that line herself for years.

She had wanted a private investigator who would take her concerns seriously. That was why she had tracked down Anson Salinas. She had hoped he could advise her, and she had been hugely relieved to discover that he was now in Seattle and part of an investigation agency. But it was clear that, while Anson would be involved, he wasn't the one who would be actively working the case. She was pretty sure now that she would be dealing primarily with Cabot Sutter.

As if he had read her mind, Cabot met her eyes.

"What's the matter?" he said. "Having second thoughts?"

She tapped her finger on the desk. "It just occurred to me that it's one thing for me to wonder if Zane is still alive and if he murdered Hannah Brewster. After all, I'm the

51

client. I'm entitled to my suspicions."

"But it's something else altogether if the investigators are on board with your personal conspiracy theory, is that it?"

"I think we need to be concerned about maintaining a degree of objectivity here," she said, trying for a diplomatic response.

"Sorry," Cabot said. "You've picked the wrong investigation agency if you want objectivity. When it comes to Quinton Zane, this is Conspiracy Central."

Anson scowled at him. "Stop trying to scare the client, Cabot." He turned back to Virginia. "Don't worry. Appearances to the contrary, he's a very good investigator. In fact, after he got out of the military, he spent a couple of years as a chief of police."

"Really?" Virginia looked at Cabot. "Why did you leave the police chief job?"

"I was fired," Cabot said.

She did not know where to go with that. "I see."

"Now, let's get back to our conspiracy theory," Cabot said. "Looks like the first step is to pay a visit to the island where Hannah Brewster died. I'll pull up the ferry schedule and see how soon I can get there."

It dawned on Virginia that she was losing control of the situation. It was time to take charge.

"Don't bother," she said. "I've visited Lost Island so often I've got the schedule memorized. The island is served by a private ferry. Service is only once a day in the early afternoon. Reservations are suggested if you're bringing a vehicle."

"Right," Cabot said. "I'll be on the next available ferry."

She gave him a cool smile. "So will I."

He went absolutely still for a moment. She knew he was trying to decide how to deal with her.

"That's not a good idea," he said finally.

"I didn't ask your opinion on the matter. I've got a reservation on the ferry tomorrow. You're welcome to join me if you still want to take the job."

"I'm taking the job," he said evenly.

Anson exhaled a long-suffering sigh. "I'm afraid Cabot is still learning the ropes when it comes to the fine points of client relations, but like I told you, he's a damn good investigator, Virginia. He knows what he's doing."

"I'll take your word for it." Virginia shut down her tablet and stuffed it into her tote. "It's not like I've got a lot of options, is it?"

Cabot allowed himself a small smile. "Nope."

"Fine. I'm the one with the reservation

for a car on the ferry, so I'll be driving. If you'll give me your address, I'll pick you up in the morning. We'll need to leave Seattle by seven thirty to catch the first of the two ferries it will take to get to the island."

"You don't have to worry about picking me up," Cabot said coolly. "I'll be at your door a little before seven thirty."

She hesitated and then concluded that the issue of who picked up whom was one battle she did not need to fight. She gave him her address.

"It's a condo," she added. "I'll meet you in the lobby."

"I'll be there."

It was a vow. The intensity infused in his words triggered a shiver of wariness. She had the feeling that she hadn't just hired a professional investigator — she had unleashed a force of nature.

"All right," she said, because there really wasn't anything else to say. She turned toward Anson and gave him a warm smile. "It's good to see you again, Anson."

He got to his feet and rounded the desk to help her into her trench coat.

"Good to see you, too, Virginia," he said. He opened the door. "Now, don't worry about Cabot. He doesn't exactly excel at customer relations, but he'll get the job done."

"That's all I ask," Virginia said. She moved past him into the hall. "Don't worry about the poor attitude. I'm used to dealing with temperamental, eccentric artists."

She had the satisfaction of seeing the stunned expression on Cabot's face before Anson very quickly closed the door.

For some inexplicable reason, she suddenly felt a lot more cheerful. She went on down the hall to the elevator and pushed the call button.

Chapter 5

Cabot went to the window and looked down at the rain-slick pavement of Western Avenue. He was feeling simultaneously energized and thoroughly pissed off. He couldn't remember the last time he had experienced such a weird mix of emotions. He also couldn't get Virginia's parting words out of his head.

"I'm used to dealing with temperamental, eccentric artists."

Like hell you are, lady.

Cutler, Sutter & Salinas occupied a small suite of offices on the fourth floor of a commercial building not far from Pike Place Market. It was a good address. True, it was not a flashy, high-end address in one of the gleaming downtown towers, but it was a respectable location. It also had the advantage of offering a discreet, low-profile entrance that appealed to those who were in the market for an investigator's services.

"What's your take on her?" he asked without turning his head.

Anson exhaled heavily. "I think Virginia Troy's got a lot of unanswered questions about the past." He paused a beat. "Same as everyone else who survived Zane's operation."

"Including Max and Jack and me."

"You know, after that fire at the compound, I called in every favor I had, contacted everyone I knew in law enforcement, trying to run down Zane. And then, a few months later, he's supposedly dead in a convenient fire-at-sea scenario."

"He faked his own death because he knew you would never stop looking for him."

"And now he's got you and Max and Jack on his trail. World's a different place these days. Lot more technology available. Sooner or later you'll find him, assuming he's alive."

"He's still out there, Anson. I know it."

"No argument from me. I never did buy that yacht-fire story."

Cabot turned around. "Virginia as much as admitted that Hannah Brewster was borderline if not full-on crazy."

"Here's what you should keep in mind," Anson said. "Hannah Brewster was Virginia Troy's last link to the cult, the last person who could have supplied some answers about the past. Now Brewster is dead, leaving Virginia with a lot of unanswered questions. She needs to know if Brewster really was hallucinating when she did that last painting."

"We need to know that, too."

"Yep," Anson said. "Okay, I gave you my take on her. What's yours?"

Cabot tried to sort through his initial impressions. Virginia Troy was cloaked in a cool reserve that made it impossible to get a handle on her. There were some contradictions that were hard to resolve.

It had come as no surprise to discover that she owned an art gallery. It was the first time he had met someone who actually did own a gallery, but damned if Virginia didn't look like what he expected an art dealer to look like: sharp, polished, sophisticated.

But there had been none of the elitist attitude that he'd expected from a woman who moved in the art world.

Her dark hair had been swept straight back and secured in a severe knot that made you very aware of her intelligent green-and-gold eyes. The black-framed glasses contributed to the crisp look-but-don't-touch aura.

There was, he concluded, something very fierce going on just under the surface. He understood because there was a similar energy burning deep inside him. *We've both had to learn how to channel the fire at the core, haven't we?*

Her clothes — dark trousers and a close-fitting jacket in a deep, dark rust color — looked expensive. And then there were the boots.

What was it about a woman in high-heeled boots that made a man take notice?

"She seems to be doing all right in the gallery business," Cabot said.

Anson pursed his lips. "Successful, I'd say. But I don't think she's exactly raking in the cash. I'll do a little research on her gallery and see what I can find."

"No ring."

"You noticed, huh?" Anson sounded amused.

"What?" Cabot said.

"Nothing," Anson said a little too easily.

"She said I was eccentric."

"Not exactly. I believe what she actually said was that she was accustomed to dealing with temperamental, eccentric artists."

"Which carries the strong implication that she classifies me in the same category as one of her temperamental, eccentric artists."

"Well, if it's any consolation, I'd say you're not temperamental. Just the opposite. You're not big on heavy drama, that's for sure."

Cabot groaned. "Thanks for that."

"Expect it's a result of all that martial arts training." Anson sat forward and folded his hands on top of his desk. "Moving right along, I do think that Virginia Troy's got a solid reason to want to go to that island and ask a few questions."

"So do I," Cabot said. "Think we should notify Max and Jack that we've got a possible new lead on Zane?"

"It's not a lead; it's a rumor based on the hallucinations of a woman who was, by all accounts, certifiably nuts. Jack is working a consulting gig in Chicago. He needs to focus. And why drag Max and Charlotte back from their honeymoon if there's nothing concrete? I vote we find out exactly what we're dealing with before we go off the deep end."

"Right." Cabot headed for his office. "I'll clean up the paperwork on that insurance job so you can send the bill to the client."

"One more thing. That lawyer fellow called again."

"Burleigh?" Cabot paused in the doorway. "What the hell did he want?"

"Same thing he wanted the first time. He wants to talk to you."

"You gave him my message?"

"Word for word. Told him you haven't had any connection to your mother's family in your entire life and you don't plan to change that situation now. But I can tell that he's the persistent type."

"So am I."

"You want my advice?"

"No, but I'm going to get it, aren't I?"

"Yeah," Anson said. "Because I'm pretty sure Burleigh's not going to go away. Find out what he's after and then you can make an informed decision."

"My decision is already informed by the fact that my mother's family disowned her when she ran off with my biological father."

"A new generation has come of age since your mother got kicked out of the Kennington family," Anson said. "Be reasonable. Maybe someone found out what happened all those years ago and wants to reach out to you. Reopen the lines of communication."

"If that was true, why go through a lawyer? Everyone knows that no one wants to get a call from a lawyer."

"Your choice," Anson said. "But I'm telling you, Burleigh is not going to go away."

"Fine." Cabot moved into his office. "I'll return his call. I'll listen to what he has to say and then I'll tell him to go to hell."

"That's the spirit. I left the number on your desk."

Cabot went into the office, closed the door and sat down. The only thing marring the Zen-like surface of his desk was the sticky note with Burleigh's name and a telephone number.

He contemplated the digits for a while. Anson was right. Lawyers generally did not give up and go away just because they couldn't get someone on the phone; at least not well-paid lawyers, and any lawyer calling on behalf of the Kenningtons of San Francisco would be very well paid.

His mother's family controlled a closely held empire that had been founded in California during the heyday of the gold rush in the 1800s. The original source of wealth had not been gold, however. Thomas J. Kennington had been far too smart to waste time chasing a fantasy with a pick and a shovel. Instead, he had built a nice little empire selling picks and shovels and other equipment to the prospectors who were chasing the fantasy.

Later, Kennington and his heirs had invested in oil and railroads. Eventually those old-school sources of revenue had given way to a more modern, more diversified portfolio that included a lot of valuable

California real estate. "You can never go wrong with waterfront property" had been the Kennington company motto since the 1930s. They had proven to be profitable words to live by.

For nearly five decades, the man in charge of Kennington International had been Whittaker Kennington. Cabot had never met his grandfather, and that wasn't going to change now, because two months ago Whittaker Kennington had collapsed and died. The cause of death was a heart attack. He had been eighty-five and on his third marriage. The family had kept the precise circumstances of his death vague, pleading privacy issues. But they couldn't control the rumors. The old man had been in bed with his mistress at the time of his death.

The Kenningtons were brilliant when it came to business, but they were also notorious for their family dramas. They were known for their volatile tempers. They harbored grudges, engaged in multigenerational feuds and usually racked up multiple marriages.

Cabot reached for the phone on his desk. *Get it over with,* he thought. Then he could start thinking about tomorrow morning and Virginia Troy.

A woman with a smooth, polished voice

answered on the second ring.

"Burleigh Hammond."

"Cabot Sutter returning a call from —" Cabot broke off to glance at the sticky note. "From J. L. Burleigh."

"Yes, of course, Mr. Sutter." The polished voice warmed instantly. "Mr. Burleigh is expecting your call. I'm afraid he's on the other line. Will you hold?"

Cabot glanced at his watch. "He's got thirty seconds."

Burleigh took the call immediately.

"Thank you for returning my call, Mr. Sutter."

It was a lawyer's voice: sincere; trustworthy; very, very smooth. It was a voice well suited to telling a story to the jury. *"Ladies and gentlemen, you have the rare opportunity to right a terrible wrong. My client is an innocent man."*

"I got your message," Cabot said. "What is this about?"

"You are no doubt aware that your grandfather passed away two months ago."

"I heard."

"My firm is handling the estate. As I'm sure you can imagine, it is a very complex situation."

"That's your problem."

"I'm calling to let you know that, due to a

64

small technicality in the will, you are entitled to receive a very nice sum of money."

Cabot sat very still. "Is it the customary one-dollar bequest acknowledging that I'm a descendant so I can't sue on the grounds that my grandfather was unaware of my existence?"

"I can assure you, this is considerably more than one dollar," Burleigh said. "The amount in question is twenty-five thousand dollars."

So, definitely more than the token dollar that was employed to prevent a member of the family from obtaining grounds to sue. But twenty-five grand was pocket change for the Whittaker Kennington estate — probably the equivalent of one dollar to the old bastard.

But a nice windfall in my world, Cabot thought. It would cover the rent on his overpriced Seattle apartment for a few months and leave a little extra that could be used to upgrade the agency's computer systems.

"Got to admit, I'm surprised," he said. "Any idea why the old man decided to acknowledge my existence?"

"When people reach the end of their lives, they often reflect on the past and experience regrets," Burleigh said.

"I heard he died in his girlfriend's bed. Doesn't sound like he was spending a lot of time brooding on the past."

"Don't believe everything you see in the media. Unfortunately, the circumstances of Mr. Kennington's death have become fodder for the tabloids. Your grandfather was a rather colorful personality."

"That's one way of describing him.

"Mean, unforgiving, tyrannical womanizer would be another way," Cabot added under his breath.

"As I was saying, you are to receive the twenty-five thousand dollars," Burleigh continued. "But there is some paperwork involved."

"Sure. Just overnight it to my office."

"I'm afraid it's a bit more complicated than that. The easiest and fastest way to handle it would be in person."

"I'm working a case. I'll call you when I'm free."

Burleigh chuckled. "I wasn't suggesting that you go to the trouble and expense of traveling all the way to San Francisco. It's my job to do the running around. I can fly up to Seattle with the check tomorrow, if that's convenient."

"No, it's not."

"It won't take more than ten minutes to

explain the technicality in the will. Once you sign the papers, the money will be yours."

"Fine, but, as I told you, I'm working a case. I'll be out of the office for the next few days. I'll get in touch when I return."

"I'm afraid this is a matter of some urgency," Burleigh said.

Cabot paused, absorbing that information. "What happens if I don't sign those papers?"

"In that event I'm afraid I will not be authorized to give you the check. As I said, the situation is somewhat complicated."

"How much time do I have?"

"I was hoping we could wrap this up in the next day or so."

"In my experience, a good lawyer can usually stall indefinitely when it suits him."

"Mr. Sutter, I urge you to keep in mind that there is twenty-five thousand dollars at stake here. If you delay too long, another clause in the will kicks in, voiding the bequest."

"Send copies of those papers to me. I'll take a look at them."

Burleigh cleared his throat. "As I said, the matter is complicated. I'd like to be on hand to explain the details."

"Look, I don't have time to argue about

this. Send the papers. I'll contact you after I've looked at them."

"Very well, if you insist." Burleigh sounded annoyed but resigned. "Your case must be quite important if you're willing to put off receiving a check for twenty-five thousand dollars."

"You have no idea."

"I'll look forward to meeting with you soon," Burleigh said. "Meanwhile, keep in mind that there is twenty-five thousand dollars at stake."

"I'll do that." Cabot ended the call and sat looking at the phone for a moment. After a while he got to his feet, rounded the desk and opened the door of his office.

Anson looked up from his computer.

"Well?" he said.

Cabot propped one shoulder against the doorframe and hooked his thumb in his leather belt. "According to the lawyer for the Whittaker Kennington estate, the old man evidently had a change of heart and left me twenty-five grand."

Anson snorted. "From most people that would be a nice little bequest. But considering that this is Whittaker Kennington's estate, I'd say it was a token gift."

"It is. Still, twenty-five thousand is twenty-five thousand."

"Can't argue with that."

"But here's where it gets interesting," Cabot said. "According to Burleigh, I have to sign some paperwork before I can cash the check. What's more, he's willing to fly to Seattle and meet with me here in my office to make it easy for me to sign the papers."

Anson's brows rose. "Huh."

"Furthermore, there appears to be some urgency about signing said papers. If I don't give him my signature fairly soon, I'll lose the money."

Anson lounged back in his chair. "I don't know a lot about wills and trusts. I'm sure your grandfather's estate is very complicated. Still, that does sound a little strange."

"That's how it struck me. Makes me think of the old saying, 'There's no such thing as a free lunch.' "

"Yeah, but there is such a thing as a grandfather having some serious regrets about never having had a relationship with his grandson."

"He didn't need me," Cabot said. "Thanks to three marriages, he wound up with plenty of offspring and a number of grandchildren."

"Which may explain why your bequest isn't exactly breathtaking," Anson said. "All those exes and their offspring are probably fighting over their shares of the estate."

"Can't say I blame them. It's the paper-work angle that makes me think this offer from Burleigh isn't quite as simple and straightforward as it sounds. I told him to send me copies of the documents he wants me to sign so that I could look them over."

Anson looked thoughtful. "Couldn't hurt to have your own lawyer take a look at them, too. Legalese is always hard to translate. Give Reed Stephens a call. We've done some work for him, and a while back he helped Max with a problem related to some family issues. You can trust him."

"Good idea. I'll contact him."

Cabot pried himself away from the door-frame, turned and went back into his office.

The twenty-five thousand would definitely come in handy, but right now the only thing he wanted to concentrate on was the trip to Lost Island with Virginia Troy.

CHAPTER 6

"One thing has been bothering me," Virginia said.

She was sitting behind the wheel of her car, watching the two-man ferry crew prepare to lower the ramp at the small island dock. It had been a long trip from Seattle, involving a lot of driving, two ferries, and a great deal of waiting-around time in between the crossings.

She and Cabot had been in close proximity since she had found him in the lobby of her condo building at seven twenty-five that morning. It was now going on two o'clock in the afternoon. She could not remember the last time she had spent so much one-on-one time with a man. And it had been forever since she'd experienced this edgy whisper of excitement. She told herself it was the prospect of finally discovering the truth about Hannah Brewster's death that was responsible for the sense of anticipation. But she had a feeling that Cabot was the real source of the little thrills.

This was dangerous territory. When it came to relationships she was a modern-day Cinderella. It was best for everyone concerned if she was home by midnight. Some men, of course, considered her quirk a real draw, at least initially. But eventually they came to see it as a form of rejection — which it was. True, she could buy a little extra time with her meds or a couple of extra glasses of wine, but that usually guaranteed a full-blown anxiety attack later.

She and Cabot had both been careful to keep things cool and businesslike during the trip. Theirs was an odd association, she reflected. They were, in some weird sense, intimate strangers. They had a history.

Cabot took his attention off the ramp-lowering process and looked at her.

"Just *one* thing bothering you?" he asked.

"Okay, a lot of things," she admitted. "But the question I keep circling back to is, why, assuming he is alive, would Zane take the risk of murdering a woman who couldn't possibly have done him any harm?"

"You're working from a false premise. Trust me, if Quinton Zane did come here to murder Hannah Brewster, it's because he believed that she was in a position to create problems for him."

"If he thought she was a threat, he could have gotten rid of her a long time ago."

"I can think of three possible explanations for the delay. The first is that Brewster was always a threat of some kind but Zane only recently discovered where she was hiding."

"What's explanation number two?"

"Something has changed in Zane's world. Whatever it is, it convinced him that Brewster had become a threat."

"And possibility number three?"

"Maybe Hannah Brewster really did burn down her cabin and jump to her death."

"Because she was delusional."

"Yes."

The ramp was finally in position. Virginia started the engine and prepared to follow a battered pickup and a sedan off the ferry.

"I do realize that this is probably a complete waste of time, not to mention money," she said. "My grandmother was very upset when she found out that I had hired Cutler, Sutter and Salinas. But once I saw Hannah's last picture, I couldn't stop asking questions."

"And now you've shown it to Anson and me, and we can't stop asking questions."

She drove slowly down the ramp and onto the town's narrow main street. "In other words, we were both doomed to make this trip."

"Doomed is a very heavy word," Cabot said. "How about *destined?"*

"Good thing each of us knows where the other is coming from, or one of us might conclude that the other wasn't entirely stable."

"Good thing," Cabot agreed.

She decided not to mention that there were people, including some old boyfriends, who had already concluded that she was not entirely stable. At the very least they didn't think she qualified as normal. One of the advantages of working in the art world was that "normal" was not considered an important job requirement.

She drove slowly past the small organic foods grocery and café, the tiny gas station, the herbal-tea shop and a handful of little galleries that displayed the works of local artists.

"This is one very small town," Cabot said.

"Yes."

"Do you know anyone here?"

"I've met some people but I can't say I know any of them well. I visited Hannah a few times every year, especially after her friend, Abigail, got so ill. Hannah was at her bedside night and day. She was exhausted.

My gallery is closed on Sundays and Mondays, so sometimes I came here to the island to stay with Abigail for a day or two so that Hannah could get some rest."

Cabot looked at her. "You were a good friend to Hannah Brewster."

"She didn't have any family. Abigail was all she had and she was losing her."

Cabot accepted that without comment. "Did anyone else on the island besides Abigail Watkins know about Brewster's history in Zane's operation?"

"It's tough to keep a secret in a small community, so it's quite possible that some people know about Hannah's time in the cult. But I doubt that anyone knows a lot about it. Neither Hannah nor Abigail ever talked much about Zane or the past, not even to me."

"How many B and B places are there on the island?"

"Four or five, but most are closed at this time of year. As far as I know there are only two open now, the Harbor Inn here in town and Abigail's old place, the Lost Island Bed-and-Breakfast. That's where we're staying. It's closest to Hannah's cabin, or what's left of it. I assume you'll want to take a good look around the ruins and the place on the cliffs where she jumped or was pushed."

"Someone took over Abigail's business?"

"Yes. It was closed as a functioning B and B after Abigail moved into the final stages of her illness. But dying is expensive, so shortly before her death Abigail sold the place to a woman named Rose Gilbert, who agreed to let Abigail stay in the house until she died. Now Gilbert has reopened but only on a limited basis. She told me she's planning some major renovations and hopes to be in full operation by the summer season."

Cabot considered the heavy cloud cover that was moving in over the island. "We've got some time left before the rain hits. Let's take a look at what's left of Brewster's cabin."

"All right, but I'll warn you up front there isn't much to see."

"Truth has metaphysical properties."

"Meaning?"

"It exists regardless of the presence or absence of the physical surroundings. The trick is perceiving it."

"Wow. That's impressive. Another one of those insightful martial arts sayings?"

"No, I just made it up. Figured it would annoy you."

She smiled and stopped briefly at the end of the main street.

"I suspected as much," she said. "I took some self-defense classes back in college but our instructor didn't teach us any fancy philosophical sayings. It was pretty much just the basics."

"Run if you can because, in spite of how it looks on television, it's hard to hit a moving target. If you can't run, fight and fight dirty. Go for the eyes. Think of every object around you as a weapon. Strike fast and hard when you get the chance because you'll only get one chance."

"Yep, that pretty much sums it up. Like I said, the basics."

"Do you still practice the moves you were taught?" Cabot asked.

"Yes." No need to explain that the self-defense exercises she went through nearly every day — usually in the middle of the night — were a form of therapy.

"Good therapy," Cabot said. "Empowering. Gives you a way to release the anger. At least for a while."

Like he'd read her mind, she thought.

"Is it that obvious?" she said.

"It is to someone who went through what we went through. Why the hell do you think I go to a dojo a couple of times a week?"

"You know, after all these years of trying to let go of the past, it's sort of a relief talking to someone who was actually there."

"Must have been tough trying to pretend you'd put it behind you," Cabot said. "I had the advantage of being able to talk to Anson and my brothers."

"I've had some chats with good therapists but there's only so much they can do. The reality is that it happened and we were just kids with no power to fight back."

"We're not kids anymore."

"No, we're not. That's why we're here. To get some answers about the past."

"Yes," Cabot said.

She realized she suddenly felt a lot better.

"Just so you know, if you really want to annoy me, you'll have to come up with fancier philosophical sayings than that line about perceiving the metaphysical truth," she said. "I sell art to a lot of very pretentious art collectors, and I talk to a lot of very snobbish art critics. When we really get going, the bullshit is so thick you need boots."

"Sometimes you give the impression that you don't have a lot of respect for the art you sell."

"I respect any work of art that incorporates some hint of truth, however small, and I am downright fascinated by any artist who can give that little bit of truth a physical reality."

The corner of Cabot's mouth may have twitched up a fraction of an inch.

"You're good," he said.

"Thank you. I've been in the gallery business awhile now. I've had lots of practice looking at art and marketing it."

"Do you date any of those artists who fascinate you?" Cabot asked.

He sounded genuinely curious.

"I learned long ago that it's a huge mistake to date an artist," she said. "They only want one thing."

"Sex?"

"Nope. At least that would be an honest, straightforward objective. The reality is that usually the only thing they want is for me to display their work in my gallery. And if it doesn't sell, they blame me. So I no longer date artists."

"Ah."

She glanced at him quickly and then looked away. "I'm sure you have similar problems in your line of work."

"Cutler, Sutter and Salinas has a couple of cardinal rules, one of which is, never sleep with a client."

"Sounds like a sensible policy."

And it was, she thought, a very sensible

policy. What's more, she had the feeling that it would take something of earthshaking importance to make Cabot Sutter break the rules.

For some obscure reason, some of the edgy excitement she had been experiencing faded a little.

She turned onto the unmarked road that wound along the rocky cliffs. A few miles later she found the graveled lane that led to what was left of Hannah's cabin. She brought the car to a halt. The only portions of the small structure that were still standing were the stone fireplace and chimney.

Cabot sat quietly for a time, studying the scene. Then he reached into the back seat for his jacket, opened the door and got out.

Virginia undid her seat belt, collected her own coat and got out of the car. A sharp, chill wind off the sound snapped at her hair. She pulled on the coat and went to stand next to Cabot. Together they stood looking at the desolate scene.

"That was one hell of a fire," Cabot said after a while. "Burned everything right down to the concrete foundation pad. Definitely not a normal house fire."

"I told you, the authorities who investigated believe that Hannah torched the cabin before she went off the cliff."

"Do they have a theory about why she would have burned down the house before killing herself?" Cabot asked.

"Rose Gilbert, the woman who took over the Lost Island B and B, told me that the locals believe Hannah felt compelled to destroy her art before she took her own life."

"If that was the case, why would she send you that camera with the photo of her final picture."

It wasn't a question.

"Exactly," Virginia said.

Cabot walked slowly around the concrete pad, pausing occasionally to pick up a stick of charred wood or a blackened bit of metal.

After a time he rejoined her.

"Do the authorities have any idea of exactly where she jumped?" he asked.

"Or was pushed? I suppose it could have been anywhere along the top of the cliffs. I assume it was somewhere nearby."

"The cabin faced the cliffs."

"Yes."

"Doors?"

"One in the front about where you're standing and one in back off the kitchen."

Cabot took up a position at the front edge of the concrete pad and studied the cliffs. Virginia folded her arms and watched him in silence. She sensed that he was going into

81

some private mental zone. It wasn't an act designed to impress the client. She had seen artists do something very similar when they were deep into their work and wholly focused on their inner vision.

"If she was running for her life, she would have gone down the lane toward the main road," he said. "Instinct would have taken over. She would have turned left toward town. If she was being chased, the killer would have caught up with her near that curve in the road. That's where she would have gone over the edge."

He indicated the direction with one hand.

Virginia considered briefly. "I think I would have headed for the woods. They're closer to the cabin, and my odds of losing the killer in the trees at night would have been better there."

Cabot glanced at her, brows slightly elevated as if she had managed to surprise him.

"You're right," he said. "That is very clearheaded thinking."

"Thank you," she said, careful to keep her tone excruciatingly polite.

Evidently the small bit of sarcasm went straight over his head without ruffling a single hair because he continued walking her through his logic.

"We can assume that Brewster didn't head for the woods because there were no indications of violence," he said. "If she had been killed somewhere on land and then dumped over the cliffs, there would have been signs of a struggle. Maybe an indication that she was dead before she went into the water."

"All right, I understand your reasoning. Why does it matter where she went over the cliffs?"

"Because it would give us a few more solid facts." Cabot turned to face the cliffs again. "Now, if she had already made the decision to take her own life, she would have gone toward those rocks. It's the closest point to the water and there's a sheer drop. Not much chance of accidentally surviving the fall."

He started walking toward the craggy outcropping. Virginia folded her arms, hugging herself against the sharp wind, and followed.

Cabot did not follow the graveled lane. Instead he cut straight across the muddy clearing. Virginia trailed a few paces behind, not wanting to crowd him.

He stopped just short of the jumble of rocks, reached down and picked up a small, rain-dampened carton.

Virginia hurried to catch up with him.

"What is it?"

"A box of household matches," Cabot said. "The long kind that you use to light kindling in a fireplace."

Virginia thought back to the occasions when she had visited Hannah. There had always been a fire going in the fireplace. It was the sort of detail you noticed when you had a serious phobia about open flames.

"Hannah kept a box of matches like that on her mantel," she said.

Cabot looked back toward the ruins of the cabin. "She set fire to the cabin to destroy her last painting and then she ran for this point on the cliffs. Probably didn't realize she was still holding the box of matches until she got this far. She dropped the matches just before she jumped."

Virginia took a long breath and let it out slowly. "The authorities are right, then."

Cabot looked at the box in his hand. "Yes. But the real question is why she thought she had to take such extreme measures."

"The locals will tell you that she was more than a little crazy."

Cabot's eyes were steel-cold. "The locals don't know what we know about her history."

"No," Virginia said. "I'm sticking with my original theory. Hannah believed that Quin-

84

ton Zane had come back from the dead. She sent me a warning in the form of her last painting and then she destroyed the picture."

"There's only one good reason why she would have done that," Cabot said.

"She was afraid Zane might see the painting."

"That's what this looks like."

"Maybe the hallucinations finally overwhelmed her mind."

"Maybe," Cabot said. "We can't rule out the fact that she might have gotten lost in a delirium. But we also can't ignore the possibility that she saw something or someone who made her think that Quinton Zane is still alive."

He started toward the car. She touched the sleeve of his jacket. He stopped at once and turned. He did not say anything, he just waited.

"Thank you," she said.

"For what?"

"For believing that Hannah Brewster did not kill herself because she went mad. For taking my concerns about Quinton Zane seriously."

"When it comes to Quinton Zane, I am always serious."

CHAPTER 7

Tucker Fleming had never before broken into anyone's home — the online world provided much easier and far less risky ways to steal. However, he had done the research on the Internet and it was clear that burglary was actually a surprisingly simple, straightforward business.

The trick, of course, was to not get caught.

Virginia Troy's third-floor condo had not been much of a challenge. He'd had to get past the security system at the lobby door, but that was easy. He'd waited until one of the residents, a woman carrying some large packages, had entered, and then he'd offered to hold the door. His toolbox and his spotless uniform bearing the logo of a nonexistent plumbing company had worked like a charm.

Once inside Troy's apartment, he'd gotten lucky again. The alarm system was an off-the-shelf piece of junk that used old-fashioned wireless technology — easy enough to jam with the highly illegal device he had constructed using components he'd bought online.

He stood in the center of Troy's living room and played the narrow beam of his flashlight across the space. It was decorated in various warm shades that made him think of honey and whiskey. Not surprisingly, there were some artworks scattered around the room. The ray of light danced on a glass bowl that glowed with brilliant blues and yellows. A couple of abstract paintings done in rich jewel tones framed the sofa.

He wasn't here for the art.

He walked across sleek wood floors, avoiding the area rugs so as not to leave an impression from his shoes, and started down a hallway. He was searching for a room that looked like it served as a home office. A businesswoman like Virginia Troy was bound to have one.

He found a bedroom that had been converted into a library. There was a couch that was probably a pullout bed. He was amused to see a lot of actual books on the shelves. Really, who read books these days when the online universe offered an endless array of entertainment?

Sure enough, there was a desk in the

corner. A cobalt-blue glass paperweight secured a small stack of invoices, business correspondence and gallery catalogs.

He wasn't here for the routine paperwork, either.

He opened the first drawer and started looking for the key to the past.

Back at the start it had all seemed so easy, so straightforward — right up until the moment that Hannah Brewster had jumped off the cliff.

Brewster had been his best bet, but with her out of the picture, he had been forced to find a new angle. He could hardly believe his good fortune when he discovered that a gallery owner named Virginia Troy had been Brewster's only real link to the outside world.

He had known immediately that the name Troy could not be a coincidence. When he learned that Virginia was Kimberly Troy's daughter, he'd been almost giddy with excitement.

He had immediately started looking into Virginia Troy's world. He'd told himself he could not afford to rush the process, but he had experienced a jolt of panic when he discovered that she had contacted Anson Salinas within a week of Brewster's death. There was only one explanation that made sense — Troy had stumbled onto something that made her realize there was a lot of money stashed away. She was looking for the key. Obviously she didn't know that she possessed it or she would have already unlocked the missing fortune.

The desk did not yield any useful information.

He abandoned the search a short time later and let himself out into the hall. When he went past one neighbor's apartment, he heard a muffled footstep on the other side of the door. He pulled the cap lower over his eyes. Ignoring the elevator, he went quickly toward the stairs.

Once inside the garage, he let himself out through the service door that opened onto the alley. His car was waiting a couple of blocks away on a side street.

He got behind the wheel and eased slowly away from the curb. There was one other place he needed to search before he gave up. It would probably be a waste of time but he had to be thorough. There was too much at stake. Brewster's death had been an unforeseen disaster. Now he could almost hear a clock ticking. He had to get out in front of the situation.

The next step was to get inside the Troy Gallery. He had cruised slowly past the entrance earlier and seen a middle-aged woman working behind the counter — Troy's assistant, no doubt. He would have to wait until later that night.

Brewster's last words rang in his head. *"You were a fool to come back. The key belongs to the children. Did you really think that they would forget what you did to their families? You're a dead man. You just don't know it yet."*

Crazy bitch.

CHAPTER 8

"Yes, there were some guests staying here the night Hannah died," Rose Gilbert said. "Not many. Third floor is still closed for renovations. But I had a pair of honeymooners who never left their room except at mealtime and a retired couple who were into birding. Why do you ask?"

Cabot let Virginia answer the question.

"Cabot is a private investigator," Virginia said. "I've asked him to look into Hannah's death."

Rose grunted. "Had a feeling you weren't satisfied with what those off-island cops told you."

"I just want a more thorough investigation," Virginia said.

Rose nodded somberly. "I understand. It was a shock, that's for sure."

Rose was a chunky, solidly built woman in her early sixties who had an aging biker babe vibe, complete with a booze-and-cigarettes voice. Her gray hair was cut short and spiky. She wore denim pants and a faded denim shirt accented with a rugged leather vest. Her belt was studded with a lot of metal hardware that matched the metal studs in her ears.

Cabot figured the big four-by-four parked behind the Lost Island B and B belonged to her. Virginia's sleek little compact was the only other vehicle. He and Virginia were the sole guests that night.

They had eaten dinner at a small café in town — a thick vegetarian stew and rustic, whole-grain bread. He'd ordered a beer. He was not surprised when Virginia had ordered a glass of wine. It went with the sophisticated gallery owner persona.

When they returned to the B and B, Rose invited them to join her in the vintage parlor for a glass of whiskey. She had apologized for the limited selection. "No point stocking the bar, not at this time of year. Not enough guests. I only drink whiskey, so that's all I can offer."

The parlor was decorated with an astonishing array of needlework. There were several large, elaborately embroidered scenes hanging on the walls. He was no expert but the quilt on the back of the sofa looked handmade. So did the area rugs.

Crocheted doilies covered almost every surface. Rose Gilbert did not look like the arts-and-crafts type. He figured the needlework had probably been left by the former owner of the B and B, Abigail Watkins.

Rose had lowered herself into the big rocking chair on one side of the hearth. Cabot noticed that Virginia chose a chair that was several feet away from the crackling blaze in the fireplace. He understood. He didn't have a phobia about fire but he sure as hell had a profound respect for its lethal power.

He had selected a large reading chair across from Rose. He stretched out his legs and sipped the whiskey in a casual manner. Long ago he had discovered that people talked more freely to someone who was sitting across from them, sharing a drink.

"Did any of the guests go out that evening?" he asked.

Rose squinted a little, thinking. "They all drove into town for dinner, same as you two did tonight. But they were back here by eight thirty or nine. The older couple had some whiskey with me but the honeymooners went straight upstairs."

"When did you hear about the fire at Hannah's place?" Virginia asked.

"Well, I heard the fire sirens much later

that night, so I knew something had happened. And then, early the next morning, one of the volunteers who was searching for Hannah stopped by to ask if I had seen her. At first everyone was sure she had died in the fire, but when they didn't find a body, they hoped she escaped. Figured she might have run into the woods and gotten lost. But her body washed up in one of the coves later that day. That's when they decided that she had jumped."

"Did any of your guests show any interest in the situation?" Cabot asked.

"Some." Rose rocked slowly in her chair. "They were curious but not overly concerned. None of them had ever met Hannah. They all left on the afternoon ferry that day."

"Is there any chance one of your guests left the B and B that night and came back without you knowing?" Cabot asked.

Rose peered at him and then looked at Virginia. "You think someone set fire to Hannah's cabin and then pushed her off that cliff?"

"I don't know what to think," Virginia admitted. "That's why I hired an investigator."

Cabot waited for Rose to come to a decision. Eventually she turned back to him,

94

shaking her head.

"Why would anyone want to kill Hannah Brewster?" Rose asked. "She was crazy but she was harmless."

"I'm trying to eliminate possibilities," Cabot said.

Rose exhaled heavily, drank a little whiskey and rocked some more. "I go to bed early but it's real quiet around here at night. Almost no traffic, not at this time of year. I'm pretty sure I would have heard someone leave. The parking area out back is covered in gravel and so is the driveway. A car, even one with a quiet engine, would have made some noise. And anyone trying to drive would have had to use headlights. No street-lamps on the island."

Virginia looked at Cabot. "If there was a killer, he would have had to use a car. I can't see anyone walking all the way out to Hannah's cabin, certainly not at night."

"Especially if he was carrying a large container of accelerant," Cabot added.

Rose eyed Cabot. "What makes you think Hannah Brewster might have been murdered?"

"*If* she was murdered," Cabot said carefully, "there's a chance that the killing was linked to something that happened a long time ago. Hannah Brewster was once in a

95

cult that was operated by a guy who used fire to get rid of evidence and murder several people."

"Oh, shit," Rose muttered. She turned and looked into the fire on the hearth. "I was afraid you were going to mention that cult business."

Virginia tightened her grip on the glass of whiskey. "Hannah told you about her time in a cult?"

"No." Rose did not take her attention off the fire. "I didn't know Hannah Brewster well. I don't think anyone here on the island did. Also, I'm a newcomer here, so the locals still consider me an outsider. But people talk, just like they do in any small community. After Hannah jumped, a lot of people said that she had always been a little mentally unbalanced. They mentioned that she had once joined a cult."

"Abigail Watkins, the woman who owned this place before you bought it, was in the same cult," Virginia said. "That's why Hannah moved here to Lost Island in the first place. She wanted to be close to someone who had shared the trauma in her past."

"Yeah, heard something about that, too." Rose rocked gently. "I can tell you that there was a lot of speculation that Hannah and

Abigail were both suffering from that PTSD thing."

"Virginia mentioned that there is another B and B open at this time of year," Cabot said.

"That's right," Rose said. "Barney Ricks and Dylan Crane have a place in town, the Harbor Inn. I understand they keep it open most of the year, but they were closed that whole week for some remodeling."

Virginia sat quietly, her expression bleak. Cabot wanted to offer some comfort but there was nothing he could say that would give her cause for optimism. The odds were very, very good that they were chasing a shadow.

He knew all about chasing shadows. He and Anson and Max and Jack had spent years doing just that. The thing about shadow chasing was that you had to keep going until you were sure there was nothing there to catch.

CHAPTER 9

Shortly after midnight, Tucker Fleming made his way to the front door of the Troy Gallery. He would have preferred to use the rear door, but that opened onto an alley. No intelligent person walked down a dark alley in Pioneer Square at night.

He paused in the vestibule that shielded the front door, and checked the sidewalk. Music blared from a nearby club. There were a few people exiting a restaurant at the end of the block, but they were heading in the opposite direction.

He took out one of the tools he had purchased online and applied it to the lock on the front door of the gallery. He was inside less than thirty seconds later.

Once again he used the jamming device to silence the silly alarm system. It was astonishing how frequently people went with cheap security junk.

The shades had been pulled down in the

front windows of the shop, so he took out his flashlight. He made his way through the stark white showroom, weaving a path through a small forest of display pedestals, and opened the door behind the counter.

The back room of the gallery was a different world. In the showroom, individual objects and paintings were elegantly arranged for maximum visual impact. But in the back room, paintings were stacked four and five deep against the walls. Sculptures littered the floor. Art glass in various shapes and sizes sat on wide shelves. There was a cluster of colorful glass paperweights on a table near what appeared to be the door to an employee restroom.

It seemed unlikely that something as valuable as the key to a fortune would be sitting around in the crowded back room of an art gallery. But he reminded himself that Troy didn't know what she had. He could only hope that, given his extensive research into the cult, he would recognize the key when he saw it. Still, the prospect of searching the cluttered back room was daunting.

He decided to start with the counter in the showroom.

He went back through the door and started opening drawers and cupboards.

The search proved futile. Nothing but

invoices, receipts, catalogs and wrapping materials emblazoned with the gallery's name.

He was about to give up when he noticed the keychain in the top drawer of the desk. There was a single key on it and a helpful label, *Storage Closet.* He returned to the back room and tried the key on the door of what he had assumed was the staff rest-room.

A little thrill pulsed through him when the key worked. He told himself not to get too excited.

He got the door open and aimed the flashlight into the darkness. The beam played across a number of large paintings covered in protective drapery. The canvases were propped against the side walls of the deep, closet-like space.

Disappointment slammed through him. Just more paintings. He was about to back out of the room but he paused, his curiosity aroused. What was so special about the paintings that were kept under lock and key?

He gripped a corner of the nearest dust cover and raised it partway to take a look at the canvas.

In the beam of the flashlight, the picture glowed with all the hot colors of hellfire. A dark, powerful-looking figure with long black hair strode through the flames.

Tucker stopped breathing for a beat. And then his pulse started to pound. He studied the picture for a moment before he dropped the cover. He went down the aisle formed by the big paintings, yanking off the covers one by one.

Each picture was slightly different, but when he reached the far end of the storage closet and looked back, he realized he was looking at a multi-canvas series that, when viewed as a whole, showed the Quinton Zane compound on fire.

Each picture was signed by the artist — Hannah Brewster.

There were two more pictures at the very back of the closet. Each had a tag that read, *Not for Sale. Client may call.*

When he lifted the covers, he saw that the paintings were signed by Brewster, but they were not part of the fire series. Each was a portrait of the same woman. She appeared to be in her late thirties, forty at most. He thought she had probably been quite beautiful in her younger days, but in the pictures she looked weak and faded.

In each painting she was shown seated in the same chair near a big stone fireplace, doing some kind of needlework. There was more needlework hanging on the wall beside her.

The setting looked vaguely familiar. It took him a few seconds to recognize the parlor of the Lost Island B and B. Finally, understanding dawned. He realized that he was probably looking at a couple of portraits of Abigail Watkins.

Curiosity made him pause to examine the woman more closely. No question about it, Watkins had been weak and pathetic. Perfect cult material.

Disgusted, he let the covers fall back into place.

Once again he turned to study the hellish scenes that Brewster had painted. He was not into art but he was thrilled by the fiery scenes. A heady excitement shivered through him. The pictures were important — they *had* to be important — but damned if he could figure out how or why.

Virginia Troy had hired a private investigator for some reason, and not just any private investigator — she had hired a man who had been at the California compound. There was only one logical explanation — Troy didn't have the key, either; not yet, at any rate. But she was looking for it. That explained why she had contacted Cutler, Sutter & Salinas. She had probably agreed to cut them in for a share of the money if they found it.

The trail was getting hot.

He took out his phone and started snapping pictures. They might contain a clue or they might simply be the work of a delusional artist who could not forget the past. Either way, they would make an excellent addition to his private collection.

CHAPTER 10

The bastard had used her and then dumped her when he had concluded that he no longer needed her. And then he had gotten her fired. Now she was going to make him pay and pay dearly.

Sandra Porter got out of the car, wrapped her fingers around the small pistol in the pocket of her long, black coat, and started toward the front entrance of the Troy Gallery. A few minutes ago she had watched Tucker break in through the front door. It seemed unlikely that he would have re-locked it after he got inside.

Earlier that day she had watched him slip into Virginia Troy's condo building dressed as a plumber. Initially she had assumed that he had gone there to have sex with Troy. That had baffled her because Virginia Troy was clearly into art, and Tucker had zero interest in that subject. And if he had started a new affair, why dress up as a plumber?

The one thing she knew for sure about Tucker was that he had a history of using and manipulating people. The question was, how did he intend to use Troy?

Discovering that Virginia Troy was out of town had raised more questions. Why would Tucker break into her condo?

There was no denying that he had undergone something of a personality change in recent weeks. He had lost interest not only in her, but in his games as well. Instead he had become obsessed with something else. At first she had assumed he had found another lover. But yesterday she had discovered his secret.

Tucker Fleming was about to learn that he could not simply toss her aside because he thought he no longer needed her.

CHAPTER 11

Tucker heard the front door of the shop open in a stealthy manner. Panicked, he switched off his flashlight and tried to stay very still in the shadows. His first semi-coherent thought was that he had been followed by someone else who was after the key.

A figure appeared in the doorway that separated the showroom from the back room.

"Tucker? What in the world is going on here?"

He recognized the voice instantly. Relief swept over him. It was followed by a cold rage.

"Don't look now, Sandra, but you've become a full-on stalker," he said. "You stupid woman. You followed me? How the hell did you do that?"

He switched on the flashlight. The beam glinted on the small gun in her hand. His insides went cold. Crazy bitch.

"I put a tracking device on your phone," Sandra said. "And I'm not stupid, Tucker. You should know that better than anyone. After all, it was my coding work that got you that big bonus at Night Watch. You were employee of the month because of me. You got the credit and the cash, and I got the shaft. You used me. Then you got me fired. Did you really think I would just disappear?"

This was what he got for fucking a crazy bitch who worked in the IT department.

"You just did a little coding for me, Sandra. That was it. Any teenager could have done it. The vision of the new Night Watch app was all mine."

"Maybe a kid could have done that coding for you, but *you* couldn't do it, could you? You're good but you're not great. People with your skill set are a dime a dozen in the tech world. What's more, you're in an industry that always wants to hire the youngest people with the sharpest skills. A couple more years in the tech world and you'll be washed up. But you've done some contingency planning, haven't you? You're running a clever little off-the-books project at Night Watch."

"I don't know what you're talking about,

Sandra." He tried to make his voice soothing. "What we had was good for a while, but it's over. Under the circumstances, it was best for you to leave the company. We both know that."

"Good for you, maybe. But for me? Not so much. I'm out of a job. But enough about me. Let's talk about your new project at Night Watch and why you're here in the Troy Gallery tonight. I assume there's a connection."

"Fine. We'll talk. But not here. We're both in danger of getting picked up for burglary if we don't get away from this place."

"No, we'll talk here. I know about your Night Watch project, so tell me why you took the risk of breaking into this gallery."

Tucker sucked in a sharp breath. "It's a long story. I don't have time to go into detail now. But I can tell you that I came here tonight looking for something very valuable that went missing twenty-two years ago."

"You expected to find it in an art gallery?"

"I'd hoped to find it here but it turns out I'm going to have to keep looking. Virginia Troy is the best lead I've got." He paused a beat. "Things are getting complicated. I could use some tech support."

"You're a real bastard."

"We'll be partners this time, Sandra.

There's a lot of money involved. Makes the Night Watch project look penny-ante. I promise you'll get your share."

"What, exactly, are you looking for?" Sandra asked.

"Take a look at what's in that closet."

"If this is some kind of trick —"

"It's not a trick, I swear it."

Sandra hesitated and then she edged toward the open door. He watched her glance into the darkness.

"I can't see anything," she said.

Without a word he aimed the flashlight into the closet. Fire danced in the shadows. She took a quick look inside and then turned back.

"Just some weird paintings," she said. "Buildings on fire. Some kids in the back-ground. A guy dressed in black. Why are they important?"

"They're a link to my past."

"I don't understand. You were in a fire?"

"Never mind. All you need to know is that a lot of money went missing around the time of that fire. I'm trying to find it. Like I said, I could use your help and I'm willing to cut you in for twenty-five percent."

"Forget it. Fifty-fifty or nothing."

"All right, fifty-fifty. Now let's get out of here."

"I want fifty percent of your Night Watch project as well, or I'll make sure Josh Preston finds out exactly why he's losing money."

Tucker grunted. "You've got me over a barrel. I'm in no position to bargain."

She gave him another icy smile. "No, you're not. You see? You really do need me, don't you?"

"Yeah. I need you."

"We're going to make a great team."

He smiled. "Yes, we are."

She dropped the pistol rather carelessly into the pocket of her coat. "You're right about one thing. We should get out of here."

So fucking predictable, he thought. Except for the part where she showed up with a gun tonight. He had to admit he hadn't seen that coming.

Crazy bitch.

CHAPTER 12

Virginia snapped awake from the all-too-familiar nightmare. She sat up abruptly, trying to orient her skittering senses. It took a few seconds to remember that she was in a guest room at the Lost Island B and B.

You're safe. There's no fire. And even if there were a fire, you've got two exits marked — the door and the window. You're on the second floor. You can use a sheet to get down. The worst that can happen is you'll break an ankle. You'll survive a broken ankle.

It was the mantra that she had established back in her teens. Before going to sleep in an unfamiliar environment, she always made certain to locate at least two exits in case of fire.

She had a third option tonight, she reminded herself — the connecting door between her room and Cabot's. Earlier he had made a point of unlocking it on his side. He hadn't asked her if she would feel safer

111

that way, he had simply told her that the door was unlocked. She had very quietly unlocked it from her side as well. She knew that neither of them expected to be over-come with uncontrollable lust. There had been no need to discuss the real reason the door was unlocked. It was all about creating a third escape route in case of fire.

So, three exits. It was okay.

Aware that she wasn't going to be able to go back to sleep for a while, she pushed the covers aside and pulled on her robe. Guided by the dim glow of the little night-light that she always brought with her when she trav-eled, she made her way across the room and pushed the small table out of the way. She needed space for the nightly routine.

It was time to run through the exercise ritual. The alternative was using the meds. She resorted to them when the anxiety overwhelmed her, but usually the exercise worked.

She summoned a vision of a figure dressed in black and reached for the nearest object, an empty flower vase. One by one she went through the series of short, slashing blows designed to smash the vase against the imaginary attacker's face. She went for the eyes and then the throat.

The old rage welled up within her, washing away the anxiety in a white-hot blaze of energy.

When she was finished with the first series of exercises, she set the vase back down on the table and grabbed the next-nearest weapon, an old-fashioned candlestick holder. Once again, she went through the moves, chopping, slashing, stabbing — letting the fury cleanse her of the panicky sensations brought on by the old dream.

Twelve minutes later she sank down on the end of the bed. The anxiety attack had been quelled, but now, of course, she was too wired to sleep. If she were at home, she would have wandered down the hall to the kitchen and made herself a cup of herbal tea. But she was stuck in a room at the B and B, and she was pretty sure that Rose Gilbert would be unnerved if one of her guests started prowling the halls.

When her pulse settled back to a normal pace, she got up, went to the window and looked out. She always slept with the curtains open. On the bad nights she found it reassuring to be able to look out and see lots of city lights. But on the island there was only the light of the moon, and tonight it was only half-full. The woods that bordered the clearing around the B and B were so dark and thick they might as well have been a jungle.

The soft rap on the connecting door startled her so badly she jumped and uttered a half-strangled yelp.

When she had herself under control, she crossed the room, opened the door a couple of inches and saw Cabot. In the pale glow of the night-light, she could see that he was dressed in trousers and a dark crew-neck T-shirt. His feet were bare.

"Something wrong?" she asked.

"That's what I wanted to ask you," he said. "Everything okay?"

"Yes, fine. I got up to get a glass of water."

Okay, so that wasn't entirely true. She had a right to her privacy.

"Heard you moving around," Cabot said. "Figured maybe you couldn't sleep."

"I'm a crappy sleeper," she admitted.

"You're not the only one. I can usually get to sleep for a few hours but I often wake up about now. Takes a while to get back to sleep."

"It's one thirty in the morning." She glanced at the clock. "Make that one forty-five."

"No kidding."

"That's the time that Zane torched the compound."

"Sure is. Damn. You think there might be

a connection?"

"Call me insightful."

"My nighttime habits ruined a lot of my relationships," Cabot said.

"I know what you mean. I've given up on what people like to call relationships. I'm what you might call a serial dater now. Haven't even done any of that for a while."

"Commitment issues?"

"Oh, yeah. Also abandonment issues and anxiety attacks," she said. "All in all I'm not good relationship material."

"Sounds like we have a few things in common."

"You're still dressed," she said. "Didn't you even go to bed tonight?"

"Yes, but now I'm up and thinking about the investigation. I've got a question for you. Want to talk for a while?"

"Now?"

"Not like either of us is getting any sleep," he pointed out.

"True." She hesitated, glanced past him into the small space and then, on impulse, stood back and pulled the door wider. "We might as well use my room. It's bigger than yours. I've got two chairs."

They sat down in front of the window, the little round table between them. Neither of them made a move to turn on the light. It was as if they had both independently reached the conclusion that it might be more comfortable to talk in the dark.

"What is your question?" she asked.

Cabot leaned forward and rested his forearms on his knees, his fingers lightly clasped. "We know that Zane started his operation in the Seattle area."

"At the house outside of Wallerton. I remember that horrible old place."

"So do I. But he kept us there for only a couple of months before he moved all of us to the California compound."

Virginia shuddered. "Fortunately for you and me, that turned out to be the town where Anson Salinas was the chief of police. Otherwise we both would have died in that barn fire."

"Yes, but my point is, Zane recruited most of his followers from the Pacific Northwest."

Virginia contemplated that briefly. "I've never really thought about Zane's past. He was always just the demon from my child-hood. A cold-blooded killer. Do you think he was from the Seattle area originally?"

"We can't be absolutely sure," Cabot said. "We never managed to identify any of Zane's family. For all intents and purposes he was a true orphan. He did a very thor-ough job of erasing his past. But he was familiar enough with the Northwest to choose the Wallerton house, an isolated place, for the first compound. In my experience, the bad guys like to operate on familiar territory whenever possible."

Virginia studied Cabot's shadowed profile. There was a dark intensity about him again, the same intensity she had witnessed that afternoon when he had worked through the logic of how Hannah Brewster had died. She could have sworn that some eerie, dangerous energy shivered in the atmosphere around him.

"Why would he move the cult to California if he felt more comfortable here in the Pacific Northwest?" she asked.

"Could be any number of reasons, but the most logical one is that there were people here who knew him. He was trying to reinvent himself as a cult leader. He preferred a location where no one would be likely to recognize him."

"So you and your brothers and Anson have concluded that there is a very good chance he was from this region," Virginia said. "That makes sense. He was still a young man when he fired up his cult."

"We've never even been sure of his age, but according to the fake ID he was using in those days, he was probably twenty-four or twenty-five when he started recruiting."

Virginia thought about that. "He must have started out with very little cash. How did he manage to acquire the Wallerton house?"

"We tracked that down easily enough through the property tax records. It belonged to one of his followers, a man named Robert Fenwick. Shortly after he gave Zane the deed, Fenwick died in a car crash."

"Convenient."

"Zane didn't need him anymore."

"No."

The room seemed to have gotten colder. Virginia wrapped her arms around herself to ward off the chill.

"Zane was a manipulative sociopath," she said. "That kind of evil shows up at a very young age, so it's safe to say he must have made some enemies before he turned twenty-four or twenty-five."

"Zane was a sociopath but he was not crazy, not in the sense that he believed himself to be a real prophet or supernatural leader. He wasn't delusional. He was in the cult business for the money and the sense of power he got when he manipulated people like our mothers."

Virginia thought about that. "You said he was in it for the money."

118

"His operation didn't last long — about eighteen months. But during that time he raked in a lot of cash or, rather, his followers raked in the money for him. Many of them turned over their life savings. As far as we can tell, he didn't take any followers who were not useful to him."

"I've always wondered why he recruited my mother. She was a young woman on her own with a child. I know she didn't have any money to give to Zane."

"I don't know why he wanted your mother in his cult, but I know exactly why he wanted to control my mother," Cabot said. "She was a trust-fund baby. Her father disowned her when she ran off with my father, but the old man couldn't prevent her from accessing her trust fund."

"What happened to your father?"

"He was killed in a car crash."

"Like the man who gave Zane the Wallerton house? I'm starting to see a pattern here."

"Oh, yeah. What happened to your father?"

"Killed in a car that was rigged to explode," Virginia said. "They never caught the person who planted the bomb on the vehicle. The authorities decided Dad must have had mob connections. It was ridiculous. He was an artist."

"Turns out there were a lot of convenient deaths around the time Zane was setting up in the cult business."

"No wonder he decided to move out of the Pacific Northwest." Virginia thought for a moment. "Did Zane manage to blow through your mother's fortune? Was he finished with her? Do you think that's why he murdered her?"

"No, he killed her well before he had exhausted her trust fund. And before you ask, no, due to some technicality in the way the fund was set up, I was never included in the trust. My grandfather couldn't stop my mother from accessing her inheritance, but he did manage to tie things up in such a way that I never got a dime."

"That's harsh."

"The old man was thoroughly pissed because Mom ran off with a man he disapproved of."

"Did you ever meet your grandfather?" Virginia asked.

"No."

"You mean your family let you go into the foster care system rather than forgive your mom for running off with the wrong man?"

"Up until his death a couple of months ago, my grandfather controlled the Kennington family with what people like to call an iron fist," Cabot said. "Anyone who wanted to keep his or her share of the inheritance had to toe the line."

"A real control freak."

"Yeah. But I got lucky."

Virginia smiled. "Anson Salinas."

"Right." There was a short pause before Cabot spoke again. "As I told you, Whittaker Kennington died recently."

"I'm guessing you didn't go to the funeral."

"No, but evidently he left me a bequest in his will."

"So he had a change of heart there at the end?"

"Maybe, but I doubt it," Cabot said. "I think it's more likely that his first wife — my grandmother — left the bequest to me before she died. Maybe something the old man couldn't touch. Who knows? It's not a lot of money. Twenty-five thousand dollars."

"Still, twenty-five grand is twenty-five grand."

"True. It will buy some upgrades for our computer system. I'll find out the details soon enough. I've got an appointment with a Kennington family lawyer. But let's get back to the real question here. I know why Zane found my mother useful."

"Her trust fund."

"Right. Do you have any idea why he might have recruited your mother?"

Virginia turned that over in her head for a moment.

"I've never asked the question from that point of view," she said. "I've often wondered why my mother joined the cult, but I've never thought about why Zane lured her into his web."

"You were just a kid, but what do you remember about the situation?"

"My mother fell in love with an artist. She got pregnant and dropped out of college. They eloped. Her parents were furious. There was a huge quarrel. Things were very strained between my parents and my grandparents after that. And then my father was killed and Mom somehow fell under Zane's influence. She never explained why."

"You grandparents must have been shocked."

"Horrified is more like it. They were both college professors, you see. They moved in serious academic circles. The fact that their daughter had gotten sucked into a cult was not only emotionally devastating for them, it was also enormously embarrassing."

"You said your mother didn't have much money, but maybe your father had a life insurance policy that was worth a lot of cash," Cabot suggested.

"No, I'm sure there was no insurance money. Mom was smart — my grandmother always says she could have had a brilliant career as a mathematician — but she certainly didn't have access to a fortune."

"Did your mother work?"

"Of course. I told you, my dad was an artist. He never did make any money."

"What did your mother do?"

"She became a bookkeeper. Why?"

"Zane's scam was, in essence, an old-fashioned pyramid scheme," Cabot said. "One of those operations that depends on a lot of people at the bottom sending money up the chain to the people at the top."

"The people at the bottom never get rich but the guy at the top does. All right, so that explains the business model. Go on."

"Zane would have needed the basic infrastructure that any successful scam or legitimate business requires, including someone who could handle the money that poured in."

Understanding slammed through Virginia.

"He would have needed a bookkeeper," she whispered. "One he could control. My mother. He needed her skill set."

"Zane built a highly profitable business,

123

but he was the CEO. He couldn't spend his time dealing with the day-to-day financial aspects of his operation. He needed someone he could trust to handle the money."

"No one knows the secrets of a business operation as intimately as the bookkeeper," Virginia said. "Mom must have realized what was going on."

"Yes."

"But if Zane was running a successful business, why did he torch the compound and destroy the people who were bringing in the cash for him?"

"Good question," Cabot said. "My brothers and I have given that a lot of thought. The only conclusion we've been able to come to is that for some reason, Zane decided that it would be in his own best interests to pull the plug on the cult operation and move on. He used fire to destroy as much as possible."

"Covering his tracks and silencing witnesses," Virginia said. "But that all happened twenty-two years ago. Why kill Hannah Brewster now, after all this time?"

"Because something has happened," Cabot said evenly, "something that has brought Zane or someone else out of the shadows. Whoever that person is, he either viewed Hannah Brewster as a threat or else he wanted some information he thought she had. Given that I think Brewster took her own life, I'm almost certain that it was the latter."

"She had some dangerous information and she died in an effort to take her secret to the grave. But at the same time she sent me a warning."

"She must have believed that you were in danger."

CHAPTER 13

A double tap, just like a pro. Sandra Porter, aka crazy stalker bitch, was no longer a problem.

Tucker couldn't get the scene out of his head. He prowled through his house, a glass of ice-cold vodka in one hand. It was not his first. Talk about a real-world video game. It was thrilling. Exciting. Over the top. He was definitely playing in the big leagues now.

The problem was that the killing of Sandra Porter had left him riding a razor-sharp edge of panic. Some part of him kept waiting for the cops to knock on his door.

He was still amazed that the two shots hadn't drawn any attention. Well, it was Pioneer Square, after all. Gunshots at night weren't exactly unheard-of, and in this case the noise had been muffled by the old brick walls of the gallery and the reverberating music of the nearby clubs.

Just two shots. Like a damned pro.

Belatedly he remembered the gun. It was in the pocket of his jacket. He should probably get rid of it. After a couple of moments of close thought, he decided he would hang on to it. He could always ditch it in Elliott Bay if it became necessary.

He stopped in front of the living room window and looked out at the small bungalow across the street. The only light was the one that burned over the front door. The elderly couple had gone to bed hours ago.

The neighborhood was incredibly boring. He would have preferred to live in one of the downtown condos or apartment towers near the cafés, coffeehouses and bars. But he'd inherited the house from the drug-addicted woman who'd called herself his mother. He was going to make a lot of money when he eventually sold the place. Meanwhile it offered the advantage of privacy. He was the youngest person on the street and no one paid any attention to him.

For what had to be the thousandth time, he went over every detail of the scene in the gallery. He was sure he had left no trace of himself behind, but the body would be discovered when the shop opened on Monday morning — if not sooner. And then the cops would be involved.

It was only a matter of time before the

police showed up at the offices of Night Watch and started asking questions. It was, after all, what cops did. And they always looked hard at the boyfriend or the husband.

He had told Sandra that they had to keep their relationship a secret because everyone knew that Josh Preston, the head of Night Watch, was a real prick who strongly disapproved of office romances. Sandra had agreed. But now he had to wonder if she had become careless or downright vindictive when the relationship ended.

He turned away from the window. He had some cleanup work to do. Earlier he had tossed Sandra's phone into Elliott Bay. They had never had sex in her apartment — he had insisted they go to hotels for that, and he had always used a fake ID to check in. Nevertheless, just to be on the safe side, he'd detoured by her place a short time ago and taken a quick look around. He had been relieved to see no obvious evidence of their relationship. Not much evidence of any kind of a life at all. Sandra had been obsessed with her online games, but aside from that she had been a real loser.

He had never intended for the affair to last any longer than necessary. Sandra Porter was hardly any man's idea of a sex goddess. She was a loner with no family or friends and had zero social skills. But he had needed her coding talents to get the app working. Seducing her had been so easy. He had assumed getting rid of her would go just as smoothly. He had been wrong.

Mentally he ran through the checklist. He had taken care of her phone and he was sure her apartment was clean. Now he had to fire up his computer and spend a few hours making certain the bitch had not left any clues to their relationship online. It wasn't like he had to scrub all traces of a connection between them, he reminded himself. He and Sandra had been colleagues, after all. It was only natural that their paths had crossed occasionally. He just needed to make sure that nothing pointed to him as an ex-lover.

He would plant a few clues that would send the police in an entirely different direction, he decided. The killing had taken place in Pioneer Square. The most logical story would involve drugs and a mystery man. He could invent an online ghost. The police would waste days or even weeks chasing Sandra's unknown lover. Eventually they would give up.

He thought about that some more. Yes, he

liked that idea very much. The cops would look for a man. He would point them toward one who didn't exist.

He returned to the freezer, took out the chilled bottle of vodka and poured himself another glass. He reran the scene in the back room of the gallery. Again. A dark thrill shuddered through him.

Two shots, just like a pro.

Crazy bitch.

CHAPTER 14

The smell of freshly brewed coffee greeted Virginia the next morning when she opened her guest room door.

There was a familiar face in the hall.

"Good morning, Louann," Virginia said.

Louann Montrose was a small, whip-thin, sharp-faced woman in her early forties. Virginia had gotten to know her because Louann had worked first for Abigail Watkins and was now handling the B and B housekeeping for Rose Gilbert.

Today, Louann was dressed in jeans and a flannel shirt. Her graying hair was pulled back and secured with a rubber band. She was pushing a large cart bristling with cleaning utensils.

She paused when she saw Virginia.

"Hey, there, Virginia," she sang out in her cheery, singsong voice. "When I arrived this morning, Rose told me that you were back on the island. She said you had a friend with you this time."

Louann's face had the tight, weathered look of a woman who'd endured a tough past and had probably overcome more than one addiction. She radiated what Virginia considered an unnatural air of perpetual bliss and serenity. She was a devoted student of yoga and meditation.

The door of the neighboring room opened. Cabot appeared.

Louann brought her cart to a halt. "So you're Virginia's friend. Welcome to the island."

"Thanks," Cabot said.

Virginia stepped in quickly. "This is Louann Montrose, Cabot. She's worked here at the B and B for years."

Cabot inclined his head. "Nice to meet you, Louann."

"A pleasure," Louann sang. "Will you two be staying long?"

"No," Virginia said. "We're leaving on the afternoon ferry. Cabot is a private investigator."

Alarm flickered in Louann's pale eyes. She stared at Cabot.

"Why are you investigating Hannah's death?" Louann's voice lost some of its singsong quality. "You think there was something suspicious about it?"

"At this point I'm just asking questions," Cabot said mildly. "Did you know Hannah Brewster?"

"Of course I knew her. Everyone on the island knew her."

"Any reason to think someone might have wanted to hurt her?" Cabot asked.

"None of the locals, that's for sure," Louann said, very firm now. "Hannah wasn't what you'd call the warm and friendly type. Her only real friend was the woman who used to own this place, Abigail Watkins. But Hannah wouldn't have hurt a fly and no one on the island had a problem with her."

"I believe you," Virginia said hastily. "But I'm wondering if someone from Hannah's past might have come to the island to do her harm."

Louann's mood changed again. Now she was curious.

"You're talking about that cult she and Abigail used to belong to, aren't you?" she said.

Virginia nodded. "Yes."

"But that was ages ago," Louann said. "Why would someone come after Hannah after so much time?"

"I don't know," Virginia said. "But I can't get the idea out of my head."

Louann's blissful serenity snapped back into place. She gave Virginia a beatific smile.

"I know what it's like to get dark thoughts in your head and not be able to get rid of them," she said, once again using her musical voice. "You know what you should do?"

"What?" Virginia asked.

"You should take up meditation. It will do wonders to calm your mind."

"Thanks for the advice," Virginia said. "I'll look into it."

"You said you were checking out today?" Louann asked.

"That's right," Cabot said.

"Mind if I go ahead and make up your beds now? I can do the rest of the cleaning later after you leave."

"Sure," Virginia said. "Go ahead and make the beds."

"Thanks," Louann said. "I'll get the fresh sheets."

She left the cart where it was and walked a short distance down the hall. She disappeared into the laundry room.

Cabot closed the door of his room and waited while Virginia shut hers. They walked toward the stairs. At the door of the laundry room Cabot stopped. Virginia did, too.

The big house had been designed originally as a summer residence for a wealthy timber baron with a large family. The owners had entertained lavishly. In those days there would have been several servants on the staff, Virginia reflected. The laundry room contained a deep sink designed for soaking soiled linens, shelves stacked high with towels and sheets, and a large laundry chute.

Louann was in the process of taking some sheets down from a shelf.

"Mind if I ask you a question, Louann?" Cabot said.

"What?" she said.

"Do you remember any of the people who were staying here the night that Hannah Brewster died?" Cabot asked.

Louann frowned. "Why?"

"Just curious," Cabot said. "It's what you might call an occupational hazard."

"Well, I can't help you because I didn't meet any of the guests — didn't even know there were some staying here. You see, I wasn't on the island at the time. I was attending a weeklong yoga retreat down in Oregon."

CHAPTER 15

"I don't understand, Mr. Sutter." Octavia Ferguson regarded Cabot with an expression of aloof disapproval. "Why in the world do you want to open up the past? No good can come of it. I assume you're doing this for the money. How much is my granddaughter paying you?"

In Cabot's experience, the people who were most afraid to open up the past were usually the ones most shackled to it.

Three minutes after being introduced to Octavia Ferguson, he had concluded that Virginia owed her edge and her streak of determination to her grandmother. Octavia was a formidable woman. He was sitting across from her now, and it was easy to imagine her as a stern professor in front of a room full of students. She wouldn't have had any patience with those who failed to study for an exam or the ones who turned in their papers late.

Toned and fit, she was in her late sixties or early seventies. Her hair was cut fashionably short and tinted a discreet shade of blond. She was dressed in a pair of dark trousers and a blue-and-white-striped sweater. She wore small gold studs in her ears but no wedding ring.

It was early evening and Cabot realized he was hungry. After catching the last of the two ferries required to get back to the mainland, he and Virginia had driven straight down the interstate to Seattle. Octavia Ferguson's Victorian house on Queen Anne Hill had been their first stop.

Octavia had clearly been pleased to see Virginia, and she had initially regarded Cabot with a welcoming air. He got the impression that she had been both surprised and possibly even a little relieved to see Virginia in the company of a man. Evidently, Virginia was not in the habit of bringing men by to introduce them to her grandmother. He was pretty sure that Octavia would frown upon the serial dating thing.

The welcome hadn't lasted long. Octavia's barely veiled curiosity about him had been transformed first into shock and then deep wariness when she had learned that he was a private investigator.

Virginia spoke from a window that overlooked a magnificent garden. "Octavia, please, just listen to what we have to say before you jump to conclusions."

Watching the two strong-willed women deal with each other was both fascinating and a little scary, Cabot thought.

"From everything you've told me, Hannah Brewster had serious mental health issues," Octavia said. "The authorities made it clear that she took her own life. Why would you waste time and money looking into her death?"

"I think there is at least a reasonable chance that Hannah was murdered," Virginia said, "or perhaps driven to take her own life. As far as I'm concerned, it amounts to the same thing."

"That seems highly unlikely," Octavia said. "But even if it's true, it's a matter for law enforcement. You have no business being involved in a private investigation."

She shot Cabot another disapproving look. He kept his mouth shut. A smart man did not step between two quarreling lionesses.

Virginia turned away from the view of the gardens and faced her grandmother.

"This is my business," she said. "And it's Cabot's business as well. Here's the bottom line: if Hannah was murdered, then there is a very real possibility that her death is connected to what happened at Quinton Zane's California compound. Our biggest concern is that Zane himself may still be alive."

Octavia flinched as if she had been jolted by an electrical charge. Pain, rage and horror flashed across her face. An instant later the emotions vanished behind a mask of cool control.

"That's impossible," she said. "It's been twenty-two years since that monster murdered your mother and so many others. How could anything that happened so long ago affect the present?"

"We don't know," Virginia admitted. "But Cabot has a theory."

Reluctantly, Cabot decided it was time to speak up.

"I agree that it's possible Hannah Brewster was a victim of her mental health issues," he said. "But I think that, under the circumstances, the situation needs to be checked out."

Octavia eyed him, making no secret of her opinion. She blamed him for encouraging Virginia to stir up the past.

"The authorities assured me that Quinton Zane was dead," Octavia said. "I was told that he attempted to escape the country on a private yacht that he stole. There was a fire on board. They found the wreckage."

"They found the wreckage of the burned-out yacht but they never found Zane's body," Cabot said.

Octavia clasped her hands very tightly together. "They told me that wasn't uncommon in disasters at sea."

Virginia looked at her. "I think Hannah Brewster was convinced that she saw Zane shortly before she died."

Octavia froze. "Impossible," she whispered.

"Hannah painted a picture showing him in modern dress. She even included a portion of his car."

"Why would she paint his picture?" Octavia demanded. "Surely if she saw him, she would have told you or said something to the authorities. She wouldn't have painted a portrait."

"I think she painted the picture because she couldn't be sure of what she had seen," Virginia said. "She was well aware that she suffered from hallucinations. She always told me that the only way she could get at the truth was to paint it. After she finished the last painting of Zane, she took a photo of it and then sent the camera with the photo to me. She destroyed the original because she was terrified that Zane would see it."

"Those are the actions of a very disturbed woman." Octavia clenched the arms of her chair and switched her attention back to Cabot. "You still haven't finished telling me your theory, Mr. Sutter."

Mostly because I wasn't given the opportunity, he thought. He let it ride.

"I'm still working on it," he said. "But the bottom line is that if Hannah was murdered, it was most likely because there's something new in the equation."

"Such as?" Octavia demanded.

He glanced at Virginia, silently asking her approval before he moved on to more dangerous ground. She gave him one short, curt nod.

He turned back to Octavia. "Virginia tells me that her mother was a bookkeeper before she joined Zane's cult."

"She worked as a bookkeeper because that no-good artist she insisted on marrying couldn't make enough money with his silly sculptures to put food on the table," Octavia said through her teeth. "Kimberly was a gifted mathematician. If she were still alive, she would be teaching math at the college level."

Virginia's jaw tensed but she said nothing.

"A lot of money rolled in off Zane's operation," Cabot said. "At the time, my brothers and I were too young to pay attention to that aspect of the matter. But later when we started looking into the cult's finances, we discovered that all the money disappeared right around the time Zane did."

"Of course. He was in it for the money right from the start. He was a thief and a scam artist."

"Yes, but he probably didn't keep his own books," Cabot said, trying to sound patient. "They would have been very complicated books because he needed to find ways to hide the money — offshore accounts, maybe."

Octavia looked stricken. "You think my daughter helped him hide the money? How dare you suggest that she was a criminal. She was one of Zane's victims."

"What I know," Cabot said, "is what I just told you. A lot of money disappeared at about the same time that Zane did. If he did die at sea, he never got a chance to cash in on the profits from the cult. That means that money might still be out there, somewhere. If your daughter worked as his bookkeeper, she would have known where the money was hidden."

"But Kimberly is dead," Octavia said.

"Maybe because she knew too much about the cult finances," Virginia suggested quietly.

Octavia seemed frozen with pain, unable to respond.

Out of the corner of his eye, Cabot saw Virginia squeeze her eyes shut and turn back to the view out the window.

"According to Virginia, Hannah Brewster was your daughter's closest friend in the compound," Cabot continued. "If Kimberly did hide the money for Zane or if she knew where it was hidden, the one person who might also have known the location of the funds was Hannah Brewster. And now she's dead, too."

"Twenty-two years later," Octavia said. She shook her head, bewildered now. "There can't be a connection."

"Maybe not," Cabot said. "But in my business, money is always a powerful motive."

A long silence fell on the room. The old-fashioned tall clock ticked relentlessly.

Eventually Octavia stirred. "But you and Virginia just said that Zane might still be alive. If you're right, he got his money twenty-two years ago. That makes your theory utter nonsense. He'd have no reason to come looking for it now."

"Not unless my mother hid it and took her secret to the grave," Virginia said quietly.

Octavia digested that for a moment. "There's still the question of the passage of time. If Zane didn't get his hands on the money twenty-two years ago and if he is still alive, why would he wait so long to go after Hannah Brewster?"

"That brings us back to the essence of my theory," Cabot said. "Something has changed. When we identify the trigger incident, we'll get some answers."

Octavia sighed. "I don't understand. How will you even know where to start looking?"

"We've already begun the process," Cabot said. "But the more we know about the past, the better. Would you be willing to answer a few questions?"

Virginia did not move. He knew she was expecting her grandmother to tell him to go to hell. But he didn't think that was going to happen. Octavia had tried to close the door on a painful part of the past, but now that door had been pried open. She was a trained academic. It was her nature to seek answers.

"Ask your questions," she said quietly. "I doubt if I can give you any helpful information, but I certainly don't want Virginia to blame me for standing in the way of the truth."

Virginia had the good sense to hold her tongue.

"Thank you," Cabot said.

Octavia met his eyes. "If you're right, if that bastard Zane is still alive, I will be happy to get a gun and kill him myself."

"You'll have to get in line," Cabot said. "And I'd better warn you, it's a very long line."

"Who's at the front?" Octavia asked. "You and your brothers?"

"No," Cabot said. "My foster dad, Anson Salinas."

CHAPTER 16

"Got to tell you, that went much better than I expected," Virginia said. "Octavia has refused to answer most of my questions about the past."

"Probably because she doesn't have many answers and she doesn't like the ones she does have," Cabot said.

They were alone in the elevator of Virginia's condo building. It was located only a few blocks from the Space Needle, but the view of the iconic Seattle landmark had been obstructed by a host of new business and residential towers.

The building had a large footprint — it covered a big chunk of a city block — but it was not a tower. In fact, it was only six stories high. The ground floor was home to some small shops, cafés and a coffeehouse.

The elevator stopped on the third floor. When the doors opened, he gripped the handle of the small, wheeled overnight bag that Virginia had taken to Lost Island and followed her out into the corridor.

"My place is at the end of the hall," she said.

Cabot looked toward the far end of the corridor and noted the Exit sign marking the emergency stairs. No surprise. When he had gone apartment hunting after arriving in Seattle, he had only looked at units that were located near the fire stairs.

"What do you mean when you say Octavia doesn't like the answers she does have?" Virginia asked.

Octavia had responded to the questions he'd asked, but she wasn't able to supply anything that was new or substantive. She hadn't even been aware of the death of her son-in-law or the fact that her daughter and granddaughter had been swept into Zane's cult until after Kimberly had taken Virginia to live in the first compound outside of Wallerton.

"Your grandmother blames herself for having driven your mother into the cult," he said.

Stunned, Virginia went very still, her key half inserted into the lock.

"No, you've got it all wrong," she said. "Octavia blames my father for having destroyed my mother's life. And she blames me for being the cause of my parents' marriage. She thinks that if my mother hadn't gotten pregnant, everything would have turned out differently."

Cabot reminded himself that he wasn't a trained psychologist. "Maybe I read her wrong," he said. "Families are complicated."

Virginia's mouth tightened. "No kidding."

"It's just that there was something about her expression and her tone of voice when she answered my questions."

"She's angry and bitter."

"That, too. But she doesn't hold you responsible. Like I said, she blames herself."

Virginia shoved the key into the lock. "Trust me, she blames me and my father. And she's got a point. If it hadn't been for me, my mother probably wouldn't have ended up in Zane's cult."

"My mother's father blamed me and my dad, too. The old man figured that if he disowned my mother, she would see the light, dump my father and go home. Instead, she wound up in the cult."

"What makes you so sure you're not wrong about your analysis of your grandfather? Maybe deep down he blamed himself for being so hard on your mother. That's probably why he left you a little bequest."

"Maybe."

"At least my grandmother and I are still speaking to each other," Virginia said.

"Don't ever forget that."

"Okay."

The door of the neighboring apartment opened. A tiny, wiry woman who appeared to be somewhere between eighty-five and a hundred peered out. She was dressed in a sky-blue velour tracksuit and sturdy walking shoes. There were a lot of rings on her wrinkled fingers. She studied Cabot with undisguised curiosity and then beamed at Virginia.

"Oh, you're back, dear," she said. "I see you have a new friend. Are you going to introduce me?"

Virginia looked at her. "Hi, Betty. This is Cabot Sutter. Cabot, this is Betty Higgins."

"How do you do, Ms. Higgins," Cabot said.

"Call me Betty, dear. How long will you be staying?"

"I'm not staying," Cabot said. "This is Virginia's overnight bag. I've my own apartment on Second Avenue."

"Just a few blocks away. Very convenient." Betty switched her attention back to Virginia, eyes narrowing in a speculative manner. "He doesn't look like one of your artist friends, dear."

"No," Virginia said. "Cabot's in another line of work."

"You mean he has a steady job? Oh, how nice. A position with benefits, perhaps?"

"It has a few," Cabot allowed.

Betty smiled approvingly.

"Don't get any ideas, Betty," Virginia said. "Cabot is a . . . friend. From the old days."

"What old days?" Betty snorted. "You're too young to be able to talk about the old days."

"Cabot and I were acquaintances for a time when we were kids," Virginia said. "We lost track of each other until recently."

"Ah, childhood friends," Betty said. She brightened. "And now you're reunited. Are you married, Cabot?"

"No, ma'am," Cabot said.

Betty was practically sparkling now. "Excellent."

"If you'll excuse us, Cabot and I have had a long day," Virginia said. "We're going to go out, have a drink and get something to eat."

"Lovely," Betty said. She winked. "Don't let me interfere with your date." She made to close her door and stopped. "By the way, next time you schedule a repairman, feel free to leave the key with me. I'll be happy to supervise. A woman who lives alone ought to be careful about letting strangers into her place when she's not home. You just never know these days."

Virginia went very still. "What are you talking about? I didn't schedule any repairs while I was gone."

"Are you sure?"

"Positive."

"Well, then, it must have been someone the manager sent up. He looked like a plumber. He let himself in and your alarm didn't go off, so obviously he had a key and the code."

Virginia stared at her. "Yesterday was Saturday."

"Yes, so I assumed it was an emergency of some sort. Can't even imagine what plumbers charge for weekend jobs these days." Betty paused. "Something wrong, dear?"

"No," Virginia said, her voice strained. "You're right, the manager must have sent someone up to check out an emergency."

"What did the plumber look like?" Cabot asked.

Betty made a dismissive motion with her hand. "Like a plumber. He was wearing a uniform. Had a toolbox."

"What color was his hair?" Cabot asked.

"What?" Betty frowned. "I'm not sure. Dark, I think, but I can't say for certain. He was wearing a cap so I didn't get a good look at him. He was on the tall side."

"Any idea of his age?" Cabot pressed. "Young? Old?"

"Well, he moved like a young man but I can't be sure of his age. Say, do you think there was something off about him?"

Virginia pulled herself together with a visible effort. "Probably not. I'll check to make sure nothing is missing and then I'll call the manager's office tomorrow and find out what's going on."

"Yes, you do that," Betty said. "See you tomorrow, dear. Maybe both of you."

She winked at Cabot and closed her door.

Virginia got her door open. Cabot saw lights blink on the control panel of an alarm system. Virginia quickly punched in some numbers.

"Ever given out your code?" he asked neutrally.

"No. Well, my grandmother has it, but she's the only other person who does."

"Except for the security firm that installed your system."

He followed her into the small foyer, set the bag aside and closed the door.

Virginia turned on the lights. "Let me take a wild guess. You think this plumber development is not a good thing."

"What I'm thinking is that you had better have a look around your condo. But I'll go first."

He did a quick sweep of the small two-bedroom, two-bath space, checked the tiny balcony and then nodded at Virginia. Without a word she walked through the condo, going room by room. Along the way she opened closets and drawers.

A short time later she came to a halt in the living room and looked at him.

"There doesn't seem to be anything missing," she said. "If he did go through my stuff, he was very neat about it. But the thought of a stranger in here, touching my things . . . It makes me feel a little ill."

"After a burglary or a break-in people often say they feel violated," Cabot said. "It's a natural reaction."

Virginia glanced back toward the foyer. "My alarm system . . ."

"Is just an off-the-shelf piece of junk. Wouldn't take a genius to put it out of commission for a while."

She winced. "I was told it was top-of-the-line." She took a deep breath and let it out slowly. "All right, let's go with the worst-case scenario. Say someone dressed as a plumber did break in while I was out of town. What on earth could he have been looking for?"

"The break-in can't be a coincidence. Whoever he is, he must be linked to Brewster's death. We'd better assume he came here looking for something and that he has some reason to think you might have it."

Virginia put up both hands, palms out. "Wait, hold on, you're going way too fast here. I think it's called leaping to conclusions."

"We conspiracy theorists tend to do that."

"Okay, you've made your point," Virginia said. "What's our next step? No point calling the police. Nothing is missing."

"We need to take a look around your gallery."

"At this hour? Why?"

"If I was looking for something and didn't find it here, my next stop would be your place of business," he said patiently.

"I've got an alarm system installed there. I haven't been contacted by the security company or the police so . . ."

"Same brand as the system in here?"

She sighed. "I got a deal in exchange for adding the second system."

CHAPTER 17

Traffic was light downtown. The result was that a short time later Virginia eased her car into an empty space at the curb near the front of the gallery.

She got out. So did Cabot. Neither of them spoke as they walked quickly to the front door. Virginia's hands shook a little when she tried to insert the key into the lock. *It's the adrenaline,* she told herself. *Perfectly natural under the circumstances. You're not having a panic attack. You're just extremely tense. You've got a right.*

She got the door open on the second — or maybe it was the third — attempt. Cabot had the good sense not to offer to take the key away from her and perform the simple task himself. That would have really pissed her off.

Once inside she hurried to the box on the wall and forced herself to concentrate long enough to punch in the code. Mercifully she got it right the first time. She flipped the wall switch. The overhead display lights came on. A quick look around reassured her.

"It doesn't look like anything has been disturbed in here," she said.

Cabot looked at the rear of the long gallery. "You said Brewster's pictures are stored in a storage locker."

"In the back. Right. I'll show you."

She went behind the elegant steel-and-glass sales counter and opened the door to the back room. A strange, disturbing sense of wrongness wafted out of the opening. It was followed by an odor that some primal part of her recognized. Instinctively she clasped a hand across her nose and mouth, took a step back and came up hard against Cabot's immovable frame.

"What in the world?" she whispered.

"Stay here," Cabot said.

He moved her aside and hit the switch on the wall. The overhead fixtures came on, illuminating the jumble of packing crates, draped canvases and art objects that littered the back room.

Cabot moved slowly into the space. Ignoring his order, she followed him. He did not try to stop her. The door of the storage closet was open. The light was off inside.

Virginia tried to connect the dots but her brain seemed to have gone numb.

"He was here," she said. "He found Hannah's paintings. But what is that smell?"

Cabot went around the end of a row of packing crates. He stopped and looked down.

"He was here but he wasn't alone," Cabot said.

The shivery feeling got more intense. She knew she did not want to see whatever it was that Cabot was looking at, but she forced herself to go around the crates and confront the truth.

For a heart-stopping moment she stared at the body lying in a pool of dried blood.

Cabot crouched beside the dead woman and reached out to check for a pulse. It was obvious he wasn't going to find one. He looked up at Virginia.

"Recognize her?" he asked.

"No. I've never seen her before in my life."

CHAPTER 18

"The cops have confirmed the ID of the victim," Cabot said. He put his phone down on the dining counter that overlooked the kitchen. "Sandra Porter. She was a computer programmer who, up until a few days ago, worked in the IT department at a local company called Night Watch. Evidently, Porter recently left the company to pursue other opportunities."

"That's usually a euphemism for getting fired," Virginia said.

They were eating a midnight dinner of pizza and red wine in her condo because by the time the police had cut them loose, neither of them had felt like trying to find a restaurant that was still open.

Just as well, Virginia thought. She was too wired to try to pass for normal in a public place. She wasn't very hungry, either. After a couple of bites of pizza, she had decided to focus on the wine.

"It's possible she really did quit," Cabot said. "Good programmers often move around a lot simply because they can. Their skills are in high demand."

"Sandra Porter certainly didn't show up in my back room because she wanted to apply for a job."

"True. The question is, who else was in your back room?"

Virginia swallowed some more wine and slumped back in her chair. "Think it might have been the phony plumber who broke into my condo yesterday?"

Cabot picked up another slice of pizza. "I'd say that's a definite maybe. Too early to tell. We don't have enough information."

"This thing is getting very complicated, isn't it?"

"Yes, but we now have a couple more facts than we had earlier."

"The name of the dead woman?"

"And her place of employment."

"I suppose the police will chase down all the obvious leads and connections."

"Sure."

Virginia examined her almost-empty wineglass. "The cops are not going to buy into our conspiracy theory, are they? They'll think we're crazy if we try to convince them that a onetime cult leader has emerged from the past and, for reasons yet to be explained, started murdering people."

"The police will spend their time investigating more plausible explanations. That's their job. It's up to you and me to try to find a connection to the past."

"Think there's a chance that Sandra Porter was in Zane's compound with us?"

"No. According to her profile she was only twenty-four years old. That means she would have been two at the time we were all in the compound. I don't remember any kids that young. Do you?"

"No."

"You were one of the youngest on the list of cult members that my brothers and I have compiled. Zane didn't want the problems that very young children or infants would have caused him. He wanted kids he could lock up at night."

"We were hostages, weren't we? We were insurance for our mothers' obedience."

"Yes."

Virginia set the empty glass aside, sat forward and folded her arms on the table. "Okay, so Sandra Porter wasn't at the compound. That doesn't mean she didn't have a connection to it. Maybe one of her relatives got sucked into the cult."

"A possibility. But the real questions are,

what was she doing at your gallery and why did someone kill her?"

"We need to find that fake plumber, don't we?"

"That would be helpful," Cabot said.

"So what's our next step?"

"We start turning over rocks but we stay out of the way of the police. They will be extremely unhappy if they think we're interfering in their investigation. And if they are unhappy, they won't provide us with any insider information."

"I understand. But where do we find the rocks to turn over?"

"Up until a few days ago Sandra Porter had a job," Cabot said. "That means she had colleagues, people who knew her. She may have had a boyfriend."

"She'll have had neighbors and probably some relatives, too. Won't the police be talking to all of them?"

"Sure," Cabot said. "But they will be asking questions that are very different from the ones we'll be asking. They'll be looking for a relationship gone bad, a drug problem or maybe an indication of corporate espionage."

"Got to admit, those sound like reasonable avenues of investigation — except none of them explain why Sandra Porter wound up dead in my back room."

"It also doesn't explain why Sandra Porter was killed in what television and the movies would have you believe is a classic hit-man style. Two shots, one to the chest to take the victim down, the second to the head to make sure of death."

"Good grief. Do you think we're talking about a professional hit man?"

"No, just someone who watches a lot of television. A real pro would have made the hit somewhere else and dumped the body into Lake Washington or Elliott Bay or driven it up into the mountains. There's too much evidence associated with a body."

Virginia exhaled slowly. "Good to know we're not dealing with a hired killer."

"According to my brother Jack, who studies this stuff, there aren't a lot of actual professional hit men in the real world. The few that do exist tend to be affiliated with specific gangs or mobs. There are trained snipers, of course, but, by definition, they work from a distance."

"I see."

"That said, it doesn't mean there aren't a lot of people who think they're smart enough to get away with murder."

Virginia poured herself a little more wine, trying to suppress the wired sensation.

"What now?" she asked.

"Now I go downstairs and get my overnight bag out of the trunk of your car."

She stilled. "You're spending the night?"

"Do you want to stay here alone?"

She did not have to think very hard about that. "Under the circumstances, no."

"Good choice," Cabot said.

CHAPTER 19

The old nightmare struck out of the darkness.

The rear wall of the barn was on fire now, and there was no way out because Zane had locked the big front door for the night. The other children were screaming but she was too terrified to utter a sound. One of the older boys was ordering all of them to get down on the floor to avoid the smoke. She crouched, clutching her prized possession, the book her mother had given her a day earlier . . .

Virginia came awake on a full-blown panic attack. The crashing waves of anxiety were made even worse by the maddening knowledge that she could not control the terrible rush of energy. The experts said that, from a physiological point of view, it was as if her system was suddenly jolted into full fight-or-flight mode but with no obvious threat. The disconnect was unnerving. But as far as she was concerned, that explanation didn't even begin to describe the infuriating sensation.

She was too far into the deep, dark waters of the anxiety attack to even attempt to stave it off with the self-defense routine. *You've been here before. This isn't your first rodeo. Do what you have to do.*

She pushed the covers aside, made it to the bathroom, yanked open the cupboard and grabbed the bottle of meds. She got the lid off, shook out one pill and washed it down with a glass of water. Shivering, she gripped the edge of the sink and tried to breathe.

She hated having to resort to the meds. Doing so made her feel weak. But lately the panic attacks had been coming on more frequently, and there was no question that they were getting worse.

She went back into the bedroom, pulled on her robe and went out into the hall. In the weak glow of the night-light she could see that the door of Cabot's room was closed.

Relieved, she hurried down the hall to the living room. But she came to an abrupt halt when she saw the otherworldly glow of a computer screen coming from the vicinity of the kitchen counter.

"How bad is this one on a scale of one to

ten?" Cabot asked from the shadows.

And suddenly, the stone-cold normal way in which he was dealing with her weirdness had a calming effect.

"How did you know?" she asked.

"Let's just say I've been there."

"Nine point nine," she said, her voice very tight.

She was still jittery but she was regaining control.

"Did you take the meds?" Cabot asked.

"Oh, yeah."

"Good. Do whatever you need to do until they kick in and then I've got a question for you."

"Okay."

She started pacing. Cabot went back to work. It was a relief not to have to explain everything to him, she thought. He knew better than to try to hold her or even touch her. He didn't tell her to get a grip or attempt to soothe her with calming words. He just gave her the space she needed to deal with the attack.

To outsiders the scene probably would have appeared bizarre, she thought — one person having a serious anxiety attack while the other one acted as if such attacks were perfectly normal.

After a while she got her pulse and her

breathing back under control. She drifted across the room and perched on one of the stools at the counter.

"I'm all right now," she said. "What was the question?"

"I've been thinking about Zane's first compound."

"That ghastly old house outside Wallerton? What about it?"

"Early on when my brothers and I started looking for Zane, we checked out that first house. Like I told you, one of his followers handed it over to him. Zane sold it to raise cash to make the move to California."

"So?"

"It was a dead end as far as leads go," Cabot said. "But tonight when I got my one thirty a.m. wake-up call, I decided to review some of our old files on Zane. Out of curiosity I looked up the Wallerton house to see what had happened to it."

"And?"

"It went through a number of hands but eventually wound up in foreclosure. The bank took possession. It stood empty for years but it suddenly sold — an all-cash deal — late last month."

"Really? Who bought it?"

"That's where things get interesting," Cabot said. "I can't ID the buyer."

"What do you mean? That kind of information is public."

"Not when the buyer purchases the property under the cover of a trust. It isn't uncommon for wealthy people to buy real estate through a trust, but usually it's possible to get some idea of the identity of the owners. Not in this case, however. Whoever constructed this trust wanted to be sure his identity remained hidden."

Her anxiety was under control, but Virginia was aware of another kind of excitement sparking somewhere inside her.

"After years of rotting into the ground, the Wallerton house is suddenly sold to an unknown party," she said. "What we've got here is another amazing coincidence."

"It's the kind of thing we conspiracy buffs take very seriously." Cabot closed his laptop and looked at her. "Want to drive to Wallerton in the morning? Have a look around for old time's sake?"

She shuddered. "Not really. But given all the things that have happened lately, yes. No stone unturned, et cetera, et cetera. My gallery is closed on Sundays and Mondays anyway and my back room will be a crime scene for a couple of days. So, yes, I'm free to accompany you on a little trip down memory lane."

He smiled.

"What?"

"You've got plenty of what Anson calls grit. You know that?"

"Are you kidding? I've suffered from anxiety attacks off and on for most of my adult life."

"That's got nothing to do with grit."

"What's your definition of grit?"

"Murder goes down in your back room, followed by an anxiety attack that ranked at nine point nine on the scale of one to ten, and yet you're up for taking a trip to the place where your nightmares got started. That, my friend, is grit."

She grimaced. "Not like there's much of an alternative. I need to know if Quinton Zane is still out there. I need to know what really happened to Hannah Brewster."

"So do I."

She saw the shadows in his eyes and knew that when he dreamed about the past, he, too, heard the echoes of the other children screaming and felt the heat of the flames. They had both lost their mothers to the fires of hell, but Virginia had been one of the lucky ones. Her grandmother had come to claim her. No one had stepped forward to claim Cabot.

Driven by an impulse she did not stop to

analyze, she leaned forward and brushed her lips gently across his.

A great stillness came over him.

"Please don't do that again," he said.

Shocked, she sat back quickly. In that next instant a furious tide of embarrassment swept through her.

"Sorry," she mumbled. "That was a mistake. I apologize for putting you in a difficult position. Please, just forget that happened. If you'll excuse me, I'm going back to my room now."

He got to his feet, moving in the smooth, fluid manner that somehow managed to cross the invisible line from the merely well coordinated to the intensely sensual, and stood in her path. He closed his hands around her shoulders.

"What I'm trying to say is, please don't do that again unless you mean it," he said. "I don't need to be comforted. I don't need your gratitude."

His voice was husky, as if he was exerting a fierce control over some dangerous emotion. His eyes were stark with desire. She could feel the need radiating from his hands on her shoulders. But there was also a lot of raw willpower, a lot of control.

She raised a hand and touched the side of his face with her fingertips.

"I don't generally kiss people unless I do mean it," she said.

"Did you kiss me because you felt sorry for me? For what happened in the past?"

She hesitated, telling herself he deserved honesty. "Well, maybe it started out that way. I was remembering you as a fatherless boy who had just lost his mother and how no one from your family came to claim you."

"Yeah, that's pretty much what I thought was going on. For the record, I do not want you to kiss me for that reason. I don't want any pity kisses."

"Okay." Feeling more certain of herself now, she flattened her palms against his chest. "But just to be clear, you don't object to me kissing you for other reasons?"

"Depends."

"I want to kiss you because I would like to find out what it's like. Is that a good enough reason?"

He gave that half a second's thought and then used his grip on her shoulders to pull her hard against his chest.

"That's the only reason you can come up with?" he asked.

"No." She gripped fistfuls of his T-shirt. "Here's the bottom line: I know some of your secrets, Cabot Sutter. And you know some of mine. A long time ago you and I spent some time in hell together. We were both wounded while we were there but we both survived. I'd say that's reason enough for a kiss."

"That works," he said. "For now."

He tightened his grip, pulled her even closer and covered her mouth with his own, all in one swift, relentless, irresistible motion.

The kiss went hot and deep, overwhelming her, swamping her senses. She was not sure what she had been expecting, but this shattering, disorienting sensation was not it. She clung to him, holding on for dear life.

She had learned long ago not to get her expectations raised too high at the start of a relationship. She made it a rule to go in clear-eyed, anticipating very little in the way of actual fireworks and, sure enough, she had never been surprised. A little mild heat and a fleeting sense of intimacy were as good as it got for her.

"Home by midnight" was her rule.

Lately she had been forced to shelve even those limited expectations because the anxiety attacks had started to become more frequent, striking with unnerving unpredictability. The turning point had occurred one memorable night a few months ago.

Brad Garfield was a very nice man but she

knew he had probably been traumatized for life when an anxiety attack exploded through her just as things reached the intimate stage.

In the wake of the disaster, she had sworn off dating, at least until what she thought of as the Storm Season had passed.

Tonight was not the time to rethink her decision, she thought. The last thing she wanted to do was wreck the fragile bond she was developing with Cabot.

Kissing him had probably been a mistake.

But it was Cabot who ended things. He eased them both out of the kiss before it could drag them under.

"We should probably stop here," he said, his voice more than a little rough around the edges.

He was right, although his reasons for calling a halt were probably quite different from her own. "Never sleep with a client" was one of his rules.

"Yes," she said, going for a bracing tone. "We're involved in a very serious situation. We don't want to make things more complicated than they already are."

He appeared to give that some thought.

"You think going to bed together would complicate the situation?" he asked.

"Well, yes. Don't you?"

"No."

She glared at him. "Then why did you stop?"

"Because I could tell you were having second thoughts."

"I see." She drew a breath. "That was very . . . intuitive of you."

"That's me, Mr. Intuitive. Mind telling me why you were having those second thoughts?"

She spread her hands. "For all the obvious reasons, starting with we hardly know each other."

"Seems to me we know a whole lot about each other. Let's cut to the chase. You're scared to go to bed with me, aren't you?"

Now she was getting angry. She made to step around him, heading for her bedroom.

"I'm not afraid," she said over her shoulder. "I'm a serial dater, remember? But I do learn from experience. And for the past year, all of my experience has been bad. The last time I got to the hot-and-sweaty stage with a man, I had a full-blown panic attack. Poor Brad thought I was having a nervous breakdown. I had to talk him out of calling nine-one-one at the same time I was trying to find my meds in my purse."

"Virginia, wait —"

She reached the bedroom, moved through

174

the opening and turned to face him. "The word *humiliation* does not even begin to describe what I experienced that night. It happened months ago and I still can't get that scene out of my head. So, yes, I'm having second thoughts about trying to have sex with you."

She closed the door with rather more force than was necessary and stood for a moment, seething.

When she had her emotions back under control, she opened the door again. Cabot was standing right where she had left him.

"I apologize for that incredibly ridiculous display of high drama," she said.

"No problem."

"I deal with a lot of dramatic artistic types but I'm not usually into the theatrics myself."

Cabot propped one shoulder against the wall and folded his arms. "Like I said, not a problem."

"Yes, it is a problem, but it's my problem, not yours, so, again, my apologies."

"No prob—"

"Don't say it."

She closed the door again, this time with exquisite control. She crossed to the window and stood looking out at the city lights for a long time.

CHAPTER 20

"Last night after you went back to bed, I did some research on Night Watch, the tech company where Sandra Porter worked," Cabot said.

He was behind the wheel of his gunmetal-gray SUV. Virginia was in the passenger seat. They were forty minutes into the roughly one-hour drive to Wallerton and the site of Quinton Zane's first compound. He had exited Interstate 5 a while back and now they were on a two-lane road and deep into rural country. Tiny towns, farms and small ranches dotted the landscape.

Thus far conversation in the front seat of the SUV had been polite but stilted. He figured he now knew the precise meaning of the phrase *walking on eggshells.*

He knew he couldn't blame all of the brittle tension in the front seat on the searing late-night kiss. It was the sight of the holstered gun he had picked up at his place on the way out of town that had made Virginia's eyes narrow.

"We may be dealing with a killer," he had said.

"I know," she said.

That was pretty much all she had said for the past several miles.

Virginia took her attention off the road long enough to give him a quick, curious glance. "You mentioned that Night Watch was a tech company."

"It is in the sense that it's selling products online and has no brick-and-mortar presence, but as far as I can tell, it's just a straight retail operation."

"What do they market?"

"According to the website, they offer a variety of personalized sleeping aids. Herbal products, guided meditations that are supposed to help insomniacs get to sleep, one-on-one online sleep therapy sessions, special music designed to help you sleep — that kind of thing."

Virginia thought about that. "Zane's cult sold a program that he claimed would allow people to control their dreams and channel the latent powers of the mind."

"Zane's operation was your basic pyramid scheme. It had several tiers. Customers had to keep buying their way up to the next level. In addition, they only made progress if they brought in new customers."

"It sounds somewhat similar to selling insomnia therapies."

"Night Watch may be selling junk cures for insomnia, but from what I can tell, the business is not a pyramid scheme."

"Well, it's probably all bogus, but given the number of people with sleep disorders who are desperate for a good night's rest, I'm guessing that business is brisk."

"It was doing well enough to catch the attention of a venture capital firm a year ago," Cabot said. "Night Watch burned through that first round of funding and is rumored to be getting ready to go out for another."

"I assume you checked out the people who are running Night Watch?"

"I did. Like most start-ups, it's still a small organization. The founder and CEO is Josh Preston, a former wunderkind tech whiz who made his first fortune before he was thirty. He designed a social media app that was hugely successful. Got bought out by one of the big companies. Looks like he kicked around for a while, enjoying his money, and then decided to reinvent himself with Night Watch."

"He wants to see if he can catch lightning in a jar twice?"

"Probably. But here's the bottom line: according to the business media, Preston is only in his midthirties and none of his employees are over thirty."

"In other words, there's no one involved with the company who might be Quinton Zane," Virginia said.

"No."

"I suppose that would have been too easy."

"Yes. That's why we're going back to the beginning again."

Virginia gave him another searching look. "Because you're sure there must be some connection between Hannah Brewster, Sandra Porter and the past."

"I think so, yes."

They stopped for coffee at a small restaurant in Wallerton and then Cabot drove the last few miles up into the heavily wooded foothills. The closer they got to the old house, the more tense Virginia became. She wasn't the only one, he thought. He was on edge, too.

The last stretch of road was a strip of badly weathered pavement that was barely wide enough for the SUV.

The big house was a three-story stone-and-wood monstrosity that had been built back in the previous century. It sat at the end of a long, mostly-washed-out drive. It was a structure that, thanks to its location in a long valley, never saw much daylight even in high summer. Now, at the end of a Pacific Northwest winter, it existed in shades of twilight.

Virginia studied the house with a grim expression. "It looks like something out of a horror movie."

"One with a bad ending," Cabot said.

He drove between the twin stone pillars that marked the front of the drive. The remains of the old gate sagged on rusted-out hinges.

"I remember the gate was always locked and guarded," Virginia said. "Zane told us it was for our own protection."

"The first rule in establishing a cult is to isolate your followers," Cabot said.

"He was a total sociopath."

"Oh, yeah."

Cabot brought the SUV to a halt in the clearing. He and Virginia sat silently for a moment, contemplating the ugly house.

"This is where it all started," Cabot said. "Hard to believe so many people fell for his lies."

"You're hoping to find some clue to the identity of the new owner, aren't you?"

"That would definitely be interesting."

He grabbed his windbreaker and the holstered gun off the back seat, opened the door and got out.

Virginia collected her parka and joined him at the front of the big SUV.

"I don't want to tell you your business," she said, "but this is technically private property."

"Don't worry, I'm not going to break in. I just want to take a look around. But if someone does happen to show up, we are a couple of city people who got lost out here in the country. Our GPS isn't working so we stopped to ask for directions."

"Okay, I guess that sounds sort of reasonable. Do you do this kind of thing a lot?"

"No, but I'm still new at the private investigation business. Did it a lot in my last job, though."

"That would be when you were a police chief?"

"Uh-huh."

"Did you really get fired from that position?"

"Long story."

"Which means you're not going to tell me, right?"

"Maybe some other time."

He walked across the weed-covered clearing to the front door of the old house. Virginia trailed after him.

He went up the steps and rapped several times on the front door. Not surprisingly, there was no response. The gleam of untarnished metal caught his eye. He looked down at the door handle.

"New lock," he said.

"The new owner probably had new locks installed to discourage transients and squatters from moving in."

"Either that or he's planning on spending some time here."

"I doubt he's doing that yet," Victoria said. "If this place has been standing empty for several years, it can't possibly be fit for habitation. The new owner will have to do a lot of work. Probably needs new wiring, for starters. The kitchen and bathrooms will have to be renovated."

"Depends on what the new owner intends to do with the place," Cabot said.

She watched him come down the front steps and go to the nearest window.

"You're really suspicious about the new owner, aren't you?" she said.

"It's the timing that bothers me. Why, after years of sitting in foreclosure, did someone decide to buy it now?"

"We have to allow for the possibility that someone figured it was a steal and picked it up with the idea of remodeling it and selling it at a profit." She looked past him toward the main house. "I hate this place."

"I'm not real fond of it myself."

"I wonder if the new owner knows that it once housed a murderous sociopath and his cult," Virginia said.

"Good question," Cabot said.

The windows were all shrouded by faded curtains. He could see very little of the interior.

"I'm going to take a look around back," he said. "Why don't you wait in the car? It will be warmer."

"All right."

She went back to the SUV, opened the passenger-side door and angled herself onto the seat. She left the door open and watched him with a brooding, anxious look.

It occurred to Cabot that it might have been a big mistake to bring her with him today. On the other hand, he doubted that he could have talked her into staying in Seattle. She was in this thing with him. They had only been in each other's company for a very short time, but he already knew her well enough to know she was going to stick with him until it was finished.

He rounded the back of the house and went cautiously up the rotting steps of the rear porch. The sight of the outside door of the covered woodshed made his stomach knot. One of the duties that he and the other boys had been assigned was stacking logs and hauling them into the house through the door inside the shed that opened onto a mudroom.

He went down the length of the porch to the kitchen door. There were no curtains on the window. There was no indication that any remodeling had been started.

The old-fashioned kitchen was in serious disrepair. But there was a small pile of empty energy drink cans on the counter near the sink. The new owner had evidently been visiting his property.

The lock on the kitchen door was new, like the one on the front door. Cabot tried the knob. It did not turn.

He glanced back at the woodshed. There was no lock on it. Maybe the new owner didn't know about the inner door.

He started back across the porch. The small flicker of movement deep in the trees stopped him cold. He had just enough time to think *not a deer* and drop to his belly before the first bullets slammed into the wall of the house a couple feet above his head.

Handgun. Not a rifle.

He yanked his pistol out from under his

windbreaker and fired into the trees, aiming high because he could not see his target.

The return fire had the effect of startling the shooter in the woods. There was a lot of thrashing around in the undergrowth.

Cabot used the opportunity to roll off the far end of the porch, slipping under the railing. He ran for the cover of the side of the house.

There were more shots behind him but they went wild.

He rounded the corner to the front of the house and saw Virginia. She was still in the passenger seat, looking stunned.

There was a lot of open ground between him and the vehicle. He could make a run for it, but that would put Virginia at risk.

"Key is in the ignition," he shouted. "Get out of here."

The order broke the spell that seemed to have transfixed her. Jolted, she scrambled into the front seat of the SUV.

Cabot heard another staccato series of shots. He turned and fired into the trees again, hoping to distract the shooter long enough for Virginia to get to safety.

CHAPTER 21

Virginia cranked up the SUV's powerful engine and drove toward the side of the house where Cabot was braced, gun in hand, his back against the wall. As she watched through the windshield, he leaned around the corner and fired another shot into the trees. He was focused on providing covering fire. For a few seconds he did not realize she was driving toward him.

She did a tight turn that brought her alongside Cabot, and slammed on the brakes. She had not bothered to close the passenger-side door. It swung open.

Cabot whipped around and saw her. He fired one more shot around the corner of the house and then leaped into the passenger seat.

"Go," he said.

She was already flooring the accelerator.

He had the passenger-side window down now. He fired again. As far as Virginia could tell, there were no more shots coming out of the trees, but her ears were ringing from the noise of the gunshots, so she couldn't be sure. In any event, it didn't matter. The only thing that did matter was getting the hell away from the evil house.

The SUV bumped and bounced over the pocked and pitted driveway. She thought she heard Cabot say something but she ignored him.

She finally reached the smoother surface of the road.

"Easy," Cabot said. "It's okay. No one is following us."

He spoke gently, as if he understood that she was in a very strange place in her head.

She realized there was a curve coming up and that she was heading into it much too fast. Basic driving habits took over. Automatically she took her foot off the accelerator, allowing the big vehicle to slow to a more reasonable rate of speed.

When she was safely on the other side of the curve, she remembered to breathe. She risked a glance at Cabot. He was in the process of reaching inside his jacket to holster his gun.

"Are you hurt?" she demanded.

"No. He used a handgun. Lousy accuracy over any kind of distance."

"Wow. Lucky us, huh?"

"Thought I told you to get the hell out of there."

"I did."

"Not fast enough," he said. "You stopped for me."

"You looked like you needed a lift."

"I did." He took a deep breath and let it out slowly, with control. "Thanks."

"Anytime."

"You're flying, aren't you?"

"Oh, yeah."

"It's the adrenaline."

"No kidding. But here's the thing: I'm not having a panic attack. Lot of adrenaline, but it feels different when there's an actual threat."

"Not for everyone. Some people just freeze when the gunfire starts."

She thought about that. "I had a vehicle and a job to do. That made it easier to focus."

He looked at her. "The job being to get us both out of there."

"All I can say is that it seemed like a good idea at the time. Are we going to mention this little incident to the local cops?"

"Not much point. Shots fired in the woods are a pretty common thing in rural country like this. We didn't get a description. Didn't even see a vehicle. No one got hurt. And, technically speaking, we were trespassing. All in all, a nonevent."

She slowed her speed a little more. "I see."

"We're both going to crash later," Cabot warned after a while. "That's how it works."

"Yeah, I have a feeling I might be looking at a particularly bad night."

"You won't be alone," Cabot said. "I'll be going through the bad night with you."

"You know, other couples usually go out to a restaurant and maybe take in a show when they do stuff together."

"Guess we're a little different."

She smiled. "You're flying, too, aren't you?"

"Oh, yeah."

CHAPTER 22

"Got to take this slowly," Anson said. "It's easy to make the case that what happened at Zane's first compound was a random thing. You and Virginia may have wandered into the wrong place at the wrong time. Some idiot was out in the woods, playing with his gun, saw a couple of tourists and decided to give 'em a scare."

"Whoever it was, he definitely wanted to give us a scare," Virginia said. "And maybe kill Cabot while he was at it."

They were in the office of Cutler, Sutter & Salinas. Anson was behind his desk. Cabot was at the window. Virginia was perched in the client chair. It was late afternoon in what was proving to be a very long day.

She was starting to sense the oncoming crash that Cabot had predicted. She was still wired but she knew from past experience that it was possible to be utterly

190

exhausted and incredibly tense at the same time. Still, she wasn't having a genuine anxiety attack. When you had to deal with those on a frequent basis, you learned to recognize the subtle nuances. *I'm a professional. Don't try this at home.*

"We're not going with the random-shots-fired theory," Cabot said. "Too many coincidences involved."

"All right, let's think this through," Anson said. "First, how could anyone have known that you two were headed for Zane's old place?"

"That," Cabot said slowly, "is a very good question." He turned around to face Anson. "I've been thinking about it ever since we left the Wallerton house. I would have noticed a vehicle following us on such a long drive. But it occurs to me that the one connection we have is a tech company — Night Watch."

"So?" Anson said.

But Virginia understood immediately. She looked at Cabot. "You're thinking that the killer may have tracked us?"

"Maybe he managed to hack into my vehicle's GPS system," Cabot said.

Anson raised his brows. "That's a bit of a stretch, don't you think? It's also possible that someone followed you the easy way,

191

Cabot — just stuck a tracking device somewhere on your vehicle."

Cabot shook his head. "I went over the SUV with a fine-tooth comb when we got back to Seattle. Didn't find anything."

"So maybe he was watching you," Anson continued. "Once he realized you were leaving town, he could have followed you at a safe distance. When he saw you take the turnoff for Wallerton, it wouldn't have required a rocket scientist to figure out where you were headed. If he knows the territory, he would be aware of any shortcuts in the area. Maybe he got to the house ahead of you and waited for his chance."

"Okay," Cabot said. "That's a possibility. I think it's interesting that he tried to take me out with a handgun from several yards away while hiding in a stand of trees. He couldn't have had a clear shot. Either he doesn't know enough about guns to realize that the odds of making a hit under those conditions were poor, or else he just hoped he'd get lucky."

"If he's the same guy who shot Sandra Porter, he may have assumed that because the handgun worked the first time at close range, it would work the second time at a distance," Anson said. "Or maybe he just didn't have time to buy a rifle and learn how to use it."

Cabot went back to the window. "Looks like we're dealing with someone who's got some tech skills but not a lot of experience with firearms."

Anson snorted softly. "Doesn't give us much to go on."

"No, but it does point to the Night Watch connection," Cabot said.

Virginia looked at Anson. "Cabot checked out the org chart at Night Watch. The oldest employee is the boss and he's only about thirty-five. As far as we can tell, there is no one at the company who is old enough to be Quinton Zane."

"Doesn't mean there isn't a link to the past," Anson said. "By the way, I had a nice chat with a Seattle police detective named Schwartz. He's young, ambitious and willing to trade information. I agreed to cooperate. He is now my new best friend."

"Did he have anything we could use?" Cabot asked.

"No." Anson turned to Virginia. "But he did tell me that they've taken down the crime scene tape in your back room. If you'll give me access, I'll get the cleaners in right away so that you can reopen soon."

Virginia shuddered. "Thank you."

Cabot turned to Virginia. "Looks like

you're going to have me as a houseguest for a while longer."

"Okay," she said, "but I think you're the one who needs the bodyguard. Whoever was in those trees today was shooting at you, not me."

Anson looked at her. "What that tells us is that the bastard may have some reason for believing that he needs you alive."

CHAPTER 23

They did takeout again for dinner. Virginia reflected on her new diet as she deposited items into the appropriate recycling and compost containers under the sink.

"You do realize that I'm not getting my customary ration of veggies," she said.

"There was tomato sauce on the pizza," Cabot pointed out. "And olives. They count."

"Technically speaking, I believe tomatoes are considered a fruit."

"We needed comfort food. It's been a hard day."

"This is true." She closed the cupboard door and looked at him. "What happens now?"

"We need to talk to some of the people at Night Watch."

"I wouldn't be surprised to discover that the company's HR department has warned the staff not to talk to anyone except the police."

"Yeah, like that'll keep people quiet. Odds are ninety-nine percent of the Night Watch employees have probably blabbed everything they know on social media. I'll see what I can find online."

"I'll do what I can to help you, but we are dealing with people who work for a high-tech start-up. They're bound to be way ahead of me when it comes to navigating the online world."

"They'll be light-years ahead of me, too." Cabot sat down at the kitchen table and opened his computer. "But that may turn out to be their Achilles' heel."

"What makes you say that?"

"Because I'm not going to try to play their games online. I'm going to track them down and talk to them face-to-face. Don't be fooled by all those TV shows featuring criminals caught by fancy forensics and exotic profiling techniques. The truth is, most investigation work gets done using old-school methods."

She smiled. "Because people are people, regardless of how much technology they use, is that it?"

"That's it." Cabot started clicking keys. "But the great thing about technology is that people who rely on it often believe they are anonymous. That, in turn, makes them careless."

"Okay, I get that."

"Which is not to say that the firm of Cutler, Sutter and Salinas couldn't use someone who has some really sharp computer skills," Cabot added. "Anson, Max and I are pretty good when it comes to finding people online, running background checks and searching the standard databases. But that's not the same thing as being able to track the bad guys who hack into a company's encrypted database. That's why we don't take cybersecurity cases."

"From what I've read, catching the online bad guys is a never-ending game of whack-a-mole. So much of that kind of thing is done by pirates operating from other countries. Even if you find them, it's impossible to shut them down."

"That's why we leave that kind of work to the big companies. But there will always be low-level scam artists, fraudsters, cons, extortionists and bookkeepers who finance their retirement by embezzling their employers' profits."

Virginia froze. "Like my mother?"

Cabot looked up, his eyes very intent. "If your mother did manage to rip off Quinton

Zane, then all I've got to say is good job. It may have been the only justice the rest of us will ever see."

She turned around and braced herself against the edge of the counter. "Do you think it's possible that it was Zane who shot at you today?"

Cabot shook his head. "My gut feeling is that it wasn't him."

"What makes you say that?"

"Zane would have come up with a better plan — one that wouldn't have involved leaving a body with several bullets in it near a house that he used to own."

Virginia nodded. "As well as a witness who would have done her best to encourage the police to reopen the file on Quinton Zane."

"What happened today was sloppy. If Zane is still alive, he has managed to stay hidden all these years. Whatever else he is, we know he isn't sloppy."

"That's not exactly reassuring, but I see what you mean."

CHAPTER 24

She awoke with the sense that something had shifted in the atmosphere. Not an anxiety attack, she concluded. Just a feeling that things had changed somewhere in her condo.

Intruder? The thought iced her nerves. Then she remembered that Cabot was in the guest bedroom. No one would get past him. She was not alone tonight.

She pushed aside the covers, got to her feet and reached for her glasses. True, Cabot was nearby, but for her own peace of mind she needed to check the lock on the front door and make sure the balcony slider was secure.

She pulled on her robe and picked up the heavy-duty flashlight she kept beside the bed.

Barefoot, she opened the door and padded out into the hall. She didn't keep the flashlight close at hand because she was afraid of the dark. It was all about one of the basic principles of her personal self-defense program: *Anything can be used as a weapon.* The flashlight doubled as a very solid club. It had an additional advantage: the average intruder would not automatically view it as a threat. Flashlights looked so *normal.*

At the end of the short hall, the glow of a computer screen bathed the living room in an eerie light. She relaxed immediately. Cabot was awake and working. That explained the shift in the atmosphere.

She stopped worrying about the locks and continued down the hall. Cabot, dressed in his trousers and a gray T-shirt, was sitting at the dining counter. He looked up, his expression concerned but not alarmed.

"Anxiety attack?" he asked matter-of-factly.

"Nope. Oddly enough." She smiled. "I take it you got your one thirty a.m. wake-up call?"

"Yeah, sorry. Didn't mean to wake you. I was just rummaging around in some of the old files, killing time until I was ready to go back to sleep."

"I'm going to make a cup of herbal tea. Want some?"

"Sure."

She went into the kitchen. "Do you think we'll be getting up at this hour of the night for the rest of our lives?"

"I have no idea. But I have to tell you that it's nice to know I'm not alone. One thirty in the morning is a very weird time of night. Things feel different at this hour."

She reached up into the cupboard for the box of tea. "Tell me about it."

"Do you think you might want to kiss me again?"

Startled, she fumbled the box of tea. It tumbled to the counter. Little packets spilled out. She turned quickly and stared at Cabot. He stood in the entrance to the kitchen, watching her intently, as if the answer to his question was of vital importance.

She took a breath. "Only if you think you might want to kiss me."

He moved toward her in his easy, gliding way and stopped directly in front of her.

"I do," he said. "I want to kiss you so badly it hurts."

She did not know whether to laugh or groan. "Okay."

"Okay?"

She put her arms around his neck. "Okay, that may not have come out quite the way you intended, but I think I get the picture."

"Good, because I don't think I've got any more words. Not right now."

He used both hands to take off her glasses. He set them aside on the counter and slowly, deliberately wrapped his arms around her. His mouth came down on hers in a searing kiss that electrified all of her senses.

She abandoned herself to the delicious rush of the embrace. Whatever was happening between them might not last forever, but it was very real at that moment and that was all that mattered.

His hands closed around her waist and then moved higher, stopping just beneath her breasts.

"I want you," he said, his voice thickening. "I need to know you want me, too."

"Yes," she said. "Yes, I want you, Cabot Sutter."

"Tonight."

"Tonight," she agreed.

He lifted her off her feet, turned and started toward her bedroom. She gripped his shoulders, bracing herself.

"Just so you know," she said, "I need to be on top."

In the shadows his smile was very sexy and very, very male.

"That," he said, "can be arranged."

He got her into the bedroom and stood her on her feet beside the bed. She thought fleetingly of the bottle of antianxiety meds in the bathroom cabinet and then forgot about them. She wouldn't need them tonight.

Very gently, Cabot peeled off her robe. Then he picked her up in his arms and dropped her lightly onto the tumbled sheets. She sat up immediately, crossed her legs and watched him strip off his trousers, briefs and T-shirt. His strong, sleek shoulders and back were silhouetted against the glow of the city lights.

When he turned slightly to climb into bed, she saw his fierce erection. Okay, he definitely wanted her, at least for tonight.

Automatically she ran a check on her senses, waiting for the rush of dark, disturbing energy to uncoil within her. But all she felt in that moment was a dizzying anticipation. This man understood her. He didn't think she suffered from bad nerves. He didn't think she was weird because she woke up in the middle of the night and ran through a series of self-defense exercises. He didn't care about her past in a cult.

Before she could jinx the moment with any more internal dialogue, he was lowering himself beside her. She did have a brief moment of doubt then. He was the take-charge type and she could feel waves of desire emanating from him. If he didn't understand that she was serious about being on top — if, in the heat of the moment, he tried to take control —

But Cabot made no attempt to cage her beneath him. He rolled onto his back and gathered her against his side, letting her choose the position that she wanted.

She levered herself up on one elbow, leaned over and kissed him. He cradled her head in one powerful hand and responded with a sensual hunger that thrilled her. He groaned with a mix of pleasure and need, but he did not lose control.

Emboldened by the fact that she was not showing any signs of flipping the panic switch, she flattened her palm on his bare chest, savoring the feel of his heated skin and the hard muscle underneath. Slowly she moved her lips from his mouth to his throat. Her fingers explored him. When she reached the thick, rigid length of him, she felt him tense. But he did not attempt to force her to hurry things along.

He moved his free hand slowly up her leg, slipping under the edge of the nightgown. He gripped her bare thigh. For the first time she felt a flicker of tension. Her hand stilled on his lower body.

He immediately released her thigh and let his fingers drift slowly over the curve of her hip and up to her waist.

"You feel so good," he said, his voice very dark, almost smoldering. "Perfect."

Definitely not perfect, she thought. Any other woman who found herself in bed with this man would be thrilled. And she *was* thrilled. But some part of her was also scared, waiting for the anxiety monster to leap out of the dark cave where it hid and destroy the moment.

Don't think about it, she told herself. *Focus.*

But the more she tried not to think about it, the more she could not stop thinking about it.

Anger at her own inability to relax and enjoy the pleasure that Cabot was offering surged through her. Dismayed, she scrambled on top of him, straddling him in an effort to force her senses to ignite.

Cabot responded with enthusiasm.

"Oh, yeah."

He gripped her hips and helped her position herself. But she was suddenly very dry, and when she tried to impale herself on his thick erection, he abruptly tightened his hold, stopping her.

"It's okay," he said. "You need a little time."

She sank her nails into his shoulders. "No, damn it. I'm going to do this."

"Hush, it's all right. This isn't like going to the dentist. You don't have to do this."

"Oh, crap." She squeezed her eyes shut against the tears. *"Shit."*

He eased her off of his still-hard body. "Go take the meds."

She knelt beside him in the tangled sheets, pulled her nightgown down around herself and tried to analyze her emotions.

"I'm not having a panic attack," she said. "I'm just disgusted with myself because I was so afraid of having an attack that I couldn't relax."

"I get it." He sat up beside her. "Like I said, it's okay."

He leaned forward and brushed his mouth lightly across hers. It was a comforting kiss, a kiss of deep understanding, not an attempt to seduce her.

She was suddenly torn between tears and hysterical giggles.

"A trip to the dentist?" she managed, her voice shaking a little. "Really, that was the best analogy you could come up with?"

He sat back and gave her a wry smile. "Sorry, but it was the first one that came to mind. I'll try to have something more romantic ready next time."

"Next time?" She couldn't believe what she was hearing. She dashed away her tears with the back of her hand. "You really want to go through this again?"

"Are you kidding? I haven't gotten this close to having sex in months. Of course I want to do it again."

She glared. "Now you're teasing me."

"I am," he agreed. "But it also happens to be the truth." He pushed aside the covers and sat up on the side of the bed. "What do you say we both try to get some sleep?"

"All right." It wasn't as if there were a lot of other options, she thought wistfully, not now that she had totally killed the mood.

He leaned down, brushed his mouth lightly across hers, and then he was gone.

She listened intently as he went down the hall. He opened his bedroom door but he did not close it again. If she woke up on the wings of another panic attack, he would hear her. He would probably come to check up on her, make sure she took her meds.

But he would not judge her. He knew where she was coming from.

CHAPTER 25

Cabot awoke before dawn with the shattering conviction that he had missed something very important. He paid attention to the sensation. He had relied on the intuitive side of his nature during his time in a war zone and during his career as a cop.

He pushed back the covers, got up and headed for the small guest bathroom to shower and shave.

When he was dressed, he headed down the hall to the kitchen, trying not to make any noise. He smiled at the sight of Virginia's glasses on the counter.

He was firing up the coffeemaker when Virginia appeared. She was wearing her bathrobe, and her hair was a tangled mass. Her face was flushed from sleep. She looked sexy as hell. He felt his insides stir. He told himself to focus on measuring the coffee into the machine.

"Good morning," he said.

"What time is it?" she asked

He handed her the glasses. "A little after six."

"Oh, wow." Her voice sharpened abruptly. "I never sleep this late."

He smiled down at the coffeemaker. "Neither do I. But we did have a rough day yesterday."

She pushed her glasses onto her nose with one finger. "Yes, we did, didn't we?"

There was a note of surprise or maybe wonder in her voice. He knew she was still trying to come to grips with the events at the Wallerton house and maybe with what had almost happened between them last night. But if she wasn't going to mention the sleeping arrangements, neither would he. They'd figure it out sooner or later.

"Cabot?"

He looked at her. She visibly steeled herself.

"About last night," she said.

"We don't have to talk about it, you know."

"I know. But I wanted to say thank you."

"For what?"

She widened her hands. "For understanding." She stepped back quickly. "I'd better go take a shower."

"Sure," he said.

"Be back in a few minutes," she said. She

turned and started to rush back down the hall.

"Virginia?"

She stopped and swung around with an air of expectation. He got the impression that she was waiting for him to say something important, something meaningful. But he couldn't be sure, so he played it safe.

"I wanted to ask you about Hannah Brewster's last painting, the one she did on the wall of her cabin."

"Oh," Virginia said. She looked disconcerted for a beat or two but she recovered quickly, composing herself. "What about the painting?"

"In Brewster's last picture the little girl intended to represent you is carrying a picture book."

"Right. But there was nothing unusual about it. I'm holding the book in every picture in the *Visions* series. It's part of the standard iconography that Hannah used."

"You said your mother gave you that book?"

"Yes. It was designed to teach early math to a child. We weren't allowed to go to school in town, remember? We were home-schooled by some of the women in the compound."

"Do you still have it?"

"Of course. It's the only thing I have of my mother's. Why?"

"Do you mind if I take a look at it?"

"No. I'll get it for you."

Virginia disappeared down the hall to the guest bedroom that served as a library and home office. When she returned she carried a slim, handmade book bound with strands of frayed yarn.

"Hannah illustrated it for Mom," Virginia said. "She used good-quality paper, so the pages have not deteriorated, but it's still rather fragile."

She set the book on the kitchen counter and opened it with great care. Cabot hit the start button on the coffeemaker and moved to stand beside Virginia. He was immediately fascinated by the illustrations. They leaped off the page in a riot of colors. Fanciful animals from a magical realm trotted, flew, hopped or paced through the story. Each carried a number or a mathematical sign. In the story that accompanied the pictures, the creatures tried to impress a little girl who didn't like arithmetic with the wonders of the world of numbers.

"I loved to read but I didn't like math," Virginia said. Her voice broke a little. "So Mom came up with a story about a kid like me. Then Hannah illustrated it. The idea was to teach me some basic arithmetic."

Cabot saw the glint of tears. "I'm sorry to dredge up sad memories."

"I know, but it's not like either of us has a choice, is it? This situation that we're in is all about the past."

"I think so, yes."

She blinked away the tears. "It's just that so much has been happening lately. I feel a little . . . disoriented, I guess."

"You're not the only one."

Acting on impulse, he reached out and tugged her into his arms. She did not resist. Instead she collapsed against him and cried for what seemed like a very long time. He realized that her tears were welling up from some very deep, dark place. He knew that place. He had visited a very similar realm from time to time over the years, often at one thirty in the morning.

He didn't realize that tears were leaking out of his own eyes until Virginia gently extracted herself from his arms, stepped back and gave him a watery smile.

"Sorry," she said. "I haven't lost it like that for quite a while."

"Neither have I." He grimaced, grabbed a paper napkin and wiped his eyes. "When I was a kid, Anson used to tell me that it was no big deal. He said it wasn't like I was ever going to forget what happened at the compound, so I would have to deal with it. He told me that crying from time to time was probably a good way to keep the bad stuff under control."

"Stuff?"

"Anson isn't a trained psychologist. He didn't have all the fancy words. But my brothers and I got the message. Sometimes it was okay to cry."

"My grandmother sent me to a couple of therapists who did have the fancy words," Virginia said. "I got the same message from them, but at the same time, Octavia was sending me another, conflicting message — don't talk about the past because it's just too painful."

"So you stopped talking about it?"

"At home, yes. Later, when I went off to college and then out into the real world, I discovered no one else wants to talk about my past, either, or, if they do, it's because of morbid curiosity. They looked at me differently after they found out about my time in the cult. I could see them wondering if I was seriously warped or maybe crazy. So I shut up."

"My brothers and I figured out real fast that talking to outsiders about our past was not a good idea. But at least we had each other and Anson to talk to."

"I didn't have anyone to share my past with until Hannah Brewster showed up at the door of my gallery. We did talk a little, but by then Hannah was living in her own world. It was difficult to know what was real to her and what wasn't. And she was so secretive. Downright paranoid." Virginia glanced at the picture book of numbers. "She often asked about the book, though."

"What did she say?"

"She was very concerned that I keep it safe. She said I might need it someday. But, honestly, I've looked at it hundreds of times over the years and I still don't know what she meant. I can tell you that each of the creatures was named after one of the kids who were forced to sleep in the barn, but you have to look very closely at the designs to see that much."

Cabot chose a page at random and concentrated on the exuberant, highly decorative designs on a hat worn by one of the fantastical creatures. At first he could not make sense of what he was looking at. Then he saw an *H* followed by the letter *u*.

"Hugh," Cabot said. He looked up. "There was a Hugh with us in the barn that night. Hugh Lewis. He and his father were at the compound."

"Are their names on that list that Anson keeps?"

"Yes," Cabot said. "Max tracked them down a couple of years ago. They're living in the Midwest now and doing reasonably well as far as we know. But Max said that neither of them wanted to talk about their time with Zane. Hugh is married with a couple children of his own. His father remarried. Their wives know about their time in Zane's operation but they don't want their friends and neighbors to find out."

"For obvious reasons," Virginia said.

"You said Hannah never gave you any idea of why the book was important?"

"No. She refused to discuss it. She just wanted to make sure I still had it. Trust me, I've looked at those pictures and those numbers a million times. I've even worked through the math problems to see if the results mean anything. If there's a clue there, it's not clear to me."

Cabot looked up and met her eyes. "But until you walked through the door of Cutler, Sutter and Salinas, you didn't know that a lot of money had disappeared in the wake of the California compound fire. I find it interesting that Zane torched the place on the night of the same day that your mother gave you this book."

Virginia went very still. "You think this book is the key to the missing money, don't you?"

"If your mother was embezzling the cult's funds, she would have had to find a way to conceal the cash."

Virginia caught her breath. "Do you think that book is written and illustrated in some sort of code?"

"It's a possibility. It would explain why Hannah was so adamant about you making sure it was safe."

"If you're right, maybe her last painting — the one that shows a modern-day version of Quinton Zane — was meant to warn me not only that he's come back but also that he's after the book."

"This is all guesswork at the moment, but one thing's for sure: we don't have time to try to decipher some secret code. Not now. We need to focus on the investigation."

"All right, but what about the book?" Virginia said. "We can't just leave it lying around here, not now that we think it might be important. We should put it into a safe-deposit box."

"Yes, but the sooner we know if this book really is valuable, the better. With your permission I'd like to give it to Anson. He can photocopy the pages and then he can put the original into a safe-deposit box. Once we have a copy to study, we can get some expert help."

"What kind of expert help?"

"A lot of the people who work in the cybersecurity field are good with codes and puzzles. Max and Jack both have contacts in that world."

"Hannah was right. Quinton Zane really has come back to haunt us," Virginia said.

But she didn't look anguished or defeated, Cabot thought. She looked quietly, resolutely angry and determined.

"We may be dealing with Zane," Cabot said. "But I think the odds are good that someone else has learned about the missing money and is trying to find it."

Virginia's mouth tightened. Her eyes narrowed a little. "You don't think it's Zane?"

Cabot shook his head. "The more I think about it, the more I doubt it."

"Why?"

"Zane was a very slick con man and a very thorough killer. He didn't make a lot of mistakes. Furthermore, if he is still alive, he's done a very good job of concealing himself for twenty-two years. If, for some reason, he decided to come out of the shadows now, I think he would operate in a far more careful manner. Got a hunch we're dealing with someone who is less experienced in this kind of thing."

"But it's been over two decades," Virginia said. "Who knows what has happened to Zane during all that time? Maybe he's desperate for some reason. Maybe he's just flat-out crazy."

"Or, maybe, after all these years, someone else discovered that your mother helped conceal a large sum of money and tracked down Kimberly Troy's heir."

"Me."

"You," Cabot said. "That's the simplest answer."

"Who else could know about it? And how?"

"That's what we need to find out."

"Where do we start?"

Cabot opened his laptop and pulled up the organization chart for Night Watch.

"Might as well start at the top," he said. "Let's see if we can get to Josh Preston."

"Why would he talk to us?"

"Because we are not the police. We are a private firm pursuing questions about the dead woman who was discovered in your gallery's back room. Never underestimate the power of curiosity. Preston will want to know what we know."

"Why?

"Because his company is getting a lot of attention from the police at the moment, and it's a good bet they're not telling him a damn thing."

Anson was at his desk and on the phone when Virginia and Cabot walked into the office a couple of hours later. Cabot had the math book inside a paper bag tucked under one arm.

Anson put down the phone and looked at Cabot.

"Good timing," he said. "That was Schwartz."

"Your Seattle PD pal?" Cabot put the paper bag on the desk. "Any news?"

"Maybe. Maybe not. Seems like there are rumors of embezzlement at Night Watch. A few people in the company are wondering if Sandra Porter might have been the thief. They seem to feel she would have had the skill set required to pull off that kind of thing."

"Interesting," Cabot said. "What did you give Schwartz in exchange for that information?"

"Nothing yet, but I probably won't get much more out of him if we don't come up with something he can use."

Cabot took the fanciful math book out of the paper bag. "Whatever you do, don't give him this. It's for members of the Zane Conspiracy Club only."

Anson picked up the book. "What is it?"

Virginia looked at him. "Maybe — just maybe — the key to the money that went missing twenty-two years ago."

CHAPTER 26

Josh Preston lounged back in his chair and contemplated the two women sitting on the other side of his desk. Was one of them the thief?

Back at the start he had assumed he was looking for a techie who had the sophisticated skills required to hack into his system. But every time he thought he'd found a clue to the identity of the embezzler, he'd hit a wall.

Now he was starting to wonder if he had been looking at the wrong people. Laurel Jenner was the head of the marketing team. Kate Delbridge wrote ad copy for the Night Watch website. Neither of them could write code, but they were both smart in ways that mattered in big business.

"I assume that by now you've heard about the death of Sandra Porter?" he said.

"Yes, sir," Laurel said. "HR notified the entire staff this morning. I still can't believe she was murdered."

Josh nodded. He had been attracted to Laurel from the start, and not just because she looked like a real-life edition of an over-endowed female superhero character in a video game. The red hair was too bright to be real, but it enhanced her green eyes and catlike face.

He had not hired her for her physical assets, interesting though they were. She was sharp and savvy, and she had an intuitive sense of how to reach potential customers online. She was also as ambitious as he was and willing to work 24/7.

He liked to have driven, ambitious people working for him, but ambition had a dark side.

He realized he was drumming his fingers on the arm of the chair and tapping his foot in a jittery, agitated manner. That wouldn't have been so bad if he'd had an old-fashioned wooden desk. Laurel and Kate wouldn't be able to see his foot, in that case. But now he knew they were deliberately trying not to stare.

He should never have allowed the decorator to install a glass-topped desk.

Suddenly he wanted to do the damned handwashing thing. He fought the compulsion with everything he had.

To distract himself, he got to his feet, crossed to the window and pretended to study the view. His office was on the twentieth floor of a high-rise office tower in Seattle's South Lake Union neighborhood. From where he stood he could still see a portion of Lake Union, but he knew that situation would not last much longer. Office towers and high-rise condos and apartment buildings had been cropping up all across Seattle for the past few years, and there seemed to be no end to the construction.

When he finally sold Night Watch, he would have more than enough cash to buy a higher floor in a forty-story building and get a sweeping view of the whole damned town.

"I talked to a homicide detective from the Seattle PD this morning," he said. "Guy named Schwartz. I gather he's in charge of the investigation. At this point they don't have any leads. They want to talk to some of the people here at Night Watch who knew Sandra."

Kate clutched a file folder. "That's most of the staff. We were all shocked. People are saying that Sandra might have been into the drug scene."

"I've instructed HR to cooperate fully with the investigators," Josh said. "It's all very sad, but the fact is that Sandra was no longer an employee of Night Watch at the time of her death. Let's get to work. Laurel?"

"The new marketing strategy is being implemented today," Laurel said briskly. "The whole team is really excited. The social media elements have already launched. Orders are starting to tick up."

He nodded, trying to read her body language.

There was no getting around the fact that the qualities that made Laurel valuable to the company also put her on his list of suspects. Still, he could not convince himself that she had the skills required to pull off a high-tech rip-off.

Unless she was working with someone else, he thought. He hadn't considered that possibility before now. *Shit. Have I got two crooks on my staff?* That seemed unlikely. Embezzlers usually worked alone, but there were exceptions to every rule.

"Do you want to go over the final version of the ad campaign again?" Laurel asked.

He realized she had asked the question twice. He turned around. Both women were watching him.

"No," he said. "I signed off on the overall plan. I don't need to go through the details."

Laurel gave him her cool, self-confident smile. "Great. I'll have some initial dates for you by tomorrow morning."

Kate cleared her throat.

"Yes, Kate?" he said, not bothering to conceal his impatience.

He tightened his hands behind his back and clenched his fingers. He really, really wanted to go into his private restroom and wash his hands. Again.

"I've come up with a new angle for promoting the third level of the Deep Sleep Exploration section," Kate said. "It's available for preview and comment. I've got a meeting scheduled with the team this afternoon. Will that work for you? If not, I can reschedule."

"This afternoon is fine," Josh said. "I think that's it for now." He paused. "Unless either of you has anything to add?"

Laurel shook her head and rose from her chair. She was as cool and unflustered as usual.

"No, nothing else," Kate said.

She shot to her feet, eager to escape.

He waited until they had both left the room before he went back to his desk. He stood for a moment, staring at the closed door of his office. He had to find the thief and he had to do it soon. He was running out of time. The rumors of Night Watch's financial problems were already starting to circulate. That kind of gossip spread fast in the tech world. If it got out that he was being systematically fleeced, he could forget any hope of securing another round of venture capital. It was okay to burn through cash. That was expected with a start-up. But getting scammed by someone in your own company was a killer.

He crossed the office, opened a door and entered the sanctuary of his private executive restroom. He washed his hands exactly fifteen times, very thoroughly, under very warm water.

When the ritual was complete, a sense of relief descended. He knew it would be short-lived, but at least he could think more clearly again.

He would see someone about the OCD thing when he had some time. But first he had to regain control of his business and find out who was stealing from him.

Chapter 27

Kate Delbridge carried her latte across the lightly crowded break room to the table where Tucker Fleming was sitting alone.

Tucker was, as usual, transfixed by whatever he was looking at on his phone. He glanced up when she arrived, acknowledged her presence with a short, impatient inclination of his head and immediately returned his attention to the screen of his device.

"Everything okay in the Zero-Zero-Zero Suite?" he asked.

Somewhere back at the start, for reasons no one had ever discovered, Josh Preston's office had acquired the title of the Zero-Zero-Zero Suite.

"I'm not sure," Kate said. "The boss is really wired today. He could hardly sit still when Laurel and I briefed him on the new marketing and promo plans."

"Preston has always been the twitchy type."

"Yes, but this is the worst I've ever seen him. I swear, he's really nervous about something."

Tucker shrugged. "Maybe he's heard the rumors that have started up around the office."

"You mean about the embezzlement? I'm sure he has. Heck, even I've heard those stories and I'm usually the last to know what's going on around here. I'm surprised Preston hasn't brought in a cybersecurity firm to investigate."

"Once he does that, he won't have a chance in hell of controlling the situation. The rumors about embezzlement will get very loud and the pool of potential investors will dry up overnight."

"You're probably right."

She peeled the lid off the latte. Some people had a problem trying to carry on a conversation with a person who could not pry himself away from his phone, but she was used to it. Like most start-ups, Night Watch was populated with highly caffeinated workers who were convinced that they had evolved the ability to live two parallel lives — one on their devices and one in the real world. She was pretty sure that for a lot of them it was the real-world life that suffered. It just couldn't compete with the never-ending stimulation of the online life. Personally, she preferred the real world.

Tucker Fleming had recently received a big bonus and been made employee of the month because of his latest Night Watch app. He was in his midtwenties and there was no denying he'd hit the genetic lottery with his looks. But he had a short, unpredictable temper. He was also impulsive. Those personality characteristics wouldn't be a problem, however, so long as he kept coming up with moneymaking apps.

Ultimately, of course, Tucker Fleming was doomed to obsolescence. Like coloratura sopranos, football stars and prima ballerinas, the careers of the hotshots in the tech world were invariably fated to be short-lived. Tucker was a blazing star now, but there was always another generation of wizards coming up who were even faster, sharper and more in tune with the machines. Even the best programmers were viewed as over-the-hill at an age when their counterparts in other businesses were just starting to hit their career heights.

As for her, she just wrote content for the Night Watch blogs and social media. The thing about writing was that someone, somewhere always needed a good writer.

She drank some coffee and lowered the

cup. "Did the cops talk to you about Sandra yet?"

"Yeah." Tucker focused on the screen of his phone. "I told 'em that I was a colleague and that we'd worked together but that I didn't know her very well. I mentioned that I'd heard rumors that she was into the drug scene. What about you?"

"The cops haven't interviewed me yet. They probably won't. It wasn't like Sandra and I were close. I barely knew her. You know how it is — IT people never have any patience with those of us who got degrees in English."

"I'll bet the police will go with the theory that it was some kind of drug deal gone bad."

"Think so?"

"It's the most logical explanation," Tucker said. "Like I told the cops, Sandra had gotten weird lately."

CHAPTER 28

Josh Preston left the office shortly before five. Cabot waited for him just outside the exit door of the building's underground garage. When Preston brought his very distinctive, very expensive sports car to a halt to check traffic before pulling out onto the street, Cabot walked to the driver's-side window, wallet open, his investigator's license in full view.

Preston looked wary, but he lowered the window. "Who are you?"

"I've been hired to investigate the death of a certain person. The death may or may not be linked to the death of Sandra Porter. I'd like to talk to you about it."

"Shit. The cops haven't said anything about another murder."

"It might be a case of suicide. That's what I'm trying to confirm."

"You think one of my employees is involved?"

"I have no reason to think that — not yet, at any rate. At this point I'm just trying to gather some facts. See, here's the problem: Sandra Porter was killed in my client's place of business."

"What the hell?"

"I'm sure you can understand why I'm looking for a connection to Night Watch."

"The police are investigating Sandra Porter's murder," Josh said.

"Yes, but they aren't interested in my case because they are convinced it was suicide."

Josh snorted softly. "But your client thinks otherwise, right?"

"Yes."

"I don't know what I can tell you," Josh said. "I was not aware that anyone else connected to Night Watch has died."

"The victim may not have had a connection. That's what I'm trying to establish. I'll only take a few minutes of your time."

Josh hesitated, fingers dancing uneasily on the steering wheel. His jaw clenched. Then he nodded once.

"There's a bar where we can talk privately." Josh rattled off the name and the street. "I'll meet you there."

"Thanks," Cabot said.

He stepped back, tucked his wallet inside his jacket and walked to his SUV. He opened the door and got behind the wheel. Virginia watched him from the passenger seat.

"Well?" she asked.

"Preston agreed to talk to us. We're going to meet him at a bar in a few minutes."

"You were right about the curiosity factor."

"Works almost every time, but in this case I think we had something else going for us."

"What?"

"I got the impression that Preston is nervous."

"What did you expect? A recently fired employee was murdered and the police are questioning the people who work for him. Any CEO would be concerned. For all Preston knows, he may have a killer on the payroll."

"There's that," Cabot conceded. He fired up the big engine and eased the SUV away from the curb. "But I think there's more to it than just the natural concern about a murder investigation."

Preston was waiting for them in a corner booth at the back of the quiet bar. His phone was on the table. There was a martini in front of him. It looked like a double. He scowled when he saw Virginia.

"What the hell is going on?" he asked.

"You didn't say anything about bringing someone else along to this meeting."

"I'm Virginia Troy," Virginia said. "Sandra Porter was murdered in the back room of my shop. Mr. Sutter is working for me."

Josh gave her a curt, appraising look. "So you're the client."

"Yes."

Josh considered that briefly and then nodded once. "All right. Sit down. Tell me what you've got."

Cabot pulled out a chair for Virginia and then sat down beside her.

"That isn't how it works," he said to Josh. "We're here to exchange information."

Josh hesitated and then nodded. "Fine. You want drinks?"

"No, thanks," Virginia said very politely.

Cabot shook his head. "Can you give us some idea of why you fired Sandra Porter?"

Josh pondered that for a moment and then shrugged. "Technically, she resigned. But, yes, she was forced out. It's not exactly a state secret. I've already told the cops. Porter was good at her job but my HR people say that there was a dramatic change in her behavior in recent weeks. There were rumors that she was involved with drugs. On top of everything else, I hear she was in a relationship that ended badly and that she was probably depressed. Now, what have you got for me?"

"Not a lot," Cabot said. "I can tell you that Hannah Brewster, the woman whose death I'm investigating, was an artist. Several of her works are stored in a closet in the back room of Ms. Troy's gallery. When we found Porter's body, the door of that closet was open."

"Huh." Josh considered that for a few beats. "I can see why you're asking questions, but I can't give you much help. I just don't know of any connection between Porter and the death of that artist. What kind of art did Brewster do? Sculpture? Glass?"

"Paintings," Cabot said.

Josh got a speculative look. "Were they valuable? Maybe if Porter was into drugs, she figured she could steal Brewster's pictures?"

"There's no market for Hannah Brewster's paintings," Virginia said coolly. "At least not that I've ever been able to find."

Josh swallowed some of his martini and set the glass down on the table with more force than necessary.

"There's nothing more I can tell you," he said. "If that's all you've got, this meeting is over."

"We've heard that there are rumors of financial problems at Night Watch," Cabot said.

Josh froze, stone-faced. "Where are you going with this?"

"When did you first realize that someone in-house was embezzling from you?" Cabot asked.

For a moment Virginia didn't think that Josh was going to respond. Then he seemed to deflate.

"A few weeks ago," he said. "Why?"

"Think Sandra Porter was the embezzler?" Cabot asked.

"No," Josh said grimly. "Or if she was, she's continuing to work from beyond the grave. I checked my financials an hour ago. More money has disappeared into the ether."

"Maybe she was working with someone else," Cabot suggested.

Josh frowned. "A partner who killed her? I'll admit that possibility did occur to me."

Cabot put his business card down on the table. "If you think of anything else I should know or if you want me to refer you to a very discreet cybersecurity firm who can investigate the embezzling, give me a call."

Josh pocketed the card without looking at it. "Do me a favor. If, in the course of your investigation, you happen to turn up any leads on who is siphoning off money from my business, will you let me know?"

"Depends," Cabot said.

"On what?"

"Whether or not it turns out to be a conflict of interest."

Josh frowned. "How the hell could there be a conflict of interest?"

"You never know. But if there isn't one and if I do get a lead on your embezzler, I'll be sure to send you my bill."

Josh gave him a curt nod. "Fair enough. You get me some answers and you'll get your money."

"Out of curiosity, any idea of where I should start looking for a potential embezzler?" Cabot asked.

Josh drummed his fingers on the table. "I ran my own investigation. Took a close look at everyone in my accounting department and in the IT department. Figured the thief had to be someone who knew how to move money around."

Virginia leaned forward. "Did you find anything?"

"No. But now I'm starting to wonder if I'm overlooking some possible suspects simply because I didn't think they had the skill set required to rip me off. But if one of them was working with Porter, who certainly did have the skill set —"

"Got a name?" Cabot asked.

Josh hesitated. "There's a writer in our social media department, Kate Delbridge. There's nothing I can put my finger on, but something about her makes me wonder if she might be involved in the embezzlement."

Virginia raised her brows. "Because she's the last person you'd suspect?"

"No. Because several months ago we had a weekend fling while on a business trip to San Francisco. I warned her going in that I wasn't interested in a serious relationship. Told her the ground rules — if she breathed a word about it at the office, I'd have to let her go. She seemed okay with that, but now I'm starting to wonder if she wants revenge. I can't get a read on her."

"Does she have the skills to embezzle and not get caught?" Cabot asked.

Josh shook his head. "No, I'm sure of that much. But it doesn't mean she wasn't working with Porter. Maybe she knows enough to keep the scheme running even though Porter is dead. Hell. I knew I should have fired Delbridge when we got back from that trip."

"Why not let her go now?" Cabot asked.

Josh snorted softly. "Ever hear the old adage, 'Keep your friends close but keep your enemies closer'? If Kate is fleecing me, I'd rather have her where I can keep an eye on her."

"Got any other suspects?" Cabot asked.

Josh's jaw tightened. "Maybe. But I'm not ready to give you another name. Not yet."

Chapter 29

Cabot opened the passenger-side door of the SUV. Virginia climbed into the seat. He closed the door, looking thoughtful. She watched him walk around the front of the vehicle. There was a blast of cold air when he opened the door and got behind the wheel.

He sat quietly for a moment. *Back in the zone,* she thought. *Doing his art.*

"What are we waiting for?" she asked after a while.

"Thought it might be interesting to see how long Preston sits alone in that bar," Cabot said.

"Ah, I get it. You don't think that the CEO of a business like Night Watch spends much time drinking alone."

"It would be unusual," Cabot said. "People in Preston's position usually have friends."

"People who want to be close to the guy

at the top."

"Yeah."

Virginia settled into the corner of the seat. "Do you do this sort of thing a lot?"

"Sit around and wait for someone to do something interesting? No. Most people are eager to share their lives with the whole world online. But once in a while there's no substitute for the old-fashioned approach."

"What happens if you need to use a restroom?"

Cabot looked at her. "Do you really want to know the answer to that one?"

"Probably not."

A fleeting expression of amusement came and went in his eyes.

In the end they did not have to wait very long. A short time later Josh Preston emerged from the front door of the bar, got into his car and drove slowly through the busy South Lake Union neighborhood.

Cabot followed at a discreet distance

"Looks like he lives on the Eastside," Virginia said.

"No, the address Anson dug up for him is on Mercer Island. Looks like Preston may be going to visit someone who lives on the Eastside."

CHAPTER 30

Tucker Fleming stared at the screen of his phone. According to the tracking program, Virginia Troy was on the move again.

There were a lot of logical reasons why she might be in a vehicle that was currently on the 520 bridge, heading for one of the communities on the east side of Lake Washington. Maybe she was going to visit the home of a client.

Tucker watched the blip on the screen. Troy was off the bridge now and veering left toward Kirkland.

An unpleasant tingle of uncertainty iced the back of Tucker's neck. After Sandra Porter's death he had told himself that the situation was under control again. The cops were focused on a theory that involved drugs and an ex-boyfriend who didn't exist.

But Cabot Sutter was proving to be unpredictable. That made him dangerous.

Tucker reached for another can of his

favorite energy drink. He popped the top and took a long swallow. Back at the start he had been the master player in the game. But things kept going wrong. Hannah Brewster had escaped him by jumping off a cliff. Virginia Troy had hired a PI with links to the past. Then Sandra Porter had turned into a stalker and tried to blackmail him.

He had to regain control of the game, and he had to do it fast.

CHAPTER 31

Preston drove through the boutique village of Kirkland and stopped in front of a low-rise condominium complex on the shores of Lake Washington. He parked at the curb, got out and walked to the security gate. He pressed the buzzer. A few seconds later the gate opened. He went through it and walked along a path.

The door of number 8 opened before he could knock.

Cabot got a glimpse of an attractive redhead, and then Preston was inside the woman's condo and the door was closing.

"Looks like Preston has a girlfriend," Virginia said.

Cabot drove slowly past the condominium complex and turned a corner.

"Maybe," he said.

He pulled over to the curb and got on his phone. Anson answered immediately.

"What's up?" he demanded.

"We're in Kirkland. I've got an address for you. I need a name to go with it."

He gave Anson the address of the lakeside condominium. Anson came back a short time later.

"The owner's name is Laurel Jenner. I did a quick search on the social media sites that the professionals use and she came up right away. She's the head of marketing at Night Watch."

"Thanks," Cabot said. "Looks like Preston and Ms. Jenner have a personal relationship."

"Wouldn't be the first time a boss had an affair with one of his employees," Anson said.

"True," Cabot said.

"They're both single," Anson pointed out. "No law against it. By the way, I was just about to call you. You need to come back to the office as soon as you can."

"Something wrong?"

"No. Just someone here you should meet. Soon."

Anson ended the connection before Cabot could say anything else.

CHAPTER 32

Traffic was light for a change. Cabot made good time getting back to the office. He opened the door of Cutler, Sutter & Salinas and came to a full stop. Virginia, however, kept going, slipping past him into the reception area.

Cabot ignored her. He did not take his eyes off the young male sprawled in one of the two client chairs. The teen was transfixed by whatever he was looking at on his phone. He worked the device in a slick, smooth, single-handed manner that made Cabot feel old.

The kid had dark hair cut in the latest trendy style. He was lean and gangly in the way of a boy making the transition to early manhood. He wore running shoes, ripped denim and a gray hoodie. Cabot figured him to be about seventeen.

The stranger lowered his phone and raised his head, revealing a sharply angled profile.

He looked eerily familiar. Cabot had the sensation that he was seeing a ghost in a mirror — a ghost of himself when he had been the kid's age.

He closed the door and looked at Anson for clarification.

"Meet Xavier Kennington," Anson said calmly. "Xavier is your uncle's son."

"Uh-huh," Cabot said.

"That makes Xavier your cousin," Anson said meaningfully.

"Uh-huh."

Anson moved on. "Xavier, this is Ms. Virginia Troy."

Virginia smiled. "A pleasure to meet you, Xavier."

Xavier shuffled to his feet, ducked his head and mumbled an acknowledgment of the introduction. But his eyes were locked on Cabot.

"Hi," Xavier said to him.

Cabot closed the office door with great precision.

"Do your parents know you're here?" he asked.

"Yeah. I texted Mom a few minutes ago."

Cabot glanced at Anson.

"I think you and Xavier should talk," Anson said.

"Anson is right," Virginia added gently.

Cabot turned back to Xavier. "My office."

It was an order, not a request. Wary but determined, Xavier trailed after him. Cabot closed the door, took off his windbreaker and hung it on the hook. Xavier stared, fascinated, at the holstered gun.

He's just a kid, Cabot thought. *What happened in the past was not his fault.*

"Have a seat," he said.

Xavier lowered himself into a chair. He clutched his phone in one hand as if it were a protective amulet.

Cabot sat down behind the desk.

"Why did you come to see me?" he asked, doing his level best to keep the anger out of the words. It wasn't easy.

"Figured I'd warn you," Xavier said.

"About?"

"Burleigh."

"The lawyer for your grandfather's estate?"

"He was your grandfather, too," Xavier said quickly.

"Biologically."

"Look, I don't know what happened back when your mom and dad took off, but everyone says that Granddad was really pissed."

"I've heard that."

"I know your mom joined some kind of

cult for a while after your dad was killed," Xavier said. "I know Aunt Jacqueline died in a fire and that you went into the foster care system. But that's all I knew until recently because no one ever talked much about you."

"I gather that changed after the old man died."

"Yeah. I wasn't sure what was going on for a while, but I knew it had something to do with Granddad's estate and you. Then I heard my dad talking to that lawyer, Burleigh."

"And you found out that I was mentioned in the will, is that it?"

Xavier gave a disdainful snort. For the first time he seemed to feel as if he was on more solid ground.

"You really don't know what's going on, do you?" he asked.

"Not yet, but I assume you're about to enlighten me."

"I'm not sure of all the details, but from what I overheard, I think Burleigh is planning to screw you out of whatever you're supposed to inherit."

"Burleigh's the lawyer who is handling the estate," Cabot pointed out. "That means he's not a beneficiary. What would he get out of the deal?"

Xavier frowned while he processed that. Then he shrugged. "I dunno. Best guess is that Dad is paying him off to screw you."

"Why would your father do that?"

"Probably because his new girlfriend wants him to get you out of the picture so she can get more for herself. Guess I forgot to mention that Dad's divorcing Mom so that he can marry Lizzie."

"Lizzie?"

"Her real name's *Elizabeth* but Mom calls her Lizzie, mostly because she knows it irritates Dad. Lizzie is just a few years older than me."

"Sounds like this situation is somewhat complicated."

"Got news for you. The whole family is complicated. If it makes you feel any better, you're not the only one getting screwed. Mom made the mistake of signing a prenup."

"I see." Cabot folded his arms on top of his desk. "I appreciate the warning, Xavier, but I have to tell you that discovering that someone wants to make sure I don't benefit from old man Kennington's estate does not come as the biggest surprise of the year. If it makes you feel any better, I do plan to have my own lawyer look at whatever Burleigh wants me to sign."

"Okay. Just thought I'd tell you." Xavier surveyed the office with intense curiosity. "You're a real private investigator?"

"As far as I know."

"You're wearing a gun."

"I'm working a case at the moment, one that involves a death that occurred under suspicious circumstances."

"A murder case." Xavier nodded wisely. "So that's why you've got the gun. That lady out there, Ms. Troy, is she your girlfriend?"

"She's my client," Cabot said. He stressed the word *client*.

"Yeah?"

"Yeah. Xavier, just how and when do you plan to go home?"

"I dunno. I've never been to Seattle. Thought I'd stay awhile."

"Is that right? And just where will you be staying while you're in town?"

"I dunno. I'll figure it out."

The phone rang in the outer office. Cabot ignored it but he got a bad feeling about the identity of the caller.

"That's probably Mom," Xavier said.

There was a single knock on the door. Anson opened it without waiting for an invitation.

"Mrs. Melissa Kennington would like to speak to you," Anson said as if the call were perfectly routine.

"Shit," Cabot said. "What am I supposed to say?"

"Beats me," Anson said. He closed the door.

Cabot eyed the phone. He had gone his whole life without hearing from the Kenningtons, and now they were popping up every five minutes.

He steeled himself and picked up the phone. "Cabot Sutter."

"This is Melissa Kennington." The voice was crisp and authoritative but it was infused with anxiety. "I understand my son is there with you."

"Yes, he is. I believe he was just leaving."

Xavier looked alarmed.

"He's on his way home?" Melissa asked, urgent and hopeful.

"I'll let you discuss it with him."

Cabot held the phone out to Xavier, who groaned and reluctantly uncurled from the chair. He took the phone.

"I'm okay, Mom . . . Yeah, I know. But as long as I'm here in Seattle, I want to stay a couple of days. I can take care of myself. I'm almost *eighteen*. I've got some money and the credit card Dad gave me. Yes, I'm coming home soon, I promise. No, I'm not going to do anything stupid. Yes, sure, you can talk to him. He's right here."

Xavier held out the phone. "She wants to talk to you."

Reluctantly, Cabot took the phone. "What do you want from me, Mrs. Kennington?"

"I want you to put him on the next plane home," Melissa said.

Cabot studied the stubborn set of Xavier's shoulders. "That is a very good idea, but I can't force him to go home."

"You have to do something."

"What would you suggest?"

"I don't know, but this is your fault. You're the reason he's there in Seattle."

"You're blaming me? I never even met Xavier until about ten minutes ago."

"He's heard about you for years," Melissa said. "You're the family mystery. Of course he's curious about you."

"I don't know what you expect me to do. I can strongly suggest that he buy a ticket home but beyond that —"

"I know." Melissa sounded defeated. "His father says I should step back and let Xavier experience the consequences of his actions. This isn't the first time Xavier has run off. But he's missing school and he can't afford to do that. This is his senior year. He's sup-posed to start college in the fall."

"Like I said, there's not much I can do

from this end," Cabot said.

"He went looking for you because he's curious about you. No offense, but you are not exactly a good influence. My son is going to college. I don't want him to be distracted. I'm afraid he's developed a very unrealistic, highly romanticized impression of the sort of work you do."

"Here's the thing — I don't want to be any kind of influence, good or bad. I just want the Kenningtons to go back to their long-standing policy of ignoring me."

There was a short silence from the other end of the line. When Melissa spoke again, there was a very subdued note in her voice.

"Is it true that after your mother died, your grandfather let you go into the foster care system?" There was another pause. "I've heard conflicting stories."

"It's true."

Melissa made a disgusted sound. "Your grandfather really was a bastard."

"Something we can agree on at last. But you don't have to waste any time feeling sorry for me. I got lucky in the system. That man who answered the phone a few minutes ago happens to be my dad."

"I see. Mr. Salinas sounded very nice. Very understanding."

"He is. I'm not."

"Look, I'm sorry Xavier tracked you down, but we both have the same goals here. You want to send him home. I want him to come home. Maybe if you just answer some of his questions about the past and what you do for a living, that will be enough to satisfy him."

"I don't have an obligation to answer anyone's questions," Cabot said.

"I know you have no reason to give a damn about any of the adults in this family," Melissa said, her voice sharpening again. "But I had nothing to do with what happened all those years ago and neither did my son. I hope you will remember that and treat Xavier with some kindness. His father and I are in the middle of a very nasty divorce. Xavier is not dealing with it well. Neither am I, for that matter."

The phone went dead in Cabot's hand. He set it down with great care and looked at Xavier.

"I understand you've got questions for me," Cabot said.

Xavier flushed a dull red. "I just wanted to meet you."

"You've met me. I don't have time to answer a lot of questions. I told you, I'm working a case. Where do you plan to stay tonight?"

"I dunno."

"You do realize that it will be next to impossible for a kid your age to check into a respectable hotel without an adult?"

That was clearly news to Xavier. But after a moment of confusion, he shrugged off the problem.

"I'll find something," he said. "Maybe one of the shelters."

The vision of Xavier — a naïve kid who had grown up with money, private schools and designer clothes — spending a night in one of the city's homeless shelters boggled the mind.

"I don't have time for this," Cabot said. He pushed himself up out of his chair, went around his desk and opened the door. "Anson, can you handle a houseguest tonight?"

Anson looked past him to Xavier, who bore a startling resemblance to a really stubborn deer in the headlights.

"No problem," Anson said. "We'll send out for pizza. You and Virginia can join us."

"Love to," Virginia said.

I'm doomed, Cabot thought.

Anson smiled at Virginia. "I've got some good news. The cleaners have finished up in your gallery. You should be able to open tomorrow. Business as usual."

"Except that there was a murder in my back room," Virginia said.

Anson nodded. "Except for that."

Xavier stared at Virginia, fascinated. "Someone got murdered in your shop?"

"Long story," Virginia said. "I'll tell you all about it at dinner."

"Excellent," Xavier said.

CHAPTER 33

The following morning Virginia unlocked the front door of the gallery shortly after eight. She had been dreading the moment. Murder had been done in the back room of her gallery. She would never again be able to enter the space without remembering the dead woman lying in the pool of blood.

The pizza dinner with Xavier and Anson had gone fairly well, she thought. True, Cabot's contribution to the conversation was minimal, but he had not been rude. He just seemed withdrawn. Later, when they had returned to her apartment, he immersed himself in research on his laptop. He was still at it when she went to bed. Eventually she'd heard the door of his room close.

Sooner or later they would have to talk about how he was going to deal with his cousin, but intuition told her that it was too soon to try to coax him into that particular discussion. Cabot needed time. There was steel in the man, but steel did not bend easily.

At breakfast that morning neither of them had mentioned Xavier.

Cabot followed her into the back room of the gallery. He surveyed the surroundings with a professional eye and then nodded once.

"The cleaners did a good job," he said.

Virginia looked at the place on the floor where they had found Sandra Porter's body. Astonishingly, there was no trace of blood.

She shivered. "You know, until recently it never occurred to me that there were people who specialized in cleaning up after crimes."

"It's another one of those career paths that high-school guidance counselors often neglect to mention," Cabot said.

He walked deliberately through the space.

"What are you looking for?" Virginia asked.

"Nothing in particular," Cabot said. "I'm sure the forensics people were thorough. Still, you never know."

The front door opened again. Jolted, Virginia turned quickly. When she saw the familiar figure standing on the threshold, she took a deep breath.

"Sorry, Boss," Jessica said. "Didn't mean

to startle you."

"Not your fault," Virginia said. "I'm a little jumpy today, that's all."

Jessica grunted. "I don't blame you. I'm not the one who found the body, but I'm feeling rather twitchy myself this morning. To be honest, I'm very glad you got here before I did. I wasn't looking forward to being the first one through the door."

Jessica Ames was in her early fifties. Tall and generously proportioned, she tinted her hair jet black and kept it cut in a razor-sharp Cleopatra style. The fringe above her dark eyes looked as if it had been trimmed with the aid of a straight edge.

Like many in the art world, Jessica wore a lot of black. Today was no exception. She wore a black turtleneck and a pair of flowy, calf-length trousers. A statement necklace fashioned of some copper-colored metal completed the look.

Virginia had not hired her because of her expertise in art. Jessica had arrived on the doorstep of the Troy Gallery knowing almost nothing about the field. But Jessica had two very important attributes. The first was that she was a fast learner. The second was that she had a talent for sales. A lot of people thought it would be nice to work in an art gallery. Very few people had the ability to match a client with the perfect object of his or her desire.

Jessica also knew how to pull people in off the street. It had been her idea to put the display of brilliant, hand-blown glass paperweights in the front window of the shop. They glowed in the carefully arranged lighting, catching the eyes of passersby. Once people opened the door of the shop, Jessica went to work. Very few customers left empty-handed.

Virginia waved a hand at Cabot. "Jessica, this is Cabot Sutter. He's the investigator I hired to look into Hannah Brewster's death. Cabot, this is my assistant, Jessica Ames."

"Nice to meet you," Cabot said.

Jessica sized him up in one quick glance and smiled approvingly. "A pleasure." She took a long, slow look around the shop. "I still can't believe someone got murdered in here. Do the cops have any leads?"

"Currently they're leaning toward a theory that involves drugs," Virginia said. "But Cabot and I are wondering if Sandra Porter's death is in any way linked to Hannah Brewster's."

"Weird thought," Jessica said. She paused. "You think Hannah Brewster might have known Porter?"

"I'm almost positive they never met,"

Virginia said. "But the door of the storage room where we keep Hannah's paintings was open."

"Maybe someone thought those pictures are worth a lot more than we assumed," Jessica suggested.

"We've had them on display from time to time," Virginia reminded her. "We've never had a single offer on any of them."

"True. They're fascinating in some weird way but they make people uneasy." Jessica got a familiar gleam in her eye. "One thing's for sure, though."

"What's that?" Cabot asked.

"In case you haven't noticed, the murder-in-the-art-gallery story is getting a real run in the local media. That kind of publicity will help get out a nice crowd for the show next week."

Virginia winced. "We don't need a lot of curiosity seekers. We need a crowd of people who are actually interested in buying art."

"Don't worry, Boss," Jessica said. "I can turn curiosity seekers into art collectors. It's my superpower."

Cabot regarded Jessica with a mix of admiration and curiosity.

"You're that good?" he said.

Jessica smiled modestly.

"She's that good," Virginia said.

Cabot studied Jessica with his usual intent expression.

"What's your secret?" he asked.

"Depends on the customer," Jessica said.

"Client," Virginia said. "We call them clients, not customers."

"Oh, right," Jessica said. She gave Cabot a winning smile. "Clients."

"What would you sell me?" Cabot asked.

"If you were passing by on the street, it would most likely be the glass paperweights that would make you enter the shop."

"Because I don't look like an art connoisseur?"

"Everyone responds to some kind of art," Jessica said. "Not everyone knows that, though. It's my job to find out exactly what type of art a person needs and then put that object into his or her hands. Between you and me, the paperweights are what I call starter art."

"What about the whole art-for-art's-sake thing?" Cabot asked.

"That's bullshit," Jessica said. "Every piece of art has a purpose, even if it's just to make someone stop and look for a couple of seconds."

"The best art tells a story," Virginia said. "That's why the Old Masters survive and a lot of modern abstract art won't."

Cabot looked at Jessica. "So I'm a paper-weight kind of guy?"

"You're a form-follows-function kind of guy," Jessica said, very serious now. "You're the type who responds to well-designed objects that have a well-defined purpose. You would admire a beautifully crafted knife or an elegant car or a brilliant paperweight that would catch the light while it was holding down a stack of papers on a desk."

She plucked a dark-blue-and-gold paper-weight from the cluster on the table near the storage locker and handed it to Cabot. He studied it for a moment, watching the light play in the heart of the glass.

"You know, Anson's got a birthday coming up," he said. "I think he might like this. It would look good on his desk."

Virginia hid a smile.

Jessica nodded. "Excellent choice for a man's desk. Masculine and useful. It will complement any style of décor."

Cabot whistled softly. "Virginia's right. You're good."

"Everyone has a talent," Jessica said.

CHAPTER 34

"What do you want from me?" Kate Delbridge demanded. "The police already took my statement. HR sent out a memo telling everyone at the company that we aren't supposed to talk to anyone except the cops."

"Which is, of course, why the news of Sandra Porter's death is all over the social media sites that the local tech crowd likes to use," Virginia said.

They were standing in the hallway outside Kate's apartment. Cabot had agreed to let her take the lead. She was following a hunch because neither she nor Cabot had been able to go deep into the latest social media sites that the young tech crowd favored. But given the way the world worked these days, she figured it was a safe bet that employees from Night Watch had done a lot of communicating about the murder.

Kate frowned at Cabot. "Who are you guys? Local TV? I don't see any cameras."

"I'm a private investigator," Cabot said. "I'm investigating a case that may have a connection to the death of Sandra Porter."

Kate switched her attention back to Virginia. "Are you his assistant or something?"

"No," Virginia said. "I'm his client. Sandra Porter died in the back room of my gallery."

"Oh." Kate absorbed that information. "I read somewhere that the gallery owner found the body."

"That's right," Virginia said. "You can understand why I'm interested in Sandra Porter's murder."

"Okay, I guess that makes sense," Kate said. "But the fact is, I didn't know Sandra Porter very well. She was a loner and she worked in IT. When I ran into her in the halls, she ignored me. All I can tell you is what I told the cops. People at work are saying that Sandra was seeing someone but she was very secretive about it. I got the impression that she'd been dumped recently. She was always intense but after that she got a little scary."

"We know she lost her job at Night Watch," Virginia said. "We know the official reason — she left to pursue other career opportunities. We also know that's not the real reason. Why do you think she was fired?"

Kate shrugged. "Some people are saying she got into drugs. But there have been rumors that she might have been embezzling funds. Management probably couldn't prove it, so they just let her go."

"That's often the way big firms deal with embezzlers," Cabot said. "It avoids the bad publicity."

"What did you mean when you said that Sandra got scary?" Virginia asked.

"It's hard to explain," Kate said. "She seemed to be seething all the time. And she had mood swings. One day I found her sobbing in the restroom. I asked her if she was okay. She told me to fuck off."

"Do you think she might have been the embezzler?" Cabot asked.

"I guess we'll all find out soon enough," Kate said. "If she was the one who was skimming off money, the losses should stop, right?" Kate started to close the door. "Look, that's all I can tell you. I really don't know anything else."

"Wait," Virginia said quickly. "One more thing — did Sandra have any close friends at the company?"

"Not that I know of. She wasn't the type who attracted friends."

Once again Kate started to close the door. Cabot took out a card and handed it to her.

"If you think of anything else that might be helpful — anything at all — please call me," he said. "Day or night."

"All right." Kate took the card and closed the door.

Virginia heard the lock click into place. Without a word, she and Cabot walked down the hall to the elevators. She pressed the call button.

"Well?" she said. "What's your take on her?"

"I think she's nervous," Cabot said. "But that doesn't give us much to go on."

His phone beeped. He unclipped it and checked the screen. His jaw tightened as he read the message. Without a word he clipped the phone back on his belt.

"What?" Virginia asked.

"A message from Anson. We're expected for dinner again this evening."

"Okay," Virginia said.

"Okay?"

"You can do this, Cabot. You are a tough crime fighter. You can handle a teenager who just wants to know more about you."

"What the hell am I supposed to do with a seventeen-year-old boy?"

"Give him a job."

"A job? He's seventeen."

"Exactly," Virginia said. "He's seventeen.

That means he probably knows a lot more about the online world than you and me and Anson put together. Ask Xavier to do some online research for you."

She thought Cabot was going to come back with a hard no to that suggestion. But he didn't. Instead he appeared to give the idea some serious thought.

"Huh," he said.

Chapter 35

"It's going to be all right," Virginia said. "I'm not saying it will be comfortable, but it will be okay. All families are dysfunctional in one way or another."

They were back in her condo, sitting on her sofa. The second dinner with Xavier and Anson had gotten off to a rocky start, but when Cabot had suggested that Xavier help Anson work on the little math book, Xavier lit up with enthusiasm. He had asked an endless string of questions while wolfing down half the pizza.

By the time Cabot and Virginia left, Xavier had been deep into the photocopied pages of the book.

"Easy for you to say all families are dysfunctional," Cabot muttered. He swallowed some of his beer and set the bottle down. "You're not the one who is suddenly developing a lot of connections with a family that, until recently, didn't give a damn whether you were alive or dead."

"I understand," she said. "But it occurs to me that what you are witnessing is a change of generations in the Kennington family. The old man, as you call him, is gone. Now that he's dead, the younger family members are taking charge. They may know some of the history of your relationship with the rest of the Kennington family —"

"That's just it. I don't have a relationship with the Kennington people."

"Well, you do now. My advice is to deal with it."

He glared at her. "Are you on the Kennington side of this thing?"

"I'm not taking sides. I'm offering advice."

"I don't need advice."

"Doesn't mean I'm not going to give you some. Don't worry, it's free."

Cabot raised his eyes. "And worth exactly what you're charging?"

She looked at him. "Do you want my advice or not?"

He groaned. "I know you're trying to be helpful. What's your advice?"

"We both know that Xavier had nothing to do with what happened all those years ago."

"I'm not arguing that point."

"So try to look at him as an individual in

his own right. He's a young man who is going through some perfectly natural growing pains while simultaneously becoming the collateral damage that always comes down when divorce happens. With things in a bad way at home, it's not surprising that he has suddenly developed a deep curiosity about his long-lost, mysterious cousin."

"I'm not mysterious and I was never lost. The lawyer, Burleigh, sure knew how to find me. So did Xavier."

"Well, it's not as if you were trying to stay hidden," she said. "Not like Quinton Zane."

"Assuming he's still alive."

"Assuming that, yes." She swallowed some of her wine and lowered the glass. "Speaking of our investigation, where do we go next?"

"Good question." Cabot seemed relieved by the change of subject. "I've been thinking about that. We can keep talking to people who worked with Sandra Porter. Sooner or later we might catch a break. But, as you said, the cops are already pursuing those leads. I think we need to refocus on our own case."

"Hannah Brewster's death?"

"If there is a connection between Brewster and Porter, we might have better luck finding it from our end."

Virginia rested one arm along the back of the sofa. "I'm listening."

"I've told you from the beginning that if we're right that someone is looking for the missing money, it's because something changed in the equation — something that must have happened fairly recently. It occurs to me that Brewster was not the first person connected to Zane's operation who died on that island up in the San Juans."

"You're talking about Abigail Watkins? The woman who owned the Lost Island B and B? But I told you, there was nothing mysterious about her death. She had cancer."

"You said she sold the B and B shortly before her death to raise a little cash."

"That's right. Rose Gilbert bought it. She allowed Abigail to stay there until the end."

"The Seattle housing market is hot, but that's not so true up in the San Juans. Properties on the more remote islands can sit on the market for months or even years, especially a big, old Victorian that needs a lot of upkeep."

"Sometimes you just get lucky when you're trying to sell property. The right buyer comes along at the right time. In this case it was Rose Gilbert. Are you saying there's something suspicious about the transaction?"

"I'm saying we need to go back to the start of this thing and question every co-incidence," Cabot said.

He leaned forward and opened his laptop on the coffee table. Virginia watched him search real estate databases.

"Nothing," he announced after a few minutes. "There's no record of the sale. The B and B was never on the market. As far as the property tax records are concerned, the Lost Island B and B still belongs to Abigail Watkins, which means it is now part of her estate."

"I don't think Abigail had a will. Like Hannah, she didn't want anything to do with legal stuff that could be used to track her down."

"Yet Rose Gilbert moved in shortly after Watkins died and told everyone she did a private transaction with the previous owner."

"No one on the island would have questioned that," Virginia said. "Certainly Hannah never did. As far as I know, Rose Gilbert didn't show up on the island until after Abigail's funeral."

"Maybe there never was a deal between Watkins and Gilbert," Cabot said.

Virginia frowned. "Are you suggesting that

Rose Gilbert just moved in one day and started running the B and B business?"

"Ever heard of squatters? They move into foreclosures and vacant properties all the time. But I'll admit it seems unlikely that the average squatter would take over a bed-and-breakfast operation."

"Well, she's not exactly running it on a paying basis," Virginia said. "She keeps talking about needing to make some major repairs to get ready for the summer season. You saw for yourself, the top floor of guest rooms is closed."

"It might be interesting to know a little more about Rose Gilbert. I'll have Anson go to work on that in the morning. Meanwhile, thanks to you, we do know two very important things about Abigail Watkins. The first is that she had a connection to Zane."

"And the second?"

"She's dead," Cabot said. "No matter who you are or how much you try to hide, there's always paperwork and records associated with dying."

He concentrated intently on his laptop. When he looked up again, Virginia could tell by his diamond-sharp eyes that he had found something.

"Abigail Watkins had only one surviving family member, a half sister," he said. "Rose

Elaine Gilbert."

Comprehension whispered through Virginia. "Rose wasn't just some casual buyer who showed up at the right moment to buy the B and B. She knew her half sister was dying. She probably figured she was Abigail's legal heir."

"Probably."

"But it doesn't make any sense. Why would Rose keep quiet about her connection with Abigail Watkins?"

"Maybe because Rose has been lying to us from the beginning."

"I assume we're going to talk to her again?"

"Yes," Cabot said. "As soon as possible."

Virginia took out her phone. "I'll see if I can get reservations on the private car ferry tomorrow. Shouldn't be hard at this time of year. I'm assuming you don't want me to call Rose and make reservations at the B and B?"

"No," Cabot said. "We'll take her by surprise."

CHAPTER 36

Rose Gilbert hit the switch on the ancient coffeemaker and went to stand at the kitchen window. She thought about how much she hated the island.

It was seven o'clock in the morning. She was still in her robe and slippers. There was no reason to get dressed in a hurry. The most thrilling event of the whole damn day — the arrival of the ferry and departure of the ferry — wouldn't take place until midafternoon.

Not that she cared about the arrival of the ferry. She wasn't expecting any guests. It was a weekday and there were no reservations. She didn't know which was worse, spending the days alone in the big house or making polite chitchat with the customers.

The only reason she kept one floor of rooms open was so that she could maintain the illusion of being a real innkeeper. The locals were suspicious enough as it was.

She had certainly never expected to stay this long. She had been trapped on the island since December, faking her way through the bed-and-breakfast business while she waited for Tucker to find the key.

It had all seemed so simple back at the start. After Abigail's death she had come to the island to pack up her half sister's things and make arrangements to put the old Victorian on the market. She had hoped to make a little money on the sale of the house.

But she had discovered Abigail's diary, and that had changed everything.

She had flipped through it, expecting to find it dull reading at best. Abigail had been a weak, pathetic screw-up all of her life — just the kind of naïve idiot you'd expect to get swept up into a cult. But the details of Abigail's time in Quinton Zane's cult had proved to be downright riveting.

So much money had been raked in and most of it had vanished into a secret account. In the end, of those who had once known the location of the key, only crazy Hannah Brewster had been left alive.

The plan to get the information out of Brewster had failed. She had jumped to her death rather than deal with what she believed to be the reincarnation of Quinton Zane.

The only lead left was Virginia Troy, who seemed entirely unaware of just how valuable she was. But Troy had complicated things by hiring Cabot Sutter.

The coffeemaker finished the brewing process. Rose turned away from the window and poured herself a mug full of coffee.

Just another boring day on the island from hell.

She was startled by the sound of gravel crunching under tires. That made no sense. The ferry wasn't due to arrive for several hours. Maybe one of the locals had stopped by for some reason.

Reluctantly, she got to her feet and went through the lobby. She twitched the curtain aside and frowned when she saw who was coming up the front steps.

She opened the door.

"What are you doing here?" she asked.

CHAPTER 37

The small parking lot behind the Lost Island Bed-and-Breakfast was empty except for Rose's big four-by-four.

"No surprise," Virginia said. "It's still February."

She did not know why she felt compelled to explain the obvious to Cabot. The Lost Island B and B had always seemed sad and forlorn, even before Abigail Watkins had died. It had not improved since Rose Gilbert had taken over.

But today, for some inexplicable reason — maybe it was just her nerves — the old Victorian appeared more unwelcoming than ever. The drapes were pulled across the windows and there was a No Vacancy sign behind the glass in the front door.

Cabot continued on around the old house and brought his vehicle to a halt in the front drive. He sat quietly for a moment, contemplating the gloom-filled structure. Then he reached into the back seat for his windbreaker and gun. He adjusted the windbreaker so that it covered the holstered pistol on his hip, but he did not fasten the front. A chill went through Virginia when it dawned on her that he wanted to be able to get to his gun in a hurry if necessary.

Well, there isn't much point wearing a gun if you can't get to it quickly, she told herself.

"Ready?" he asked.

"Yes," she said.

She unclipped her own seat belt and reached into the back for her parka and her cross-body bag. She got her door open, jumped down and walked around the front of the vehicle to join Cabot.

Together they went up the front steps. Cabot pressed the buzzer.

There was no response. Cabot waited a few seconds and then rapped sharply on the front door. Again there was no answer.

"Rose must be inside," Virginia said. "Maybe she's in her room upstairs and can't hear the buzzer."

"Or maybe she's trying to discourage business." Cabot tried the knob. It turned easily in his hand. He opened the door and walked into the small lobby.

Virginia followed him. "That's weird. Feels like the heat is off." She glanced into the parlor. "No fire going, either."

Cabot went to the foot of the stairs. "Rose Gilbert? This is Cabot Sutter. I'm here with Virginia Troy. We need your help."

There was no response. Virginia did not hear any footsteps overhead.

Cabot glanced back over his shoulder. "Wait here."

She wanted to ask why but when he reached inside his jacket and took out his gun, she decided she probably would not like the answer. *He used to be a cop,* she reminded herself. *Old habits.*

He went quickly through the downstairs rooms, checking the office, the kitchen and the parlor.

A short time later he returned. "The place feels empty but I'm going to check upstairs. Stay here until I get back."

"All right," Virginia said. "But it's starting to feel like something is very wrong. Be careful, okay?"

Cabot took the stairs two at a time, his gun in his hand. When he disappeared on the landing above, she heard the muffled sound of his footsteps. After a moment he knocked on a door. She assumed he was standing at the entrance to Rose's private quarters.

Cabot called from the top of the stairs.

"No answer at her door. I'm going in."

"Not alone." Virginia went swiftly up the stairs. "Something has happened. Let me try talking to her before you do anything else. You'll scare the living daylights out of her if you open that door with a gun in your hand."

Cabot did not argue.

She joined him at the top of the stairs. Cabot motioned her to move to one side of the door before he flattened his back to the wall and reached out to grab the knob. Then he signaled her to speak.

"Rose, it's me, Virginia. I've got Cabot Sutter with me. We just want to be sure you're okay."

No answer.

Cabot turned the knob. The door was unlocked. It swung open with a few squeaks of the hinges. A cold draft of air carrying an all-too-familiar odor floated out into the hallway. Virginia got a little sick to her stomach.

"No," she whispered. "Not again."

But she was speaking to an empty hallway. Cabot was inside the room. She forced herself to follow him.

Rose's body was crumpled on the floor just outside the entrance to her private bath. Her robe and nightgown were stained with a lot of blood. There was more blood on the floor under her head.

Cabot crouched beside the still form and touched the throat. "Two shots. One in the chest. One in the head."

Virginia's stomach clenched. She hoped she wasn't going to throw up.

"Just like Sandra Porter," she whispered.

"Gilbert's been dead for a few hours. Looks like she was killed this morning. Hard to be certain because the room is so cold. I'm going to take a quick look around before we report this."

"I'm not even sure who we should report it to," Virginia said. "There's no police station on the island. There's a volunteer fire department. The man who runs the general store is in charge of handling emergencies. I suppose we should contact him."

Cabot stood, crossed to the dressing table and took some tissues out of a box. He went into the bathroom and started opening drawers.

Virginia pulled herself together, opened her handbag and removed some tissues. "I'll take a look through her bureau and closet. Any idea what we're searching for?"

"No," Cabot said. "But anything that connects Rose Gilbert to Quinton Zane or someone at Night Watch would certainly be useful."

"What do we do if we find something? There are rules about disturbing crime scenes."

"We're not going to steal anything. We're going to use our cameras to take pictures of whatever we find."

"Right."

Virginia went quickly through the bureau. The top two drawers contained an assortment of nightgowns, sweaters, socks and underwear. All of the garments looked as if they were about the right size for Rose's chunky frame.

There was more clothing in the lower drawers but the items were not folded. Instead, they looked as if they had been scooped up in a hurry and dumped into the drawers. They also looked much older and faded from years of washing.

Curious, she unfolded one of the nightgowns and held it up to take a closer look.

"It's the wrong size," she said, baffled.

Cabot came to the door of the bathroom. "What?"

"The clothes in the top drawers look like they would have fit Rose, but the things in the bottom drawers are much too small for her. They probably belonged to Abigail

285

Watkins. It looks like Rose never bothered to get rid of them after she moved in here."

"So?" Cabot went back into the bathroom and opened the cabinet.

"So, a woman might keep a dead woman's sweaters, but only if they fit. She certainly would not wear a dead woman's underwear or her nightgowns."

Cabot came back to the doorway, intrigued.

"Maybe it was just too much trouble to get rid of Watkins's things," he suggested.

"Maybe. But it feels creepy to keep a dead woman's underwear. At the very least I would have thought that Rose would have packed up the stuff and stored it in the basement."

"I think what this tells us is that, initially, at least, Rose wasn't planning to hang around for long," Cabot said. "But something made her change her mind."

Virginia finished the search of the bureau and went to the nightstand. There were some old needlework magazines inside. She picked them up, not expecting to find anything useful.

Underneath the magazines was a large, unsealed envelope. There was no address. She raised the flap and looked inside. There were several sheets of paper and another, smaller envelope.

"Cabot?"

"Find something?"

"I don't know." Virginia tipped the envelope over the bed and looked at the pages that cascaded out onto the quilt. "Photocopies," Virginia said.

Cabot moved toward her. "Of what?"

"I'm not sure. Letters, maybe. Looks like Abigail Watkins's handwriting. She had amazing handwriting. Very neat, very precise — just like her needlework."

"Use your camera," Cabot said. "Get pictures of every page."

"Okay." Virginia was about to reach into her handbag for her camera when she remembered the smaller envelope. Unlike the larger envelope, it was yellowed with age. It, too, was unaddressed and unsealed. She opened it. A photograph slipped out and fell onto the bed.

It was a casual, candid shot showing two people, a man and a woman, standing arm in arm at the railing of a ferry. The skyline of the city of Seattle was behind them. The woman looked rapturously happy, practically glowing. The good-looking man who had his arm around her was smiling a warm, charming smile, but there was something reptilian about his eyes.

Virginia stopped breathing.

"Cabot," she said. "Look at this."

He came to stand at her shoulder.

"Shit," he said. "Quinton Zane."

"All these years I've tried to remember exactly what he looked like. I could never quite describe him because I saw him with a kid's eyes. But, yes, I'd know him anywhere."

Cabot took a closer look. "Is that Abigail Watkins?"

"I'm almost positive that it is. She looks about sixteen or maybe seventeen in this picture. That would make her a couple of years younger than when we knew her, but I remember that glorious red-gold hair. She was a spectacularly beautiful woman. Reminds me of Botticelli's Venus. So innocent looking."

"An easy target for a bastard like Zane." Cabot turned over the photograph. "This is dated a couple of years before Zane went into the cult business. I wonder what —"

A thin, muffled explosion shuddered through the old floorboards.

Jolted, Virginia looked at Cabot.

"Did you feel that?" she asked sharply. "Earthquake?"

They were common enough in the Pacific Northwest, she reminded herself. But the

288

tremor hadn't felt like any earthquake she had ever experienced.

"No," Cabot said. "Stay here."

He was already moving, gun in hand, toward the door. He did a quick survey of the hallway.

"Clear," he said over his shoulder. "But something is wrong. We need to get out of here now."

Virginia hesitated. There was no time to take pictures of the letters or the old photo. She scooped up the whole lot and shoved everything into her handbag. She promised herself that she would apologize to the authorities later.

She rushed out into the hall. The second muffled blast sent another shudder through the old house.

"Gunshots?" Virginia whispered.

"No," Cabot said. "Explosions. We walked into a trap."

They made it to the top of the stairs just as the third blast rattled the windows. Cabot stopped on the landing and looked down.

"We've got a problem," he said very softly.

Virginia saw the wisps of smoke unfurling up the staircase.

A fourth blast echoed through the walls. The old house groaned as though in mortal agony.

The fire exploded first on the ground floor. The roar of the flames was horrifyingly familiar. Virginia had heard it often enough in the hellish dreamscapes of her nightmares.

CHAPTER 38

Cabot holstered his gun, wrapped a hand around Virginia's upper arm and steered her toward the nearest bedroom.

"We can use sheets to get down to the ground," he said. "And just hope like hell that there is only one person out there. He can't watch all four sides of the house at once. Odds are he'll focus on the front door or the back door. Human nature."

Cabot opened the door of the nearest bedroom. Virginia saw the flames leaping up the windows.

Panic threatened to choke her.

"Not that way," she gasped.

Cabot hurried to the end of the hall and tried another room. He shut the door almost immediately.

"No good," he reported. "The bastard rigged explosions around the perimeter of the house. The ground floor is engulfed."

Virginia was vaguely aware that her heart

was beating much too fast and she could scarcely catch her breath. Not because of the smoke, she thought. It wasn't that bad on the second floor — not yet. It was smoke that killed you in a fire, and they still had a little time before they faced that death sentence.

No, it was raw fear that was roiling her senses. She and Cabot were trapped, just as they had been all those years ago when they were locked up in the barn that Quinton Zane had torched. But this time there was no Anson Salinas to come to their rescue.

"The fire is burning up through the house," Cabot said. "There's no way out from here or the third floor. Our only option is to go down to the basement."

"Down?" Virginia gasped. "But that's where the fire is."

"It's on the first floor, not the basement. Odds are he wouldn't have tried to set the fire from down there. It's concrete. There should be some sort of exit from there."

"The old coal bunker," Virginia said. "There are steps there now. But how do we get down to the basement? The staircase is functioning like a chimney."

"The laundry chute." Cabot grabbed her wrist and went swiftly back down the hall. He shoved open the door of the linen room.

"It's our only chance."

Virginia followed him inside and slammed the door shut. She whirled around, grabbed some towels off the shelves and shoved them up against the bottom of the door in hopes of temporarily blocking the smoke that was now drifting down the second-floor hallway.

Cabot went straight to the big soaking sink and turned on both faucets full blast. He yanked two large sheets off a shelf, whipped them open and plunged them into the rapidly filling tub.

"Wet sheets are stronger," he explained. "Check the chute. See if it's clear."

Virginia yanked open the door of the large, old-fashioned laundry chute. Relief overcame some of her fear when she realized there was no smoke billowing out of the wide chase.

"I don't see any signs of fire," she said.

Cabot hauled one of the soaked sheets out of the sink. Virginia found a corner while he fished out the second sheet.

"They're king-sized sheets," he said. "Two should do it."

He found one of the corners of the second sheet and tied it to Virginia's sheet with a tight, square knot.

"You're going first," he said. "I'll lower you down."

"What about you?" she said.

He angled his chin toward the small table near the sink. "I'll tie off one end to that table. It's a lot bigger than the chute. It'll catch at the entrance. All right, time to move."

She hurried to the entrance of the laundry chute. The thought of going down into the darkness with no idea of what was waiting at the bottom was terrifying — but not as terrifying as the fire that was eating the house. She could smell the smoke now. It was seeping around the edges of the door-frame.

At the last moment she realized she still had her handbag. It was attached to her by the cross-body strap. She yanked off the bag and tossed it into the chute. There was no sound when it hit the bottom.

"Good sign," Cabot said. "With luck there's a laundry cart filled with dirty towels and sheets down there."

"It would certainly beat landing on a concrete basement floor."

Cabot helped her scramble through the wide entrance of the chute, gripping one of her wrists to secure her while she got oriented. She clung to the edge of the chute with both hands, dangling above the un-known, terrified of falling into the deep darkness at the bottom of the chase.

Cabot wrapped a corner of the sheet around her wrist and held her while she got a secure grip.

He did not give her time to let the fear build any higher.

"Hang on, and whatever you do, don't let go," he said.

He lowered her rapidly down the chase. Instinctively she closed her eyes. The trip did not last long, probably no more than a few seconds, but it seemed like an eternity.

The interior of the chute was surprisingly spacious; the sides had been polished by several decades of laundry. Nevertheless, it felt close and airless. *Like a coffin,* Virginia thought. *No, damn it, like an escape hatch. Got to think positive.*

Her shoulders and hips bumped against the sides of the chute from time to time, but she did not get stuck.

And then, without any warning, her feet touched a mound of bed linens and towels.

She released her grip on the knotted sheets.

"I'm down," she shouted. "No fire here. Not yet."

"On my way."

She groped around, found her handbag and clambered out of the laundry cart. The basement was not completely dark. The weak light of the waning day was dimmed by years of accumulated grime on the narrow ground-level windows, but there was enough to illuminate the concrete space.

She heard a muffled thud from the second floor. At first she thought Cabot had not been able to escape. The panic returned in a sickening wave.

Then she heard more thumps and thuds. She forced herself to breathe again. Cabot was making his way down the chase. With his bigger frame and broader shoulders, he did not fit inside as easily as she had.

Seconds later he landed in the heap of sheets and towels that filled the cart. He climbed out quickly.

"The coal bunker," he said.

The old bunker that had once been used to store coal had been empty for years. Somewhere in the distant past, a previous owner had installed wooden steps designed to allow gardeners and handymen access to the basement without having to tromp through the house.

"I'll go first," Cabot said.

He took out his gun again, went up the steps and cautiously opened one side of the slanting doors.

Virginia smelled smoke but there were no

flames in sight. The coal bunker doors were set a few feet away from the house, concealed by a badly overgrown garden.

She covered her nose and mouth with the edge of her parka. Cabot covered his lower face with his windbreaker.

He went through the door first. She rushed up after him.

"Head for the trees," he said. "I'll be right behind you."

She ran for the safety of the nearby woods, expecting to get slammed to the ground by a bullet in the back. But there was only the furious roar of the fire beast as it devoured the house.

Somewhere in the distance she thought she heard the muffled spatter of gravel spitting out from under tires. She was vaguely aware that a vehicle was speeding away from the scene.

She stopped to catch her breath. Cabot caught up with her. Together they turned around to look at the burning house. The B and B was nearly engulfed now.

Eventually Virginia became aware of a siren in the distance. The island's volunteer fire department was on the way.

CHAPTER 39

They spent the night at the only bed-and-breakfast that was open — the Harbor Inn. It overlooked the bay and the town's small marina.

Fortunately, Cabot's SUV had been parked several yards away from the Lost Island B and B. Some of the paint had been charred, but the car had survived the blaze, and so had the overnight bags stashed in the back. Virginia had never been more grateful for clean underwear and a change of clothes.

The owners of the Harbor Inn were a middle-aged married couple from Seattle. The two men, Barney Ricks and Dylan Crane, wore matching gold rings. There was a wedding photo on the wall behind the front desk that showed the couple dressed in elegant tuxedos, smiling with joy.

The picture of the glowing newlyweds sent a little whisper of wistfulness through

Virginia. All wedding photos had that effect on her. They reminded her that her own chances of establishing a home and having a family were slim at best. She countered the sentiment the way she always did — by recalling the divorce statistics.

Barney and Dylan were solicitous and did not so much as blink when Cabot requested two rooms with a connecting door on the second floor. After a warm, comforting meal of homemade lasagna and a salad of organic greens, they offered sherry in the parlor.

The sherry was accompanied by a lot of questions and some interesting gossip.

"Word on the island is that Rose Gilbert was probably deep into the drug business," Barney said. "The theory is that one of her competitors took her out."

Barney was a slender man who was going bald in a sleek, elegant fashion. His husband was on the solid, well-built side, with a closely trimmed beard and a friendly, out-going manner that was well suited to an innkeeper.

"Pretty spectacular way to get rid of the competition," Cabot said.

"We couldn't help but notice that whoever wired the house to explode waited until Cabot and I were inside," Virginia added.

Barney frowned. "Good point. Any chance

someone other than you two got caught in that fire?"

"There was no one else in the house," Cabot said. "Not unless he was hiding up on the top floor, which was closed off. But I don't think so. When we got out, we did hear someone driving away, though."

Dylan looked intrigued. "Did you see the car?"

"No, unfortunately," Cabot said. "Sounded like something small, though."

"Heading toward town or the other way?" Dylan asked.

"That," Cabot said, "is a very good question. Whoever it was did not drive away down the main road toward town. It sounded like he was going in the opposite direction. It will be interesting to see who gets on the ferry tomorrow afternoon."

"Don't count on seeing the car that belongs to the guy who torched the B and B," Barney said. "This is a pretty big island and most of it is covered in forest. Plenty of places where someone could ditch a car or even push it over a cliff into the water."

"Still, it seems likely that whoever set the fire would want to get off the island as soon as possible," Virginia said.

"Sure. But there is another way off this island," Dylan said.

Cabot looked at him. "By boat?"

Dylan nodded, his expression grim. "Right. A lot of people who live here have their own boats. Some of the regular visitors who come for long weekends do, too. After we heard about the explosion, Barney and I walked around the marina. Didn't see any boats missing. But there are a lot of private docks scattered around the island. They mostly belong to people who only come here during the summer."

Cabot nodded thoughtfully. "So you could steal or rent a boat from a marina on the mainland, bring it in to a private dock here on the island and then steal a local vehicle to drive to the Lost Island B and B to torch the place."

"Sure," Barney said. "Doubt if you would even need to hot-wire the vehicle. People here on the island usually leave their keys in the car."

Virginia looked at him. "Can you tell us anything at all about Rose Gilbert?"

Barney lounged deeper into his chair, stretched out his legs and sipped his sherry. "Dylan and I had a few conversations with Rose Gilbert about the B and B business but she never seemed interested in taking our advice. We got the feeling she didn't plan to stick around for long."

"Did she tell you that Abigail Watkins was her half sister?" Virginia asked.

Barney and Dylan exchanged startled looks.

"No," Barney said. "She never mentioned that. Just said she'd bought the place from Abigail and that the deal was finalized shortly before Abigail died."

"Turns out that's not true," Cabot said. "From what we can tell, Rose just moved in after her half sister's death and took over the business."

"There wasn't that much business to take over," Dylan said, "not at this time of year. After Abigail got very ill, she couldn't handle a lot of guests. Over time most of her regulars began making reservations with us."

"Rose Gilbert did have a few guests from time to time," Virginia pointed out. "I stayed there on a couple of occasions whenever I came to see Hannah."

"Gilbert occasionally took in tourists off the ferry, but aside from you, there was only one person who stayed at her B and B whenever he visited the island," Dylan said. He paused. "Now that I think about it, he drove a small car. Nothing special. Looked like a rental."

"How would you describe him?" Cabot

asked. "Young? Old?"

"Young, early to midtwenties," Dylan said. "Never saw him up close. He didn't spend any time in town. When he arrived he just drove straight off the ferry and went directly to Rose's place."

"You wouldn't happen to know if he was on the island the night that Hannah Brewster died, would you?" Virginia asked.

Dylan seemed surprised by the question. "He was here. In fact, he was the only guest at Rose's that night."

Virginia sensed the sudden stillness that had come over Cabot.

"You're sure of that?" he asked. "Because Rose distinctly told us she had two couples staying at the B and B that night."

"I'm sure there was just the one guest," Dylan said. "I know that because I was part of the search team that looked for Hannah the next morning. I stopped by the Lost Island B and B to ask Rose if she had seen Hannah. She said no. She didn't want to talk. Said she had to get back to making breakfast for her guest."

"One guest," Virginia said. She looked at Cabot. "A man in his early to midtwenties."

Cabot's mouth tightened. She knew he was thinking the same thing that she was thinking. Rose's guest might well have been

303

a killer, but he was far too young to be Quinton Zane.

"One thing we do know about Rose Gilbert," Cabot said quietly. "She lied to us."

Dylan reached for the sherry decanter. "I can give you another small fact — Rose's one and only guest left on the ferry the day after the fire. I saw him drive his car on board."

CHAPTER 40

Virginia didn't expect to sleep much that night, so she was not surprised when she drifted in and out of a restless haze for a couple of hours after going to bed. What astonished her was that she did not have a panic attack. Under the circumstances, that seemed strange because every time she closed her eyes, she thought about how close she and Cabot had come to dying in the inferno. The memories should have sparked a storm of anxiety. She and Cabot had, after all, relived their worst nightmare from childhood.

At about one thirty in the morning it finally hit her. *This time was different. This time we saved ourselves.*

She gave up trying to sleep, pushed aside the covers and swung her feet to the floor. For a while she sat there, trying to sort through her feelings and sensations. She had her meds in her handbag but she didn't need them. She was definitely wired but, astonishingly, she seemed to be dealing with the fallout from the harrowing experience. Perhaps there would be some kind of delayed reaction in the future, but for now she was, oddly enough, relatively okay.

She stood, pulled on her robe and went to sit in a chair at the window. Most of the marina lay in darkness, but there were a few lights strung along the docks. A cluster of private boats and a small sightseeing vessel bobbed gently in the dark water.

A soft knock sounded. Cabot was awake, too. She glanced at the bedside clock. It was one thirty-five. No surprise.

She rose and opened the connecting door. Cabot, dressed in trousers and a T-shirt, loomed in the shadows. His dark hair looked as if he had raked his fingers through it. His eyes were deep pools of midnight. She sensed the edgy energy prowling through him.

"Let me guess," she said. "You couldn't sleep, either."

"Business as usual for me. How are you doing?"

"I'm okay, strangely enough. I keep thinking about what happened today, of course. How so many things could have gone wrong, but didn't."

"What happened today was that we made one hell of a team."

"And we got very, very lucky."

"As Anson would say, we made our own luck."

She thought about that and then smiled a little. "Yes, we did."

Cabot retreated a step. "If you're sure you're okay —"

And just like that she knew she did not want him to go.

"Do you mind if I ask you a question?" she said.

"What?" He sounded a little wary.

"Why did you get fired from your job as chief of police? I know it's none of my business, but I have this theory, you see."

Cabot braced one hand on the doorframe.

"You've got a theory," he repeated, his tone utterly neutral.

She was on dangerous ground now, but she was very sure she would not retreat.

"Yes," she said.

"What is your theory?"

"I'm guessing you were probably a little too good at your job. It was a small town. That means small-town politics. You might bend the rules if you thought that was the only way to see that justice was done, but you wouldn't give an inch if some local mover and shaker tried to lean on you. If you bent a rule, I'm guessing you would have found a way to keep it quiet. So, what did you do? Arrest the mayor's son?"

For a second or two she didn't think he was going to answer. Then he whistled very softly.

"How the hell did you figure it out?" he asked.

"You and I have been through a lot lately. I've learned a few things about you."

Cabot was silent for a few beats.

"It wasn't the mayor's son," he said finally. "The mayor didn't run the town, a man named Ashcroft did. He owned the biggest local business. Employed a lot of people. Half the town owed him in one way or another. His son, Nick, came home from college for a long weekend. He brought some friends with him. They got high, picked up a couple of local girls — high-school kids — and got them blackout drunk. Probably used drugs. They raped the girls. One of Nick's pals made a video with his phone. The father of one of the girls came to me for help. I looked at the video and arrested Nick and his buddies."

"What happened?"

"Ashcroft threatened to have me fired if I didn't get the charges dropped. Said I was going to ruin his son's future. I ignored him. In the end, Ashcroft finally made a deal with the families of the two girls. Paid them off. They dropped the charges."

"And you lost your job."

"I was ready for a change. By then I had already figured out that if you want to pursue a career in law enforcement in a small town, you have to be good at playing politics."

"Which is not your strong suit."

"No," Cabot said.

"All in all, the private investigation business sounds like the right career path for you."

"It feels like a good fit."

Another short silence.

"Would you mind very much if I kissed you?" she said.

"It's okay so long as it's not one of those pity kisses."

"Nope. I just want to kiss you. But I should warn you that it probably won't go anywhere, given my intimacy issues. I don't want you to think of me as a world-class tease."

"You're world-class but you are definitely not a tease," Cabot said. "You've got a few issues. So do I."

"Different kind of issues, though."

"Issues are issues. We're wasting time here. Are you going to kiss me or not?"

She took a step forward, gripped his shoulders and crushed her mouth against his.

Except he didn't crush. Instead, he caught her face between his hands and raised his head so that his mouth was an inch away from hers.

"Remember what I said," he whispered, his voice a little ragged. "It's not a trip to the dentist."

"I know." She clutched at his shoulders. "I just don't want to screw up again."

"Then quit trying so hard. Relax. Go with what you feel. When you stop feeling it, we'll stop whatever it is we're doing at that moment."

"You make it sound so simple."

"It is simple. Don't worry, you'll get the hang of it."

She giggled. It was ridiculous. Totally inappropriate. But for some reason, the urge to laugh was irresistible.

Cabot did not laugh, but in the glow of the night-light, she could see him smiling a very sexy, very masculine smile.

The part of her that had been locked in ice for so long started to heat. She leaned into Cabot's strength and kissed him again, not trying to force the pace; taking her time, testing the waters.

She sensed his response — his mouth was hot, his body was hard and his erection was rigid — but he made no attempt to overwhelm her. He did not tighten his grip on her nor did he try to rush her.

Encouraged by her own reaction as well as his, she pressed herself against him, caught hold of his wrist and moved his hand to her waist.

A deep longing rose within her. She wanted to touch and be touched. She wanted to be free to enjoy the sensual side of herself.

The kiss got more intense. Thrilling. It charged all of her senses.

After a moment or two she guided one of Cabot's hands inside her robe, just under her right breast. He settled his fingers there but he did not try to touch her in more intimate ways.

She slipped her hands up under his T-shirt, thrilling to the feel of him. To hell with feeling guilty for sending out mixed signals. Cabot could handle it if she lost her nerve again. He could handle it if she experienced a panic attack. He would not hold it against her. He would not judge her. He would not think she was weird.

An unfamiliar excitement ignited her blood. She began to explore Cabot with a growing sense of urgency.

"Virginia," he whispered.

Carefully, cautiously, he drew the pad of his thumb across the tip of her breast. It was as if he had flipped a switch. Desire crashed through her.

"Yes," she said. She kissed Cabot's throat, the curve of his shoulder; closed her teeth around his ear. "Yes."

"There's no rush," he whispered.

"Yes. There is."

"We've got all night."

"You might have all night. I don't. I need to do this now, before something goes wrong."

"That's it. Think positive."

"You're laughing at me."

"Maybe," he admitted. "Just a little. Mostly I'm trying to tell you that you don't have to be afraid. We can go this far and stop as often as you want."

"I don't want to stop, damn it. That's what I'm trying to tell you."

"Whatever you say."

She seized his hand and started to haul him into her room, aiming for the bed.

"No," he said.

He didn't try to free his hand but he did

not follow her. Instead he simply stood there in the doorway between the two rooms, as immovable as a large rock.

The first flicker of fear sparked through her. She'd screwed up somehow.

"What?" she said.

He tugged her gently back toward him. "We don't need a bed."

Her heart sank. This was worse than she'd thought. He might not blame her for leading him on, but he had evidently lost interest in the entire project.

He led her across the room and stopped at the padded reading chair. He unzipped his trousers and lowered himself into the chair.

"Let's try it this way, instead," he said. "You did say you liked to be on top."

He drew her down slowly, giving her time to figure out a comfortable position. And then she was kneeling astride his thighs, her nightgown riding up above her hips.

Desire rushed back with the force of an incoming wave. She wrapped her fingers around his shoulders to steady herself.

He moved one hand along the inside of her leg and then he was touching her, stroking her in ways that made her want more. She closed her eyes against the fierceness of her need. Everything inside her went tight.

She sucked in her breath and dug her nails into his shoulders.

He did something with his fingers, something that shocked her senses in the most delightful way, and in the next instant the intense, tightly wound sensation inside her was released in a series of deep waves.

"Cabot. *Cabot.*"

He eased her down onto his rigid erection before she had finished climaxing. She was so sensitive now she could scarcely catch her breath. Another little ripple of release sparkled through her, an echo of the first cathartic sensation.

She heard Cabot's hoarse, muffled groan. His heavy climax shuddered through both of them.

The night became very still and quiet.

CHAPTER 41

Virginia stirred and eased herself to her feet. She was a little unsteady, but she could not recall the last time she had felt so good. Cabot lounged in the chair, utterly relaxed. There was just enough light seeping through the doorway of her room to let her see that he was watching her with half-closed eyes.

"Are you okay?" he asked.

She thought about it and then smiled, feeling pleased and more than a little smug. "Yep. I do believe I am okay. And you are positively brilliant."

"I am? Well, I feel very good at the moment, but not sure what you mean by brilliant."

"How did you know?" she demanded.

"How did I know what?"

"That a chair would be a solution to my issues?"

"Ah. The chair thing. Lucky guess?"

She waved that aside with a magnanimous

sweep of her hand and began to pace the room.

"Somewhere along the line I must have begun to associate beds with panic attacks," she said. "Some people can't get on an airplane without having a panic attack. Maybe that's how it is for me with beds."

"Are you suggesting we should have sex on an airplane? Join the Mile-High Club? I'm willing to give that some serious consideration."

She shushed him with another wave of her hand. "I've experienced some of my worst attacks while I was in bed. And then there are my commitment issues. A therapist would probably say that somewhere along the line sex and bed got fused into a trigger that set off my anxiety. I figured out a while back that I needed to be on top, but obviously that didn't always work."

"Are you sure you're not overthinking this?"

She went back across the room, leaned down and kissed him on his forehead.

"You're better than any therapist I've ever had," she announced, straightening.

"Good to know. A possible career path for me if this PI gig doesn't work out."

He reached for her but she slipped away.

"I need to wash up," she said.

She hurried into her own room, went into the bathroom and turned on the light. When she caught sight of herself in the mirror she was a little startled by her flushed cheeks, tangled hair and overbright eyes.

"Good news, Cinderella," she said softly. "It's after midnight, you just had great sex and there are no signs of a panic attack. You are almost normal, at least for tonight."

She didn't remember the sheaf of photocopied papers and the photo that she had found in Rose's nightstand until she emerged from the bathroom. She crossed the room to the table where she had left her handbag. Unzipping the bag, she reached inside and took out the envelope and the papers.

She switched on the reading light, put on her glasses and shuffled through the photocopies.

A name leaped off the page. *Kim.*

Her euphoric mood evaporated in a heartbeat. Dread shivered through her.

"Cabot?" she called quietly.

He materialized in the doorway, zipping up his trousers. "Right here. Are those the papers and the photo you found in Gilbert's nightstand?"

"Yes," she whispered, stunned by what she was reading. "What with everything that's happened since the explosion, I forgot about them until now."

Cabot changed gears in an instant, transitioning from satisfied lover to intense hunter mode. He crossed the room to the table and looked down at the papers and the photo.

"I assumed they'd been destroyed by the fire," he said.

"I shoved them into my bag on the way out the door. It was instinctive. I wasn't really thinking."

"You've got great instincts."

"We'll have to give these to the investigators when they arrive in the morning, won't we?"

"If they want them. For all we know they may not consider them important. The dates on these letters go back a couple of decades."

"Twenty-two years, to be exact," Virginia said very evenly. "And they aren't letters, they're pages from a diary. The name Kim appears on some of them. I think it may be short for Kimberly."

"Your mother?"

"Yes." Virginia flipped through a couple more pages. "Hannah's name appears as well. There's also a Jacky."

"My mother's name was Jacqueline Kennington Sutter."

Without a word, Virginia handed him one of the pages. He read a few sentences and then he put the paper down on the table.

"This isn't just a collection of memories of life in Zane's cult," he said. "This is hard evidence. Your mother and mine, together with Hannah Brewster and Abigail Watkins, came up with a plan to steal from the devil himself."

CHAPTER 42

Cabot drew up a chair and sat down at the table, his phone at the ready. Virginia sat beside him. Together they went through the papers.

"There are only half a dozen pages here," Virginia said. "And they're just photocopies. I wonder what happened to the original diary?"

"No way to know. But obviously Rose Gilbert must have considered these pages important. She didn't throw them into the bottom drawer of the bureau along with the rest of Abigail's things, and she didn't throw them away."

Every page contained a fresh shock. Virginia had to keep wiping the tears from her eyes.

. . . We know the plan is terribly dangerous but what choice do we have? Kim and Jacky are right. As long as Zane holds the children hostage and as long as his thugs control the compound, there is no escape. We need leverage that we can use to force the monster to give up the kids and let us go. All he cares about is the money . . .

. . . We know that he is capable of murder. Jacky and Kim are certain now that he murdered their husbands . . .

Virginia turned over the last photocopied page.

. . . Kim says the money has been deposited in the secret bank account that Jacky set up using her trust fund. Regardless of what happens to us, the money will be safe, held in trust for the children. Only the four of us know the location of the key. Tomorrow we will confront Zane.

Virginia looked at Cabot. For a moment neither of them spoke.

"They had a plan," Virginia said eventually. "They were going to try to force Zane to free the children. They were so daring, so brave. So desperate. They must have been terrified of Zane."

"Somehow he must have discovered that some of the cult members were plotting against him. He decided to destroy the

321

whole operation and kill as many people as possible on his way out the door. At that point he probably didn't know that the money had disappeared into a secret account. He made the mistake of murdering most of those who could have told him where it was hidden."

"Except for Hannah and Abigail."

"It was sheer luck that they survived that night. They weren't locked up with the mothers of the children. Zane kept them in a different section of the compound. He evidently saved it for last. Someone driving past out on the old highway reported the fire. Anson and the local fire crew responded immediately. Zane must have heard the sirens. He had vanished by the time the first responders arrived on the scene."

"Yes. But after Zane realized that the money was gone, why didn't he go after Hannah and Abigail?"

"Best guess is that he probably didn't think they knew about the plot or, if they did, he assumed they hadn't been entrusted with the information needed to access the money. Neither of them had any experience in the financial world. Abigail and Hannah were just the cult's housekeepers and cooks."

Virginia did not say anything; she couldn't

speak. Without a word, Cabot got to his feet and pulled her up into his arms. She did not feel trapped. Maybe that was because she was holding him as tightly as he held her.

After a while, she raised her head. "I wonder what happened to the original diary. And why did Rose have only photocopies of those pages?"

"No way to know where the diary ended up, but I have a hunch Rose only bothered to photocopy the pages that described the plot to hide the money and use it as a ransom payment to free the kids."

"Because all she cared about was the money. What are we going to do with the diary pages and the photograph?"

"I was planning to give them to the authorities, but I've changed my mind," Cabot said.

"Why?"

"There's no information in those pages that will give the investigators a lead on the guy who set off that fire today. But the main reason I don't want to mention them to the authorities is because I don't want whoever is chasing the key to know that we found part of Abigail Watkins's diary. You'd be in even more danger than you are already."

She got a little misty-eyed again. "You're

bending the rules. For me."

He shook his head. "There are only two rules on this job: keep you safe and find out if Quinton Zane is still alive."

She smiled. "In other words, you make your own rules."

"Are you okay with that?"

"You're an artist. A very good artist knows when to follow the rules and when to break them. It's how creativity works."

"I am not an artist but I'll take that as a yes," Cabot said. He glanced at her phone, which was lying on the table next to her handbag. "One more thing."

"What?"

"From now on we don't discuss this on our cell phones. No texts. No e-mail."

The heat was on in the room but Virginia suddenly felt very cold. She looked at her phone.

"Oh, crap," she said. "Do you really think that someone is tracking us?"

"Given what happened yesterday, we have to assume a worst-case scenario."

"Do we ditch the phones?"

"No. If someone is following us around, that would be an immediate red flag. We're just going to be very, very careful about using our phones. I doubt if someone has been able to hack my phone. Max asked some of his connections in the cybersecurity business to assist us with the encryption. But it's possible that yours has been compromised."

She looked at her phone and shuddered. "Lately, from time to time, I've had the creepy sense that I'm being watched. I just chalked it up to the fact that my anxiety attacks have been getting worse."

"Sounds like your intuition was trying to tell you something."

"Do private investigators believe in women's intuition?"

"This PI believes in intuition, period."

CHAPTER 43

Kate left the door of her office open and kept an eye on the hallway for nearly an hour. Eventually Laurel went past. Unlike some of the other employees, she did not pause in the doorway to make friendly conversation. No surprise, Kate thought.

She and Laurel had had a prickly relationship for months. Except for the occasions when they were obliged to work together, Laurel mostly ignored her. But lately Laurel's disinterest had undergone a subtle change. Kate was pretty sure it was animosity that she saw in the other woman's eyes these days.

She knows that I know, Kate thought, *or that I'm suspicious.* Maybe it was time to get the issue out into the open.

She waited a few seconds and then got up and went out into the hall. She was in time to see Laurel disappear into the women's restroom.

Kate followed her into the stainless-steel-and-tile room. Only one stall was occupied. She and Laurel were alone.

Kate fussed with her hair and watched the closed stall door in the long mirror above the row of sinks. Laurel finally emerged. When she saw Kate, an expression of wariness flashed across her face but she recovered quickly. She went to the nearest sink and turned on the faucet.

"Hi," she said. Her tone was barely civil.

"Hi," Kate said. She tried to inject some warmth into her own voice. "Did you hear the latest on Sandra Porter? They're saying she may have been involved in a drug deal that went bad."

"I heard," Laurel said.

She rinsed her hands very quickly and reached for a paper towel.

"I never suspected that Sandra had a serious drug problem," Kate said. "Did you?"

"I barely knew her. She was in IT." Laurel dropped the crumpled towel into the wastebasket and went toward the door. "I only talked to her when I had a computer glitch."

"Same here," Kate said.

Laurel paused at the door. "If I were you, I'd keep my mouth shut. Spreading gossip and rumors is a dangerous business, especially for someone in your position."

Kate sighed. "This isn't about poor Sandra, is it? You're the one who's afraid of gossip. You know that I have a pretty good idea that you're sleeping with the boss. Talk about a dangerous business."

Laurel flushed a furious shade of red. "I swear, if you start a rumor like that, I'll make sure you pay."

"Are you saying it's not true?"

"I'm telling you that my personal life is none of your damned business."

"Sure. But you might want to remember the first rule of workplace affairs: when they're over — and sooner or later they always end — it's always the lower-ranking employee who gets fired. In this case, that would be you."

Laurel looked as if she was about to explode in fury. But in the next instant stunned comprehension lit her eyes. She smiled an ice-cold smile.

"You're jealous," she said. "That's what this is all about. You want Josh Preston. You think that if I'm out of the way, he'll notice you again."

"That's not true."

"Bullshit. I get it now. Trust me, you were nothing but a weekend fling. And speaking of workplace rules, here's one you might want to keep in mind — you can be replaced. Anyone can write content."

She spun around, yanked open the door and went out into the hall. The staccato tap of her footsteps faded quickly.

Kate stared at her reflection in the mirror. There was no escaping the reality of the situation.

Confronting Laurel had been a very big mistake.

CHAPTER 44

"No way the local cops could go with the theory that you just happened to be in the wrong place at the wrong time," Anson growled.

"Keep in mind that there aren't any local cops on Lost Island," Cabot said. "The investigator who showed up to look into the fire and the death of Rose Gilbert was from one of the neighboring islands. He said it looked like a gang hit. He reminded me that the area has been notorious for drug running since the days of Prohibition."

Anson grunted.

"It used to be liquor that was shipped from Canada to the West Coast of the U.S.," Cabot continued. "These days it's meth, cocaine, heroin and, lately, exotics from the other side of the world. There's also some human trafficking going on as well. The smuggling business flows both ways, and the islands offer ideal places to dump a hot cargo or pick up a shipment."

"Cabot and I talked to the couple who operate the B and B where we stayed last night," Virginia said. "They had no problem believing that Rose might have been in the drug business and that she might have made some dangerous enemies."

It was late afternoon. They were gathered in the offices of Cutler, Sutter & Salinas. She was sitting in one of the client chairs. Anson was behind his desk. Cabot was standing at the window.

Xavier was hovering in the doorway of one of the darkened offices, trying to be inconspicuous. But Virginia could tell that he was following the conversation very intently, clearly fascinated.

Neither she nor Cabot had gotten much sleep, and they had spent a long morning talking to the investigator who had showed up to take charge of the crime scene. She had napped a little during the ferry crossings but she was starting to become aware of the heavy weight of stress and exhaustion. It occurred to her that she and Cabot were seriously sleep-deprived.

Not that all of the factors that had contributed to her current state of exhaustion were negative, she reminded herself. Every time she thought about the passionate lovemaking in the chair, she got a little thrill. *Yes. You can do normal, woman.*

Cabot had called ahead to tell Anson that they were on the way home, but he had saved the harrowing details and the news about the discovery of the diary pages until they were all in the same room. It was clear he had meant what he said when he told her that they would no longer trust the security of their phones.

"Did you remind the investigator that this was the second major fire on the island in the past few weeks?" Anson demanded.

"Sure," Cabot said. "He said to let him know if any new evidence came to light, but until then, he's sticking with the rival-smugglers theory."

"Cops like the easy answer because it's usually the right one," Anson said.

"Occam's razor," Cabot said grimly.

Xavier stared at him. "What's that?"

"Never mind," Cabot said. "I'll explain later."

"Point is, in this case, the simple answer is bullshit," Anson growled. He winced and glanced apologetically at Virginia. "Apologies for the language."

His old-fashioned manners made her smile a little.

"I may have mumbled something just as

bad or worse when Cabot was in the process of lowering me down that laundry chute," she said.

Anson blew out a small sigh. "You two had one hell of a close call. Good thing you remembered the laundry chute."

Xavier stirred a little, clearing his throat. "What's a laundry chute?"

They all looked at him.

"Just what it sounds like," Virginia said gently. "A long chute that runs from the basement straight up through a house. You chuck dirty laundry into it on the upper floors. It falls into a cart at the bottom. In the old days, most multistory houses had one. The bigger the house, the bigger the laundry chute. The Lost Island B and B had a large one."

Xavier regarded Cabot with something close to awe.

"Excellent," Xavier said.

Cabot did not seem to notice the little flash of hero worship. He was focused on the view outside the window.

"The trip was not a complete loss," he said. "Virginia discovered some photocopied pages of a journal that Abigail Watkins kept. They date from the days of the California compound and they confirm that we're on the right track. Among other things, there are references to a secret bank account that Virginia's mother and mine used to hide at least some of the money that Zane's operation raked in. Evidently four women in the compound knew where the key was hidden: Kimberly Troy, my mother, Hannah Brewster and Abigail Watkins."

Anson whistled softly. "And now all four are dead."

"Which leaves Virginia," Cabot said. "I am convinced now that someone thinks she can lead him to the key."

"Well, well, well," Anson said. He sounded very satisfied. He turned to Xavier. "Tell 'em what you found."

Cabot turned around at that and pinned Xavier with a piercing look.

"You came up with something?" he said.

Xavier reddened under the close scrutiny and he stammered a little at first.

"You were r-right," he said. His voice firmed quickly. "The little children's book turned out to be a simple code, but it's got nothing to do with computers, at least, I don't think so. Mr. Salinas and I did the math problems and put the answers together. Mr. Salinas said the result could be a numbered account in a bank — maybe one of those places the mob guys and drug runners use to hide their money."

Virginia looked at Anson. "An offshore account?"

"I believe so," Anson said. "Once we decided we might be looking at a bank account, we went back through the picture book and started looking for some clues that would give us the location of the bank. We came up with a possibility. There's an island in the Caribbean with the same name as that of the magical kingdom in the math book. For several decades it's been doing a very brisk business with folks who like to conceal their money offshore, no questions asked."

Cabot's eyes heated a little. "That fits. Did you try to access the account?"

"No," Anson said. "Figured we'd hold off until we could talk to you and Virginia. Technically the account probably belongs to her now. She is her mother's heir."

Xavier looked at Cabot. "Also, I was afraid that if I started poking around online and screwed up, I might alert the bank's security department. Mr. Salinas said that would not be a good idea, not at this point in the investigation."

Cabot smiled a wolfish smile. "That was very good thinking. Nice work, Xavier."

Xavier grinned. "Thanks. In that case, I

guess it's okay to tell you my other good news."

"You made reservations to go home?" Cabot said.

"No," Xavier said. "I asked my mom if I could stay here in Seattle for a couple more days. Told her I had a job. She said it was okay with her if it's okay with you."

Cabot shot a wary glance at Anson and then turned back to Xavier.

"What's the job?" he asked.

"I'm an intern here at your agency," Xavier said. He was practically bubbling over with excitement.

"We don't have a position for an intern," Cabot said.

"We do now," Anson announced. "Turns out the kid's good with computers and we just happen to need an in-house IT department."

Cabot gave Xavier a considering look. "How good are you?"

"Pretty good," Xavier said. His eyes lit with hope. "Why?"

"Do you think you could tell if someone had planted some kind of tracking device on Virginia's phone?"

Xavier switched his attention to Virginia. "Maybe."

She took her phone out of her handbag

and gave it to him.

"Go for it," she said.

"I'll need some password info," Xavier warned.

"Not a problem." She smiled. "I trust you."

Xavier was almost glowing now. "Thanks. I'll get right on it."

Virginia took out the photo of Abigail Watkins and Quinton Zane standing with their arms around each other on the ferry. She put it down on Anson's desk.

"We also found this in Rose Gilbert's room," she said. "I'm sure that the girl is Abigail Watkins and the man —"

"Quinton Zane," Anson said, his voice very grim. "I'd recognize him anywhere. That poor kid. Looks like she was in love with him."

"Yes," Virginia said. "She was very young and very naïve. Zane would have found it easy to seduce her and manipulate her."

Chapter 45

"I shouldn't have come here this evening,"
Josh said. "I need to be alone. I've got some
work-related problems I need to think
about. I can't concentrate on them when
I'm with you." He managed a ghost of a
sexy smile. "You're a major distraction."

Laurel watched him from the kitchen
doorway. Josh was sitting on the couch,
leaning forward, forearms braced on his
widespread thighs. He looked weary, beat.

He wasn't drunk but she could tell he'd
had a drink somewhere between the office
and her place. That was not like him. Their
affair had started a couple of months ago.
She knew him well enough by now to know
that work was Josh's drug of choice. He was
driven by one passion: the desire to make
Night Watch a dazzling success.

He was desperate to repeat the brilliant
performance he'd given back at the start of
his career when he'd been one of the young

guns of the tech world, a real wunderkind. But that kind of a comeback almost never happened in their industry, a world in which even the smartest guys in the room had a use-by date stamp. Josh was in his midthirties. That made him an old man in the eyes of his much younger competitors.

"You're here now," Laurel said gently. "Let me get you a beer. We can talk. You always say I make a good sounding board."

"No, I don't want anything else to drink. Like I said, I need to think."

"About what?"

For a moment she thought he wasn't going to answer. Then he surged to his feet and started pacing the room.

"How well did you know Sandra Porter?" he asked.

"Not well at all. Why?"

"Do you think she was doing drugs?"

"I have absolutely no idea. Josh, why are you suddenly so concerned about Sandra Porter? Did the police come up with some new evidence?"

"No." Josh stopped in front of the floor-to-ceiling windows and looked out at the view of the Seattle cityscape on the far side of Lake Washington. "But I talked to a private investigator named Cabot Sutter a couple of days ago. His client was there, too. Virginia Troy."

"Troy? The owner of the gallery where Sandra was killed?"

"Yes. Sutter told me that he was investigating the death of an artist named Hannah Brewster. She lived on one of the islands up in the San Juans. Sutter's client thinks Brewster was murdered."

"What does that have to do with Sandra Porter?"

Josh turned around. "Sutter thinks there's a link between Porter's death and the death of that artist."

Laurel absorbed that news. "I see. Where are you going with this, Josh?"

"Where am I going? I'll tell you where I'm going. I'm afraid Sutter will find a connection between the two deaths, and if he does, it could bring down my company."

"I doubt that there's a connection. Sandra never had any interest in art. But even if for some crazy reason the two deaths are linked, it will probably prove to be something involving drugs. It won't have anything to do with Night Watch. Sandra wasn't even working for you at the time of her death."

"No, but it doesn't mean that she wasn't still ripping me off."

Laurel watched him for a while. "You think this might be about the embezzlement that's going on at Night Watch, don't you?"

"More money went missing within the past twenty-four hours."

"Oh, shit."

"Yeah."

"I suppose that means that Sandra Porter wasn't the embezzler, then."

"Or it might mean that she had a partner who decided to cut her out of the deal."

"How could that have anything to do with that dead artist?"

"I don't know." Josh turned around. "But if I don't find whoever is bleeding me dry and shut down the embezzlement, I can forget going out for expansion capital. The rumors in the financial industry are getting stronger."

"How is your investigation going?"

"Nowhere."

"Josh, I'm so sorry. Maybe it's time to bring in one of the big cybersecurity firms."

"That would be the kiss of death. I'd become a laughingstock in the tech community." Josh abruptly started toward the door. "I can't stay here, not tonight. I need to clear my head and come up with a plan to find the embezzler."

"Josh, wait —"

"I'll see you at the office tomorrow." He ran his fingers through his hair, pulled on his jacket and opened the door. "Goodbye."

He went outside, shutting the door behind him.

Laurel started to follow him but common sense made her change her mind. Josh did not like clinging women.

But she wanted Josh Preston. She wanted him very, very much. And back at the start he had wanted her badly enough to break his own rules about dating his employees. Someone or something had changed his mind.

The way Josh had looked at her just now gave her chills. She could almost read his mind. He was starting to wonder if she was the embezzler.

She thought about the scene with Kate Delbridge in the women's restroom that day.

Delbridge was just a writer. Writers were a dime a dozen. The ability to produce chatty blogs and catchy posts was hardly rare. Anyone who could string two sentences together could create content. But writers did have one special skill — a good writer who also happened to be jealous might be able to spin a story that an anxious CEO who was being robbed by a clever embezzler would be all too willing to believe.

Maybe Delbridge had planted the seeds

of doubt in Josh's mind.

Laurel went back into the kitchen and poured herself a large glass of wine. She carried it into the living room and stood where Josh had stood earlier, looking out at the lights of Seattle on the far side of the lake.

She had worked too hard to get where she was. The brass ring was within reach. She would not allow a jealous woman to destroy her plans.

She took her time with the wine and contemplated the best way to get rid of Kate Delbridge.

CHAPTER 46

"I couldn't help but notice that you didn't put up much of a fight when Xavier announced that he was going to be your intern for a few days," Virginia said.

She and Cabot were seated on the sofa in her living room, going through the photocopies of Abigail Watkins's journal again in an attempt to glean some additional information. The pages were spread out across the coffee table.

Cabot did not look up from the time line of events that he was creating on his laptop.

"The way I see it, the kid earned the job by helping Anson figure out the code in your mom's book."

Virginia smiled. "You know what I think? I think you're feeling sorry for Xavier. He's drifting at the moment. He came looking for you because he needs an anchor."

"If there's an anchor involved, it's Anson, not me. He's the one keeping an eye on

Xavier."

"Still, you could have put Xavier on the next plane home. You didn't do that."

"Haven't had time. Been a little busy lately."

Virginia smiled and said nothing.

Cabot finally looked up, his eyes tightened a little at the corners. "Xavier can't stay here in Seattle indefinitely."

"But for now?"

"For now it's okay as long as Anson is willing to watch him," Cabot said.

His phone pinged before Virginia could say anything more on the subject. He glanced at the screen. A great stillness came over him for a split second. And then he was on his feet.

"It's Kate Delbridge," he said. "She says she needs to see us immediately."

"Where? Her place?"

"No, she's on the way to the airport." Cabot picked up his holstered gun and headed for the front door. "Wants to talk to me. There's an address. Looks like it's a restaurant located a few blocks south of Pioneer Square."

"The SoDo neighborhood?" Virginia leaped to her feet and hurried after him. "That's mostly an industrial area. It will be practically deserted at this time of night."

"I get the feeling she doesn't want to be seen talking to me."

"Us," Virginia said. "I'm coming with you."

Cabot paused at the door, his hand wrapped around the knob. "There's no need."

"Yes, there is. You're the one who said I shouldn't be alone until this thing is over."

He groaned. "Yeah, I did say that."

"There's no time to call Anson and have him come babysit me. Besides, I'm your backup. We're a team, remember?"

"Backup. Right."

He didn't sound thrilled, but he did sound resigned. He opened the door.

Virginia grabbed her handbag and followed him out into the hall.

CHAPTER 47

The restaurant was an aging fast-food establishment located between two warehouses. It was closed for the night. There was only a single vehicle in the parking lot. It was parked at the far end, its lights off.

"You know," Virginia said, "I admit I'm new at the investigation business, but this does not look promising."

"Speaking as someone who has had a little experience in the field, I can guarantee you that it doesn't look good," Cabot said.

He cruised slowly past the entrance and kept going.

Virginia glanced back at the lone car in the parking lot. "We're not going to stop?"

"We're definitely going to find out what's going on, but the first rule in a situation like this is to control the meeting point," Cabot said.

He turned the corner and eased his vehicle to the curb. Virginia realized they were now hidden behind the massive bulk of a warehouse.

Cabot took out his phone and called the most recent number. Kate answered immediately. He put the phone on speaker so that Virginia could hear everything.

"This is Sutter," he said.

"I don't see you," Kate said, her voice tight and anxious. "Where are you? I told you, I'm on my way out of town. I can't stay in Seattle. I think I'm in danger."

"Listen closely," Cabot said. "Drive your car out of the parking lot. Turn right at the end of the block. The SUV parked at the curb is mine. Drive past it. You'll see a loading zone. Pull into it. Get out of the car and walk back toward me. I'll meet you halfway."

"Look, I don't have time for games. I called you because I've got some information that may or may not be useful to you. Are you interested or not?"

"I'm interested but I'm sure you can understand that under the circumstances, I'm inclined to take precautions. The body count in this case is starting to climb. I'd rather not add to it. This meeting is your idea but we do it on my terms."

There was a short hesitation. Then the soft, muffled sound of a car starting.

"All right," Kate said. "I'm on my way.

But no more games, understand?"

"No more games," Cabot agreed.

He ended the connection.

"She certainly sounds scared," Virginia said. "I notice you didn't tell her that I'm here, too."

"That's because you're my backup," Cabot said.

"Oh, yeah. Right."

"It's always best if the person who arranges the meet doesn't know there's a backup."

"Got it. But what does the backup do in this situation? I don't even have a gun."

"The backup gets into the driver's seat and keeps the engine going in preparation for a fast takeoff in the event that something looks the least bit wrong."

"In other words, I'm the wheelman. Wait. Make that wheelwoman."

"Not sure that term is still in use, but yeah, that's the general idea."

"Doesn't sound like much of a job for the backup person."

Cabot did not take his eyes off the rear-view mirror. "We all have a role to play."

Virginia was about to argue the point but the sight of headlights coming slowly down the street behind them silenced her.

The vehicle drifted past the SUV and

pulled into the loading zone. Virginia realized that the position put Kate's vehicle squarely in the glare of a towering streetlight. That was not an accident, she decided. By forcing Kate to reposition her vehicle, Cabot had gained some control over the territory.

"She's following instructions," Cabot said. "That's a good sign."

There was a tense pause and then the headlights of the other car winked out. The driver's-side door opened. Kate emerged. She was clearly illuminated in the glow of the streetlight.

Cabot cracked open his door and got out. "Remember the backup's job."

"I'm on it," Virginia said.

Cabot closed the door.

Virginia scrambled into the driver's seat and lowered the window so that she could overhear whatever Kate had to say to Cabot. She realized she was shivering ever so slightly. Adrenaline, she thought, not nerves. Okay, maybe it was nerves. But not an anxiety attack, so it was all good.

She watched Kate start walking quickly toward Cabot.

In the eerie silence of the almost deserted street she could hear Kate's footsteps echoing faintly on the pavement.

Kate came to a halt at the edge of the ring of light cast by the streetlamp.

"Cabot Sutter?" she said uneasily. "Is that you?"

"Yes," Cabot said. He was about twenty feet away, still in deep shadows. "That's far enough. Why are you leaving town, Miss Delbridge?"

"Because I think someone is setting me up to take the fall for the embezzlement that's going on at Night Watch. Look, I don't have a lot of time. I think you need to take a close look at someone else in the company."

"Got a name?"

"Yes, as a matter of fact. That's why I called —"

She broke off as the growl of a rapidly accelerating car engine shattered the unnatural stillness of the night.

Virginia automatically looked around, trying to see the other vehicle. For a beat she saw nothing. In the next instant, a car roared around the corner at the far end of the street and rocketed forward. The twin beams of the headlights lanced the darkness.

Virginia had a split second in which to realize that the oncoming vehicle was rushing forward in the wrong lane and that, if it did not change course, it would slam into Kate and Cabot.

Kate half turned to see what was happening behind her. She must have been stunned by the headlights because instead of trying to get out of the path of the oncoming vehicle, she froze.

"Kate," Cabot shouted. *"Move."*

He broke into a run, heading toward her.

Virginia did the only thing she could think of — she switched on the SUV's powerful headlights, hoping to distract or even temporarily blind the driver of the speeding car. For good measure, she hit the horn.

The maneuver must have caught the driver of the oncoming car by surprise. Whoever was behind the wheel reacted instinctively, swerving out of the wrong lane and into the other one.

Cabot grabbed Kate's arm and hauled her out of the street and around the rear of her vehicle.

The driver of the attacking car, having lost sight of the target, roared away down the street and kept going.

Virginia tried to get a look at the driver as the vehicle raced past, but all she could make out was a vague silhouette.

It took her a second to realize that whoever

was behind the wheel was wearing a ski mask.

CHAPTER 48

"I think we can assume that was not a drunk driver," Kate Delbridge said.

She was huddled in the rear of Cabot's SUV. There was a tremor in her voice.

"Agreed," Cabot said. He was back behind the wheel of the SUV. He had his phone in his hand. "I'm going to call the cops."

"Wait, please." Kate wrapped her arms around her midsection. She rocked slowly back and forth. "I think I'm going to be sick."

Kate appeared to be hovering on the edge of hysteria. Cabot looked at Virginia, trying to send a message. He knew she got it because she turned in her seat and looked at Kate.

"We can wait to notify the police, Kate," Virginia said. "What was it you wanted to tell us?"

She kept her tone quiet but firm. Kate visibly steadied.

"I told you, there have been rumors about embezzlement circulating around Night Watch for weeks," she got out in low tones. "A few days ago I found a large cash deposit in my bank account. I was sure it was a mistake. I called the bank. They looked into it and said it was a legitimate deposit. As far as they were concerned the money was mine. For a while I told myself I had just been on the lucky end of a banking error. I was sure the bank would figure it out sooner or later, so I was careful not to spend the money. But today it happened again."

"There was another big cash deposit?" Virginia asked.

Kate nodded weakly. "I wasn't stupid enough to believe I'd gotten lucky twice. Both deposits were sizable but under the limit that banks are required to report."

"What, exactly, do you think is going on?" Cabot asked.

"I admit I'm not very tech savvy," Kate said. "But I'm not as dumb as everyone at Night Watch seems to think. Someone is setting me up to take the fall for the embezzlement scheme."

"If that's the case, why try to kill you tonight?" Cabot asked.

Kate shook her head. "I don't know. Probably because I made the appointment to talk to you. Someone is watching my every move. I have to get out of town."

"Got any idea of who might want to use you for the fall guy?" Cabot asked.

Kate was silent for a few tense seconds.

"Maybe," she said finally. She took a deep breath and seemed to regain some control. "But I have absolutely no proof."

"Go on," Virginia encouraged.

"When the rumors of embezzlement first started, I assumed it was someone in the accounting department or in IT. We all did. I mean, those people must know every possible way to skim money off the top, right? And they're all pretty tech savvy, at least when it comes to dealing with money. After Sandra Porter was fired, we all thought it was because she was the embezzler and management had decided to let her go quietly. But today, when I realized that someone was trying to make it look like I was embezzling, I realized Sandra couldn't have been the one stealing the money — or, at least, not the only one involved."

"Who, then?" Virginia prompted.

"This is just a guess, you understand, but Laurel Jenner, the head of marketing, is really pissed at me."

"Why?" Cabot asked.

Kate rocked a little in the seat. "I'm

356

almost positive she's sleeping with the boss, Josh Preston. And she knows that I know. I think she's afraid I'll ruin her cushy situation. Preston has made it clear that he doesn't approve of workplace romances. Those things happen, but at Night Watch people get fired if the relationship becomes common knowledge."

"So you think Jenner might be willing to murder you in order to keep you quiet?" Virginia asked.

"I just don't know," Kate whispered. "But if she's using her relationship with Preston to get the kind of inside information she needs to steal from his company, and if she thought that rumors of the affair might put her scheme at risk — maybe. Like I said, it's just a theory. I've got no proof. I can tell you one thing, though. Laurel has a gun."

"How did you find out about the gun?" Cabot asked.

Kate grimaced. "She told me about it a few months ago. That was before she and Preston started their affair. Laurel and I were friends back in those days. She said she bought the gun because she'd just gone through a nasty divorce. She was afraid her ex might become a stalker. Look, I really have to get to the airport. My flight leaves in less than two hours."

"Where will you go?" Virginia asked.

"Mexico," Kate said. "When I was younger my family vacationed down there every year. I know my way around. Please, I've told you everything I know. I need to go now."

"We'll follow you to the airport," Cabot said. "Make sure you get safely past security."

"Thanks," Kate said. "I would appreciate that."

"What about your car?" Virginia asked.

"It's a rental. I'll turn it in at the airport. When I realized that someone might be watching me, I decided it might be smart to leave my own car in the garage at my apartment building. Obviously that brilliant plan didn't work. Shit. Still can't believe someone tried to kill me."

"It's a weird feeling, all right," Virginia said.

A short time later Virginia and Cabot stood inside the bustling Sea-Tac terminal and watched Kate wend her way through the airport security screening lines. When she disappeared, they went back over the sky bridge into the parking garage.

They got into the SUV and sat quietly for a moment.

"It feels like we're chasing shadows," Virginia said.

Cabot cranked up the engine. "Old shadows and new ones."

The cool, distant tone of his voice told her that he had moved into his zone. She glanced at him. In the harsh light of the parking garage his profile was hard, fierce. This was the man she had glimpsed the first day in the offices of Cutler, Sutter & Salinas, a man who could be your best friend or your worst nightmare of an enemy.

Any brute could be dangerous, she thought. What she found so deeply compelling about Cabot was that he adhered to a code, one that involved gritty, old-fashioned qualities like honor, determination and loyalty. This was a man who would walk into hell for those he loved and those whom he felt bound to protect.

"We need to find the intersection between the past and the present, don't we?" Virginia said.

"Yes."

"Got any ideas?"

"One."

"I feel a cryptic martial arts saying coming."

"Nope, this is a pragmatic detective saying."

"What is it?" Virginia asked.

"Follow the money."

"Wow, that's old-school, all right. But we've already followed the money. We know our mothers hid it twenty-two years ago in a secret account."

"That's one money trail," Cabot agreed. "But we are dealing with two, and the second one goes directly to Night Watch."

"How could the embezzlement that seems to be going on at Night Watch be connected to the money that disappeared all those years ago?"

"I don't know yet, but there has to be a link," Cabot said. "I can almost see it."

Virginia smiled.

"What?" Cabot asked.

"In your own way, you're an artist, Cabot Sutter."

"I keep telling you, I'm no artist."

"You're wrong. But never mind. Where do we go next?"

"Obviously we need to take a closer look at Laurel Jenner, but first I want to try to get a handle on what Sandra Porter was doing in your back room on the night she was killed."

"I take it you're not buying Sandra Porter in the role of drug dealer?"

"Nope. Doesn't fit. Nothing else in this

case is actually about drugs, but it's interesting that people keep trying to point us in that direction."

"Porter is dead, so where do we look for answers?"

"In my experience, the home of the dead person is always illuminating. The crime scene tape should be down by now. Tomorrow we'll see if we can get inside Porter's apartment."

"All right. You know, it occurs to me that whoever was driving that hit-and-run car tonight might have been aiming for you," Virginia said. "Maybe Kate wasn't the target."

"Funny you should mention that," Cabot said. He put the SUV in gear and reversed out of the parking stall. "The possibility did cross my mind."

CHAPTER 49

Virginia lay awake for a long time, waiting for sleep or an anxiety attack. When neither occurred, she gave up on both and pushed the covers aside. It was one thirty in the morning. For a couple of minutes she sat on the edge of the bed, listening to the night. After a while she heard the door of Cabot's room open. She knew he was probably headed toward the living room with his laptop.

She found her glasses, got to her feet, pulled on a robe and went out into the hall. Sure enough, her living room was illuminated by the cold light of a computer screen. Cabot was on the sofa, his laptop in front of him on the coffee table.

"You know, the experts say that it's a bad idea to stare at a computer screen before going to bed," Virginia said. "Something about the blue light."

"Yeah, I've heard that," Cabot said. "It's

on the standard list of good sleep hygiene rules. Right up there with 'go to bed at the same time every night' and 'don't watch television in bed.' "

"None of those sleep hygiene rules have ever worked for me."

"Didn't work for me, either." Cabot looked up. "You don't look like you're having an anxiety attack."

"I don't feel like it, either. But I can't sleep. I keep thinking about how someone tried to kill you tonight."

"We don't know I was the target. There's a very good possibility the driver was aiming for Kate Delbridge."

"In which case, you might have been collateral damage. Doesn't change anything. I don't think I'm going to get much sleep tonight. I think I'll make some herbal tea. Want a cup?"

"Sounds good."

Virginia went into the kitchen and made the tea. The little ritual — for years a lonely one — seemed very different tonight. *Because I'm making tea for both of us.*

When she carried the mugs of steaming tea back into the living room, Cabot closed his laptop, leaned back and stretched out his legs. Virginia set the mugs on the coffee table and sat down on the sofa. She curled

363

one leg under herself and picked up her tea.

The lights were off but the glow from the cityscape illuminated the space. She and Cabot sipped their tea in a companionable silence for a while.

"What was it like, growing up with Anson as your foster dad?" she asked.

"Good," Cabot said. "It wasn't always easy, but it was good. From day one he made it clear that he would be there for us until hell froze over. Took us a while to really believe him, but one thing we learned about Anson Salinas — if he gave you his word, you could take it to the bank."

"Was he married at the time?"

"No. His wife had died a couple of years earlier."

"He never remarried?" Virginia asked.

"No. There was a woman once. For a while my brothers and I thought that Anson would marry her. But in the end she married someone else and left town. After that Anson had a few discreet relationships, but he never got serious about any other woman."

"Did you ever find out why Anson and the first woman didn't marry?"

"Anson never talked about it, but Jack and Max and I knew why she chose someone else. She didn't want to take on the task of raising three teenage boys who were all carrying a few scars."

"And Anson would never have abandoned the three of you."

"No," Cabot said.

They went back to drinking their tea in silence. At some point Virginia put her empty mug down on the table. Cabot set his mug beside hers. He put his arm around her. She settled against his side, savoring the heat of his body.

She did not remember closing her eyes.

She awoke to the early morning light. It took her a few minutes to realize that she and Cabot were both stretched out on the sofa, entangled in each other's arms. Cabot was still asleep.

She extricated herself very carefully and got to her feet. For a time she stood looking down at Cabot. A sense of wonder swept through her.

"What?" he asked without opening his eyes.

"Nothing," she said. "I'll go put on the coffee."

She had gone to sleep in her lover's arms. No anxiety attack involved.

Life was good.

CHAPTER 50

Sandra Porter's apartment was located in an anonymous downtown apartment tower. The lobby was sleek, modern and covered in a lot of hard surfaces — black granite and glass, for the most part.

"Yeah, sure, you can take a quick look around," the manager said. According to the little tag on his white shirt, his name was Sam. "Cops took the crime scene tape down yesterday. No one has shown up to claim Porter's stuff. I'm getting ready to have her things removed and put in storage so I can get the place cleaned and back on the market."

"What number?" Cabot asked.

"Twelve ten." Sam handed Cabot a key. "If anyone asks, tell 'em I sent you up. You're prospective renters. Got it?"

"Got it," Cabot said.

He slipped Sam a couple of large bills. Sam made the money vanish with an expertise that told Virginia it wasn't the first time he had accepted a gratuity in exchange for looking the other way.

Virginia did not say anything until she and Cabot were in the elevator.

"That was slick," she said. "Do that a lot?"

"You'd be amazed how far old-fashioned cash goes in a world where most transactions are done online or with credit cards," Cabot said. "It's still the perfect medium of exchange if you want to protect your privacy."

Virginia nodded. "Untraceable. No need to explain things to the tax people. No awkward questions about your credit history."

"There's a reason why criminals and private investigators prefer the old-fashioned methods in certain situations," Cabot said.

She could feel the icy energy charging the atmosphere around him. He was back in the zone.

"You live for this," she said.

He shot her a quick, wary look. "For what?"

"For the moment when the vision starts to come together."

"Do me a favor, stop comparing me to one of your oddball artists."

"Okay," she said. "But for the record, I

don't think you're an oddball artist."

"No?"

"No. Just an artist. No oddball qualities involved."

Fortunately the elevator doors slid open before Cabot could think of a response. He instantly refocused and led the way out of the elevator.

She followed him down the hall and waited while he got the door of 1210 open.

Sandra Porter's apartment was a studio with an alcove for the bed and a bath. Virginia's first thought was that someone had searched the place. The room was definitely in an untidy state. Drawers looked as if they had been emptied and then had the contents dumped back inside. Cupboards and closet doors stood open. The furniture had been pushed around in a random manner.

"Good grief," Virginia said. "Either Sandra Porter wasn't much of a housekeeper or someone got here before us."

Cabot handed her a pair of gloves. "I think you can blame the crime scene people for most of this mess. After they go through a place looking for evidence, they don't refold clothes or put items neatly back on shelves. Not their job."

"I see what you mean."

Cabot headed for the small kitchen area.

Virginia pulled on the gloves and went into the alcove. The bed had been stripped. The clothes in the closet had been shoved to one side. A collection of shoes littered the floor.

"What are we looking for?" she called.

"I have no idea," Cabot said. "But I'll know it when I see it."

She heard the refrigerator door open. There was a pause and Cabot appeared.

"There's almost nothing in the refrigerator," he reported. "Nothing in the freezer, either. Looks like she lived on takeout. Any luck in here?"

"No. Well, there are some clothes, but that's about it. Nothing of a personal nature. No books. No pictures on the walls. If there was something important here, the cops found it."

"Maybe. If so, Anson's good pal Schwartz is no longer passing along the information."

Virginia closed a drawer. "Do you really think Sandra Porter's death is connected to Zane's cult?"

"Everything in this case is connected."

"Because you can see it," she said, smiling a little.

"Yes."

Virginia went into the bathroom. The

process of going through the dead woman's things was not only frustrating, it gave her the creeps.

"Remember why you're doing this," Cabot said quietly behind her.

Startled, she turned to face him.

"It gives me a weird feeling," she said.

"I know. That's why you have to remember that you're going through a dead woman's stuff because you're trying to find out why Hannah Brewster died and because you're trying to identify the person who tried to murder us."

His words had a bracing effect. She took a deep breath.

"Right," she said. She looked around. "I think I'm done in here. Maybe you should take a look. You're the professional."

"Yes, but that only means I see things from a particular point of view. Your observations are just as valid because you look at them from an entirely different angle."

"Because I'm a woman?"

"No, because you come from the art world. You know how to look beneath the surface."

"Right. Maybe I should try that approach."

She went past him and moved into the main room of the studio. For a couple of minutes she wandered through the space, just looking at her surroundings, as if the studio were a work of art. Waiting for some small kernel of truth to speak to her.

She was about to give up when she noticed the cardboard shipping box on the floor in the kitchen. It stood next to the recycling containers. Her first thought was that it had been destined to be flattened and taken down the hall to be discarded in the trash room.

She lifted the box lid and looked inside. Light glinted on pieces of a broken mug. There was also a man's black T-shirt that looked as if it had been attacked with a pair of scissors. A couple of small, smooth rocks that looked as if they had been picked up on a beach, a smashed picture frame and a photograph that had been ripped in half completed the strange collection.

She picked up a couple of pieces of the mug and examined it closely. When she fit the pieces together, she was able to read the words written in bold red letters: *Happy Birthday.*

Cabot came to stand next to her.

"I assumed the stuff in the box was junk that Porter intended to recycle," he said.

"Maybe." Virginia dropped the shards of the mug back into the box and held up a piece of the T-shirt. "This belonged to a man. It was cut with scissors, not accidentally ripped."

"Everything in that box is broken," Cabot said thoughtfully.

Virginia studied the contents of the box. A chill of knowing whispered through her.

"Not accidentally broken," she said. "Shattered. Destroyed."

"There's a difference?"

"Oh, yes," Virginia said softly. "There's a difference."

She reached back into the box and picked up the ripped photograph. She put it on the kitchen counter.

"It's the right size to fit inside the picture frame," she said.

Carefully she smoothed out the page.

The picture had obviously been taken at an office party. A crowd of people was gathered beneath a banner that read, *Night Watch Employee of the Month for January: Tucker Fleming.*

Virginia stared at the picture, shock icing her blood. She felt Cabot go very still and knew that he, too, was stunned.

In the festive scene a smiling Josh Preston was handing a coffee mug and an envelope to a tall, good-looking man with a disturbingly familiar face.

"Tucker Fleming is not quite a dead ringer for Quinton Zane," Cabot said, "but he's got to be a relative — a son or a nephew, maybe. Same height, similar build, although not as lean."

Virginia shuddered. "Same profile."

"Dress him in black and the resemblance would be very close to the Zane we knew twenty-two years ago."

"Why didn't the cops take this as evidence?" Virginia asked.

"Evidence of what? It's just a picture of an office party for an employee of the month."

"Hannah Brewster must have seen Tucker Fleming on Lost Island," Virginia said. "No wonder she painted that picture of Zane in modern clothes and added a late-model car. She probably believed that he had come back from the dead."

"Or she may have figured out that his son was searching for the missing money."

"Either way, she was trying to warn me."

CHAPTER 51

The rain was coming down hard by the time Xavier got off the bus. He paused in the shelter to check the screen of his phone again. His excitement spiked when he saw that he was very close to his objective. It looked like the subject was inside the small bungalow at the end of the block.

The neighborhood was very quiet. The houses were small and most of them needed a fresh coat of paint. The cars parked on the street were all older models.

All he had to do was make a note of the address, he thought. He was about to crack the case. Cabot and Anson would be impressed. They'd probably want to give him a permanent job at the agency. As for Virginia Troy, she would think he was brilliant, a real hero.

It occurred to him that a photograph of the target who lived in the house, or at least the license plate of his car, would be even better than just an address. Armed with that information, Cabot and Anson would know exactly what to do.

He tucked the phone back into his pocket and pulled up the hood of his sweatshirt. Although the skies were heavy and gray, he put on his sunglasses. Just one more teen in a hoodie and shades.

He slouched along the sidewalk, trying to look like he belonged in the neighborhood. When he passed the front door, he made a mental note of the number of the house. Unfortunately there were several cars parked on the street. No way to know which vehicle belonged to the target.

He took out his phone and surreptitiously began snapping pics of license plates.

When he reached the end of the block, he paused, thinking. To really nail the case, he needed to get a photo of whoever was inside the house.

He could knock on the door and — assuming someone answered — pretend to be lost. But that sounded weak. He needed a better plan.

A straight-up lost-my-phone-and-the-tracking-app-says-it's-here story sounded like the only sure approach. Whoever answered the door would deny that the missing device was in the house, which would be the truth. But there would be a couple of minutes of confusion and irritation while the resident of the house denied having the piece of tech.

Xavier figured he could put his phone on silent mode and maybe get a short video, all while pretending to realize that his app had led him to the wrong house.

He walked back along the sidewalk, went up the front steps and started the video. He could feel his pulse racing. He didn't think he had ever been so scared or so excited in his life.

He pressed the doorbell and held his breath. Part of him was already regretting the plan. But he could not back out now. He gripped his phone very tightly.

Maybe whoever was inside would not answer.

The door opened. A guy in his mid-twenties looked at him. He had an energy drink in one hand. He was clearly irritated.

"What do you want?"

Xavier had to try twice before he got the words out. "I'm l-looking for my phone. Got a tracking app that says it's here."

"Yeah? What's that in your hand?"

"A friend's phone. He let me use it to find mine."

"You think I stole your phone?"

"I was using it at a Starbucks. Left it on the table while I went to get another latte. When I turned around it was gone. Probably just a mistake."

"I sure as hell don't have it. Come on inside and take a look."

Xavier hesitated and then took one step over the threshold. He pretended to study the screen of his phone.

"I think I made a mistake," he said.

"Funny you should say that." The man closed the door. "I came to the same conclusion."

Panicked now, Xavier half turned. But something hard and metallic was pressed against the back of his head. He froze, so frightened he couldn't catch his breath. *Just like in a video game, except the gun is real. He's going to kill me.*

"Don't move," the subject said quietly. "The house on one side is empty. Neighbors on the other side are gone for the day. If I pull this trigger, no one will call nine-one-one."

CHAPTER 52

Virginia knew from the hard look in Anson's eyes that something was very wrong.

"Xavier is gone," he announced.

"Back to California?" Cabot closed the office door. "I knew he would eventually get tired of hanging around, but I thought it might take a few more days before boredom set in."

"Pretty sure he didn't go home," Anson said. "His pack is still at my house. Far as I can tell, the only thing he took with him is his phone."

Virginia was still trying to get past the shock of the discovery that she and Cabot had made in Sandra Porter's apartment. Reluctant to trust their phones, they had headed directly to the offices of Cutler, Sutter & Salinas with the intention of telling Anson the news about Tucker Fleming. It was Saturday, but no one was taking any time off. The situation was too fluid and dangerous.

When they had walked into the room a few seconds ago, Anson was not ensconced behind his desk. Instead, he had been pacing the room, which struck Virginia as very un-Anson-like behavior. The deep concern in his eyes was more than enough to make it clear that he was very worried.

She stood quietly near the desk and listened to the conversation with increasing alarm. Cabot's entire attention was suddenly focused on Anson.

"What do you have?" Cabot asked.

Anson ceased his restless pacing.

"I don't have much," he said. "That's the problem. He took off a couple hours ago. Said he was bored. He told me that he wanted to see the Space Needle and maybe Pike Place Market. They're all within walking distance. I asked him if he needed directions. He held up his phone and said he could find his way around town."

"Did you try calling his phone?" Virginia asked.

"Twice," Anson said. "Got dumped into voice mail both times. Under other circumstances I wouldn't be too concerned, but this just doesn't feel right. He was having a blast digging into Virginia's phone, trying to see if someone had planted a tracking app.

At least I thought he was really involved with that project."

"Okay, let's not get ahead of ourselves," Cabot said. "This is Xavier we're talking about. He's got a history of taking off and not letting anyone know where he is until after he's at his destination."

Virginia stirred a little. "For what it's worth, I don't think Xavier would just up and disappear. He has to know that would annoy both of you. He wouldn't want to do that, not at this stage."

Both men looked at her.

"What do you mean?" Anson asked.

"He's been working hard, trying to prove himself to you and Cabot," Virginia said. "He wants to be part of your pack."

Cabot's brows rose. "Pack?"

"Sorry, slip of the tongue," Virginia said quickly. "I meant that Xavier wants to be a member of your crew, your team. I think it's more likely that he's trying to impress both of you. He wouldn't go out of his way to piss you off now."

Anson looked at Cabot. "She's right."

"Yeah," Cabot said. "I know. Shit. We did not need this problem. All right, let's assume that he thinks he's working the case. Maybe he did find a tracking app on Virginia's phone. Maybe the kid found a way to follow the trail back to the individual who enabled the app."

Virginia went cold. "Oh, no, surely he wouldn't take a risk like that."

Anson looked startled. "Is that even possible?"

"Theoretically, yes," Cabot said. "It wouldn't be simple. I'm sure it would take some real skills, but, obviously, Xavier is good. I think we need to assume the worst-case scenario here."

"What, exactly, is that?" Anson asked.

Virginia cleared her throat. "I think Cabot is afraid that maybe — just maybe — Xavier found Tucker Fleming."

"Who the hell is Tucker Fleming and why is that a problem?" Anson demanded.

"Fleming works for Night Watch," Cabot said. "He's not on the org chart because he's just a regular employee in the IT department. We found a picture of him in Porter's apartment. He looks a hell of a lot like Quinton Zane. He's the right age to be Zane's son or nephew."

Anson was thunderstruck. "What?"

"I'll let Virginia explain," Cabot said. "I need to get moving."

Virginia looked at him. "Shouldn't we call the police and tell them that Xavier has disappeared?"

"No good," Anson said. "We don't have any evidence of a kidnapping, and as a rule, the cops don't take a missing person case seriously until the individual has been gone for a day or more. That's especially true with teenagers who are known runaways."

Virginia winced. "Xavier does fit that profile, doesn't he?"

"Hang on," Anson said. "I'm coming with you."

"No," Cabot said. "Two reasons. First, I need you to keep an eye on Virginia. I can't look after her and deal with Tucker Fleming at the same time. Also, someone needs to be here in case we're wrong about what is going on. Who knows? Xavier might actually be at the top of the Space Needle snapping pictures. Call me if he decides to wander back into the office."

"How are you going to find Tucker Fleming?" Virginia asked.

"That's the easy part," Anson said. He turned back to his computer. "Fleming should be on the list of Night Watch employees that I compiled after you found Sandra Porter's body. Yep, here he is."

"Give it to me," Cabot said.

Anson jotted down the address on a sticky note and handed it across the desk.

Cabot took the note, opened the door and

let himself out into the hall. In a heartbeat he was gone, leaving Virginia alone with Anson.

Anson looked at her. His lawman eyes were bleak.

"The kid's not at the top of the Space Needle," he said.

Virginia thought about the carefully curated collection of destroyed objects that she and Cabot had discovered in Sandra Porter's apartment.

"No," she said, "he's not. That poor kid is in trouble and it's because of me."

"Nope." Anson shook his head. "It's my fault. I shouldn't have let him take off like that. He's a seventeen-year-old kid. They do dumb stuff, like try to play hero."

Virginia gave him a rueful smile. "From what Cabot tells me, I gather you've had some experience with teenage boys."

"Always figured it was a miracle that Max, Cabot and Jack made it to adulthood, what with having me for a dad and all. Not like I knew what the hell I was doing. My own pa took off when I was two. I just winged it with my boys."

"I think it's safe to say you figured it out."

"All I did was try to give them the tools and the skills I knew they'd need to make it," Anson said. "The rest was pure dumb luck. Gives me cold chills whenever I think of all the things that could have gone wrong."

"There's some luck involved in everything, but you didn't just get three orphaned boys safely to adulthood. Judging by what I know about the situation, you created three good men. You were obviously an excellent role model."

"I'll let you in on a little secret," Anson said. "Role models or not, in the end every man has to decide for himself just what kind of man he will be."

"I never thought about it but I suppose that goes for all of us, women as well as men."

Anson nodded thoughtfully and gave her a long, knowing look. "It's clear you made your choice somewhere along the line."

"It wasn't a conscious choice. I got lucky in my role model, too. My grandmother made it clear that you do whatever you have to do to be able to face yourself in the mirror."

"Reckon that's where it gets complicated," Anson said. "Some people can live with a real murky version of themselves. Which brings us to this new, younger edition of Quinton Zane. Tell me what you found out about him."

"If we're right, Tucker Fleming is a chip off the old block."

CHAPTER 53

Unlike the other aging bungalows on the street, Tucker Fleming's house felt cold and empty.

Cabot stood in the living room and absorbed the vibe. He held Xavier's sunglasses in one hand. There was an empty energy drink can on an end table. It was the same brand as the empties he had spotted at the Wallerton house.

Two minutes ago he had forced a bedroom window, expecting the screech of an alarm. The prospect hadn't worried him because he was certain he could be in and, if necessary, out before the police or the neighbors bothered to investigate. Alarms went off all the time. People rarely reacted.

But there had been no blaring alarm. There was a security system installed in the house — a good one — but it had been deactivated. Evidently Fleming had left in a rush and had either forgotten to reset the device or hadn't wanted to waste the time.

That made sense. A man who had been surprised by a kid who had tracked him to his home address would not have been thinking clearly. Fleming had believed himself to be in control of the game from the start. The realization that Xavier had found him would no doubt have pushed him close to the edge of panic.

Speed was the most important factor now, Cabot thought. But he forced himself to think through the logic of the situation. There was no way that Fleming could have had time to plan for such an unforeseen kidnapping scenario, let alone figure out how to dispose of a body.

He would head for a location where he felt safe and in control, a place where he could get rid of a teenage boy who was now a witness.

Cabot took one last look around the living room. The space was crammed with electronics — a massive, state-of-the-art television and various pieces of equipment designed for computer games. But there was no desk, no pile of magazines — nothing of a personal nature that might tell him where Fleming was headed with Xavier.

He had already done a quick prowl of the two small bedrooms, but he forced himself to take the time to go back through the house a second time. There was always something, he reminded himself, and the most likely place to find it was in the most personal space in a house — the owner's bedroom.

He stopped in the doorway. There was another large-screen TV on the wall and some more electronics on the bedside table and on top of the dresser.

Fleming was not a complete slob but he was not the neatest person in the world. A shirt and a pair of jeans hung over the back of a chair. There was a single athletic shoe on the floor. The hamper was overflowing.

The closet was long and narrow and fitted with sliding doors. Cabot opened one of the doors and took a quick look around. More jumbled clothes hung on the rod. There were several pairs of shoes tumbled on the floor.

It occurred to him that the second bedroom had been much neater. Clearly it had gone largely unused. But that seemed odd, given the general clutter in the bungalow. In his experience most people allowed stuff to accumulate to fill the space available. It took self-discipline to maintain a well-ordered household.

He went back down the hall and into the

other bedroom. *Why so neat and orderly in this room, Fleming? You've been living in this house for a while and you've filled up most of it with your stuff. There isn't even a TV. You haven't emptied the garbage in the kitchen for at least a couple of days, yet this room is so clean and tidy.*

He crossed the bedroom and slid open the closet doors.

There were no clothes inside, no shoes on the floor. The interior walls were covered with scenes from his old nightmares.

Press clippings of the fire at the California compound papered one side wall. There were some pictures of the small handful of the dazed survivors who had agreed to talk to the reporters. There were no images of the children. Anson had refused to allow any of them to be interviewed by the journalists who had covered the story.

A framed picture of Quinton Zane hung in a place of prominence. It was discolored with age. In the picture Zane looked to be in his early twenties. Cabot decided that it had probably been taken around the same time as the photo of Zane and Abigail Watkins on the ferry. Zane had a warm, open smile for the camera. You had to look closely to see that his eyes were ice-cold.

Most of the images and articles dated back

twenty-two years but there were some recent additions — full-color printouts of Hannah Brewster's *Visions* series. It looked like the photos had been taken with a cell phone.

There was also a printout of a picture of the Lost Island B and B going up in flames.

There was a small filing cabinet on the floor of the closet. Cabot opened the drawer and saw two folders. The first contained a well-worn leather-bound journal. The handwriting was the same as that on the photocopies that Virginia had found in Rose Gilbert's nightstand.

The second folder contained a lot of paperwork relating to a recent real estate deal. The property that had been purchased was the old house outside of Wallerton — a location where a panicked Tucker Fleming would feel safe and in control, a place where he could get rid of a witness.

Cabot ran for the door, Abigail Watkins's journal in his hand.

Outside he got into the SUV, shoved the journal under the passenger seat and fired up the engine.

When he was rolling, he used a new disposable phone to call the office landline.

Anson answered halfway through the first ring.

"Fleming has Xavier," Cabot said. "Can't be positive but I think it's a good bet that he took him to the Wallerton house."

"I'll call the local cops," Anson said.

"No. If they show up at the front door of the first compound, we'll probably be looking at a hostage situation. I think Fleming may be more than a little crazy, Anson. He's obsessed with Zane. Constructed a shrine to the bastard. No telling what he'll do if he's cornered."

"Where are you?"

"I'm on my way to the first compound outside of Wallerton."

Cabot ended the connection and concentrated on his driving.

CHAPTER 54

It was Xavier's first experience with real, gut-level fear. He didn't think he was handling it very well.

He was also cold. He was still wearing his sweatshirt but it provided only limited protection against the chill that gripped the old house. Tucker Fleming hadn't bothered to build a fire in the big stone fireplace in the huge living room. Xavier figured that was not a good sign.

He was on the floor in front of the darkened hearth. Fleming had used duct tape to bind his wrists and ankles. After arriving at their destination, Fleming had cut the tape that secured his feet, and forced him to walk into the old house before once again taping his ankles together.

He had expected an interrogation of some kind. It seemed likely that Fleming would want to know if the others were on his trail. Xavier had concocted what he hoped was a believable story designed to make his kid-napper think that Anson and Cabot would descend at any moment. But so far he hadn't had an opportunity to try out the lie.

After dumping him in the living room, Fleming had returned to the SUV to collect a bulging duffel bag. He had rigged up some kind of explosive devices at various points on the ground floor and then hauled the bag upstairs. Xavier could hear him moving around on the floor above the living room.

Xavier struggled to a sitting position and propped himself up against the stone hearth. He tried to imagine what Cabot would do in such a situation. Probably pull a knife out of a hidden sheath strapped to his ankle.

Cabot would use the knife to slice through the duct tape, and then he would wait for Fleming to return to the ground floor. True, Fleming had a gun, but Cabot had one, too. Fleming wouldn't stand a chance.

The floorboards overhead creaked. Fleming was on the move again. Xavier twisted around to survey his surroundings. The only thing he saw that looked remotely like a weapon was an empty camping lantern. It was sitting on the end table at the side of the sagging couch.

CHAPTER 55

The old house was locked in the deep shadows of the surrounding woods.

Cabot stood in the shelter of the trees and contemplated his strategy. The wind was picking up. He remembered how the old structure had wailed and moaned whenever a storm had struck. He and the other kids had huddled under the covers and imagined ghosts howling in the basement.

The noise of the gusting wind would be useful, he thought. He and the others had been frightened by the storms of their childhood, but now the wind was his ally. With luck it would partially mask any sounds he made when he gained access to the house.

He had left his car on an unpaved side road and made his way through the heavily forested area behind the big house. The sight of the vehicle parked in the front drive had been somewhat reassuring. It was a good indication that he had come to the right place. Now he could only hope that Fleming had not yet murdered Xavier.

The problem with dead bodies was the issue of disposal. Fleming might be in a panic, but surely he was thinking clearly enough to realize that it would be risky to kill his victim inside the house. There would be a lot of evidence left behind.

But Fleming had to be seriously wired, running flat out on adrenaline and desperation. Xavier was a huge problem for him. He would act quickly.

Cabot knew he could not wait any longer. He had to make his move. The one advantage he had was that he knew his way around the old house.

He took his gun out of the holster, slipped out of the woods and went swiftly toward the long rear porch. For a few tense seconds he was in the open. If Fleming happened to glance through one of the few windows that were not boarded up on that side of the house, he would have a clear shot.

Judging by the results of the first shootout at the old mansion, Fleming was a lousy shot unless he was very close to his target. But even if he missed, Cabot knew the element of surprise would be lost. Fleming would have time to grab Xavier and use him as a human shield.

There were no shots.

He made it up onto the porch and flattened himself against the side of the large wood-storage shed. The outer door sagged on its hinges. He opened it wider, exerting great care, and let himself into the shadowed space. He could make out a jumble of old, rotted logs and kindling. No one had built a fire in the house in a very long time.

He moved toward the inner door in the shed, the one that had been installed to allow firewood to be brought into the house without the necessity of going outside into the teeth of a winter storm.

It opened onto a room that had been used to store muddy boots, wet rain gear and assorted household cleaning supplies. He hoped the door would be unlocked. If it wasn't, he would have to take the risk of forcing it.

Very little light seeped into the shed via the sagging outside door, but his memory of the layout proved accurate. He crossed the space and put out a hand to feel for the knob on the inner door.

He found it almost immediately. He tested it gently. It turned easily in his hand. He forced himself to wait until another gust rattled the remaining windows and whistled through cracks in the wooden walls. When he got his cue — a wailing wind accompanied by the first blast of rain — he raised the gun, crouched, opened the door and went into the old mudroom.

He winced when he heard the squeak of rusty hinges, but there were no running footsteps, no shots.

Now that he was inside he could hear another sound — footsteps on the floor above. Fleming was upstairs. It seemed logical that he would have left his captive downstairs.

Cabot pulled up memories of the layout of the big house. There were a lot of rooms upstairs but not many on the ground floor. Most of the space was taken up by a large kitchen and pantry, a sizable dining area and a vast living room.

He moved quickly but methodically from one room to the next.

Xavier was half propped up against the stone hearth of the big fireplace. There was a storm lantern on the floor beside him. He stared at Cabot, first in shock and then in overwhelming relief. Then he jerked his head upward and mouthed the words, "He's up there."

Cabot nodded once, reached down and took the knife out of his ankle sheath. Fleming either had no experience with taking people captive or he had been in too much of a rush to think about technique. Regardless of the reason, he had bound Xavier's wrists in front, not in back. That meant that the kid had not lost feeling in his hands and arms. He would be able to move quickly once he was free.

Cabot crossed the room and used the blade to slice through the duct tape that bound Xavier's hands and feet.

He hauled Xavier upright and put his mouth to Xavier's ear.

"We're going out through the kitchen. Anything happens to me, you keep going, understand? I tell you to run, you run. Get out of the house and don't stop."

Xavier swallowed hard and nodded in a jerky manner. He was clearly scared and disoriented, but he was trying to focus on the orders.

Cabot started to give him a push toward the kitchen, but at that moment he heard the purposeful footsteps at the top of the stairs. Time had run out. In the next second or two Fleming would appear on the staircase. When he did, he would have a clear view of what was going down in the living room.

There was no point trying to keep silent now. Cabot yanked Xavier back and shoved him up against one side of the massive stone fireplace.

Fleming froze at the top of the staircase, gun in hand. He was clearly trying to make sense out of the fact that his captive was no longer lying on the floor in front of the hearth.

Then he saw Cabot.

"What the fuck?" he said.

"Drop the gun," Cabot ordered. "Now."

But Fleming scrambled backward, firing wildly to cover his retreat.

The shots were all over the place, but that didn't make them any less dangerous. Cabot moved next to Xavier and flattened his back against the side of the fireplace.

He squeezed off a couple of shots but Fleming was already disappearing into the hallway at the top of the staircase.

"That money is mine, Sutter," he screamed. "Do you hear me? That money is my inheritance. *I'm Quinton Zane's son.*"

Cabot kept his attention on the staircase. He heard pounding footsteps overhead. It sounded like Fleming was fleeing along the upstairs hall. He was intent on escape. He would go down the back stairs and most likely make a run for his vehicle, which was parked at the front of the house.

"Change of plans," Cabot said to Xavier.

"We wait until he's gone. Then we leave."

"Okay, but I think there may be a problem."

"What?"

"The guy is full-on crazy," Xavier gasped. "I think he was wiring this place to explode. He said something about a blast from the past."

"We need to leave. Now."

The muffled whoosh of the explosion rumbled through the house. The fire exploded around them.

"How far did he get setting the explosive devices?" Cabot asked.

"He did the downstairs first. Then he went upstairs."

Cabot thought about the woodshed.

"It's a big house," he said. "And he was in a hurry. He didn't have time to cover every exit point. Let's go."

He ran for the mudroom, Xavier hard on his heels.

CHAPTER 56

"I knew you'd have a knife," Xavier said.

Cabot glanced at him. "You did?"

He and Xavier were in the front seats of his SUV, watching the fire crew deal with the remnants of the blaze that had destroyed the big house. The rain was falling steadily now, soaking the surrounding area and ensuring that the fire would not spread.

He had called Anson immediately after he contacted the local authorities. Anson had put Virginia on the phone.

"You're sure you're both okay?" she had asked.

"Xavier is a little shaken up, but yes, we're both all right," he said.

"You saved his life, Cabot."

"It's my fault he got into trouble."

"No," she had said.

"Yes," he said.

He'd ended the call before she could pursue the argument because a detective from the Wallerton Police Department had arrived. Meanwhile the search for Tucker Fleming was under way.

"I kept thinking that if I'd had a knife, I would have been able to cut the duct tape," Xavier said. "I told myself that you would have had one."

Cabot did not take his eyes off the smoldering ruins of the first compound.

"Fleming would have found a knife when he wrapped the tape around your ankles."

"Yeah. Probably."

"The lantern?"

"It was sitting on a table at the end of the couch," Xavier said. "I rolled across the floor until I could sit up and reach it. Probably wouldn't have done me any good but I couldn't see anything else that looked useful."

"Smart move," Cabot said.

Xavier gazed morosely through the windshield. "I fucked up, didn't I?"

"I should have kept an eye on you."

"It's not your fault. Not Mr. Salinas's fault, either. I fucked up."

"You found Tucker Fleming. That was good work."

Xavier brightened a little at that. "I followed his trail. Reversed the app he'd installed on Ms. Troy's phone."

402

"So, there was a tracking app on Virginia's phone?"

"Oh, yeah. He hid it in a subfolder so she never saw it. By enabling it he opened the door for me to track him."

"Nice job. But at Cutler, Sutter and Salinas we're a team. Going off on your own the way you did not only puts you in danger, it puts other people in harm's way as well. Next time keep your team members informed of your findings at every step."

"Yeah, sure," Xavier said. "A team. I get it." He paused. Cleared his throat. "Next time?"

"Forget I said that. There won't be a next time because when your mother finds out what happened, she'll make sure you're on the next plane back to San Francisco, even if she has to come to Seattle to put you on it."

Xavier groaned. "We don't have to tell her."

"Yes," Cabot said, "we do have to tell her. And what's more, we have to do it soon, before the cops get in touch with her. She's going to be mad as hell at me and she'll have every right."

"But it wasn't your fault Fleming grabbed me."

Cabot exhaled slowly. "Yes, it was my

fault. Forget that part. Let's get back to the case."

Xavier frowned in confusion. "The case?"

"We're working a murder and arson case," Cabot said. "Remember?"

"Oh, yeah." Xavier perked up again. He went so far as to straighten in his seat. "Right. The case."

"I heard what you told the detective a while ago. Before this is over he'll want both of us to go through it again in more detail. But right now I want you to tell me every single thing that happened from the time Fleming opened his door until you saw me arrive."

"Okay," Xavier said.

He started to talk.

Cabot listened. From time to time he asked questions but, for the most part, Xavier did a good job of recounting the ordeal. He had a keen eye for detail — much better than the vast majority of witnesses that Cabot had interviewed.

"What was your overall impression of Tucker Fleming?" he asked when Xavier reached the end of his tale.

Xavier thought for a moment. "Like I told the detective, he didn't talk much, but when he did, he sounded scary-crazy most of the time. I figured he might be on drugs."

"What, exactly, did Fleming say that made you believe he was on drugs?"

"It was like he heard voices or something."

"Voices?"

"You know, like those crazy people on the street who talk to themselves."

Cabot turned to meet Xavier's eyes. "Fleming talked to someone only he could hear?"

"Not exactly. He said something about getting messages from his dad on his phone. But if we're right, Fleming's father is that old cult guy, right?"

"Quinton Zane."

"Yeah. Him. But you told me that Zane is dead."

"Welcome to the wonderland of conspiracy theories, kid."

CHAPTER 57

Jessica was getting ready to close the gallery when Virginia and Cabot walked through the door.

"Welcome, strangers," Jessica said. "How goes the big case?"

"Things got interesting today," Virginia said. "You'll be hearing all about it on the evening news."

Jessica winced. "Bad?"

"Could have been worse," Cabot said. "But it wasn't, so I'm prepared to call it a good day. I've got a question for you."

Jessica tipped her head to one side. "About art or your investigation?"

"It's about the computer system you use here in the gallery." Cabot nodded toward the equipment on the front counter. "Had any trouble with it lately?"

"No, it's been working fine," Jessica said. "Funny you should ask, though."

Virginia got a cold feeling in the pit of her

stomach. "Why?"

"Someone from the customer service department of the company that sold us the software package called the other day with a new update to fix a potential bug. He said they were calling all of their customers to patch the software. It only took a few minutes. You remember we got that great deal when we bought the complete system? Turns out we get great tech support, too."

Cabot's jaw tightened. "Did you answer all his questions? Give him the info he needed to log in from a remote location?"

"Sure. He walked me through the whole process. There weren't any problems. We're clean."

Cabot looked at Virginia. "That answers that question."

Jessica's eyes widened. "What's going on here? What are you talking about? Did I do something wrong?"

Cabot turned back to her. "Do me a favor. If you get any more calls from a helpful tech support guy who wants to walk you through another software update, tell him you're busy and that you'll call him back when you're free. Then hang up and call me."

Jessica's eyes widened. "Oh, shit."

CHAPTER 58

Virginia poured some whiskey into one glass and some wine into another. She set both glasses on the coffee table and sat down beside Cabot, tucked one leg under her thigh and rested her left arm along the back of the sofa cushions.

"How bad was the conversation with Xavier's mother?" she asked.

"Bad." Cabot picked up the whiskey, took a healthy swallow and set the glass down. "At first she didn't believe me. She thought it was some sort of bizarre joke and that Xavier had put me up to it. When she realized I was telling her the truth — that Xavier had gotten tangled up in an ongoing investigation — she was shocked and then furious."

"Predictable. She's a mom, after all."

"Xavier got on the phone. He tried to calm her down but that only made things worse. She got back on the phone with me and made me promise that I would put Xavier on the first available flight tomorrow morning. I explained that the police would want to interview Xavier again. She said she was going to fly to Seattle herself to deal with the cops. I said that was fine by me. Then Xavier's father, Emerson Kennington, called."

"Your uncle?"

"Biologically speaking, yes. He yelled at me for a while. Said something about having his lawyer deal with me. I told him his son had helped identify a man wanted on murder charges. That just made him even madder. Then he yelled at Xavier."

"Is Emerson Kennington getting on the next flight to Seattle to see Xavier and make sure he's okay?"

"Yep. The happy family will be reunited sometime tomorrow in the offices of Cutler, Sutter and Salinas. Reality TV can't begin to compete with the Kenningtons when it comes to drama."

"Well, at least Xavier will realize that his dad does care about him, even if Emerson is divorcing Xavier's mother."

Cabot drank some more whiskey and lowered the glass. "It's the comment about the lawyer that I found interesting."

"Do you really think that Xavier's father

will try to sue you because Xavier got kidnapped? That seems pretty far-fetched."

"You know as well as I do that you can sue somebody over anything. That's not what I found curious."

"What, then?"

"Emerson mentioned the lawyer by name — Burleigh."

"Who is Burleigh — oh, wait. Is that the lawyer who is going to fly up here to have you sign some legal papers as soon as you're free?"

"The very same."

"So it looks like Xavier's father will probably try to make sure you don't get that twenty-five-thousand-dollar bequest."

Cabot shrugged. "Easy come, easy go."

"You don't care about the money, do you?"

"Got to admit it would have come in handy. But, no, I don't give a damn about the money. The bequest means that, in the end, the old man decided not to disown my mother."

"It means more than that," Virginia said. "It means that your grandfather acknowledged you as a full member of the Kennington family."

Cabot drank some more whiskey.

"Yeah," he said. "I guess it means that, too."

Virginia smiled. "Whether or not you want to be a member."

Cabot grimaced. "There is that part."

"But that's how it goes with families, isn't it? Sometimes you get a choice but most of the time you don't."

He looked at her. "And when you don't get a choice?"

"You deal with it." Virginia paused a beat. "Helps to have some family on your side, though."

"I've got plenty on my side," Cabot said. "Anson, Max and Jack."

"True. And now you've got Xavier, too."

Cabot thought about that. "The kid's okay. He kept his head today."

"I think he's decided who he wants to be when he grows up."

Cabot eyed her warily. "Who?"

"Got a hunch he's going to pattern himself after his long-lost cousin Cabot."

Cabot groaned. "His parents won't like that."

"No," Virginia said. "But that's only because at this point they don't know how lucky they are that Xavier is choosing you as a role model."

"I don't want to be anyone's role model."

Virginia swirled the wine in her glass. "You had one."

"Anson."

"Yep. Looks like it's your turn."

Cabot turned his head and fixed her with his intent gaze. "Something you should know."

"What?"

"By now the cops will have searched Fleming's house. They'll have tagged and bagged almost all of the Quinton Zane memorial crap that I found in the closet."

"Almost all?"

"I discovered Abigail Watkins's journal in a file cabinet in that closet."

Virginia took a breath. "You didn't tell the cops about it, did you?"

"No. They don't need it to build a case against Tucker Fleming. But we do need it."

"Because it might give us more background about Quinton Zane," Virginia said. "Judging by the photo we found in Rose Gilbert's nightstand, Abigail Watkins knew Zane at least a couple of years before he founded his cult."

"Which means she probably knew more about him than anyone else we know who is still alive. And we need all the information we can get."

"Where is the journal now?" Virginia asked.

"Anson stashed it in his safe-deposit box at his bank along with your mother's math book. We don't have time to study it now. Got to wrap things up with Tucker Fleming first. Still a lot of loose ends."

"Do you think that Abigail Watkins was Tucker Fleming's mother?"

"I think that's a very real possibility," Cabot said. He paused for a beat. "It fits with everything else that's happened, and the timing works. Fleming is twenty-four, according to the cops. That would mean that he was born a couple of years before Zane founded the cult."

"Abigail never mentioned having a child — which would make sense if Zane forced her to give the baby up for adoption."

"That would definitely explain a few things," Cabot agreed. "Still leaves us with the interesting question of just how Fleming discovered the truth about his biological father."

Virginia mulled that over for a moment. "Tell me again about how he thinks he's been getting messages from Quinton Zane."

"I told you everything I know. The one thing I'm sure of is that Zane was not sending messages to Tucker Fleming."

413

"Really? What makes you so certain?"

"He's too smart to risk exposing himself by sending messages about a missing inheritance to a son he's never even met."

"Don't be too sure. After all, if Tucker Fleming really is his son —"

"Fleming may actually be Zane's son," Cabot said. "But Zane is a card-carrying sociopath. He wouldn't give a damn about anyone else, including his own offspring."

"Unless he thought he could use Fleming as a stalking horse to find the money that our mothers hid all those years ago," Virginia said.

"I don't think so. Tucker Fleming is the working definition of a loose cannon. I don't think a cold-blooded strategist like Quinton Zane would have wanted to take the risk of trying to manipulate him in order to carry out such a delicate task. Fleming is just too unpredictable and impulsive."

"Maybe Zane assumed he had no choice and went with the best available option."

"Maybe, but it doesn't feel right. I need to keep looking."

"We," Virginia said.

"What?"

"*We* need to keep looking."

Cabot was silent for a few seconds. She knew he was going into his zone. She waited, willing him to understand.

After a moment he raised his hand and touched the side of her face. His eyes got a little hot.

"Yes," he said. "We need to keep looking."

"If you don't mind, I would like you to come to bed with me tonight," she said.

"Is this an experiment?"

"Yes."

"You don't have to do this, you know," he said.

"I want to sleep with you," she said.

She took his hand and led him down the hall to her bedroom.

CHAPTER 59

Tucker Fleming stood at the end of the private dock and watched the small boat cruise cautiously toward him. It was close to midnight. He was wearing a heavy jacket, but the cold wind coming off the night-darkened waters of Lake Washington was as sharp as a knife.

The vessel was running without lights, but the night was clear and the moon cast a swath of silver across the water. Tucker used a flashlight to give the person at the wheel the all clear.

Several hours had passed since the disaster at the Wallerton house, but he was still shaky, still edgy. The least little noise caused him to start violently. He could not believe that everything had gone so wrong. He had been the master of the game, but now he was on the run, his grand project in smoking ruins.

Looking back he realized things had

begun to come apart the night Hannah Brewster jumped to her death. That was the turning point. It had been one bad outcome after another. Today he'd been tracked by a teen with a phone and a low-rent private investigator.

For a time this afternoon he'd allowed himself to hope that Sutter and the kid had not made it out of the burning house. But it wasn't long before he realized he hadn't caught a lucky break. He'd ditched the car as soon as possible and used his fake ID to rent an anonymous Ford, just as he had when he'd made the trips to Lost Island. Seemed like a lifetime ago.

He'd considered heading for Canada — the border was less than three hours away and there were places he could cross without having to risk dealing with the authorities. In the end he'd pulled into the vast parking lot of a busy shopping mall where the Ford was just one more car in a sea of vehicles.

He'd gone into the mall, bought some coffee at a Starbucks and sat down at a table. He'd spent an hour trying to come up with a plan of action, some brilliant new move that would allow him to regain control of the game. But he could not seem to think clearly. Bizarre schemes — each more implausible than the last — danced erratically through his head.

At last he had forced himself to face the truth. He had only one viable option. Sending the emergency code was the last thing he wanted to do, but he had no choice. When you needed help, you turned to the only people you could really trust — family.

He had sent the emergency code.

The answer did not come immediately. The wait had been excruciating. He hadn't been able to catch his breath, and his pulse beat so fast he wondered if he might do something really crazy like faint right there in front of Nordstrom. That would have been the end. He would have awakened in an emergency room and there would have been a cop waiting to take him into custody.

Just when he had begun to wonder if Quinton Zane was going to turn his back on his son, the message came through. He had been given the address of a house on the shores of Lake Washington and told to wait on the private dock at a quarter to midnight. A boat would pick him up and take him to the one person who could help him — his father.

The house was located on a secluded stretch of waterfront property. There were no lights in the windows. A discreet For Sale sign had been planted in the front yard. Dad thought of everything.

This wasn't how he had wanted to meet Zane. He had wanted to show up with the money that the old man had lost all those years ago, wanted to prove that he had inherited Zane's ambition, talent and raw nerve. More than that, he had been determined to succeed where Zane had failed. That dream had gone up in the flames of the Wallerton house.

But it wasn't as if Zane had been any more successful, he reminded himself. Zane had allowed himself to be conned by a few members of his own organization — a bunch of women, no less. They would have gotten away with it, too, if they hadn't been betrayed. Zane had taken his revenge, but by then the money was long gone.

I'm as good as you ever were back in the day, Zane. Hell, I picked up the trail of the money that you lost, didn't I? It's still out there. Doesn't look like Virginia Troy and Sutter have found it yet. You and I might be able to get to it first if we work together. We'd make a hell of a team.

A father-and-son team.

He liked the sound of that. All he needed was a new identity and a fresh start. Working together, he and Zane would be unstoppable. They would set the whole damned world on fire.

The boat glided to a stop at the end of the dock. The pilot was a dark silhouette behind the wheel. Tucker clambered aboard. He had been instructed not to ask any questions. He was to get into the boat and keep silent until the craft reached its destination.

The boat took off, slowly at first, and then at speed. The chill of the wind got a thousand times worse. Not much longer now, he thought. He wondered which of the expensive houses on the lake belonged to Quinton Zane.

The boat eventually came to a halt at the end of another dock in a secluded cove. The pilot cut the engines.

"About time," Tucker said. "It's damn cold out here on the water."

The pilot emerged from the small wheelhouse. The moonlight glinted on the gun in his hand.

Only then did Tucker realize that he had made a terrible mistake.

"*No,*" he yelped.

He struggled frantically to scramble out of the boat and managed to get one foot on the dock.

The first shot caught him squarely in the back with such force that he was flung facedown on the wooden boards. He was vaguely aware of the pilot stepping up out of the boat.

His last conscious thought was that, like his father, he had been conned.

He never felt the second shot, the one to the head.

CHAPTER 60

Virginia awoke with a suddenness that told her something had changed in the atmosphere.

For a moment she lay still, trying to get oriented. There had been no nightmarish dream of fire, no fierce surge of urgency bordering on panic.

It took her a couple of seconds to realize that Cabot was not in the bed beside her. It came as a distinct shock to realize that after so many years of sleeping alone, she had already become accustomed to the comforting awareness of a lover sleeping next to her.

Not just any lover. Cabot.

She opened her eyes and saw him. He was at the window, looking out at the glowing night. His sleek, strong frame was silhouetted against the city lights.

I'm falling in love with him.

That brought on a deep sense of wonder.

So this is what it feels like.

Her first instinct, honed by years of failed relationships, was to use logic to dampen her sense of delight and astonishment. *Don't get carried away here. Okay, we have some old childhood history and in recent days we've been through a lot together. He understands me and accepts the bad stuff in ways that no one else ever has. And I understand him. I trust him. And, yes, indeed, there's a strong physical attraction. That doesn't necessarily add up to the real thing.*

Oh, yes, it does.

She pushed the covers aside and glanced at the clock. It came as no surprise to see that it was one thirty in the morning.

She got to her feet and went to join Cabot at the window. He put an arm around her shoulders and hugged her close against his lean, warm frame. She wrapped her arm around his waist.

"Thoughts?" she said.

"It's the money angle that's bothering me," he said.

"Why? Seems to me that it makes a crazy sort of sense that a whack-job like Tucker Fleming would have become obsessed with what he came to think of as his inheritance."

"It's not that," Cabot said. "The problem is the other money trail."

It took her a second to realize what he meant.

"Are you talking about the rumors of embezzlement at Night Watch?" she asked.

"What are the odds that we stumbled into two unrelated financial scams that somehow got tangled up in the same case?"

"I have no idea. But you said yourself, embezzlement goes on all the time. It's a fairly common crime."

"True, but it rarely turns violent. Most embezzlers prefer to keep a low profile. It's hard to conduct a profitable skimming operation when the cops are asking questions about a murder."

"Where are you going with this?"

"There's a connection between the embezzlement at Night Watch and the murder of Hannah Brewster."

"I'll bet Tucker Fleming is the embezzler," Virginia said. "He was working his scam at Night Watch before he found out about his connection to Zane. He decided to go after that money, too."

"I think you're right," Cabot said. "But that still leaves questions."

She turned and put both her arms around him.

"You're convinced there's someone else involved in this thing," she said.

"The person who posed as Quinton Zane and sent the messages to Fleming."

"Maybe Fleming really is delusional," she warned.

"Yes." Cabot framed her face with his hands. "But I think we'll know very soon if there is someone else involved in this business."

"When the cops pick up Fleming? That probably won't take long. As you said, he's a loose cannon, and loose cannons have a problem keeping a low profile. Once they arrest him we'll get all the answers."

"If I'm right, Fleming is not going to be around long enough to talk."

She went still. "Do you think he'll escape?"

"I think he'll try, but he'll be in a state of raw panic. I doubt if he had a solid backup plan. The only good news is that whoever tried to use him to find the money will be frantic, too."

"Why is that good news?"

"Because he or she will also start making mistakes."

CHAPTER 61

Cabot's phone rang just as he and Virginia were finishing breakfast. He glanced at the screen and got a rush of certainty mingled with anticipation.

"It's Anson," he said.

Virginia put down her fork and waited, watching him with somber eyes.

"What have you got?" he said into the phone.

"Just had a call from my best friend in the Seattle PD," Anson said. "Schwartz told me that a jogger discovered Tucker Fleming's body on a private dock on Lake Washington early this morning. The house is on the market. Owners are gone. It's a very secluded location. No one heard the shots."

"Shots? Plural?"

"One in the back and one in the head."

"Starting to see a pattern here."

"You bet, ace detectives that we are," Anson said.

"I did some thinking last night."

"Got a plan?"

"I'm going to talk to someone who knows all the players in this case, a person who might have had a lot to lose if Tucker Fleming had been captured alive and started talking."

"Who?" Anson demanded.

Cabot told him. Then he ended the connection and told Virginia what he intended to do.

"I'm coming with you," Virginia said.

"Not a good idea."

"If you're right, you're going to need me."

CHAPTER 62

Laurel Jenner was in a bathrobe when she opened the door. Virginia watched the expression on her face change from bewilderment to deep wariness.

"I know who you two are," Laurel said. "Josh warned me about you. What are you doing here?"

"Tucker Fleming is dead," Cabot said.

Laurel seemed genuinely startled. "Did the police shoot him? I heard he was wanted for arson, kidnapping and attempted murder. The evening news last night made it sound as if he was more than a little crazy."

"Fleming wasn't gunned down while resisting arrest," Cabot said. "But he was shot. They found his body on a dock in a cove not far from here."

"I don't understand." Laurel glanced uneasily at Virginia and then looked at Cabot. "Why did you two come here to give me the news? Tucker and I were just people who happened to work at the same company. We weren't close. What is this about?"

"Are you alone?" Cabot asked.

"Yes," Laurel said. She stiffened in alarm. "Why are you asking me that?"

"We just want to be sure you're safe," Virginia said, going into her soothe-the-temperamental-artist voice. "We were worried about you."

"You think I'm in danger?" Laurel gasped.

"Maybe," Virginia said, "but not in the way you think. To answer your questions, we're here because we think Fleming's murder is related to our investigation."

Laurel frowned. "Josh said you were looking into the death of an artist who exhibited in your gallery."

"Hannah Brewster," Virginia said.

"We came here to talk to you because I've got a hunch that the person who shot Fleming may have set you up to take the fall for his murder," Cabot said. "If I'm right, you're at risk of being arrested. Time is not on your side."

Laurel caught her breath.

"What are you talking about? You're crazy, both of you." She started to close the door. "Leave. Get away from me. I'm going to call the police."

Cabot stuck his foot in the door.

"Before you do that, answer one question," he said. "Do you still have that gun you bought when you were concerned that your ex-husband might stalk you?"

"How did you — ? Yes, I still have it and I swear I'll use it if you don't leave right now," Laurel said.

"Do me a favor," Cabot said. "Go see if it's still in your possession."

"What?"

"It's all right," Virginia said quickly. "We don't mean you any harm. We'll wait out here. We just want to be sure that your gun hasn't been stolen."

"I'd know if it had been stolen," Laurel said. "I've got a security system. Now get out of here. Leave me alone."

"Please," Virginia said. "Just make sure you still have it. If you find it, we'll apologize and leave. You have my word."

Laurel narrowed her eyes. "You really think my gun was used to kill Tucker?"

"Maybe," Cabot said. "Fleming was murdered sometime late last night. The body was found a short time ago. If your gun was stolen and used to kill Fleming, it will be missing — unless you had a late-night visitor?"

"No." Laurel shook her head. "I was alone all night."

"In that case the killer hasn't had an opportunity to return the gun so that it can be discovered in your house."

"You're both crazy," Laurel said. "I haven't even looked at that damn gun in months. It's still in the gun safe. Stay where you are. I'm going to close and lock the door. I'll open the safe. If the gun is missing, I'll let you know. If it's not, I'm going to call the police and tell them that you two are trespassing and threatening me."

Cabot politely removed his foot from the threshold. Laurel slammed the door closed. Virginia heard the bolt slide into place.

"This might not have been one of our better ideas," Virginia said. "What are we going to do if she finds the gun in the safe?"

"We'll think of something," Cabot said.

A short time later Virginia heard muffled footsteps in the hall. Laurel unlocked the door and looked at them, stricken.

"It's gone," she croaked. "That bitch stole it."

"Who are you talking about?" Virginia said.

"Kate Delbridge." Laurel shook her head, torn between rage and something that bordered on panic. "She's the one who told you I owned a gun, isn't she? I knew she hated me. She was jealous. But I never

431

thought she'd go this far. She set me up for murder just to get revenge? She must be crazy."

"What makes you so sure Kate Delbridge took your gun?" Cabot asked.

"It had to be her. She was one of the few people who knew I bought the damned thing. That was before —"

"Before you and Josh Preston got involved in an affair?" Virginia finished quietly. "When you and Kate Delbridge were still friends?"

"Kate is convinced that I stole Josh away from her. But that's not how it was. She was just a weekend fling. He got bored with her." Laurel grimaced. "Just as he's getting bored with me. That's his pattern. I can see that now. I just don't understand why Kate would murder Tucker Fleming."

"I don't think she did murder him," Cabot said. "One more question. Ever hear of Quinton Zane or the cult he founded a couple of decades ago?"

"Oh, shit." Laurel shuddered and wrapped her arms tightly around herself. "I was afraid this had something to do with that old cult."

CHAPTER 63

On a clear day the big house on Mercer Island would have had a stunning view of the Seattle skyline. But fog cloaked the scene in a featureless gray mist.

Cabot knocked on the front door. There was no answer. He hadn't expected one.

He went around the side of the house, through the professionally tended gardens and down the sloping lawn to the private dock.

A sleek boat bobbed at the end of the wooden dock. Josh Preston, dressed in a dark windbreaker, was in the back of the boat. He was concentrating so intently on wiping down the wooden railing that he did not notice his visitor until Cabot stepped onto the dock.

"Doing a little cleanup work, Preston?" Cabot asked. "Blood spatter is always a problem. The stuff flies everywhere."

Josh straightened abruptly, gripping the

wet rag in one hand. "Sutter. What the hell are you doing here?"

Cabot came to a halt at the far end of the dock. "I thought we should have a little chat."

"If this is about your investigation, forget it. I answered your questions. I don't have anything else to say. As you can see, I'm a little busy at the moment."

"You're wasting your time. No matter how much you scrub down that boat, you'll miss some traces of Tucker Fleming's blood. The forensics people are really good. All they need is a trace amount and they'll be able to nail you for the murder."

Josh watched him, unmoving. "I have no idea what you're talking about. Get off my property before I call the cops."

"I don't think you're going to call them, at least not until you get the boat cleaned up. But I used to be a cop and I can promise you that you'll never get all the blood. My advice is to sink the boat. That's your only chance of getting rid of the evidence."

"You're not making any sense. What's all this talk about Fleming's blood? Are you telling me he's dead?"

"Yep, and by the way, you waited a beat too long before you asked that question. You might want to be a little faster off the mark when the police come around asking about the death of yet another Night Watch employee. And, sooner or later, they will come around."

"If the police thought I killed Fleming, they would be here by now. Instead, I find myself talking to you. Why is that?"

"You know why. I'm here to talk business. I know you murdered Fleming and planned to pin the blame on Laurel Jenner. Maybe, under other circumstances, you would have let Kate Delbridge take the fall. But she left town, so you were forced to use Laurel."

"That's pure bullshit. You can't prove any of it."

"Maybe not all of it, but I don't have to do that. All I need to do is give the cops a reason to suspect that you were the killer. See, I know how cops think. They like the basics — motive, opportunity and the weapon, preferably with fingerprints and gunshot residue."

"You don't have any of those things, but I'd be interested to hear exactly what you think you've got."

"Sure. Let's start with motive. Your company is in trouble. You burned through the first round of venture capital months ago and you need more. But a while back you realized that someone on your staff was embezzling from you. You couldn't go out for more cash until you stopped the bleed. But you were desperate to keep the financial situation as quiet as possible. The rumors of embezzlement would have ruined your chances of attracting new money. You didn't dare hire an outside cybersecurity firm. Too much chance of a leak to the financial press. So you set out to find the embezzler yourself. After all, you used to be one of the hotshot wonder boys of the tech world."

"For your information, I'm still damn good."

"I don't doubt it," Cabot said. "You conducted a secret investigation of your own employees. In the course of prowling through their online lives, you didn't find the embezzler, but you did discover that Tucker Fleming was on the trail of what might be a fortune — the money that went missing when Quinton Zane's cult was destroyed. You found out that Fleming believed he was Zane's biological son."

"Sounds like Fleming was mentally unbalanced."

"The fact that Fleming was obsessed with Zane and Zane's cult made it easy to manipulate him, didn't it? You sent him a series of well-disguised messages. You made him think that his father was communicating with him. Fleming desperately wanted to believe that he really was chatting with his father. You thought you could just sit back and let Fleming run, maybe lead you to the missing money."

"You're sounding as mentally unbalanced as Fleming."

"You figured you'd let Fleming take all the risks. You planned to wait until he found the money. At that point you would have moved in and grabbed the cash. Of course, you would have had to get rid of Fleming in the process, but that wouldn't have been complicated."

Josh grunted in disgust. "You really are crazy."

"Unfortunately for you, things started going wrong. That's the problem with trying to control an obsessed individual like Fleming. He was erratic and unpredictable, and ultimately he screwed up everything. After he burned down that house outside of Wallerton and tried to murder a young man in the process, you knew you had to end the game. The cops were looking for him. If they found him, there was a very real risk they might find you."

"You can't prove any of this."

Cabot ignored him. "You murdered Fleming sometime late last night or early this morning. But you made a few mistakes. Probably because you were in a hurry. One of your mistakes was using Laurel Jenner's gun. I'm sure you planned to return it to her gun safe sometime today. After that you intended to call in an anonymous tip to the cops."

"I'm going to be charitable and go with the theory that you're delusional. You're just not making any sense."

"How about we talk business now? Will that sound more sensible?"

"What business could I possibly have with you?"

"Back at the start of this thing, I had the same goal as you," Cabot said. "I thought Virginia Troy would lead me to the money her mother tucked away all those years ago. But things didn't work out as I planned. You were right. It was all a fantasy."

"You're saying the money is gone?"

"As far as I can tell, Kimberly Troy, with the help of some friends, did manage to conceal a fortune in an offshore account. But someone got to it — probably years ago."

"It's gone?" Josh went still. "Who found it?"

"I have no idea. Maybe one of Quinton

438

Zane's followers. Hell, maybe Zane himself."

"Quinton Zane is dead."

"So they say. But you know how it is with
those Internet rumors. Can't believe any of
them. The bottom line here is that the
money disappeared. That brings me to you."

"Yeah? How the fuck did that happen?"

"You were the person who was sending
messages to Fleming, pretending to be his
father."

"Bullshit."

"I know you did a lot of research into the
history of Zane's cult in order to sound
authentic."

Josh's eyes burned with a cold fury. "How
do you know that?"

"One of the first things you learn in my
business is that lovers always know more
about each other than even they realize."

"Are you talking about Laurel Jenner?"

"She didn't take kindly to having her gun
stolen and used in a crime, by the way,"
Cabot said. "Turns out she caught you
searching online for information about
Zane's cult a few times. But let's get back
to our business arrangement."

"What business arrangement?"

"Here's my offer. I'll keep quiet about the
game you were playing with Tucker Flem-

ing. Hell, I'll even throw in a freebie — he was the guy who was embezzling from you, so now that he's dead, Night Watch will stop bleeding cash. In exchange, I want fifty percent of whatever you get when you go out for your next round of funding for Night Watch."

"Do you really believe you can blackmail me?" Josh asked very softly.

"I prefer to think of it as a business arrangement."

"You are just a dumb PI who is playing way out of his league, Sutter. There's no way you can prove that I spoofed Fleming, let alone that I killed him."

"Now, see, that's where you're wrong. I admit I'm not a red-hot cybersecurity investigator, but I've got this intern — a young wonder boy, just like you used to be. He said to tell you that you obviously haven't gotten on the Darknet lately to read up on the last couple of software and firmware updates for your phone. Apparently there were some issues that were not fixed. I won't pretend I understood all the details. All I know is that he was able to get me what I needed on you. Has your phone been a little slow lately?"

"You're bluffing."

"Believe whatever you want to believe. I'll

give you a little time to think about it. But don't take too long. There's not a chance in hell that you can sneak the gun back into Laurel's house. She's already talking to the cops. Probably giving them a list of people who might have known the code on her gun safe. It will be a very short list, won't it? You'll be right at the top."

Preston's face contorted with the full force of his fury.

"You are causing me way too much trouble," he said. "I'm done with you."

He reached down under a seat. When he straightened, he had a pistol in his hand.

But Cabot had already grabbed the boat hook. He swung it in a sweeping arc as Preston tried to take aim.

The boat hook slammed into Preston's shoulder just as he squeezed off a shot. The gun roared, the sound echoing in the fog.

Preston had been going for a chest shot, but the impact of the boat hook knocked him off balance, ruining his aim. The bullet caught Cabot in his left arm. The jolt sent him reeling.

So much for the Kevlar vest Schwartz loaned me, he thought. *No such thing as a perfect plan.*

Preston was bringing the gun up again, going for another shot. With his left arm

441

out of commission, Cabot knew he would not have the leverage and power he needed to take another swipe with the boat hook.

He rolled to his feet, seized a heavy coil of rope with his right hand and hurled it at Preston.

Preston managed to dodge the uncoiling rope, but in the process he lost his balance and went down on one knee. The boat rocked violently.

Cabot launched himself into the craft before Preston could recover. His weight and the sudden impact caused the small vessel to bounce and shudder in the water. He went down, taking Preston with him.

"Freeze," someone yelled.

Preston tried to toss the gun over the side, but Cabot was sprawled on top of him, using his good arm to pin Preston's gun hand to the bottom of the boat.

Two uniformed officers appeared at the end of the dock. They looked down into the boat, guns drawn.

"Drop the gun," one of them barked.

"Fuck," Preston hissed.

But he released his grip on the gun. One of the officers got into the boat to collect the weapon.

"Careful with the gun," Cabot said. "It's stolen. Pretty sure it's the same gun that was used to kill Tucker Fleming."

Anson jogged across the lawn. He was accompanied by a young man in plain clothes who had a gun in one hand and a badge in the other.

Schwartz eyed the growing stain on Cabot's windbreaker. "So much for the vest."

"Yeah," Cabot said. He was suddenly aware of the ice and fire in his upper left arm. "The same thought occurred to me."

"The medics are on the way," Schwartz said.

The officers got cuffs on Preston and hauled him up onto the dock.

Anson helped Cabot out of the boat.

"Sit down," Anson ordered.

He started to remove the jacket. Cabot groaned.

"Take it easy," he said. "That hurts."

"I'll bet," Anson said.

He got the jacket off and clamped a hand around the bleeding wound.

"Virginia isn't going to like this," Anson said. "I seem to recall you assuring her that your big plan to confront Preston was perfectly safe because you would be wearing a vest."

"Tell me the truth, Anson. Do you think this little incident is going to hurt my image as a hotshot private eye?"

"Doesn't do it any good," Anson said. "Lucky for you, Virginia has noticed that you have other qualities."

Cabot realized he was greatly cheered by that thought. "You're right. Lucky me. Still, she isn't going to like this."

"No," Anson said. "She won't."

Chapter 64

"You conned Josh Preston, didn't you?" Virginia said. "You made him believe that Xavier had hacked into his phone and found proof that Preston was sending the messages to Tucker Fleming."

They were sitting in her living room. Anson was at the window. Cabot, his left arm in a bandage and a sling, was sprawled on the sofa. Virginia thought he looked exhausted, but she knew he was in no mood to sleep — not yet, at any rate. She was feeding him a steady diet of hot soup and herbal tea, but she could feel the vibes generated by hand-to-hand combat coming off him in waves.

She was still in the process of reentry herself. She had arrived at the emergency room before they'd had a chance to dispose of Cabot's blood-stained clothes. It was a sight she knew she would revisit in her dreams from time to time.

"Preston thought he was the smartest guy in the room, but he was rattled because he had recently killed a man and had been discovered in the act of trying to destroy the evidence," Cabot said. "Under those circumstances, it wasn't hard to make him believe that someone had hacked into his phone."

Anson turned away from the window. "The trick to running a con is to tell a good story, one that plays to the hopes or fears of the person you're targeting. It has to be a story with just enough truth in it to make it feel real."

"Sounds like an art form," Virginia said.

Anson looked at Cabot. "Never thought about it like that, but, yeah, just another kind of art."

Chapter 65

The following morning, Reed Stephens cranked back in his desk chair, propped his elbows on the armrests and put his fingertips together. "Young Xavier is right," he said. "Someone or maybe several people in the Kennington family are trying to screw you."

Cabot stopped prowling the office and turned to examine the view out the window. Stephens specialized in business law. His firm was not affiliated with any of the big national outfits. Instead, he catered to small local companies and start-ups.

"Anson and Xavier both warned me there was probably a catch," Cabot said.

"This document you're being asked to sign is full of legal fog, but there was enough here to make me suspicious." Reed continued. "I talked to some people I know in San Francisco. Evidently your grandfather was what folks like to call a colorful figure in the business world. The result is that there is a lot of squabbling going on among the ex-wives and various offspring. That means there are also a lot of rumors and leaks about the terms of the estate. From what I can determine, you are entitled to your mother's share of the company. The document you brought to me is an attempt to get you to sign away your rights to your inheritance."

Cabot swung around, blindsided. "I was told that my grandfather disowned his daughter after she married my father."

"Evidently he changed his mind at the end." Reed sat forward and tapped the document. "It's complicated and, I will say, rather cleverly done. The bottom line, however, is that if you sign this document and take the twenty-five thousand, you'll be giving up a major interest in the Kennington business empire, which is worth a hell of a lot more than twenty-five grand. Potentially you'll be walking away from millions."

"What happens to my mother's share of the company if I sign that document?"

"It will go to Xavier's father — your uncle, Emerson Kennington."

"Who is about to move on to Wife Number Three."

"Emerson Kennington has a son and a

daughter by his first marriage; and another son, Xavier, and a daughter, Anna, by his second marriage. The next Mrs. Kennington has no doubt been working behind the scenes to ensure that she and her future offspring secure a chunk of the company just in case she, too, gets dumped."

"What about Xavier's mother?"

"My contacts in San Francisco say it's no secret down there that by the terms of the prenup she gets a nice condo, which she can live in as long as she can afford to pay the taxes and homeowner's fees. Under the circumstances, that seems unlikely. She'll make some money when she sells the condo, of course, but that's it."

"What about Xavier and his sister?"

"Hard to say. I'm sure that Kennington will be on the hook for his offspring's college expenses, but aside from that there are no guarantees. I suspect young Xavier's inheritance depends on how much influence the next Mrs. Kennington exerts over her husband. The fact that she is rumored to have avoided signing a prenup would seem to indicate that she's got a talent for strategy. Whatever happens, she will do very nicely."

"What are my options?"

"You've got two. You can accept your mother's stake in Kennington International or ditch your claim to a share of the company in exchange for twenty-five thousand dollars."

Cabot considered that briefly. "Maybe there's a third option."

"I'm listening."

CHAPTER 66

"I don't understand," John Burleigh said. He seemed deeply offended and a little bewildered. "Why did you insist that Xavier and his parents be present for this meeting? They are not involved in this matter. And there was no need for all of these strangers, either. This was supposed to be a private business meeting between you and me."

Cabot looked around at the crowd that had gathered in the reception area of Cutler, Sutter & Salinas. Virginia lounged against the edge of Anson's desk, her arms folded. Anson was in his chair behind the desk.

Xavier's mother, Melissa, was perched tensely on one of the two client chairs. Everyone else, including Burleigh, Reed Stephens, Xavier, Emerson Kennington and Cabot, was standing.

"To be clear," Cabot said, "Virginia, Anson and my lawyer, Mr. Stephens, are present because I wanted lots of witnesses.

As for Xavier and his parents, they're involved in this thing, so I figured they should be present."

"I thought you agreed to sign the documents that I sent to you," Burleigh said firmly.

"No, I agreed to take a look at them," Cabot said. "And naturally I showed them to my lawyer."

Reed Stephens cleared his throat politely. "That would be me."

"I see." Burleigh's jaw hardened. But he opened his briefcase and took out a folder. "We might as well get on with this meeting. I have four copies of the agreement for you to sign, Mr. Sutter. Two of the parties present can serve as witnesses. I have a cashier's check for the agreed-upon amount already made out."

He held up the check.

"That's a very nice visual aid," Cabot said. "But there was no agreed-upon amount. You made an offer. After due consideration I have decided not to accept it."

Xavier grunted in approval. "I told you they were going to try to screw you."

"Yes, you did mention that," Cabot said. "And my lawyer confirmed it."

Emerson Kennington gave Cabot a baleful glare. "What kind of game are you trying to play, Sutter? Whatever it is, I guarantee I'll fight you every step of the way."

Reed looked at him. "I have been assured that the terms of the late Mr. Kennington's estate are quite clear. My client, Cabot Sutter, is to inherit his mother's share of Kennington International."

"We have made a serious offer to buy out Cabot Sutter's shares of the business," Burleigh said smoothly. "There is, of course, room for negotiation. What number did you have in mind, Mr. Sutter?"

"I'm not much into negotiation," Cabot said. "But I am willing to do a deal."

"Name your price," Burleigh said evenly.

"I've asked Mr. Stephens to draw up a document that transfers half of my shares of the business to Xavier, his sister and my other cousins. Those shares will be divided equally among them. Naturally, Melissa Kennington will hold Xavier's and his sister's shares in trust and administer them until the kids turn twenty-one. I intend to sign the document in front of all of you today." He smiled at Burleigh. "Plenty of witnesses that way."

With the exceptions of Virginia, Anson and Reed, the news was met with stunned expressions.

Emerson Kennington recovered first.

"You can't do this," he sputtered. "All of those shares should have come to me in the first place. My father never intended for Jacqueline to inherit. He cut her out of the will the day she ran off with your father."

"And later, at some point, he put Cabot into the will," Reed said. "What's more, he did it in the form of a trust that is very well constructed. You can fight us if you want, but I'm sure Mr. Burleigh will tell you the simple truth — wills are broken all the time, but it's virtually impossible to dismantle a solidly protected trust."

"You don't have to do this," Melissa Kennington said to Cabot. She shook her head and locked her fingers together. "In fact, you *shouldn't* do it. Your mother would have wanted you to inherit all of her shares of Kennington International."

"Mom's right," Xavier said. He shot to his feet. "You shouldn't give me and the others any of your shares. That's not fair."

"Turns out," Cabot said, "that my mother was part of a small group of women who left me and the other surviving children of Zane's operation a very handsome inheritance. Evidently, Mom got the Kennington family talent for handling money. If she were alive, she would probably be running Kennington International today. Trust me

454

when I tell you that I won't starve."

They hadn't found a huge fortune in the offshore account, not by Kennington family standards, and it was going to be divided eight ways among the adult children of the cult, but that still meant a nice round number with a lot of zeros after it for all of them.

"We need to discuss this in more detail," Burleigh said quickly. "There are extenuating circumstances here. As I'm sure you're aware, Emerson Kennington and Melissa Kennington are currently in the process of dissolving their marriage. The situation is complicated."

"Yeah, I heard about the divorce," Cabot said. "That kind of thing can get messy. But fortunately for all of us, there is nothing complicated about the document that my lawyer has ready for me to sign."

"Let's talk about this," Emerson Kennington said.

"What's to talk about? I have every right to make a financial gift to my cousins. This way if your next wife takes you to the cleaners, as everyone seems to think will be the case, you won't have to worry about Xavier and your other kids. They'll be protected. Consider this a win-win."

"I have every intention of taking care of

my own children, damn it." Emerson shot a quick look at Xavier. "I've made that clear to Melissa and her lawyer."

"I'm sure you have the best of intentions," Cabot said. "But evidently you weren't willing to put those intentions in writing."

"That is a matter to be settled by Melissa and me."

"There's plenty of stuff for you and Melissa to work out," Cabot said. "But this way there won't be any question of Xavier and his siblings receiving a share of the company."

Reed opened his own briefcase, took out a folder and handed it to Cabot. "You're sure you want to do this?"

"Absolutely certain," Cabot said. He looked at Xavier and winked. "Never let it be said that I can't do family drama as well as the rest of the Kenningtons."

Xavier grimaced. "Guess I've been a real pain in the ass for you."

"It's okay," Cabot said. "You're family."

CHAPTER 67

Three days before the show, Virginia and Jessica stood in the back room, making final decisions about which objects and paintings to display.

"For the last time, I am not going to put the glass paperweights in the show," Virginia said. "I agree they work wonders when it comes to drawing customers in off the street, but this is a very serious show for very serious collectors. If we treat the paperweights as serious art, the serious collectors will be deer in the headlights."

"Maybe they'll think it's a charmingly original concept," Jessica said. "You know — a way to soften the elitism of the art world."

"Don't kid yourself. Serious collectors love the elitism of the art world. They thrive on it."

Jessica gave a little snort. "Maybe we should print up name tags with the words

'You're Special' on them for each guest."

Virginia smiled. "It's a thought." She crossed her arms and walked around the room, taking one last look at the objects and paintings she had selected. She stopped in front of a glass bowl.

"I'll tell you what," she said. "No paperweights, but I'll add the Billings glass. Will that make you happy?"

Jessica brightened. "I love that piece. In the right light it looks like molten gold."

"Light makes art glass come alive," Virginia said. She glanced at her new phone. "It's after five. Time for you to go home."

Jessica collected her jacket and handbag and headed for the front door. "We've got some wonderful pieces. Can't wait for our clients to see them. They will be absolutely wowed."

"I hope so. See you in the morning."

Jessica paused at the door. "How is Cabot doing?"

"He's fine, thanks," Virginia said. "His wound is healing nicely. Right now he and Anson are tidying up some loose ends in the case."

She didn't see any reason to mention that Cabot and Anson were starting work on Abigail Watkins's journal. Jessica knew a lot about recent events, but she wasn't a mem-

458

ber of what Anson referred to as the Zane Conspiracy Club. *Family secrets,* Virginia thought.

Jessica let herself outside and disappeared into the rainy afternoon. Virginia waited until the door closed. Then she began another walk-through, trying to see the objects and paintings she had selected through the eyes of serious collectors and art critics.

When she was satisfied that she had made the right choices, she went to where her jacket hung on a wall hook. It was time to go home. She and Cabot were planning to meet Anson for dinner. She was eager to hear what the two men had learned from Abigail Watkins's diary.

She looked at the door of the large storage room that contained Hannah's paintings. She toyed with the notion of putting a picture from the *Visions* series on display with an NFS — Not for Sale — tag on it.

You did all you could to protect me, Hannah. It's not your fault that the past would not stay buried. You gave me a warning that probably saved my life.

If not for the photograph of Hannah's last painting, she would never have understood that she was in danger, Virginia thought. She would not have gone looking for Anson

Salinas. She would not have found Cabot.

I might never have known the joy of falling in love.

Yes, she decided. She would hang one picture from the *Visions* series in a tribute to a brave, emotionally wounded artist who had jumped to her death in a desperate effort to keep a promise to a friend who had died twenty-two years ago.

She put down her jacket and handbag, got the key from the desk and opened the door of the storage closet. Mentally she braced herself as she always did when she entered the small antechamber of her own private hell and flipped the wall switch.

She walked down the aisle formed by the paintings and pulled off the tarps that covered each of them one by one.

The fiery paintings of the *Visions* series flared to life around her. The only one that was missing was Hannah's final picture, the one that had been destroyed when she had burned down her cabin. Virginia made a note to have the photograph printed, mounted and framed. It would finish the series.

She stopped at the far end of the closet, where the two covered paintings of Abigail Watkins rested against the wall. Each was clearly marked: *Not for Sale. Client may call.*

So many questions about the past had been answered in the last few days, she thought, but one remained. *Why two paintings of Abigail Watkins, Hannah? You said Abigail asked you to paint them, and then you told me to keep them in case someone came looking for them.*

But no one had come looking.

A shiver of knowing swept through Virginia. Had Abigail, at the end of her life, entertained a fantasy that Quinton Zane might someday come looking for her? But that explanation didn't feel right. Like Hannah, Abigail had been terrified of Zane.

What did feel right was another kind of fantasy — the dream of a mother who had been forced to give up her baby at birth.

"You hoped that Tucker might someday come looking for you, didn't you, Abigail?"

But that had not happened, either. Instead, Tucker had become obsessed with the father he had never known. It was just as well that Abigail had died with her fantasy. It would have broken her heart if she had learned the truth — that her son had been a deranged killer.

Except . . .

Why two paintings?

An ice-cold flicker of anxiety whispered through her. For a few frantic seconds she tried to reason with herself. *Don't let your imagination take control.*

But the conclusion was inescapable. If the two paintings had not been done for an old lover who had betrayed her, or a long-lost son, there was another possible explanation.

There was only one way to be certain. She started back out of the storage closet, intending to get to the phone in her handbag.

But the alley door opened abruptly, bringing with it a draft of cold, damp air and Jessica, who stared at Virginia with stricken eyes.

Startled, Virginia stopped in the middle of the back room.

"Jessica? What's wrong?"

"I'm s-sorry," Jessica whispered.

She stumbled forward a few steps. Not under her own free will, Virginia realized. Jessica had been pushed into the room.

Kate Delbridge came through the doorway. She was using both hands to grip a gun.

"Don't move, either of you," Kate said. She kicked the alley door closed.

She kept the barrel of the gun aimed at Jessica's head, but she was wholly focused on Virginia.

"Everything went wrong because of you,"

Kate said. "*Every damn thing.* But now you're going to pay."

CHAPTER 68

"Killing me won't bring back your brother," Virginia said. "Besides, I'm not the one who shot him. Josh Preston is responsible for Tucker's death. Or haven't you been paying attention to the news?"

Kate stilled. "You know?"

"That you and Tucker were fraternal twins? It occurred to me that there may have been two babies who were given up for adoption."

"No one ever guessed," Kate said. "Fraternal twins don't look any more alike than other kinds of siblings. Tucker got the bastard's looks. I got the brains."

Virginia's phone rang, the sound muffled because it was in her handbag.

"Ignore it," Kate said through clenched teeth. "And just to be clear, Tucker and I were not *given up* for adoption. Rose Gilbert *sold* us in an off-the-books transaction. What's more, she did the deal with two different couples. Tucker and I didn't even know about each other until a couple of years ago."

"How did you and Tucker find each other?"

"Shortly before she died, the woman who had raised Tucker told him the truth. She said there had been two babies offered for sale but she could only afford one. She had enough information to send Tucker in the right direction. He came looking for me after he learned the truth."

"He wanted to know his sister."

"No, he was just curious to see if I might be interested in going into business together. Figured he could trust family. He was already running low-level online cons. He taught me the tricks. We made a good team. Night Watch was going to be our big score."

"You and Tucker were the ones doing the embezzling, weren't you?"

"We took a lot of money out of that company and were getting ready to shut down the operation and move on. Josh Preston was getting too close."

"Was he the person who tried to run you down with a car the night you met with Cabot and me?"

"No, that was Tucker, and he wasn't aiming at me," Kate said.

"He tried to murder Cabot. Make it look like a hit-and-run accident."

"I told Tucker it was a risky idea, but he was right: if it had worked, it would have been an easy fix for at least one of our problems, so I agreed to go along with it. But Tucker screwed up, as usual. When I realized it had all gone wrong, I tried to point you at Laurel."

"When did Rose Gilbert come back into your lives?"

"In December she contacted Tucker out of the blue and told him the truth about our parents," Kate said. "Turns out dear Aunt Rose had kept track of us just in case we might prove useful someday."

"She waited until your mother was dead before she got in touch?"

"She had no reason to contact us before Abigail Watkins died. She didn't need us. But she knew that she was Watkins's only legal heir, because, thanks to her, there was no record of Abigail having given birth or of the adoptions. Rose had no intention of becoming an innkeeper, but she rushed to Lost Island to take charge of the B and B because she figured she could make some money if she sold the place."

"She found the diary," Virginia said.

"That journal changed everything. Rose

contacted us because she concluded that she needed help finding the missing money. Tucker and I agreed to get involved because it looked like there was a fortune out there somewhere and it belonged to us."

"All you had to do was find it. But that's where things got complicated, isn't it?"

"We realized that Hannah Brewster knew what the key was and where it was hidden, but she was crazy. Rose was the one who came up with the idea of using Tucker to convince Brewster that Quinton Zane was still alive. Turns out Tucker looked a lot like the bastard back in the day. Brewster was panic-stricken when she saw him. She really did believe that Zane had come back from the dead. Rose and Tucker were sure they could control her, but they fucked up."

"They went too far, didn't they? Hannah jumped to her death rather than risk falling under Zane's control."

"I'm the one who realized that you were our only hope of finding the missing money," Kate said. The gun shook a little in her hands. "According to the diary, your mother gave the key to you. But Abigail Watkins didn't describe the key in her journal. We had no idea what we were looking for. And you, you stupid woman, didn't even know you had it."

"Hannah never told me the truth because she thought it would put me in danger."

"Tucker made Rose give him the diary," Kate said. "He went a little crazy then. He became obsessed with everything and anything that linked to Quinton Zane. He wanted to find the lost money to prove that he was as brilliant as Zane."

"Josh Preston discovered that obsession and pretended to be Zane."

"Tucker was always a little unstable, but believing that dear old Dad was alive and communicating with him pushed my brother right over the edge," Kate said. "Still, he was smart when it came to the tech stuff. He even managed to get into your account through your computer, and your computer is connected to your phone through the cloud. He didn't just install a tracking app. He was able to see some of your messages and your e-mail."

"Which one of you took the shots at Cabot that day when he and I went to the house?"

"That was me. I'm the one who realized that Sutter was going to be a huge problem. Tucker took Sandra Porter's gun the night I killed her, but he never bothered to learn how to use it."

"He liked fire, though, didn't he?"

"Oh, yeah. He was a real pyro."

"You're the one who shot Sandra Porter."

"I knew she was stalking Tucker, so I followed her that night. When I saw her go into your gallery, I knew we had to get rid of her. She had discovered the embezzlement, you see. She actually had the nerve to try to blackmail Tucker. He really freaked out after I got rid of her."

"You shot Rose Gilbert, too."

Kate snorted softly. "We had the diary. We didn't need her. Why split the money three ways? When you made the ferry reservation online, we realized you and Sutter were headed to Lost Island. Tucker and I decided that we had to get rid of both of you. It was obvious you didn't know any more than we did. We decided we might have a better chance of finding the money if both of you were out of the picture. I was raised on the water. I know how to handle a boat. We used one to get to Lost Island that morning, hours before the ferry was due to arrive. We took care of Rose. Tucker wired the house and then we waited for you and Sutter to show up. We figured the locals would just write it off as a drug gang hit."

"But things went wrong. Again."

"Nothing worked out," Kate said, her voice rising. "Everything went wrong because of you and that damned Cabot Sutter. But this is where it ends."

"You're risking everything now for revenge?"

"It's all that's left," Kate said.

"You're going to kill me and then disappear, is that it?"

Kate's mouth curved in a humorless smile. "I'm willing to negotiate. Give me the key to my inheritance and I'll think about letting you and your very helpful clerk live."

"Now why would you do that?"

"Because I don't need to kill you. I'm very good at disappearing, you see. I've had lots of practice. In fact, I'd just as soon not get rid of you. Dead bodies are always a problem. Give me the key to the money and we'll call it a day."

This was probably not the time to tell Kate that she was a lousy liar, Virginia thought.

"I'll do better than that," she said. "I'll let your mother give you the key to the money."

Kate stared at her, her jaw unhinged in shock. After a second or two she managed to pull herself together.

"What are you talking about?" she hissed.

"This afternoon it finally dawned on me that your mother had the key all along. It's in the portraits that Hannah Brewster painted. I was going to take a closer look at them when you showed up with Jessica."

"What portraits?"

"There are two of them. I wondered about that from time to time. Why did Hannah paint two very similar portraits of her good friend? But now I understand. There was one for you and one for Tucker. Each contains a portion of the information needed to find the missing money. I suppose poor Abigail wanted to leave something to the children she had never known. The only thing of value that she knew about was the missing cult money."

"You're lying. Why would she commission portraits for us, let alone leave us the money? She never wanted us. She told Rose Gilbert to get rid of us. She let Gilbert sell us."

"I think Quinton Zane made Abigail give you up for adoption. She did it because she was totally under his control. Rose no doubt promised her that you would both go to a loving home. I'm certain that Abigail never knew that Rose sold you."

"Bullshit."

Virginia thought about Anson's advice on running a con. Come up with a good story, one with just enough truth in it to make it sound real.

"I think that, deep down, Abigail always hoped that someday her children would come looking for her," she said. "When she was diagnosed with cancer, she commissioned the portraits so that if you and Tucker ever showed up asking questions, you would have something of her — a portrait and the key to the money."

"That's a touching story but I don't believe it. If you knew about the key, you would have used it to get hold of the money."

Virginia shook her head. "I told you, I only realized the truth tonight when I took another look at the portraits."

"You're lying," Kate said.

But she wanted to believe. It was there in her eyes. *Time to close the sale,* Virginia thought.

"See for yourself," she said. She motioned toward the open door of the storage closet. "The two portraits of Abigail Watkins are in there at the very back. Your mother embroidered your real names on a wall hanging and also the name of an offshore bank. There's a string of numbers on each portrait. I think they go together to form the key to a numbered account. The money has been sitting there all these years waiting for someone to claim it."

"I don't believe you." Kate moved the gun in a jerky fashion. "Get the portrait that you say has my name on it."

"All right, but it's big and heavy. I'm going to need Jessica's help to drag it out here."

Kate hesitated and then she gave Jessica a shove.

"Go on," Kate ordered. "Get the picture. Try any tricks and I'll shoot both of you. I can be blocks away before anyone comes to investigate."

Jessica steeled herself and fixed her attention on Virginia. "How do you want to do this?"

"There's not a lot of room in there," Virginia said. "I'll go first. You follow me. We can get the portrait out lengthwise if we each take an end."

"Right."

Virginia moved into the closet. With one last, nervous glance at Kate, Jessica followed her.

Kate took a few steps closer to the closet, stopped and peered into the space. A strange excitement burned in her eyes.

When Jessica reached the back of the closet, she stopped beside Virginia. They both looked at the covered portraits.

"Which one?" Jessica asked.

"I think the picture on the left is for Mary." Virginia raised the drape partway. "Yes, this is it."

"Mary?" Kate said. "She named me Mary?"

"Yes," Virginia said. "She embroidered your name very clearly on the needlework in the picture. *For my beautiful daughter, Mary Elaine.*"

"Let me see the picture," Kate said. "Bring it out here. Hurry."

Virginia let the drape fall back over the picture. She looked at Jessica.

"You go first," she said. "I'll take this end."

Jessica was mystified but some of her panic was giving way to a desperate hope. At the very least she seemed to comprehend that there was a plan of some sort. It was always good to have a plan, Virginia thought, even a weak one. The plan she had in mind was as weak as they came.

She thought about her late-night drill and the mantra that went with it. *Any object within reach is a weapon.*

Jessica hoisted one end of the painting. It was unframed and, therefore, not very heavy, but it was a fairly large canvas. Virginia thought it would look reasonably hefty or, at the very least, awkward to handle.

She picked up her end of the picture. Together she and Jessica slow-walked the portrait sideways down the aisle of *Visions* pictures. The closer they got to the entrance, the less hopeful Jessica looked.

She edged reluctantly through the doorway. Virginia maneuvered her end of the portrait at an angle as if trying to avoid hitting the doorframe.

For a critical few seconds Kate's view was partially obscured by the large picture.

Gripping the back of the portrait with one hand, Virginia reached toward the pile of heavy glass paperweights and picked up the nearest one. It was about the size of a baseball, but the blazing yellow-and-green-glass sphere was thick and heavy.

She held the paperweight out of sight behind the portrait.

"Put the picture down and take off the drape," Kate ordered.

She still had a tight grip on the gun but her attention was riveted on the painting.

Virginia looked at Jessica. "Let's put it down on that workbench."

Together they maneuvered the picture to the workbench and positioned it upright, the bottom edge resting on the bench, so that Kate could view it.

"All right, Jessica, you can let go of your end," Virginia said. "I've got it."

Jessica released the canvas. Virginia angled her head slightly, trying to signal her to step back. Jessica obeyed, edging away from the workbench. Kate did not seem to notice. She was wholly focused on the covered painting now.

"Hurry," she said. "Take off the cover."

"Why don't you do it?" Virginia suggested. "I need both hands to hold the painting upright."

She had done her best to set the stage. Now it was time for the dramatic reveal. In the art world, as in so many areas of life, presentation was everything.

"Keep in mind that you are about to see your mother as she was in the last year of her life," she continued. "She was still lovely, but she was also quite ill. The message that she left for you is on the framed embroidery that hangs on the wall beside her chair. This is your inheritance, Kate. Or should I call you Mary Elaine?"

Kate reached out, grasped a corner of the dust cover and tore it aside. She gazed at the portrait of Abigail Watkins, evidently fascinated.

"That's her?" she said. "My birth

mother?"

"Yes," Virginia said. "She was quite beautiful."

Kate seemed to shake off some emotion she did not know how to express. Her jaw tightened.

"She looks weak. No wonder Zane was able to manipulate her. Where is the embroidery with the name of the bank and the account number?"

"On the left. See the framed wall hanging? That's your name at the top. The smaller stitching contains some of the information you need to claim your inheritance. The rest is on the second portrait."

Kate leaned forward eagerly, trying to read the lettering on the embroidery.

It was, Virginia decided, the only chance that she and Jessica were going to get. She released her grip on the painting. It started to topple forward.

Kate yelped in dismay. Instinctively, she reached out with her free hand to catch the canvas before it could fall to the floor.

Virginia slammed the paperweight in a short arc, aiming for the side of Kate's head.

Sensing the sudden movement, Kate started to turn, trying to duck and scramble out of reach at the same time. Her hand tightened on the gun. She got off a shot just as the paperweight struck.

The roar was deafening. Virginia was vaguely aware that the world had gone eerily silent and that something was terribly wrong with the right side of her waist, but there was no time to process the information. Not that she could think rationally, anyway. She was on fire with a wild, elemental fury.

It was as if the anger and frustration generated by years of nightmares and anxiety attacks had been channeled into this moment of cathartic violence.

Revenge was all now. She was no longer fighting only to defend Jessica and herself. She wanted to maim, punish and destroy the woman who had helped drag all the darkness of the past into the present. She did not care if she died in the battle. It only mattered that Kate Delbridge died with her.

The paperweight had found its mark, but because Kate had been partially turned at the instant of impact, the heavy glass ball had struck only a glancing blow on the side of her head — hard enough to draw blood and send her staggering but not hard enough to take her down.

She struggled to catch her balance and aim the gun at the same time. But by then Virginia was charging straight into her. The violent impact took them both down. Kate landed on the bottom.

Virginia managed to get both hands around Kate's forearm and wrench it aside just as the gun roared a second time. Kate screamed as Virginia smashed her arm again and again against the floor.

Kate screeched and finally lost her grip on the weapon. The pistol skittered across the floor.

"I've got it," Jessica shouted. "I've got the gun."

Somewhere a door crashed open. Virginia heard footsteps pounding across the floor but she ignored them. Kate was clawing at her, yelling in a panic-stricken voice.

"Get her off me. Get her off me. She's crazy."

And then strong hands were reaching down to hoist Virginia to her feet.

"It's all right," Cabot said. He braced her with a strong arm around her shoulders. "Everything is under control. You're safe. Jessica is safe. You can stand down now. It's over."

Virginia saw Anson moving forward to take charge of Kate. He glanced at Jessica.

"Give the gun to Cabot and then call nine-one-one," he ordered.

"Yes," Jessica gasped. "Right."

Cabot kept one arm around Virginia and

reached out with his free hand to take the gun.

Virginia looked at Jessica.

"Are you okay?" she asked.

"Yes," Jessica said. She fumbled with her phone. "I'm okay." She stared at Virginia, eyes widening. "But you're not."

"What?"

Confused, Virginia looked down. There was a rip on the right side of her gray cashmere sweater. A dark, wet stain was starting to spread. She was suddenly aware of the pain.

"Oh," she said. Her head swam. "Oh, hell."

"Shit," Cabot said. "Jessica, tell the operator we need an ambulance. Now."

"Yes," Jessica said. She concentrated on her phone.

Virginia was vaguely aware of Cabot lowering her down on the floor and pulling up her sweater. Jessica knelt beside him and handed him the wadded-up cloth cover that had been used to cover the portrait of Abigail Watkins.

"Is she going to be all right?" Jessica asked.

"Yes," Cabot said. He clamped the makeshift bandage over the wound. "She's going to be fine."

For some reason Virginia found the forcefulness of his words amusing.

"Thought you said handguns aren't very accurate," she said.

"Not over distance," Cabot said. "They work just fine when your target is only a couple of feet away." He raised his voice. "Where the hell is that ambulance?"

"On the way," Anson said. "Hear the siren?"

Cabot looked down at Virginia. "Don't you dare faint on me."

"I have never fainted in my life," Virginia said.

"Hold that thought."

Virginia thought she heard a door open, and then there were more voices and a lot of commotion in the back room.

The world was starting to spin. Virginia wondered somewhat disinterestedly if she was dying. If that was the case, there was something important that she needed to say to Cabot.

"I love you," she said.

"Good to know," he said. "Because I love you, too."

"That bitch is fucking crazy, I'm telling you," Kate shrieked.

Cabot looked down at Virginia. His eyes were very fierce.

"You just have to get to know her," he said.

Virginia wanted to laugh but she could not seem to muster the strength. The world went away.

CHAPTER 69

"Look at us," Virginia said. "Are we a couple of hotshot investigators, or what?"

She surveyed the small group gathered in her condo with a sense of deep affection.

Her grandmother, Octavia, was bustling around in the kitchen. Earlier she had made a large pot of tea and now she was constructing sandwiches. It was late and none of them had eaten dinner.

Anson lounged on the sofa. Cabot was prowling the living room. Virginia was dressed in pajamas, robe and slippers and was ensconced on the big reading chair, her feet propped on a hassock. In spite of Cabot's concerns, the wound in her side had been declared a clean through-and-through, non-life-threatening. She had been stitched up, bandaged and sent home with a bottle of pain pills and a page of instructions on wound care.

She had been surprised to discover that

she was taking an unfamiliar satisfaction in the knowledge that she had such a concerned circle of family and friends. After the shooting, Cabot had never left her side. Anson had picked up Octavia and driven her to the hospital. All three of them had stayed with her until she was released.

The police had dropped by to take statements. Virginia knew there would be more interviews in the morning. The Troy Gallery was once again a crime scene. Jessica had consoled her with the reminder that the publicity would no doubt be good for business.

Virginia took another fortifying sip of tea and looked at Cabot. "What made you and Anson come racing to my gallery this afternoon?"

Cabot halted his pacing and looked at her. "Abigail Watkins's diary. Anson and I started going through it as a team. I read it out loud while Anson made notes on the computer. We were just trying to establish basic facts and nail down a time line. When we got to the part about Abigail being forced to give up twins for adoption, I tried to call you. But I was thrown into voice mail. Let's just say I got a bad feeling at that point. Anson and I got into the car and drove over to see what, if anything, was going on."

Anson snorted. "As it turns out, you and Jessica had the situation in hand by the time we arrived. Any truth to that story you told Delbridge? Was there some hidden info in the embroidery that appears in the portraits?"

"No," Virginia said. "I made it up."

Anson nodded. "You conned a professional con artist. Nice work."

Virginia smiled ruefully. "Jessica was right. At least one of those glass paperweights deserves to be in the show."

"I couldn't agree more," Octavia said. She carried a plate heaped high with sandwiches into the living room and set it on the coffee table.

Anson and Cabot brightened at the sight. They both reached for a sandwich. Octavia smiled as the men dove into the food.

"One thing I'm curious about," she said.

"What's that?" Cabot asked around a mouthful of his sandwich.

Octavia looked at him. "You learned some more about the past. You know that Quinton Zane fathered fraternal twins, one of whom is now dead. But did you discover anything in that diary that might tell you whether or not Zane is still alive?"

"No," Cabot said, "but thanks to Tucker Fleming, we might have some new leads.

He went deep into the Darknet and he found some very intriguing information. Most of it relates to scams and cons that someone has been running in other parts of the world for several years. They all have a few things in common when it comes to style and technique."

"They're all pyramid schemes of one sort or another," Anson said.

"Pyramid schemes have been around forever," Virginia pointed out.

"True," Cabot said, "but every con artist has his or her own way of constructing the scheme. Zane's style is distinctive."

"Even the smartest crooks take the if-it-ain't-broke-don't-fix-it approach to their work," Anson said dryly.

"Tucker Fleming believed that his father was alive, so he compiled a detailed file of scams and cons that looked like they had Zane's signature," Cabot said.

"The bottom line," Anson said, "is that, thanks to Tucker Fleming, we've got a whole new file on crimes that have a reasonably high probability of having been carried out by Quinton Zane. The file is massive, though. We're going to need some serious expertise."

"Xavier, I assume, will be eager to help," Virginia said.

"If his parents will let him, which is an open question," Cabot said. "I'll admit we could use his talents, but in the end the machines can only give us raw data. Finding out the truth about Zane will take some old-fashioned detective work."

"Max and Charlotte are coming back from their honeymoon soon," Anson said. "Max used to be a criminal profiler. He'll be able to offer some insight. We're also going to need Jack's help."

"Jack?" Octavia asked.

"Jack Lancaster," Cabot said. "My other brother."

"I see," Octavia said. "And what particular expertise does he bring to the investigation?"

Cabot and Anson exchanged looks.

"It's sort of hard to explain Jack," Cabot said.

Virginia noticed that he seemed to be choosing his words with great care.

"He's an academic," Anson offered with a touch of pride. "Writes books about the criminal mind. He does some consulting, too."

"But his approach is a little unorthodox," Cabot said.

"Define unorthodox," Virginia said.

Anson snorted softly. "Can't define it. Not

when it comes to Jack. All I can tell you is that most people think he's weird."

Virginia smiled. "The older I get, the more I realize that everyone is weird in one way or another."

"The difficulty in getting a handle on Zane is that — if we're right and he's still alive — he's learned a few things since the disaster with his cult," Cabot said. "He's a lot more careful about risking his own neck now. He uses proxies and cutouts and pawns. When things fall apart, as they always do sooner or later, it's someone else who takes the fall. Not Zane."

Virginia shuddered. "The puppet master behind the scenes."

"Yes," Cabot said.

Octavia looked at him. "Is there anything else you know about him?"

"He likes to use fire to clean up the evidence," Cabot said. "Several of the projects we have tentatively attributed to him ended with a fire in a warehouse or an apartment or some other structure. Sometimes people died."

Virginia thought about that. "Zane doesn't use fire just to destroy the evidence. I'll bet he sees himself as an artist. Like any artist, he can't resist signing his work. Sounds like fire is his signature."

CHAPTER 70

She came awake on the dark tide of a rising anxiety attack.

"Crap, not again," she said aloud into the darkness. "Damn it to hell."

It was time to run through the exercise routine. Except she couldn't because of the stitches in her side.

That left the meds.

It dawned on her that she was alone in the bed. She didn't need to glance at the clock but she did so anyway. It was one forty-five in the morning. Cabot had probably been gone for a few minutes.

With a sigh, she pushed back the covers and started to sit up on the side of the bed.

Pain lanced through her side. She sucked in her breath on a sharp gasp and froze.

"Okay," she whispered. Gingerly she touched her side. "That's not an anxiety attack. It's actual pain."

Obviously the pain meds had worn off.

She was surprised to realize that the incipient anxiety attack was receding. Nothing like real, honest-to-goodness physical pain to distract the brain, apparently.

She let out the breath she had been holding and cautiously touched her bandaged side. When she thought she had things under control, she pushed herself to her feet.

She was struggling to get herself into her robe when she became aware of Cabot's presence in the doorway. He moved closer to help her with the robe.

"Need some pain meds?" he asked.

"Yes, but I think the over-the-counter stuff will work. And maybe a medicinal dose of whiskey. How is your arm doing?"

"I'm good, but I will admit that whiskey sounds like an excellent idea."

"Do private investigators get shot often, or was this case something of an aberration?"

"This case is definitely not the norm."

"I'm glad to hear that."

They went down the hall to the living room. Cabot eased her carefully into the big reading chair.

"I'll get the whiskeys," he said.

He went into the kitchen and opened a cupboard. His laptop was open on the dining counter. The screen was illuminated.

Virginia could see what looked like old newspaper clippings.

"Are you going through some of Tucker Fleming's files?" she asked.

"Yeah." Cabot carried the glasses into the living room and handed one of them to her. "Fleming had one major advantage when it came to digging into Zane's background. Rose Gilbert."

Virginia swallowed some of the whiskey and lowered the glass. "She would have had more background on Zane than the rest of us because of her relationship with Abigail Watkins."

"Right. And Abigail Watkins knew Zane better than anyone we've ever come across because she fell under his spell early on. According to the journal, she was only sixteen when they met. Zane was in his early twenties. Her diary offers us a glimpse into the way the bastard's mind works."

"I know we're in this conspiracy theory together and I'm on board, believe me. But we do have to keep in mind that Zane really might be dead."

"He's alive," Cabot said. "I sent some of Fleming's files to Max and Jack. They agree with me. Fleming was on the trail of his old man and now we are, too."

Virginia nodded, accepting that without

further argument. "What about Kate Delbridge?"

"I doubt that we'll get much out of her."

"Because she has no incentive to help us find Zane?"

"No, because she doesn't appear to have been all that interested in finding her long-lost father. She was in it for the money, not because she wanted to be reunited with dear old Dad."

"I wonder if Quinton Zane was aware of Tucker and Kate," Virginia said.

"If he's alive, then we have to assume that he knew of the existence of his offspring."

"Yes, I suppose so. But he never made any attempt to contact them over the years."

"Why would he? This is Quinton Zane we're talking about. He wouldn't have had any interest in his own flesh and blood unless he thought he could make use of them."

Virginia eased herself back into the chair and concentrated on her whiskey. Both the pain in her side and the last remnants of the anxiety attack were fading. Cabot sat on the sofa, his knees apart, his forearms resting on his thighs. He cradled his glass in both hands.

"I meant what I said this afternoon," he said after a while. "I love you."

She knew a sense of warmth that had

nothing to do with the whiskey. "I meant what I said, too. I love you."

"You thought you were dying."

"Doesn't change the facts. I meant it. I love you."

"I think you should know that I have a lousy track record with relationships."

"No kidding. So do I. We'll figure it out together."

"Yes," he said. "We will. You know, under other circumstances, I would pick you up and sweep you off to the bedroom and we would engage in some hot and sweaty sex."

"Under other circumstances, I would be thrilled to be carried off to the bedroom. However, given our current physical conditions, I guess we'll just have to sit here in the dark and tell each other how much we love each other."

"Works for me. But just so you know, as soon as we get the stitches out, I intend to go back to plan A."

"That would be the plan in which you sweep me off to the bedroom and we engage in hot and sweaty sex?"

"Right."

She smiled. "It's good to have a plan."

"The plan includes asking you to marry me after the hot and sweaty sex."

She drew a breath and released it with a

sense of certainty.

"Does your plan allow for some modifications?" she asked.

Cabot's jaw tightened. "It's too soon. I understand. But I think you should know that sooner or later I will ask because I won't be able to stop myself."

"The modification I was about to suggest is that we reverse the sequence of events. You could ask me to marry you now instead of waiting until after we get the stitches out."

Cabot did not move, but it seemed to Virginia that there was a lot of energy in the atmosphere. It was the vital, intoxicating energy of joy.

"That first day, when I walked into the office and saw you sitting there with Anson, I felt as if I'd had the breath knocked out of me," Cabot said. "For a couple of seconds all I could do was just stare at you."

"I noticed. I thought it was because you thought I was suspicious."

"No," he said. He shook his head very slowly, utterly intense, fully in his zone. "No, it was because I knew I'd found something I'd been looking for all my life. I just hadn't realized what it was I wanted until I saw you. Will you marry me, Virginia?"

"I guess you didn't notice that I stopped

breathing for a couple of beats that day when you walked into the office carrying those two cups of coffee and some pastries. It was as if I'd been walking through an endless gallery filled with boring abstract paintings and suddenly, there on the wall, was an old Renaissance masterpiece."

"Old?"

She smiled. "I mean that in the nicest possible way. Yes, I will marry you, Cabot Sutter."

He got to his feet, pulled her gently to her feet and kissed her. It was not a hot tango of a kiss; it was not a kiss that seduced and enthralled. It was a vastly more meaningful kiss — the kind that sealed a vow.

CHAPTER 71

"I worry about them," Octavia said.

Anson paused his glass of sparkling wine halfway to his mouth. Generally speaking he was not a fan of small bubbles in his alcohol, but the gallery event was a class act and he was determined to show respect.

He looked at Octavia, who was standing next to him. She, too, had a glass of bubbly in one hand. She was dressed in a sleek black pantsuit and high heels. A fine-looking woman, he thought. Smart, too. He had always been attracted to smart women.

"Virginia is your granddaughter," he said. "Naturally you're going to fret about her. I worry about Cabot. But for what it's worth, I think he and Virginia suit each other. They share some serious history. There's a connection between them. You can feel it when you're around them. No way to see into the future, but I think that what Cabot and Virginia have is as solid as it gets."

Octavia hesitated and then nodded once. "You're right. You are very intuitive, Anson."

"Don't know about intuitive, but I do know something about Cabot," Anson said.

He and Octavia were standing close together in a corner at the back of the crowded gallery. He was no expert on such matters, but to his untrained eye, the show looked like a roaring success.

The publicity about the confrontation between Virginia and Kate Delbridge in the back room had probably done wonders to ensure a big turnout. Nevertheless, the guests who were swilling the sparkling wine and wolfing down the fancy canapés seemed to be genuinely impressed with the show.

Although there was a lot of art on display, it was the picture from Hannah Brewster's *Visions* that got his attention. The fiery scene was displayed against a stark white wall. The local media had gone all out to dig up the old story about Zane's cult. Television crews and cameras had descended on the gallery shortly before the doors had been opened. It seemed like every guest in the room had his or her cell phone camera out and was snapping pictures like mad.

Anson had to admit that he was as fascinated as everyone else by the *Visions* painting. Even standing on the far side of the room, it was hard to take his eyes off the blazing scene. With her brushes and paints, Hannah Brewster had somehow captured the terrible events of the night of the compound fire in a way that was far more revealing than any photograph or video, as far as he was concerned.

He remembered Virginia's words the day she had walked into the offices of Cutler, Sutter & Salinas. *"Here's the thing about Hannah Brewster. She had trouble dealing with reality, but that was why she painted. She said it was the only way she could get at the truth."*

"She was right," Anson said quietly.

"What?" Octavia asked.

"Hannah Brewster painted the truth. That's how it was that night out at Zane's compound. That's exactly how it was."

"Dear heaven," Octavia whispered. She gazed at the painting. "I've always known it must have been a nightmare."

Anson thought about the screams of the children that he still heard in his worst dreams.

"Yes," he said.

Octavia sighed. "I hoped Virginia would be able to forget it or, at least, put the memory behind her. She was so young, after all."

"Some things you can't forget."

Octavia looked at the painting. "No."

Anson forced himself to look away from the *Visions* picture. He focused on the crowd.

Most of the artists looked to be both bewildered and thrilled by all of the unaccustomed attention.

Virginia was elegant and charming in a black dress with a little black jacket that effectively concealed the small bulge of the bandage that covered her wound. Her hair was in a sleek twist. *You'd never know she had nearly been murdered a few days ago,* Anson thought. One tough lady.

The fancy affair was an alien environment for Cabot, but he appeared to be holding his own. Virginia had taken him shopping before the event. The result was a laid-back but surprisingly sophisticated-looking Cabot in a stylish steel-gray jacket, black trousers and a black pullover. At the moment he was deep in conversation with a very earnest, very intent-looking man who was wearing heavy glasses and a rumpled jacket.

"I have no doubt but that there's a strong bond between Virginia and Cabot," Octavia said. "That's not what I meant. It's this obsession with hunting for that monster, Quinton Zane, that worries me. How can

Cabot and Virginia ever be truly happy if they don't find a way to put the past behind them?"

"What matters is how they deal with the past."

"I suppose so," Octavia said. "Virginia still has nightmares about what happened the night Zane burned down his compound and murdered my daughter and those other people."

"She's not the only one who has bad dreams. So does Cabot. Hell, so do I, for that matter."

Octavia gave Anson a long, considering look. "You have nightmares because you couldn't save them all, don't you?"

He knocked back some of the effervescent wine. "Reckon so. I'm sorry, Octavia."

"That you weren't able to save my daughter? You made the choice I know my daughter and I'm sure the other mothers who died that night would have wanted you to make. You saved their children."

He thought about trying to explain that he hadn't made a conscious decision that night. He'd acted purely on instinct. He had known the kids were forced to sleep in the barn because he'd kept an eye on Zane's compound for months. The children had been his first priority on that terrible night.

In the end he didn't say anything. He knew that Octavia understood.

They watched the crowd in a companionable silence for a time.

"Don't know much about the art world, but I'd say this looks like a good crowd," Anson said after a while.

"Yes, it does," Octavia said. She smiled, quietly pleased. "I wonder what Cabot and Hector Montgomery are talking about. They appear to be very deep in conversation."

"I noticed. Who is Hector Montgomery?"

"One of the local dot-com tycoons. Made a fortune in the high-tech world and then retired last year."

Anson snorted. "Doesn't look a day over forty."

"He isn't. Probably more like thirty-five. He's in the process of setting up some kind of charitable foundation. The headquarters are here in Seattle. Having him show up this evening is a coup for Virginia. Perhaps he's decided to start collecting regional art."

"That would be a good thing for Virginia, I take it?"

"Nothing arouses interest in the art world like finding out that a high-profile collector is attracted to the works displayed in a small, previously low-profile gallery such as this one."

Anson grinned. "A variation on auction fever?"

Octavia chuckled. "Yes, indeed. It's human nature, I suppose. Almost anything appears to be a lot more interesting and more valuable if someone else is willing to pay a lot of money to acquire it."

On the other side of the room, Virginia joined Cabot and Hector Montgomery. Hector fixed his very focused attention on Virginia and said something to her. She inclined her head and led the way across the room to a large metal sculpture that had been twisted into what Anson considered a very strange shape.

Cabot propped one shoulder against the wall, drank a little champagne and watched Virginia with the eyes of a man who knew damn well that he had found the woman of his dreams.

"I just want my granddaughter to be happy," Octavia said.

Anson snorted. "If you ask me, happiness is overrated."

Octavia rounded on him with an expression of disbelief. "I beg your pardon?"

"Most people don't even recognize happiness when it hits them over the head. They only appreciate it when they find themselves unhappy. There's something a lot more important than happiness."

Octavia regarded him with intent curiosity. "About your theory of happiness. Perhaps you would care to explain further?"

"Sure," Anson said.

And he did.

CHAPTER 72

"I gather the show was a success," Octavia said.

"Better than I could have hoped." Virginia set her teacup down on the saucer. "Hector Montgomery, the tech mogul who is firing up his own foundation, was there."

It was midafternoon. She and Octavia were having tea in the sunroom of Octavia's house. The space overlooked the large garden.

She was off the pain meds but the doctor had suggested that driving was probably a bad idea until her side had healed. Cabot had taken the suggestion as law. He had insisted on driving her to Octavia's house before heading to the office.

"I saw Montgomery chatting with you," Octavia said. "He appeared quite animated."

Virginia smiled. "Between you and me, he's the type who gets wildly enthusiastic whenever he discovers a new passion. Currently, that passion is art, so I'm not complaining. He wants to hire me as a consultant."

"That's wonderful. He has become a collector, then? I assumed as much when I spotted him in the crowd."

"Yes. He wants to build a personal collection with a focus on Pacific Northwest artists, but he also wants to have a series of installations in the headquarters of his new foundation. That means that the artists involved will get a lot of public exposure. It's a fantastic opportunity for them and for me."

"Yes, it is." Octavia hoisted her teacup in a small salute. "Congratulations, dear, you're on your way. The Troy Gallery is going to flourish. Once word gets around that Montgomery has hired you as a personal consultant, you will have people standing in line outside the gallery. Interior designers and serious collectors will be desperate for your advice."

"Well, collectors are a fickle lot and artists are inherently complicated. Still, you're right, last night provided a wonderful launching platform. Now it's up to me to take my business to the next level."

"You will," Octavia said. "The gallery is your passion. I understand that now and I am grateful that you stuck to your own path, even when I was pressuring you to take another one."

"I know you wanted me to be happy. You thought that would only happen if I stuck to the family script and went into academia."

Octavia smiled. "I have it on good authority that happiness is an overrated condition."

Virginia raised her brows. "Good grief, where did you get that bit of advice?"

"Anson Salinas and I had a rather illuminating chat last night," Octavia said. "When I told him that I just wanted you to be happy, he gave me his opinion of happiness. He claimed it was a superficial, fleeting sensation that most people don't even recognize when it happens to them. They only pay attention when they find themselves unhappy. And then they tend to feel resentful and angry."

"He has a point, I suppose."

"He went on to say that what really mattered was the ability to experience joy. He seems to feel that is the more powerful emotion because it endures, regardless of circumstances. Once you've known joy, you are never quite the same. It changes a person."

"Do you think he's right?"

"I know he's right. I was devastated when I lost your mother. I blamed myself."

"I thought you blamed me," Virginia said. "She got married because of me. She was vulnerable to Quinton Zane because of me. Later you and Granddad got divorced because of me."

Octavia shut her eyes in an expression of grief and regret that was far more poignant than words. Alarmed, Virginia reached across the small table to touch Octavia's hand.

"Octavia . . . Grandma. Please. You were right. We shouldn't talk about the past. It just opens up all the wounds."

Octavia's eyes snapped open. They burned with resolve.

"Pay attention, Virginia," she said, "and never forget what I am going to tell you. You are not to blame for the choices that your mother made, and you are not responsible for the choices that your grandfather and I made. We were the adults. We made our own decisions. You bore the fallout of those decisions, and for that I can only say I am truly sorry. I have no right to ask for your forgiveness. I just want you to know that I'm sorry."

Virginia gripped Octavia's hand very

tightly. "There is nothing to forgive. You were there for me when I needed you. You gave me a home. You provided me with stability and structure when I needed it most. And I always knew that you loved me, no matter how much we argued. I know I often disappointed you but I hope you know that I love you, too."

"Virginia. Oh, my dear girl. You do not know the half of it. You were the one who saved me. If it had not been for you, I do not think that I could have survived the loss of Kimberly and, later, Paul's betrayal. You brought love and purpose back into my life. Those are gifts that I have never taken lightly. And for the record, you have never disappointed me. When we argued, it was because I was terrified that you would make a choice that would cause you pain. I was so afraid that I would fail to protect you, the way I failed to protect Kimberly."

"You were right. My mother made her own choices. In the end, she and the other women who defied Quinton Zane were very brave and very daring. Their plan failed but their children were saved."

"I told Anson that he made the right decision when he rescued the children from the barn that night. He made the choice that Kimberly and the other mothers would have wanted him to make."

Virginia could no longer hold back the tears. She did not even try. Neither did Octavia.

When the storm passed, they stood close together, looking out into the mist-drenched garden.

"Cabot asked me to marry him," Virginia said after a while.

Octavia smiled. "Took him long enough."

"How can you say that? Cabot and I have only known each other for a short time."

"You and Cabot share some history. And you two can envision a future together. That is a wonderful thing."

"I was thinking we could have the wedding here in your garden."

"An outdoor wedding in Seattle is always a bit risky. It might rain."

"So what? If it rains, we'll just move things inside. This sunroom would make a lovely venue for a wedding."

"Yes, it would," Octavia said.

Virginia smiled. "Cabot and I are going out to dinner tonight. Can you join us?"

"Love to, but I'm afraid I've got other plans."

"One of your club meetings?"

"No, dear. Something a bit more interesting. Anson invited me to have dinner with him this evening."

Virginia was speechless for a couple of seconds. This was probably what it felt like to be struck by lightning, she decided.

"*What?*" she finally managed. "You and Anson Salinas? *Dinner?*"

"Makes a nice change from bridge and the garden club, don't you think?"

CHAPTER 73

"Anson has a *date?*" Max Cutler's disbelief echoed through the phone. "Are you serious?"

"Let me take a wild guess here," Jack Lancaster said. "Anson's hot date is some fast-moving blonde half his age who discovered that he is part owner of a security business that just got a big infusion of cash."

His voice was laced not so much with disbelief as it was with cool, detached cynicism. Jack always suspected the worst of people until proof to the contrary appeared. It was, Cabot thought, the predictable side effect of a career spent in academia studying criminal behavior.

"You can both relax," Cabot said. "Anson's date is my fiancée's grandmother."

"Grandmother?" Max repeated. "Just how old is she?"

"Early seventies, I think," Cabot said. "Virginia told me that her grandmother married young — while she was still in college."

"Anson just turned seventy-one," Jack observed. "So at least he's dating age-appropriately. But what do he and Virginia's grandmother have in common?"

"You mean, aside from the fact that Octavia's going to be my future grandmother-in-law?" Cabot asked.

"Aside from that," Jack said.

"You could say that Octavia and Anson have some history," Cabot said. "Octavia was the one who showed up to collect Virginia the day after Zane torched the compound."

That was all he needed to say.

Jack exhaled slowly. "So she was one of the many people Anson had to face the morning after."

"As long as I live," Max said, "I'll never be able to wrap my head around what it must have been like for Anson that day."

"Octavia has made it clear that, given a gun and an opportunity to shoot Zane, she would pull the trigger in a heartbeat," Cabot said.

"Sounds like she'll make a fully accredited member of our little Zane Conspiracy Club," Jack observed.

"Oh, yeah," Cabot said. "She's on board."

"I can't believe we're discussing Anson's love life," Max said. "He'd be pissed off if he knew about this conversation."

"Well, I, for one, don't plan to say anything about it," Cabot said.

"Neither do I," Jack said.

"Agreed," Max said. He paused. "Are you sure he can't overhear you?"

Cabot looked through the door of his office and contemplated Anson's empty desk. He smiled.

"Anson went home early to get ready for the date," he said.

Max chuckled. "Good sign."

Jack cleared his throat. "As interesting as this topic is, it's not why I called. I've been going through my copy of the new files on Zane that you sent, Cabot. I still can't say definitively that he's alive, but I can tell you one thing."

"What?" Cabot asked.

"We've assumed that if Zane is still out there, he's been living as an expat in various foreign locations," Jack said.

"So?" Max prompted.

"I think there's a very real possibility that the failure of his son and daughter will draw him out of hiding."

"Because he wants revenge for the death of his son and the fact that his daughter is going to prison?" Cabot asked.

"Quinton Zane isn't capable of caring enough about anyone, including his own offspring, to risk his neck in an effort to exact revenge," Jack said. "No, if this situation brings him back to the U.S., it will be because he's concluded that the catastrophic results of Fleming and Delbridge's project reflect badly on him. Make him look weak."

"Huh," Max said. "Some kind of twisted view of the supposed superiority of his personal gene pool?"

"Hard to say exactly how he'll rationalize it," Jack said. "But if he's out there, I think he will be looking for a way to prove to us and to himself that he really is the smartest, most powerful guy in the room."

"To do that, he'll have to destroy us," Max said.

"Yes," Jack said. "What's more, he'll try to do it with fire."

Cabot remembered Virginia's words.

"It's Zane's signature," he said.

CHAPTER 74

It was time to go home.

The man who had once been Quinton Zane stood on the pristine white sand beach and contemplated the foaming waves of the turquoise-blue sea. By any measure his new life was perfect, but in the past few years he had been forced to accept the bitter truth — perfection inevitably induced boredom.

Twenty-two years ago he had pulled off the perfect escape. Officially he had been lost at sea in a fire that had consumed the stolen yacht.

Back at the start he had naïvely assumed that he would soon be able to return to the States under a new identity. After all, the fire at the compound had been investigated by a small-town police chief with few resources. He had failed to anticipate that Anson Salinas would not accept the lost-at-sea verdict.

It had come as a shock to discover that

Salinas had quietly kept the case open. Still, there was little that Salinas could do under the circumstances. He was, after all, just a small-town cop — not exactly the FBI.

Salinas had never been a serious threat, Zane thought. And the press had soon grown tired of the story of a crazed cult leader who had torched his own compound and died in a fire at sea.

After a few years had passed, he had judged it safe to slip back into the country. He had been careful, sticking to the East Coast. There was so much money sloshing around New York.

He had set up a very successful hedge fund operation that was basically a pyramid scheme before drawing the attention of the SEC. He had not been overly concerned at first. He could have handled the feds. But there was the uncomfortable possibility that a serious investigation might lead to questions about his past. He could not risk being exposed as Quinton Zane.

He had been forced to slip out of the country one step ahead of the SEC. He had reinvented himself again in Europe.

It wasn't as if he did not have a very nice life as an expat. He had made a lot of money running various operations in Europe and Asia. The explosion of the Internet had brought with it unlimited financial opportunities.

He had a pied-à-terre on the Amalfi Coast, an apartment in Paris and a town house in London. His clothes were bespoke and his wines were the best. He slept with very expensive, very beautiful women. Currently his headquarters were the exclusive private island where he now stood contemplating his utterly predictable, utterly boring life.

He had expected to be able to return to the U.S. again long before now. The SEC threat had faded but, as the years passed, it had become crystal clear that he had a new problem — three of them to be exact. The boys who Salinas had fostered after their mothers died in the compound fire had come of age, and it was soon obvious that they did not believe the yacht-fire story, either.

What was far more worrisome was that all three had pursued careers linked to law enforcement. At first he assumed it was because they had been raised by an old-school lawman and had followed in Salinas's footsteps because they lacked the imagination to do anything else.

But each of the three had started searching for him online before they even graduated from high school. They had continued to watch for him even as they took up their careers. He had been forced to acknowledge the truth. None of them would let the past stay buried.

For years he had told himself that it did not matter that he could not return to the United States. He had been occupied with building a fortune abroad and living his glittering dream life. But all the while the rage and the frustration had burned deep within him.

He needed a strategy. He also required some pawns who could be sacrificed. That was the easy part. He had a talent for manipulating people, a gift for playing to their fantasies. The hard part was controlling them in such a way that he did not put himself at risk.

He turned away from the postcard-perfect view and walked back to the elegant white villa. He crossed the tiled floor, went into the room he used as his office and fired up the computer.

The latest news from Seattle was disappointing. He had watched the entire project from his secure island hideaway with the detached curiosity of a lab researcher observing the outcome of an experiment.

He had to admit that he had expected different results. After all, the twins had inherited his DNA. But instead of proving the superiority of his genes, the pair had gone down like a brother-and-sister version of Bonnie and Clyde.

Very disappointing.

But, then, Abigail had contributed her share of genes to the twins, and she had been a weak, pathetic creature. Even after all these years, he still found it astounding that she and the other women had not only worked up the nerve to defy him, they had managed to steal what, at the time, had amounted to a small fortune.

He had gone on to make vastly more money in the years following the destruction of the cult, but he had never been able to forget the past.

He sat back in the chair and looked out at the sparkling sand and the jeweled ocean. The old rage welled up, threatening to choke him. He beat it back with the power of his will. He could not think clearly when he was in the grip of such a strong emotion — one of the few he actually experienced in full measure. And he needed to think clearly.

He needed more than a good strategy and a few pawns. He needed people he could trust. That meant he needed people who had secrets — dangerous secrets that they would do anything to keep.

After a while he took his phone out of his pocket and called a number.

The voice that answered was male, midthirties. It was infused with the cold arrogance that was the natural result of the combined forces of money and power.

"Who are you and how did you get this number?"

"Is that any way to greet your long-lost older brother?"

When you needed people you could count on, you turned to family.

CHAPTER 75

It did not rain on the day of the wedding.

Virginia looked out the window of her old upstairs bedroom and concluded that her grandmother's garden had never looked more beautiful.

A white canopy framed with flowers stood at the ready. There were only a few rows of white folding chairs set up on the lawn, but they were all filled. Those on the groom's side were occupied by Max Cutler's new bride, Charlotte, and Charlotte's stepsister, Jocelyn Pruett, as well as some friends and business colleagues. Reed Stephens was seated on that side of the aisle. The surprise guests were Xavier and his mother.

The bride's side was full, too, with friends and acquaintances from the art world.

Octavia and Jessica fussed with the simple veil and the skirts of Virginia's ankle-length white gown one last time and then stood back to admire their handiwork.

"You look so beautiful," Octavia said. "And so happy — no, I take that back. You look as if you are overflowing with joy."

Virginia blinked back the moisture that had somehow collected in her eyes.

"So do you," she said.

"I am." Octavia leaned forward briefly to brush her lips against Virginia's cheek. "Anson was right. Happiness is overrated, but joy is a lasting gift."

"You look spectacular," Jessica said. She waved a cosmetic brush in triumph. "Don't you dare cry and ruin all my hard work."

"Time to go," Octavia announced.

The three of them made their way downstairs and stopped in the doorway of the sunroom. Octavia and Jessica moved outside. The musicians struck a chord. Octavia and Jessica made their way along the carpet to the canopy.

Virginia's pulse was dancing, but she was very certain she was not having an anxiety attack. She should know, she reminded herself. She was an expert on the subject. Octavia was right; the sensation she was experiencing today was joy.

Anson appeared in the doorway. He smiled at the sight of her and offered her his arm.

"You look beautiful," he said. "Ready to

do this?"

Virginia smiled. "Oh, yes."

Together they went out into the sunshine and stopped at the top of the petal-strewn carpet. The musicians struck another chord. The guests rose. Virginia saw Cabot waiting for her. His foster brothers stood with him.

"Welcome to the family," Anson said to Virginia.

She tucked her hand under his arm and walked with him down the aisle and into her future.

ABOUT THE AUTHOR

Jayne Ann Krentz is the author of more than fifty *New York Times* bestsellers. She has written contemporary romantic suspense novels under that name, as well as futuristic and historical romance novels under the pseudonyms Jayne Castle and Amanda Quick, respectively. There are more than 35 million copies of her books in print. She lives in Seattle.